DENIS DIDEROT (1713–1784) was born at Langres in Champagne, the son of a master cutler who wanted him to follow a career in the Church. He attended the best Paris schools, took a degree in theology in 1735 but turned away from religion and tried his hand briefly at law before deciding to make his way as a translator and writer. In 1746, he was invited to provide a French version of Ephraim Chambers's *Cyclopaedia* (1728). The project became the *Encyclopaedia* (*Encyclopédie*, 1751–72), intended to be a compendium of human knowledge in all fields but also the embodiment of the new 'philosophic' spirit of intellectual enquiry. As editor-in-chief, Diderot became the impresario of the French Enlightenment. But ideas were dangerous, and in 1749 Diderot was imprisoned for four months for publishing opinions judged contrary to religion and the public good. He became a star of the salons, where he was known as a brilliant conversationalist. He invented art criticism, and devised a new form of theatre which would determine the shape of European drama. But in private he pursued ideas of startling orginality in texts like *Supplement to Bougainville's Voyage* (*Supplément au Voyage de Bougainville*) and *D'Alembert's Dream* (*Le Rêve de d'Alembert*), which for the most part were not published until after his death. He anticipated DNA, Darwin, and modern genetics, but also discussed the human and ethical implications of biological materialism in fictions—*The Nun* (*La Religieuse*), *Rameau's Nephew* (*Le Neveu de Rameau*), and *Jacques the Fatalist* (*Jacques le fataliste*)—which seem more at home in our century than in his. His life, spent among books, was uneventful and he rarely strayed far from Paris. In 1773, though, he travelled to St Petersburg to meet his patron, Catherine II. But his hopes of persuading her to implement his 'philosophic' ideas failed, and in 1774 he returned to Paris where he continued talking and writing until his death in 1784.

RUSSELL GOULBOURNE is Professor of Early Modern French Literature at the University of Leeds. He has published widely on seventeenth- and eighteenth-century French literature and has contributed to the new critical edition of Voltaire's complete works.

OXFORD WORLD'S CLASSICS

*For over 100 years Oxford World's Classics have brought
readers closer to the world's great literature. Now with over 700
titles—from the 4,000-year-old myths of Mesopotamia to the
twentieth century's greatest novels—the series makes available
lesser-known as well as celebrated writing.*

*The pocket-sized hardbacks of the early years contained
introductions by Virginia Woolf, T. S. Eliot, Graham Greene,
and other literary figures which enriched the experience of reading.
Today the series is recognized for its fine scholarship and
reliability in texts that span world literature, drama and poetry,
religion, philosophy and politics. Each edition includes perceptive
commentary and essential background information to meet the
changing needs of readers.*

OXFORD WORLD'S CLASSICS

DENIS DIDEROT

The Nun

Translated with an Introduction and Notes by
RUSSELL GOULBOURNE

OXFORD
UNIVERSITY PRESS

OXFORD

UNIVERSITY PRESS

Great Clarendon Street, Oxford OX2 6DP

Oxford University Press is a department of the University of Oxford.
It furthers the University's objective of excellence in research, scholarship,
and education by publishing worldwide in

Oxford New York

Auckland Cape Town Dar es Salaam Hong Kong Karachi
Kuala Lumpur Madrid Melbourne Mexico City Nairobi
New Delhi Shanghai Taipei Toronto

With offices in

Argentina Austria Brazil Chile Czech Republic France Greece
Guatemala Hungary Italy Japan Poland Portugal Singapore
South Korea Switzerland Thailand Turkey Ukraine Vietnam

Oxford is a registered trade mark of Oxford University Press
in the UK and in certain other countries

Published in the United States
by Oxford University Press Inc., New York

First published as an Oxford World's Classics paperback 2005
Reissued 2008

British Library Cataloguing in Publication Data

Data available

Library of Congress Cataloging-in-Publication Data

Diderot, Denis, 1713–1784.
[Religieuse. English]
The nun/Denis Diderot; translated with an introduction and notes by Russell
Goulbourne.
p. cm.—(Oxford World's classics)
Summary: 'This novel takes the life of a young girl forced by her parents to enter a
convent as its subject matter and provides an insight into the effects of forced
vocations'—Provided by publisher.
Includes bibliographical references.
I. Goulbourne, Russell. II. Title. III. Oxford world's classics (Oxford University
Press)
PQ1979.A76E5 2005 843'.5—dc22 2004024150

ISBN 978–0–19–955524–6

10

Typeset in Ehrhardt
by RefineCatch Limited, Bungay, Suffolk
Printed in Great Britain by
Clays Ltd, Elcograf S.p.A.

CONTENTS

ACKNOWLEDGEMENTS

I should like to thank David Coward for encouraging me to undertake this translation, Jennifer Cooper, Nicholas Cronk, Nick Hammond, Olive Sayce, and Tom Wynn for generously giving me their help and advice, and Judith Luna for being such a kind and patient editor. My greatest debt, though, is to Michael Hawcroft, whose help and support have been as selfless as they have been ceaseless: to him this volume is gratefully dedicated.

INTRODUCTION

Diderot: An Enlightenment Polymath

BY the time *The Nun* (*La Religieuse*) was first published in book form, in 1796, Diderot had been dead for twelve years. The timing would have suited him perfectly. In an age of enlightened self-publicists and literary celebrities, Diderot dared to be different. Unlike his near-contemporary Voltaire, for instance, who was loath to leave any piece of writing unpublished and who positively enjoyed courting controversy, Diderot avoided conflict with the authorities by composing works like *The Nun*, *Jacques the Fatalist* (*Jacques le fataliste*), and *D'Alembert's Dream* (*Le Rêve de d'Alembert*) without thought of conventional publication in his lifetime, 'writing for the desk drawer' ('pisat' v yashchik'), as it was known in Stalin's Soviet Union. The result is that many of what we now regard as his best and most important works were unknown to his contemporaries.

So how was Diderot viewed by his contemporaries? They saw him first and foremost as the joint editor, together with the mathematician and scientist Jean d'Alembert, of the *Encyclopaedia* (*L'Encyclopédie*). What began in 1746 as a project to translate into French and expand Ephraim Chambers's *Cyclopaedia*, the first true English encyclopedia, published in 1728, quickly grew into something much more ambitious. In fact, it grew into seventeen large volumes of text, together with eleven volumes of plates, published between 1751 and 1772. The result is a vast and collaborative dictionary of the knowledge of the day (some 72,000 articles by more than 140 contributors), an extensive account of the arts, sciences, and technology of modern Europe written from the reforming standpoint of the *philosophes*, the free-thinking intellectuals of the day.

The *Encyclopaedia* became the Bible of the Enlightenment, the name given to the intellectual tidal wave that washed across Europe, and particularly France, in the eighteenth century, eroding superstition, conventional thinking, and received wisdom, and ushering in new modes of critical thought. The Enlightenment set out above all to challenge and demystify traditional religious authority, in particular the authority of the Roman Catholic Church. But this was an age when thought and expression were still rigorously policed. In the late 1750s the authorities stepped up their war against the *philosophes*, whose possible subversive influence had been highlighted by François Damiens's attempt to assassinate Louis XV on 5 January 1757, the eve of the Epiphany, *la fête des Rois*. In 1759 the Parlement of Paris banned further publication of the *Encyclopaedia* (a ban that proved ineffectual, since, thanks to the collusion of the authorities, the remaining volumes were published unofficially), and the work was put on the Roman Catholic *Index of Prohibited Books*. The persecution of the *philosophes* may have contributed to the virulence of the satire in *The Nun*.

But editing, and contributing to, the *Encyclopaedia* was not enough for Diderot. He was a great all-rounder, a true polymath. By the time he wrote *The Nun* in 1760, he had already made his name in a number of other domains. By the 1740s he was known as a philosopher. His first major publication was an annotated translation of Shaftesbury's *Inquiry concerning Virtue, or Merit* (1745), preceded by an open letter to his brother, who had become a priest, in which he offers a critique of religious intolerance. This was followed, in the late 1740s and early 1750s, by a series of philosophical works of his own, notably the *Letter on the Blind* (*Lettre sur les aveugles*, 1749), Diderot's first radically subversive work, which earned him a brief spell in prison, from where he was released only when he promised to do nothing subsequently which was in any way contrary to orthodox religion or morality.

Throughout these philosophical works Diderot moves away from English-inspired deism, which posited the existence of an intelligent creator as proved by the order and harmony of the universe, and towards a more radical position which can be best described as materialist atheism. Materialism holds that whatever exists is either matter or entirely dependent on matter for its existence; it consequently denies the existence of non-material things, in particular God. God is irrelevant; matter is all that matters. Since matter is the only reality and everything that exists is the product of molecular chemistry, it follows, for Diderot, that each individual is preprogrammed by their physiology and determined by the particular environment in which they find themselves. Diderot's materialism would find its most powerful expression in a group of dialogues entitled *D'Alembert's Dream*, written in 1769 but unpublished until the nineteenth century; it would also inform one of the underlying premisses of *The Nun*.

In the second half of the 1750s, Diderot also made his name as a dramatist. He was the driving force behind the *drame bourgeois*, or bourgeois drama. The *drame* was intended as a serious play in prose about contemporary middle-class life. Diderot wanted to sweep away the traditional French generic division, which had existed since the seventeenth century, between comedy and tragedy: comedies were designed to make audiences laugh at ordinary people; tragedies were designed to make audiences cry by feeling pity and fear for the likes of kings and queens. Diderot wanted to create a genre mid-way between these two extremes: he wanted audiences to feel pity for ordinary people. So he wrote two such *drames*, *The Natural Son* (*Le Fils naturel*, 1757) and *The Father of the Family* (*Le Père de famille*, 1758), to show his ideas in practice, and he attached to each play a theoretical work, the *Conversations about 'The Natural Son'* (*Entretiens sur le Fils naturel*) and the *Discourse on Dramatic Poetry* (*Discours sur la poésie dramatique*) respectively. Diderot's approach to drama was innovative, and it was to lay the foundation stone for modern European drama.

Also in the late 1750s Diderot became increasingly interested in the visual arts. In 1759 he wrote the first of his *Salons*, accounts of the biennial exhibitions of the Académie Royale de Peinture et de Sculpture in the *Salon carré* at the Louvre, in Paris. These exhibitions were a Parisian institution, major events open free of charge to all social classes. Diderot's *Salons* are generally regarded as marking the beginning of art criticism in France: Diderot turned banal journalism into a high-minded art form. Fascinated by the links between the verbal and the visual, he wrote nine *Salons* between 1759 and 1781, describing the works of art for readers who had not seen them: he transposed visual objects into words. His *Salons* first appeared in the pages of the *Literary Correspondence* (*Correspondance littéraire*), a handwritten journal, edited between 1753 and 1773 by Frédéric-Melchior Grimm and between 1773 and 1793 by Jacques-Henri Meister. It was distributed to a small number of wealthy and titled subscribers throughout Europe, including Catherine the Great. And it was in the *Literary Correspondence* that *The Nun* was first to appear.

This brings us to the last strand in the richly textured fabric of

Diderot's career: his fiction. Diderot's first foray into fiction was *The Indiscreet Jewels* (*Les Bijoux indiscrets*, 1748), an erotic novel about an African monarch, Mangogul, who has a magic ring, one turn of which will make a woman's genitals speak the truth about what the woman has been doing in the bedroom. Thirty trials of the ring fail to produce a single example of a wife who is faithful to her husband: satire and intellectual enquiry combine, as they will in *The Nun*. After *The Indiscreet Jewels*, Diderot let fiction-writing lie fallow for more than ten years, returning to it only in 1760, when he wrote *The Nun*. He began *Rameau's Nephew* (*Le Neveu de Rameau*) in 1761, though it was not published until 1821. In the late 1760s and the 1770s he wrote a number of short stories and dialogues, including *This is not a Story* (*Ceci n'est pas un conte*) and *The Two Friends from Bourbonne* (*Les Deux Amis de Bourbonne*), and he started writing his experimental anti-novel *Jacques the Fatalist*, which, like *The Nun*, was not published until 1796.

Diderot returned to fiction in the 1760s because of Samuel Richardson. Richardson's three epistolary novels, *Pamela* (1742), *Clarissa* (1748), and *Sir Charles Grandison* (1754), enjoyed a huge success in France, thanks in part to the prompt publication of translations of them. Diderot published an important *Eulogy of Richardson* (*Éloge de Richardson*) in 1762, shortly after the English novelist's death in 1761. Hitherto, Diderot argues in his *Eulogy*, novels have been scorned, relegated to the bottom division in the literary hierarchy, dismissed as so much frivolous froth, if not downright immoral. But Richardson has changed all that, writing novels that offer a lifelike rendering of the real world, a vision of human experience, a source of knowledge and wisdom, emotionally charged and morally uplifting. The reader believes in the truth of what he is reading, he becomes involved in the text, and this involvement is essential to the text's moral impact. The power of the fictional illusion brings about aesthetic participation, and that paves the way for moral renewal. It is precisely this kind of Richardsonian reading experience that Diderot seems to be trying to recreate in *The Nun*.

Nuns and Novels: Fact into Fiction

If Diderot wanted to transpose reality into art, he only had to look at the society in which he lived to find material. Diderot wrote his novel about nuns at a time when nuns were numerous and convents were commonplace. Convents were integrated to a remarkable degree into the polite society of eighteenth-century France. If respectable parents could not marry off their daughter, perhaps for lack of a dowry or because she was unattractive in some other way (for example, if she was illegitimate, as Diderot's fictional heroine is), the natural thing for them to do was to send her off to a convent to become a nun. The result was that in the middle of the eighteenth century, one Frenchwoman in every two hundred was a nun. France was home to about 5,000 convents containing some 55,000 nuns, compared to about 3,000 monasteries and about 30,000 monks. France was in fact unique in Europe in possessing so many more nuns than monks.

But if convents were commonplace, they were also enigmatic; they were places of teasing fascination for those (men) who had never set foot inside their cloistered walls; they were an intriguing no man's land. This fascination is reflected in fiction. The *Portuguese Letters* (*Lettres portugaises*), a slim volume of five letters published anonymously in 1669 and purportedly written by a deserted Portuguese nun to her unfaithful French lover, effectively fixed the view of the nun as unhappy in love, the convent setting serving to underline the cloistered victim's predicament. These letters are now generally accepted as the fictional work of one Vicomte de Guilleragues, but until relatively recently readers believed that the letters were real, an effect that Diderot seems to have been aiming to recreate in trying to pass off his work as the memoir of a real nun.

In addition to the *Portuguese Letters*, there also stretches behind *The Nun* a long tradition of male-authored libertine, quasi-pornographic novels, in which the convent, which is supposed to be a place of continence and self-denial, becomes instead a highly charged site of sexual fantasy. The starting point for this tradition seems to be Jean Barrin's *Venus in the Cloister, or The Nun in her Chemise* (*Vénus dans le cloître, ou la religieuse en chemise*), written in about 1680 but first published in 1719, a text that suggestively intertwines religious and sexual libertinism, blasphemy and lust. A flurry of similar tales duly followed, including, for example, Gervais de La Touche's *The Carthusians' Porter* (*Le Portier des Chartreux*, 1745), the story of the sexual initiation of the young and naive Suzon at the hands of a more experienced sister.

Diderot was familiar with these and similar titillating tales. But what makes his nun different from her fictional predecessors is that, whereas earlier convent novels tend to depict a nun who is unhappy because she is separated from the man she loves in the outside world, Suzanne's unsuitability to her way of life is not caused by love or by any lack of religious devotion. Rather her protest is an ideological and fundamentally humanitarian one. She has been forced to take the veil; her claim is to self-determination. This is a novel about enforced vocations, about making a young woman become a nun against her will.

While it was unquestionably contrary to the Church's law to force novices to take vows, it was by no means unheard of: Diderot's fiction is not entirely fanciful. Diderot had personal experience of the deleterious effects of the cloistered life. In 1743 his own father had his 30-year-old son locked up in a monastery when the wayward Diderot decided, against his father's wishes, that he did not want to become a priest and that he wanted instead to marry the poor but beautiful Antoinette Champion. (Diderot escaped after a month and married his beloved 'Nanette'.) Meanwhile his fourth sister Angélique, born in 1720, took the veil at the Ursuline convent in the family's home town of Langres, was driven mad, and died there in 1748. But perhaps the best-known case of a woman forced against her will to take the veil is the one that actually forms the starting point for Diderot's novel.

The origins of *The Nun* combine fact and fiction, a true story and a daring hoax. Early in 1760 Diderot and his friend Grimm, editor of the *Literary Correspondence*, together with Grimm's mistress, Madame d'Épinay, decided that their old friend, the Marquis de Croismare, had been away from Paris—and from them—for long enough (he had left the capital at the beginning of 1759 in order to retire to his country home in Lasson, near Caen). So they devised a plan to persuade him to return. They knew that in 1758 he had become interested in the fate of a nun in her early forties at the convent of Longchamp, a certain Marguerite Delamarre, who was trying to annul her vows on the grounds that her parents had forced her to become a nun. He had gone as far as to intervene in her case, but in vain: Delamarre's appeal was refused, and she was forced to remain a nun for another three decades, until the dissolution of the convents after the Revolution. Choosing to exploit his philanthropy, the plotters sent the Marquis a series of letters written by Diderot which purported to come from the nun who had supposedly escaped from her convent, and from Madame Madin, the woman she was supposedly staying with in Versailles, who was in fact one of Madame d'Épinay's friends who had agreed to pass on to Diderot any letters she received from Caen. The exchange of letters in spring 1760 did not, however, go entirely according to plan. The Marquis refused to come to the nun, preferring instead to invite her to come to him in Normandy in order to take up a position in his household. The plotters played for time, but eventually killed off their paper heroine on 10 May 1760.

But Diderot's interest in this poor nun did not die with her. He spent much of the rest of 1760 working on a longer account of the nun's life, now the memoir of one Suzanne Simonin, but he kept the manuscript to himself for the next ten years. In 1770 Grimm published in his *Literary Correspondence* the exchange of letters (the fictional letters from the nun and her guardian and the Marquis's authentic replies), together with a preamble outlining the hoax, but not the novel proper. By late 1780 Meister, Grimm's successor as editor of the *Literary Correspondence*, was looking for material for the journal; Diderot offered him *The Nun*. Meister duly published Suzanne's memoir, followed by the correspondence, now given the title 'Preface to the Preceding Work' ('Préface du précédent ouvrage'). This periodical publication took place in nine instalments between October 1780 and March 1782, with Diderot all the time making last-minute revisions to the text. The 'Preface' followed the final instalment in March 1782, by which time it had become an extension of the novel. Details in the letters were changed to bring the text into line with the novel, which is conceived of as Suzanne's memoirs in the form of a long letter to the Marquis, supposedly written, it seems, after her first (undated) letter to him in the 'Preface'.

Published in this way, of course, *The Nun* had a very small readership, limited to the small circle of subscribers to the *Literary Correspondence*. By contrast, when *The Nun* was first published separately, in book form, in October 1796, the reception was quite different. By 1796 the nun had become less a figure of sexual fun and more a figure to be pitied. In the years leading up to the Revolution the convent was increasingly seen as an emblematic form of social abuse on a par with the infamous *lettres de cachet*, sealed orders issued at will by the King, ensuring the immediate imprisonment of the unlucky recipient. Both were a form of arbitrary power wielded on behalf of the state by well-to-do families. It was in this context that *The Nun* was first published.

The novel was an immediate success, with some fourteen separate editions appearing in France between 1796 and 1800. It came to be seen as a text uncannily close to the *Zeitgeist*, a text true to the ideals of the Revolution and the First Republic: in October 1789 the taking of perpetual religious vows had been suspended; in February 1790 all the orders that required lifelong vows had been dissolved; by the end of 1792 even the congregations with simple vows had been disbanded; and barely a year later, Catholicism itself was outlawed, to be replaced by the cult of Reason and the Supreme Being. *The Nun* was an exemplary text. It came to illustrate for some what the Enlightenment stood for and the values it had bequeathed to the Revolutionary era: the pursuit of tolerance, justice, and freedom. Diderot's novel was not simply the story of a young woman with a bad habit, forced to enter a convent and to take holy orders, but a powerfully emblematic fable about oppression and human self-determination, intolerance and the ill effects of systems in general.

For very similar reasons, of course, the novel also met with opposition. It was condemned as irreligious, obscene, and morally corrupting, with one reviewer in 1796 earnestly advising mothers not to leave a copy in the hands of their daughters. This current of moral disapproval was to resurface two decades later, when, during the reactionary period of the Bourbon Restoration, *The Nun* was banned twice, first in 1824 and then in 1826, because it was judged to be an obscene work. But this only served to heighten the profile of the work, and by the 1880s it found new favour with the anticlerical movement. This was a novel with a long shelf-life.

What this sketch of the first hundred years of the novel's reception suggests is that attitudes to *The Nun* seem to be a litmus test of public opinion towards the free-thinking ideas that the novel embodies. The novel speaks, it seems, at different times and in different places to ongoing debates between faith and secularism, between conservatives and liberals. In the mid-1960s the French film-maker Jacques Rivette re-ignited these debates with the production of his film version of the novel, *Suzanne Simonin*, with Anna

Karina playing the role of Suzanne. In de Gaulle's France in 1966, the film was judged untimely and unwelcome, and it was promptly banned on April Fool's Day, apparently single-handedly, by the Minister of Information, Yvon Bourges, who considered it 'a blasphemous film which dishonours nuns'. This act of state censorship caused a huge scandal. The new wave of French cinema faced a backlash from the old guard, including the likes of the Catholic novelist François Mauriac, who complained that 'it would never occur to those who chose to film Diderot's poisoned book to make a film against the Jews—but against the Catholics, anything goes!' But liberal opinion refused to be silenced. Jean-Luc Godard, the well-known film-maker and husband of Anna Karina, published in the pages of the magazine *The New Observer* (*Le Nouvel Observateur*) a now famous open letter to the then Minister of Culture, André Malraux, in which he defined censorship as the 'gestapo of the mind' and accused Malraux, a leading intellectual himself, of blindness and cowardice. A large number of people—intellectuals, film-makers, and even sympathetic priests—added their voices to the chorus of protest. The decision of the right-wing Gaullist government, driven as much by electoral concerns as moral ones, did not prevent the astute Malraux from allowing the film to be screened at the Cannes film festival, and in May 1967, after the legislative elections, the ban was lifted, and the film was finally shown in Paris in the following November. That Rivette's film was, until very recently at least, the greatest popular scandal of French cultural life suggests that Diderot's novel has lost none of its satirical sting.

Satire and Sexuality

Diderot was no stranger to satirizing convents. Early in the *Philosophical Thoughts* (*Pensées philosophiques*, 1746), he compares convents to prisons, and in the *Sceptic's Walk* (*La Promenade du sceptique*), written in 1747 but not published until 1830, he develops this witty defamiliarization by comparing nuns to birds and convents to aviaries:

All over the place one finds big aviaries in which female birds are locked up. Here there are pious parakeets, bleating out words of affection or singing a jargon that they do not understand; over there are little turtle-doves sighing and lamenting the loss of their freedom; elsewhere there are linnets fluttering about and deafening themselves with their chatter, and the guides have fun whistling at them through the bars of their cages. . . . What torments these captives is that they can hear travellers going past but are unable to go after them and mingle with them. Nevertheless, their cages are spacious, clean and well supplied with millet and sweets.

Madame de Graffigny similarly 'makes strange' the commonplace convent in her best-selling novel *Letters from a Peruvian Princess* (*Lettres d'une Péruvienne*, 1747), in which the naive Peruvian letter-writer comments abrasively on her experiences in Paris, including temporary incarceration in a convent, which she refers to as 'a house of virgins': 'The virgins who live there are so profoundly ignorant . . . The faith they swear to their country's god demands that they give up all advantages, intellectual endeavour, feelings and even, I think, reason, at least that is the impression they give by what they say.'

The apparent echo of Graffigny's cross-cultural fiction is important. For in *The Nun* Diderot uses a device familiar from numerous eighteenth-century satirical fictions, from Montesquieu's *Persian Letters* (*Lettres persanes*, 1721) via Graffigny's *Letters from a Peruvian Princess* to Voltaire's *Candide* (1759): the device of the naive observer. Suzanne is, literally, a novice, an outsider who brings an apparently honest and disarmingly satirical perspective to bear on the dark recesses of convent life (though the extent of her honesty and innocence is crucially open to question). The satire in *The Nun* gains its incisive force from the distinctive narrative form of the novel. We see everything through the eyes of Suzanne, the suffering victim of family pressure to become a nun with no vocation. Although some of the satire comes from voices other than Suzanne's, notably Manouri and Dom Morel, even these voices are filtered through Suzanne's all-controlling voice. This serves to make *The Nun* the most sustained, most graphic, and most far-reaching literary satire of enforced seclusion in the eighteenth century.

In a letter to Meister on 27 September 1780 about *The Nun*, Diderot writes in self-congratulatory mode: 'I do not think a more terrifying satire of convents has ever been written.' His observation is important, though, as it serves to underline a crucial point about this novel: this is not a satire of the Christian religion per se, nor is it a satire of the Roman Catholic Church as a whole, which may be why it was never put on the *Index*. But the satire is perhaps more specific than Diderot implies. *The Nun* is an attack on enforced vocations, an attack on the unjust collaboration of Church, state, and family, an attack on the convent as a silencing mechanism and a means of social control. This is an anti-cloistral satire that argues for human rights and self-determination. Diderot denounces the persecution and repression of the individual who enters the religious life against his or her own will. There are examples of true devotion in the novel, and Diderot treats them uncritically. Suzanne's own faith, crucially, is in a sense unimpeachable: it is precisely at the height of her suffering at Longchamp that she feels that 'Christianity was superior to all the other religions in the world' (p. 65). His real target is the practice of enforced vocations; the real issue at stake is individual freedom. What Diderot exposes, at least implicitly, are the deleterious effects of all kinds of systems on the human beings ensnared by them. The ramifications of the novel's satire are very broad.

But if Diderot fixes his satirical gaze on enforced seclusion for what might be called political reasons, he does so for physiological reasons too. As a materialist, Diderot is interested in how human beings operate in physical terms. For him, the convent becomes a laboratory, the nuns experimental subjects: just as he uses the hypothesis of blindness in order to think about vision in the *Letter on the Blind*, so in *The Nun* he uses the hypothesis of seclusion from society in order to think about society itself. What happens, he asks, when you place people in (to him) abnormal, unnatural conditions? The concepts of nature and sociability are crucial here. Diderot is fascinated by the alienation of the natural being. For him, the natural being is a social animal. The novel describes in graphic, even startling, detail the alienating effects of the anti-social, cloistered life. Enforced seclusion violates what Diderot sees as the essential human need for sociability. The novel dramatizes the problematic relationship between the individual and society.

Diderot was not the first to dwell on this problematic relationship. Significantly, *The Nun* can be read as a response to the ideas of the proud and persecuted citizen of Geneva, Jean-Jacques Rousseau, another of the great *philosophes* in the eighteenth century. Rousseau had profound disagreements with his fellow *philosophes*, notably Voltaire and Diderot. What he rejected in particular was their belief in cultural and scientific progress. For him, humanity was free by nature but enslaved by civilization. In 1755 he published his

Discourse on the Origin of Inequality (*Discours sur l'origine de l'inégalité*), a far-reaching critique of the corrupting influence of modern manners and morals. This was followed first, a year later, by his own solitary retreat to rural Normandy from the corruption of Paris society, where he had been a close friend and ally of Diderot's, and secondly, in 1757, by the irrevocable breach between the two men, when Rousseau took exception to what he saw as a personal attack on him in an allusion to misanthropy in Diderot's play *The Natural Son*. For Diderot, unlike Rousseau, to retreat from society is to distort the individual. And so, in implicit response to Rousseau's perceived misanthropy, Suzanne stresses the importance of 'man in society': 'Such is the effect of cutting oneself off from society. Man is born to live in society. Separate him, isolate him, and his way of thinking will become incoherent, his character will change' (p. 104).

But why should Diderot focus in particular on cloistered women, as opposed to cloistered men? The answer lies, again, in physiology. Diderot is particularly interested in female physiology: what happens to women, he asks, when you bar them from normal contact with other women and, perhaps more importantly, men? The answer to this question, the novel suggests, is that women become hysterical and alienated. Here the novel chimes in with Diderot's later essay *On Women* (*Sur les femmes*, 1772), in which Diderot argues that women are ruled by their womb, 'an organ susceptible to terrible spasms, controlling her and creating in her mind all kinds of apparition', and that they are unusually prone to what he calls 'hystericism' as a result of religious fervour.

So we find madness running like a leitmotif through the novel. It is, for example, the terrifying spectacle at her first convent of a deranged nun who has escaped from her cell that makes Suzanne resolve not to take her final vows, and that nun's madness foreshadows the fate of the lesbian Mother Superior at her last convent. Nor is the last Mother Superior alone in her suffering. All the Mothers Superior are examples of the pathologically alienated, hysterical being: the mystical Madame de Moni, the sadistic Sister Sainte Christine, and the lesbian Superior at Sainte-Eutrope. Just as *Jacques the Fatalist* is about metaphysical alienation and *Rameau's Nephew* about social alienation, so *The Nun* depicts and dissects different forms of physical alienation. Diderot paints a vivid picture of how the mind and body can be twisted and deformed by hysteria in cloistered conditions.

It is perhaps the 'hysteria' of the lesbian Mother Superior at Sainte-Eutrope that has received most critical attention in recent years. Of course, the idea that convents, by shutting nuns away together, could incite women to engage in sexual behaviour with one another was well established by the eighteenth century. Locking women away, so the argument went, was 'unnatural', and so it led to 'unnatural' sexual practices. Popular medieval literature had portrayed monks and nuns as stock types of sexual licentiousness. But concern over the possibility of homosexual relationships was even expressed within the very rules governing the orders. As early as the thirteenth century in Paris and Rouen, for example, nuns were warned against excessive intimacy and encouraged to stay out of each other's cells and to leave their doors unlocked so that the Mother Superior could check on them. And since the Council of Trent (1545–63), certain practices hitherto tolerated in convents had been forbidden, in particular two (or more) nuns sleeping in the same room. In eighteenth-century France, homosexual practices became another stick with which the *philosophes* could beat monasteries and convents. Amidst contemporary (but ultimately unfounded) fears about depopulation, celibacy was seen, not least in Diderot's article on the subject in the *Encyclopaedia*, as against nature and useless, and monasteries and convents were regarded as running counter to the common good. Typical of this attitude is letter 117 of Montesquieu's *Persian Letters*, in which monasteries are described as being home to 'an eternal family which gives birth to nobody' and are compared to 'gaping chasms in which future races bury themselves'.

Given this context, what image of lesbianism does *The Nun* offer? One answer is provided by placing Diderot's novel in a purely literary (and, in a sense, ahistorical) context: that of the libertine fiction discussed earlier. This is a novel written by a man for, at least explicitly, a male reader, namely the Marquis de Croismare, and so in part it aims to titillate and excite. (The fact, though, that novel-reading was seen primarily as an activity for women in eighteenth-century France might even suggest that Diderot's novel is, in part at least, lesbian pornography for a female public.) Such a reading might be given added weight by bringing into play Diderot's own apparently erotic fascination with lesbianism. Diderot wrote *The Nun* at the same time as he was reflecting on what he imagined to be the incestuous and lesbian relationship between his mistress Sophie Volland and her sister Mademoiselle Le Gendre. In a letter to Sophie of 3 August 1759, for example, Diderot views the relationship between the two sisters as entirely welcome, even (erotically?) appealing:

We shall soon be together again, my dear, never fear, and these lips will once again touch the lips I love. Until then I forbid your mouth to everyone except your sister. It does not make me unhappy to be her successor, indeed it rather pleases me. It is as if I were pressing her soul between yours and mine.

This reading of Diderot's novel as an erotic text is certainly partial, but it has found favour with some, not least the Italian film-maker Joe d'Amato, whose crude pornographic 'nunsploitation' film *Convent of Sinners* (*Monaca nel peccato*, 1986) is, at least according to the credits, based on Diderot's novel.

Another approach to lesbianism in *The Nun*, and one more in keeping with the historical context sketched out above, is to argue that the novel presents lesbianism, quite unproblematically, as another of the monstrous psychic and physiological side effects of living an unnaturally cloistered life: the novel, according to this view, presents lesbianism on a par with madness and sadistic cruelty. The final Mother Superior is depicted as a shallow and unstable personality who preys on those for whom she is meant to be caring. *The Nun* could be read as a cautionary tale about the dangers of female intimacy, particularly within a same-sex, cloistered environment. Here again we might detect an echo of Diderot's own concerns, for he is not only titillated by the possibility of Sophie Volland's relationship with her sister; he is also angry and jealous, as his letter to Sophie on 17 September 1760 reveals:

I have grown so touchy and unreasonable and jealous; you say such nice things about her and are so impatient if anyone finds fault with her that . . . I dare not finish my sentence! I am ashamed of my feelings, but cannot prevent them. Your mother says that your sister likes pretty women and it is certain that she is very affectionate towards you; then think of that nun she was so fond of, and the voluptuous and loving way she sometimes has of leaning over you, and her fingers so curiously intertwined with yours!

Diderot, both in this correspondence and in *The Nun*, could be said to be struggling to come to terms with, even to control, female intimacy. And the fact that it is a Benedictine monk (presumably Dom Morel) who tries to rape Suzanne once she has escaped from the convent could be seen as further evidence of the novel's condemnation of the sexually damaging effects of the cloistered life: if only Dom Morel had been able to enjoy normal relations with women in society, the novel seems to imply, he would not have tried to rape Suzanne.

But an alternative approach is to say that the novel does not constitute an unambiguous attack on lesbianism, nor does it depict same-sex intimacy for the titillation of the male (or, for that matter, female) reader. Instead, the novel might be offering a positive, even liberal vision of same-sex desire. Sainte-Eutrope is a happy, even euphoric place, a haven of lesbian love. It is worth remembering that the third Mother Superior's sexual climaxes are presented subtly and sympathetically: she suffers far more than the sadistic second Mother Superior, who is so cruel to Suzanne. And she goes mad, and domestic harmony is upset, only when the Church intervenes, in the shape of the (male) confessors, and tells Suzanne that intimacy between women is wrong. In this sense, the implicitly positive portrayal of lesbianism could be said to go hand in hand with the explicitly negative portrayal of institutional repression: the Church is criticized, not just for cooperating in forcing young women to become nuns, but also for suppressing their natural sexual instincts and driving them mad.

This approach, viewing the novel as a criticism of the Church for its attitude to human sexuality, is supported by Diderot's comments elsewhere on sexuality. In his *Supplement to Bougainville's Voyage* (*Supplément au Voyage de Bougainville*, 1772), for example, Diderot uses the device of a South Sea island paradise to play off moral and natural law against each other, reserving particular criticism for ascetic Christian moral teaching on human sexuality. It is in particular the Church that tries to suppress same-sex desire and portray it negatively, to achieve stability in a world which, according to Diderot, is fundamentally unstable. Desire is a response to beauty, whatever the sex, and it cannot be divided into homo- and heterosexuality. Anticipating much recent gender theory, Diderot the materialist presents human sexuality as polymorphous, free-floating, fluid. As the scientist Bordeu declares at the end of *D'Alembert's Dream*, in which homosexuality, bestiality, and masturbation are all mentioned: 'Everything that exists can be neither against nor outside nature.' Homosexual desire is both a fact of nature and a fact of society. So, the attack in *The Nun* might be against the Church's attitude to lesbianism, not against lesbianism itself.

Such a reading also enables us to see *The Nun*, paradoxically perhaps, as one of Diderot's most feminist works. In *The Nun* there seems to be a symbolic division between masculine law and feminine desire: reason, justice, and sobriety characterize the male characters in the novel, notably Séraphin, Manouri, Hébert, and Dom Morel; madness, intrigue, and cruelty, on the other hand, characterize the majority of the women. For her part, however, Suzanne, by launching her lawsuit at Longchamp, shows that woman can also escape her hysteria and fight against social injustice. Perhaps the ultimate sign of female self-definition and affirmation in this novel is the exclusion of men that is concomitant with the expression of lesbian desire. Crucially it is precisely this power-move that the young Benedictine who helps Suzanne to escape promptly tries to subvert by trying to rape her.

Like the letters of Graffigny's Peruvian princess, Suzanne's memoir constitutes a struggle to find a voice through the written word, a fight to break the silence imposed upon her by Church and family. Suzanne becomes a bold mouthpiece, a symbol of enlightened resistance, a 'trouble-maker' as she calls herself (p. 34). Whereas Rousseau seems to be at pains to silence woman, particularly in book V of his controversial pedagogical novel *Émile* (1762), in which he extols the virtues for a young woman of a stay in a convent as a fitting preparation for her sedentary life as a breast-feeding mother, Diderot gives her a powerful voice. It is the prevailing presence of this voice that makes possible the different readings of the novel, in particular the ambiguities and ambivalences surrounding the portrayal of lesbianism. How we interpret the narrative voice is crucial.

Artful Artlessness

Suzanne's narrative is presented, at least initially, as a true story. This is Diderot emulating Richardson. The genesis of *The Nun* coincides, as we saw earlier, with Diderot's discovery of the

Englishman's novels, in particular the ingenious epistolary novel *Pamela*, and *Clarissa*, a novel about female entrapment. From Richardson Diderot seems to have derived the idea that a novel can produce a reality effect and have the same effect on the reader as reality itself: the novel as deception, hypnotic illusion, falsehood dressed up as truth. The novel could assert its validity as a genre by presenting itself as true and moral.

Similar truth claims had, however, been made since at least the end of the seventeenth century. Dissatisfied with the implausibilities of earlier fiction, novelists from the turn of the century onwards sought to win greater popular and critical esteem for their efforts by claiming that what they were writing was not fiction, but fact. They attempted to pass off fictions as memoirs, histories, journals, eye-witness accounts. In other words, they turned from third-person narratives to first-person narratives. If a third-person narrative could never seriously claim to be real—how could a narrator plausibly know everything about his characters?—a first-person narrative, such as a memoir, was much more authentic, much more plausible, much less 'literary'. Perhaps the best-known French first-person narratives from the eighteenth century before *The Nun* are Prévost's *Manon Lescaut* (1731) and Marivaux's unfinished *Marianne's Life* (*La Vie de Marianne*, 1731–42).

First-person narrators commonly do two things at the beginning of their narratives: they lay claim to honesty and naivety, and they deny any ulterior motive, such as a persuasive role. Suzanne is no exception. From the outset she stresses the confessional aspect of her memoir when she claims that she is 'writing with neither skill nor artifice, but with the naivety of a young person of my age and with my own native honesty' (p. 3). This insistence on her youthfulness occurs on a number of occasions in the novel. She states that she was 16 when the question of her taking the veil was first raised (p. 4), but though her story must extend over at least nine years, she tells us towards the end that she is barely 20 (p. 109), and in the concluding 'Preface', Madame Madin claims that her ward is barely 17 (p. 162). One effect of these apparent inconsistencies, of course, is to stress the innocence of youth. But her claim to naivety and artlessness is, in fact, an artful way of luring her reader in—both her intended reader (the Marquis de Croismare) and us. For what distinguishes *The Nun* from, say, *Manon Lescaut* is that in Diderot's novel the perspective is explicitly feminine, and the intended reader is explicitly male.

Suzanne's memoir is presented as an honest, revelatory self-portrait, but at the same time she is eager to captivate, if not to seduce, the Marquis, to move him so powerfully that he will be persuaded to come to her aid. Partly, like *Jacques the Fatalist*, this is a story about storytelling: Suzanne is telling her story to the Marquis, which becomes a kind of framing narrative, within which we hear her telling her story to a number of other listeners. Our attention is focused throughout on the character of Suzanne. She is a strong and individualized presence from the start. We see everything from her perspective: Diderot the cross-dressing ventriloquist speaks with a woman's voice. This distinctive perspective, crucially, is lost in the film version by Rivette, who abandons the subjectivity of the first-person narrative in favour of a more objective approach.

The novel is, ultimately, an exercise in rhetoric, the art of persuasion. Suzanne's narrative encourages us to share in her sufferings, to feel sorry for her, and to be persuaded by the case she is making. Despite her claims to naivety and innocence, she nevertheless demonstrates at least some self-awareness. The night before she is due to take her vows, for example, she writes self-consciously: 'I played out in my mind the role I would perform, kneeling before the altars, a young girl crying out in protest against an event to which she seems to have given her consent' (p. 12). When she is summoned before the Archdeacon, she acknowledges her advantages, physical and otherwise, including, crucially, the ability to make people believe her: 'I have a touching appearance; the intense pain I had experienced had altered it but had not robbed it of any of its character. The sound of my voice also touches people, and they feel that when I speak, I am telling the truth' (p. 67). And she directs Manouri to leave out certain details of her past when presenting her case because 'they would have made me look odious and would not have helped my case' (p. 24).

Suzanne is clearly alive to the art of self-presentation. Moreover, her sense of an audience is not limited to her convents. At one point she seems to envisage a wider readership beyond the Marquis when she refers to 'most of those who will read these memoirs' (p. 71) and even anticipates their reactions. (This might also explain why the novel opens with a reference to the Marquis in the third person: the first paragraph reads like an introduction addressed, not to the Marquis himself, but to a wider reading public.) At the end of her account Suzanne goes so far as to recognize an element of deception: 'I have realized that, though it was utterly unintentional, I had in each line shown myself to be as unhappy as I really was, but also much nicer than I really am. Could it be that we believe men to be less sensitive to the depiction of our suffering than to the image of our charms, and do we hope that it is much easier to seduce them than it is to touch their hearts?' (p. 152). The effect has been, not one of spontaneity and naivety, but one of studied control and seduction through the many devices of a first-person narrative. Suzanne is a deft narrator presenting the Marquis and us with the image of an inexperienced young girl. So what are these devices and how do they work? How persuasive is Suzanne?

Suzanne displays great narrative and descriptive skills, despite her claim to be writing in an artless way, and she uses these skills to offer the most positive image of herself possible. One of the most striking is her ability to deploy direct speech. She shows other people responding favourably to her in order to encourage the reader to react to her in the same way. At the end of the vow-taking ceremony, for example, she reports the words of her fellow nuns: ' "But look, Sister, look how pretty she is! Look how her black veil brings out the whiteness of her complexion! How her headband suits her! How it rounds off her face! How it makes her cheeks stand out! How her habit shows off her waist and her arms!..." ' (p. 7). Conversely, she reproduces her exchange with her mother in order to provoke revulsion in the reader for the mother's cruel, twisted logic: ' "don't make your dying mother suffer; let her go to her grave in peace so that she may tell herself, as she's about to appear before the judge of all things, that she has atoned for her sin as far as she could, so that she can reassure herself that, after she is dead, you won't make trouble for her family and you won't lay claim to rights that aren't yours" ' (p. 21). The technique is a clever one: offering accounts of how others see her means that Suzanne does not have to rely on putting forward her own views; the text works for her to create an illusion of innocence.

But if Suzanne appears to be good at remembering dialogue, she is also good at forgetting it. Just as she dwells on conversations which cast her in a favourable light, so too she is adept at avoiding scenes

and passing over exchanges which might show her in an unfavourable light. Her account of her first vow-taking is surprisingly brief
and undramatic: 'They did whatever they wanted with me throughout the morning, which has never been real to me, as I never knew
how long it lasted. I have no idea what I did or what I said. I must
have been asked questions, and I must have replied and made my
vows, but I have no memory of doing so. I found I had become a
nun just as innocently as I had been made a Christian' (p. 29).
Suzanne is at pains to stress that, although she went through the
ceremony of final vow-taking at Longchamp, she did so like an
automaton: her heart and mind were not engaged in what she was
doing. (In Rivette's film, there is no scene depicting vow-taking at
Longchamp, which is perhaps the definitive negative means of con-
veying Suzanne's point that she remembered nothing of that morning.) This is important: she has to counter the potential objection
from the Marquis that she knew exactly what she was doing and that
she had chosen not to resist, as she had done at the convent Sainte-
Marie. Her references to unconscious behaviour and amnesia are
part of her arsenal of narrative devices.

Suzanne's overwhelming reliance on dialogue suggests an important link between *The Nun* and Diderot's contemporary experimentation in the theatre. This is a theatrical novel in the broadest sense, a
novel full of detailed, lively, well-paced dialogues. But more specific
links can be detected between the novel and Diderot's *drames*. In his
plays Diderot was interested in showing how a character's 'conditions', by which he meant, for instance, their profession or family
role, had a large share in determining what they are and what they
can do. Likewise in *The Nun*, Diderot shows how the condition of
the reluctant nun carries with it pain and suffering, a necessary
consequence of violating what Diderot sees as the essential human
need for sociability. In both his plays and in this novel, Diderot the
materialist seems to have been less interested in individual characters
than in showing how people are shaped and determined by their
environment and their circumstances.

Diderot's conception of the *drame* also laid significant emphasis
on the emotional involvement of the audience. Diderot aimed to
offer moving and morally uplifting representations of the lives of
ordinary people as a stimulus to intellectual reflection on the prob-
lems of humanity. *The Nun*, like Diderot's ideal theatre, relies on

emotional impact for its intellectual stimulus. This is a highly senti-
mental novel which stirs the reader's emotions. It is a forerunner of
the Gothic novel with its depictions of hideous suffering. Suzanne
recounts scenes which present her as an innocent victim, even a
Christ-like victim, embarking, it would seem, on her own march to
Calvary, before being resurrected from her cell on the third day
(pp. 41–2). It is precisely this Christ-like aspect of Suzanne's character, the innocent victim at her most sinned against, that is highlighted at the end of Rivette's film: in a departure from Diderot's
text, Rivette makes Suzanne throw herself from an upper-storey
window of the brothel, and she is last seen from above lying dead on
the pavement, spread out like a penitent before the altar, but also like
Christ on the cross.

Rivette is arguably more faithful to Diderot's novel in his theatri-
cally stylized use of space and positioning of characters, evoking at
every turn Suzanne's entrapment and suffering. (Rivette's film version is in fact a cinematographic adaptation of a dramatized version
of the novel by Jean Gruault, first staged in 1960 and revived by
Rivette in 1963.) For the art of *The Nun* has close links with another
aspect of Diderot's theatrical experimentation in the 1750s: the tableau. Diderot's innovative preoccupation in the theatre with creating
an overall stage picture, with a great deal of attention paid to décor,
costumes, and the positioning of actors, extended to *The Nun*. This
is a theatrical novel with lots of physical portraits and descriptions of
gestures and movements, similar to the extensive stage directions in
Diderot's plays. Suzanne excels at painting visually striking
ensembles and group scenes, such as the death of Madame de Moni
(p. 31), where static description and the use of light and dark create
a truly 'mournful scene', a theatrical *mise en scène* with a specific
shape, and which appeals strongly to the reader's emotions.

The theatrical quality of Diderot's novel can also be related to his
art criticism. The art of the tableau is, of course, a painterly art.
Suzanne describes the décor and the nuns' gestures, positions, and
movements in a painterly way, indeed in a way that specifically
recalls Diderot's descriptions of Greuze's paintings in the *Salons*.
She refers to painting on a number of occasions in the novel. For
example, describing a scene in the convent of Sainte-Eutrope, she
observes: 'You know about painting, and I can assure you, Monsieur
le Marquis, that it was quite a pleasant picture to behold' (p. 120).

She implicitly compares the Marquis to a putative reader of Diderot's *Salons*. It is in the *Salons* that Diderot presents Greuze, in effect, as the equivalent in painting of Richardson in fiction-writing. In the *Salon* of 1763 he refers to Greuze's art as 'moral painting', and in the *Salon* of 1765 he praises the artist's ability to depict subjects ripe for treatment by a novelist: 'Here is your painter and mine, the first of our artists to have taken it upon himself to invest art with morals and to link together events in such a way that it would be easy to make a novel out of them.' Diderot was clearly fascinated by the relation between words and pictures: he conceives of paintings as telling stories, and so too he conceives of his stories as paintings. This makes Diderot's letter to Meister on 27 September 1780 about *The Nun* all the more important, as he echoes Correggio's reaction to Raphael's *Saint Cecilia* in Bologna in about 1525: 'It is full of moving *tableaux*. . . . It is a work that painters should leaf through constantly; and if only vanity allowed it, its real epigraph would be: *Son pittor anch'io* [I too am a painter].'

Playing with Truth

But Suzanne is not just the talented painter in this text; she is also the subject of the portrait, an actor in her own drama. This raises the important question of how much Suzanne actually knows about herself and about others. The novel, because of the narrative perspective it adopts, makes this question infuriatingly difficult to answer. For, as we have seen, on the one hand there is the rhetoric of the naive, innocent Suzanne, and on the other hand there is clear textual evidence of a much more knowing persona. Suzanne is both ingenuous and well informed, a character in whom there is an unsettling and paradoxical combination of apparent naivety and satirical insight. As in Rousseau's autobiographical *Confessions* (1764–70), the first-person narrative form becomes a vehicle for exploring the self in all its complexity.

The complexity surrounding Suzanne is created in the first instance by the confusion surrounding the timing of the narrative. When is Suzanne actually writing? Suzanne's perspective on her life is complex and confusing. We need only look at the opening paragraph of the memoir to be confused. Is this a beginning or an ending? Suzanne implies that she is just starting to write her memoirs ('it is for this reason that I have resolved to put aside my pride and my diffidence and write these memoirs', p. 3), but then she promptly refers to how they end, which implies she has already written them. The first paragraph reads almost like a text that has been added after the completion of the rest of the narrative. What is clear is that Diderot deliberately does not present a narrator who recounts her story from a position of distance and superior knowledge. Rather we have a sense of a narrative being written at a very short remove from the events being narrated. Diderot closes down the distance between the time of the events and the time of the narration, a distance that earlier novelists, like Prévost and Marivaux, had expanded for deliberate effect.

The uncertainty that this creates permeates the text. Ignorance and awareness coexist in a delicate tension. At times Suzanne does seem to be able to step back and offer critical comments on her experiences, such as when she declares: 'Oh! Monsieur, you simply cannot begin to imagine how devious these Mothers Superior are!' (p. 5). But more often than not, Suzanne claims to be ignorant. For example, when subjected to persecution at Longchamp, Suzanne protests ignorance then and now of the reasons for this treatment:

To be frank, I am not a man and I do not know what can be imagined about one woman and another, and still less about a woman on her own. But since my bed had no curtains and since nuns came into my room at all hours of the day and night, what can I say, Monsieur? Despite their outward reserve, their modest looks and their chaste expression, these women must have truly corrupt hearts. Or at least they know that unseemly acts can be committed on one's own, whereas I do not. So I have never really understood what they were accusing me of, and they spoke in such an obscure way that I had no idea how to respond. (pp. 59–60)

Already these protestations of ignorance relate to the question of sexual knowledge, an issue that will come to the fore when Suzanne is describing her stay in the convent of Sainte-Eutrope.

The question of Suzanne's knowingness is particularly important when considering the image of lesbianism that the novel offers. At the heart of the novel is the thorny problem of sexual self-knowledge, one reason why the text still fascinates readers today. Suzanne would have the Marquis—and us—believe that she understands nothing at all about lesbian sexuality. But how much does she really know? The signs are there from the start of her time at Sainte-Eutrope:

On the first evening, the Mother Superior came to visit me; she came in as I was getting undressed. It was she who took off my veil and wimple and brushed my hair for bed; it was she who undressed me. She said a hundred sweet things to me and stroked me a thousand times, which made me feel rather awkward, but I do not know why, because I did not know what was happening, and neither did she, and even now as I think back over it, what could we have possibly known? (pp. 95–6)

Suzanne insists on her ignorance then and now of what was happening: she pretends not to know what the Mother Superior's advances mean even as she recounts them. But at the moment of writing, she has already learnt that the Mother Superior is a lesbian, so her failure—or refusal—to make the point explicit is revealing.

Diderot's achievement in *The Nun* is to construct a naive or 'innocent' female narrator who can none the less narrate her own and others' sexual experiences, an achievement that recalls John Cleland's narrative technique in *Memoirs of a Woman of Pleasure* (1749), which was first translated into French in 1751, and which depicts the erotic activity between Fanny Hill, the 15-year-old heroine, and Phoebe Ayres, her much older instructor, who initiates her into lesbian sex. But unlike Fanny, who brings retrospective knowledge to bear and explicitly acknowledges that Phoebe was not just a harmless companion, Suzanne describes what the reader can perceive to be lesbian sexual encounters, while leaving her understanding of what was actually going on enticingly and crucially ambiguous. This is the case in her delicately euphemistic account of the Mother Superior's orgasm:

Eventually there came a point, and I do not know if this was out of pleasure or pain, when she went deathly pale, her eyes shut, her whole body tensed violently, her lips tightened at first, slightly moistened as if by some kind of foam, then her mouth opened and she gave a deep sigh, as if she was dying. I jumped up, I thought she was unwell, I was going to leave and call for help. (p. 106)

But the way the narrative continues, and in particular the words Suzanne uses to describe her own state, raises the possibility that Suzanne was in fact just as sexually aroused as the Mother Superior: 'I do not know what was going on inside me. I was afraid, I was trembling, my heart was pounding, I could hardly breathe, I felt anxious, constrained, agitated, I was frightened, I felt as if my strength had drained away and I was about to faint' (p. 106). When she describes how she reflected later on what had happened, she seems to acknowledge that awareness dawned, but she is quick to cover it up, as the suspension points suggest: 'When I woke up, I went over in my mind what had happened between the Mother Superior and me. I examined my conscience; as I did so again I thought I glimpsed... but they were such vague, stupid, ridiculous ideas that I dismissed them' (p. 108). As she makes clear to the Mother Superior, she enjoys the bliss that is ignorance: ' "I don't know anything, and I prefer that to gaining knowledge which might make me even more wretched than I already am" ' (p. 113).

Reading Suzanne's narrative necessarily involves us in an attempt to tease out the different levels of narrative illusion, that is, to distinguish between truth and fiction. This detective work reaches its climactic conclusion in the unconventional preface at the end of Suzanne's memoir. Prefaces normally claim to offer a clear statement of an author's intentions and to constitute a key to understanding the work they introduce. Diderot's preface is very different. Diderot deliberately positions it at the end of the text, refusing to use the word 'postface', coined in French by Voltaire in 1736. Doing this effectively exposes and reinstates the original relationship between a text and its preface, for, in reality, every preface is a postface, a discussion a posteriori of what has just been written, even though we conventionally read it before we read the main text.

But more than that, Diderot's preface, instead of preparing us for our first reading of the text proper, actually forces us to reread the novel, a rereading which destroys the illusion of reality which had been so artfully created. The preface plays with truth and illusion. *The Nun* appears to be a largely traditional novel—until we get to the end. The preface reveals the story of the trick played on the Marquis de Croismare. Alongside the narrative, it purports to be an authentic document, but it too is effectively fictional, as Diderot has tampered with the original letters. So the text ends with another narrative voice, another layer of fiction, another illusion of reality. The preface shows the strategy behind the narrative: to move the reader, which is the effect it has on Diderot himself, who declares himself 'deeply distressed' by the story he is engaged in writing (p. 154). The preface uncovers the workings of fiction, but at the same time it reasserts its undiminished power to move and to deceive. Diderot's preface calls into question the very genre of the novel, demystifying it by sabotaging the illusion of reality. In retrospect, we will realize that the apparent discrepancies and inconsistencies in Suzanne's age were so many means, on Diderot's part, of playing with the reader, making us feel sorry for the eternally young, innocent heroine, before revealing the illusion behind the apparent truth. The preface turns what otherwise might seem like an exercise in realism into what is now seen increasingly as an exercise in modernist (even postmodernist) fiction *avant la lettre*. The preface reveals that what we have just read is in fact a fiction. So *The Nun* is more than just Suzanne's memoir. It is that memoir plus the correspondence: it is a complex composite text.

Some critics dispute the idea that the preface is an integral part of *The Nun*, since it is originally a text assembled and published by Grimm. Following the example of Diderot's friend and editor Naigeon in 1798, some editors simply leave it out. Conversely, in the most recent critical edition of Diderot's complete works, the preface is included, but it precedes the memoir. The case for this rests simply on the fact that Diderot called that part of the text 'preface' when he could very well have called it 'postface'. But that edition is unusual, and it misses the point, which is that Diderot wanted readers to become convinced by the realism of the narrative before retrospectively shattering the illusion. Reading the preface first gives the game away, and that is not what Diderot wanted.

It is the destruction, not the creation, of the illusion that is perhaps the most challenging and fascinating aspect of *The Nun*, and it is this aspect that links *The Nun* to *Jacques the Fatalist*. These are two apparently contrasting novels, seemingly at opposite ends of the spectrum of Diderot's fictional output, the one the product of Diderot's engagement with Richardson in 1760, the other the product both of Diderot's reading of Laurence Sterne's *Tristram Shandy* and of his experiments in narrative form in the *Salons* in the 1760s and 1770s, which mark the major watershed in Diderot's career. But in fact both novels end in carefully contrived confusion and deliberate disarray. With the preface to *The Nun*, the influence of Richardson gives way to, or rather teasingly combines with, that of Sterne. It is surely no coincidence that Diderot revised *The Nun* for publication in 1780–2 immediately after *Jacques the Fatalist* had been serialized in the *Literary Correspondence* (November 1778–June 1780). Hence his comment to Meister, in his letter of 27 September 1780, that *The Nun* is the 'counterpart' to *Jacques the Fatalist*.

Diderot constantly questions and plays with the nature of illusion and the relationship between truth and fiction in his literary works. The 'Question to People of Letters' at the very end of the preface focuses precisely on the relationship of beauty to truth, of fiction to reality. There is a fundamental paradox at the heart of Diderot's fictional world: on the one hand he wants to draw readers in, to make us respond as if what we are reading is truth; on the other, he seems to acknowledge that this effect is best obtained through the art of fiction. Diderot does not so much resolve this paradox as revel in it. His desired aesthetic effect relies on the illusion of reality being lovingly created and then spectacularly dismantled. He seems to have set out both, in Richardsonian vein, to reveal how engaging and moving fiction can be, and, in a more subversive, Sternian manner, to demonstrate at the same time how easily readers let themselves be duped and taken in by the machinations of the work of art.

For Diderot, art and literature are not about the mimetic representation of reality. Rather they involve transposition and transfiguration, the object plus something more. As Diderot puts it in the *Salon* of 1767: 'The great man is no longer the one who creates truth; he is the one who knows how best to reconcile falsehood with truth.' Or, as the narrator of *The Two Friends from Bourbonne* acknowledges at the end of his tale, the writer of the *conte historique*, or historical tale, has to satisfy two apparently contradictory demands: 'to be at one and the same time a historian and a poet, a truth-teller and a liar.' Originally intended as a hoax, *The Nun* reads first like a true story, and then confounds all our expectations. Mystification is fundamental to this novel, from its genesis to its aesthetics.

NOTE ON THE TEXT

THE first version of *La Religieuse* dates from 1760 and survives as a manuscript in Diderot's own hand, a critical edition of which was published by Jean Parrish in 1963. Diderot made changes to this manuscript in 1780 before sending it to Meister to be published in the *Literary Correspondence*. Some time in 1780–1, Roland Girbal made a copy of this manuscript, on which Diderot made some corrections in 1781, and these were incorporated by Meister into his manuscript for publication. In 1782, and possibly as late as 1783, Diderot made further corrections to Girbal's manuscript. It is this latest version of the text that we know Diderot to have been involved in that forms the base text of the modern critical edition published in the definitive Hermann edition of Diderot's *Œuvres complètes* in 1975. That edition has been used for this translation, but with two important modifications. First, the Hermann edition departs from conventional practice in placing the preface before rather than after the text; I have restored the preface to its rightful position. And secondly, I have presented the frequent dialogues in the novel in modern format, that is to say, with the change of speaker signalled by a new line, rather than by dashes within the block of text.

La Religieuse has long been known in England. The novel was first published in book form by Jacques Buisson in Paris in October 1796, and such was the contemporary interest in French literature in England that by February the following year a pirated edition of the French text had been published in London. (Pirate copies of popular French texts were often quickly published in England in the eighteenth century: this was the case for Voltaire's *Candide*, Rousseau's *La Nouvelle Héloïse*, and Diderot's *Jacques le fataliste*.) The pirated edition was designed to hold the interest of the public until an English translation was ready.

The public did not have to wait long. In March 1797, only five months after the first French edition of the novel, the first English translation of *La Religieuse* appeared, entitled *The Nun* and published by Robinson in Paternoster Row, London. (In the same year translations into German and Italian also appeared.) This translation seems to be something of a rushed job, as it is littered with errors, mistranslations, and omissions. Yet the translation met with a chorus of praise in the press, notably in the *European Magazine and London Review*, which pointed out the distinction Diderot makes between enforced vocations and true devotion, and in the *Critical Review*, which offered large extracts and blistering denunciations of the Roman Catholic Church and the Old Regime in France. The only dissenting voice to be heard, it seems, was in the *British Critic*, which dismissed *The Nun* for its deplorable lack of taste and morality, and warned its readers that neither pleasure nor profit could be gained from reading it. The Jacobins nevertheless enjoyed reading Diderot: for example, William Godwin, who had just married Mary Wollstonecraft, read *La Religieuse* as early as April 1797. Tapping into the contemporary vogue for Gothic fiction (perhaps typified by Ann Radcliffe's *The Italian*, 1797), Diderot's novel went on to have an influence on Charles Maturin's *Melmoth the Wanderer* (1820). The Irish novelist appears to have copied out passages of Diderot's novel, particularly the visit of the Vicar General to the convent, and used them in the extended anti-Catholic diatribe of his own novel, albeit changing the gender of his narrator: this is a fine example of Protestant appropriation of the Enlightenment. Victorian Britain, by contrast, was less enamoured of Diderot. Only one translation of *La Religieuse* appeared in the nineteenth century: *The Nun, A Recital of the Convent*, a truncated (and, it was hoped, inoffensive) version of the 1797 translation, was included in the *Illustrated Literature of All Nations*, published in London in 1852. In this respect, at least, *La Religieuse* fared better than *Jacques le fataliste*, which was unavailable in English between 1797 and 1959.

In the twentieth century three translations of *La Religieuse* appeared: Francis Birrell's *Memoirs of a Nun*, first published by George Routledge in 1928 and incorporated in 1992 into the Everyman's Library series, with an introduction by P. N. Furbank; Marianne Sinclair's *The Nun*, published in 1966 in the New English Library series, with an introduction and foreword by Richard Griffiths; and Leonard Tancock's *The Nun* (minus the all-important preface), first published by the Folio Society in 1972 and then, in 1974, by Penguin.

SELECT BIBLIOGRAPHY

Editions

Œuvres complètes, ed. Herbert Dieckmann, Jacques Proust, and Jean Varloot, 25 vols. to date (Paris: Hermann, 1975–). Vol. xi (1975) contains *La Religieuse*, ed. Georges May, Herbert Dieckmann, Jane Marsh Dieckmann, Jean Parrish, and Jacques Chouillet.

Contes et romans, ed. Michel Delon (Paris: Gallimard, 2004).

La Religieuse, ed. Jean Parrish, in *Studies on Voltaire and the Eighteenth Century*, 22 (1963).

La Religieuse, ed. Roland Desné (Paris: Flammarion, 1968).

La Religieuse, ed. Robert Mauzi (Paris: Gallimard, 1972).

La Religieuse, ed. Annie Collognat-Barès (Paris: Pocket, 1999).

La Religieuse, ed. Claire Jaquier (Paris: Librairie Générale Française, 2000).

La Religieuse, ed. Heather Lloyd (London: Duckworth, 2000).

Correspondance, ed. G. Roth and J. Varloot, 16 vols. (Paris: Les Éditions de Minuit, 1955–70).

Diderot's Letters to Sophie Volland, trans. and ed. Peter France (London: Oxford University Press, 1972).

Biographies

Furbank, P. N., *Diderot: A Critical Biography* (London: Secker and Warburg, 1992).

Wilson, A. M., *Diderot* (New York: Oxford University Press, 1972).

Critical Studies

Adams, T., 'Suzanne's Fall: Seduction and Innocence in *La Religieuse*', *Diderot Studies*, 27 (1998), 13–28.

Byrne, P. W., 'The Form of Paradox: A Critical Study of Diderot's *La Religieuse*', *Studies on Voltaire and the Eighteenth Century*, 319 (1994), 169–293.

Carrera, R. de la, *Success in Circuit Lies: Diderot's Communicational Practice* (Stanford, Calif.: Stanford University Press, 1992).

Connon, D., *Diderot's Endgames* (Oxford: Peter Lang, 2002).

Conroy, P. V., 'Gender Issues in Diderot's *La Religieuse*', *Diderot Studies*, 24 (1991), 47–66.

Cook, M., 'Diderot's Imperfect Religious and the Language of the Senses', *British Journal for Eighteenth-Century Studies*, 11 (1988), 163–72.

DiPiero, T., *Dangerous Truths and Criminal Passions: The Evolution of the French Novel, 1569–1791* (Stanford, Calif.: Stanford University Press, 1992).

Edmiston, W., *Hindsight and Insight: Focalization in Four Eighteenth-Century French Novels* (University Park: Pennsylvania State University Press, 1991).

Ellrich, R. J., 'The Rhetoric of *La Religieuse* and Eighteenth-Century Forensic Rhetoric', *Diderot Studies*, 3 (1961), 129–54.

Fowler, J. E., *Voicing Desire: Family and Sexuality in Diderot's Narrative* (Oxford: Voltaire Foundation, 2000).

France, P., *Diderot* (Oxford: Oxford University Press, 1983).

Hayes, J. C., 'Retrospection and Contradiction in Diderot's *La Religieuse*', *Romanic Review*, 17 (1986), 233–42.

Jackson, K., '"Carnal to the Point of Scandal": On the Affair of *La Religieuse*', in Robert Mayer (ed.), *Eighteenth-Century Fiction on Screen* (Cambridge: Cambridge University Press, 2002), 139–56.

Josephs, H., 'Diderot's *La Religieuse*: Libertinism and the Dark Cave of the Soul', *Modern Language Notes*, 91 (1976), 734–55.

Mylne, V., *Diderot, 'La Religieuse'* (London: Grant and Cutler, 1981).

—— 'What Suzanne Knew: Lesbianism and *La Religieuse*', *Studies on Voltaire and the Eighteenth Century*, 208 (1982), 167–73.

Rex, W. E., 'Secrets from Suzanne: The Tangled Motives of *La Religieuse*', *Eighteenth Century*, 24 (1983), 185–98.

Rivers, C., '"Inintelligibles pour une femme honnête": Sexuality, Textuality and Knowledge in Diderot's *La Religieuse* and Gautier's *Mademoiselle de Maupin*', *Romanic Review*, 86 (1995), 1–29.

Sage, V., 'Diderot and Maturin: Enlightenment, Automata, and the Theatre of Terror', in Avril Horner (ed.), *European Gothic: A Spirited Exchange, 1760–1960* (Manchester: Manchester University Press, 2002), 55–70.

Sherman, C., 'The Deferral of Textual Authority in *La Religieuse*', *Postscript*, 2 (1985), 57–65.

Stewart, P., *Half-Told Tales: Dilemmas of Meaning in Three French Novels* (Chapel Hill: University of North Carolina, 1987).

Undank, J., 'Diderot's "Unnatural" Acts: Lessons from the Convent', *French Forum*, 11 (1986), 151–67.

Further Reading in Oxford's World Classics

Cleland, John, *Memoirs of a Woman of Pleasure*, ed. Peter Sabor.

Diderot, Denis, *Jacques the Fatalist*, trans. and ed. David Coward.

Laclos, Pierre Choderlos de, *Les Liaisons dangereuses*, trans. Douglas Parmée, ed. David Coward.

Maturin, Charles, *Melmoth the Wanderer*, ed. Douglas Grant, introd. Chris Baldick.

Prévost, Abbé, *Manon Lescaut*, trans. and ed. Angela Scholar.

Richardson, Samuel, *Pamela*, ed. Thomas Keymer and Alice Wakely.

Rousseau, Jean-Jacques, *Confessions*, trans. Angela Scholar, ed. Patrick Coleman.

—— *Discourse on the Origin of Inequality*, trans. Franklin Philip, ed. Patrick Coleman.

Sterne, Laurence, *Tristram Shandy*, ed. Ian Campbell Ross.

Voltaire, *Candide and Other Stories*, trans. and ed. Roger Pearson.

—— *Letters Concerning the English Nation*, ed. Nicholas Cronk.

A CHRONOLOGY OF DENIS DIDEROT

1713 5 October: birth of Denis Diderot at Langres, first child of Didier
Diderot (1675–1759), a master cutler, and Angélique Vigneron
(1677–1748), a tanner's daughter. There followed Denise (1715–
97), Catherine (1716–18), Catherine (II) (1719–35), Angélique
(1720–48), who took the veil and died mad, and Didier-Pierre
(1722–87), a strict churchman who could not tolerate his brother's
atheism.

1723 Enters the Jesuit college at Langres.

1726 22 August: receives the tonsure, the first step towards an ecclesiastical career.

1728 Autumn: moves to Paris to continue his education at the Collège
Louis-le-Grand, the Jansenist Collège d'Harcourt, and the Collège
de Beauvais.

1732 2 September: Master of Arts.

1735 6 August: awarded a bachelor's degree in theology but, after applying unsuccessfully for a living, abandons his plans for a career in the
Church and takes up law, with the reluctant approval of his father.

1737 Abandons law and makes a meagre living as a private tutor, translator, and supplier of sermons to the clergy. Frère Ange, at
Diderot's father's request, keeps an eye on him.

1741 Contemplates entering the seminary of Saint-Sulpice in Paris, but
falls in love with Antoinette Champion (1710–96).

1742 Meets Jean-Jacques Rousseau.

1743 January: His father refuses to allow him to marry Antoinette and
has him detained in a monastery at Langres, from which he escapes
a month later. 6 November: marries Antoinette secretly in Paris.
Publication of his translation of Temple Stanyan's *History of
Greece*.

1744 Birth of Angélique, who lives only a few weeks. Meets Condillac
and begins following a course of lectures in surgery.

1745 Translates Shaftesbury's *Inquiry concerning Virtue, or Merit*.

1746 Beginning of a liaison with Mme de Puisieux which lasts until
1751. Invited by the publisher Le Breton to translate Ephraim
Chambers's *Cyclopaedia* (1728). Meets d'Alembert. June: publishes
Philosophical Thoughts (*Pensées philosophiques*) anonymously; it is

banned in July. Birth of François-Jacques-Denis. Ordination of Didier-Pierre Diderot.

1747 June: denounced by the curé of Saint-Médard as 'a most dangerous man', he is watched by the police. 16 October: becomes joint director, with d'Alembert, of the *Encyclopaedia* (*Encyclopédie*).

1748 Publication of his first novel, *The Indiscreet Jewels* (*Les Bijoux indiscrets*). His sister Angélique dies in her convent. October: death of his mother.

1749 24 July–3 November: imprisoned at the Château de Vincennes for publishing the *Letter on the Blind* (*Lettre sur les aveugles*). There he is visited by Rousseau. On his release, he meets d'Holbach and Grimm.

1750 June: death of François-Jacques-Denis. October: birth of Denis-Laurent, who dies in December. Distribution of the Prospectus of the *Encyclopaedia*.

1751 18 February: *Letter on the Deaf and Dumb* (*Lettre sur les sourds et muets*). 1 July: publication of volume i of the *Encyclopaedia*.

1752 January: volume ii of the *Encyclopaedia* which, together with volume i, is banned by the Royal Council. The Prades affair brings Diderot into conflict with the authorities. Police raid his house. He entrusts other manuscripts to Malesherbes, the government minister in charge of the book trade, for safekeeping.

1753 November: volume iii of the *Encyclopaedia*. 2 September: birth of Marie-Angélique, his fourth and only surviving child. December: *Thoughts on the Interpretation of Nature* (*Pensées sur l'interprétation de la nature*). Not wishing to provoke the authorities, he publishes no more radical works until 1778.

1754 Volume iv of the *Encyclopaedia*. Begins following a course of chemistry lectures.

1755 Volume v of the *Encyclopaedia*. Moves to the rue Taranne, where he lives until shortly before his death. First of many contributions appear in Grimm's *Literary Correspondence* (*Correspondance littéraire*). July: meets Sophie Volland (1716–84), who may have been his mistress for a time, and with whom he corresponded regularly for many years.

1756 May: volume vi of the *Encyclopaedia*. 29 June: Diderot's letter to Landois on determinism.

1757 February: publication of the play *The Natural Son* (*Le Fils naturel*) and the *Conversations about 'The Natural Son'* (*Entretiens sur le Fils naturel*), a discussion of the play and of Diderot's views on drama.

March: beginning of the quarrel with Rousseau. November: volume vii of the *Encyclopaedia*.

1758 D'Alembert states his intention of withdrawing from the *Encyclopaedia*. October: Diderot breaks with Rousseau. November: the play *The Father of the Family* (*Le Père de famille*) and the *Discourse on Dramatic Poetry* (*Discours sur la poésie dramatique*).

1759 March: the permission to print the *Encyclopaedia* is withdrawn. 3 June: death of his father. September: the *Encyclopaedia* is condemned by Rome. Writes the first of his nine *Salons* (detailed accounts of the major art exhibitions in Paris, the last completed in 1781) for the *Literary Correspondence*.

1760 February–May: correspondence with the Marquis de Croismare, which becomes the starting point for *The Nun* (*La Religieuse*). 2 May: first performance of Palissot's satirical play *Les Philosophes*, which attacks him and the other leading *philosophes*.

1761 February: *The Father of the Family* is performed in Paris. Writes the *Eulogy of Richardson* (*Éloge de Richardson*), published in 1762. April (?): meets Jean-François Rameau, nephew of the composer. September: revises the last volumes of the *Encyclopaedia*.

1762 6 August: the Parlement orders the expulsion of the Jesuits. Works on *Rameau's Nephew* (*Le Neveu de Rameau*). D'Holbach introduces him to Laurence Sterne, who promises to send him the first six volumes of *Tristram Shandy*. The first of the eleven volumes of plates which accompany the *Encyclopaedia* appears: the last is published in 1772.

1763 Quarrels with his brother who, since 1745, had considered him the Antichrist. Meets David Hume.

1764 October: meets David Garrick. November: is furious to learn that his publisher Le Breton has secretly censored articles of the *Encyclopaedia*.

1765 Reconciled with d'Alembert, but Rousseau rejects his overtures. 1 May: Louis XV grants him permission to sell his library to Catherine II of Russia for 15,000 livres and an annual pension of 1,000 livres. She allows him to use it during his lifetime: it will revert to her only on his death. Autumn: reads volume viii of *Tristram Shandy* which contains the story of Trim's knee. Resumes, or more probably begins writing *Jacques the Fatalist* (*Jacques le fataliste*).

1766 Subscribers receive the remaining volumes (viii–xvii) of the *Encyclopaedia*.

1767   Diderot's brother appointed canon of the cathedral at Langres.

1769   August–September: writes *D'Alembert's Dream* (*Le Rêve de d'Alembert*). Falls in love with Mme de Maux.

1770   Writes a number of tales and dialogues, including *The Two Friends from Bourbonne* (*Les Deux Amis de Bourbonne*).

1771   Writes the *Philosophical Principles Concerning Matter and Movement* (*Principes philosophiques sur la matière et le mouvement*) and reads a version of *Jacques the Fatalist* to a friend. 26 September: *The Natural Son* staged in Paris. Diderot withdraws it after one performance.

1772   March: *On Women* (*Sur les femmes*). September: finishes two stories, *This is Not a Story* (*Ceci n'est pas un conte*) and *Madame de la Carlière*. Marriage of Angélique to an ironmaster, Caroillon de Vandeul.

1773   11 June: leaves Paris for Russia. 15 June–20 August: stays at The Hague, where he revises *Rameau's Nephew*, *Jacques the Fatalist*, and an article which would be published as *The Paradox of the Actor* (*Le Paradoxe sur le comédien*). 8 October: arrives at St Petersburg.

1774   In Russia, he works on various writings dealing with politics, physiology, and materialism. 5 March: leaves St Petersburg, reaching The Hague on 5 April, where he remains until 15 September. Arrives in Paris on 21 October.

1776   A dialogue on atheism, the *Conversation of a Philosopher with the Maréchale de* *** (*Entretien d'un philosophe avec la Maréchale de* ***), appears in Métra's *Secret Correspondence* (*Correspondance secrète*).

1777   Continues his collaboration (1772–80) with the abbé Raynal in the *History of the Two Indies* (*Histoire des deux Indes*), writes a comedy, *Is he Good, is he Wicked?* (*Est il bon, est il méchant?*), and further revises *Rameau's Nephew* and *Jacques the Fatalist*.

1778   November–June 1780: publication in serial form of *Jacques the Fatalist* in the *Literary Correspondence*.

1780   Revises *The Nun*, also serialized in the *Literary Correspondence*, and expands his *Essay on the Reigns of Claudius and Nero* (*Essai sur les règnes de Claude et de Néron*, 1778), his major political work.

1781   July: reads *Jacques the Fatalist* to his wife and probably makes further additions to the text.

1783   29 October: death of d'Alembert.

1784   22 February: death of Sophie Volland. The news is kept from Diderot, who is recovering from an attack of apoplexy. 15 July:

moves to the rue de Richelieu. 31 July: death of Diderot. He is buried (1 August) in the church of Saint-Roch. 9 September: Catherine II sends 1,000 roubles to Mme Diderot.

1785 Friedrich Schiller translates the Mme de la Pommeraye episode of *Jacques the Fatalist* in *Die Rheinische Thalia*. This text is translated back into French by J.-P. Doray de Langrais in 1792 as *Strange Case of a Woman's Vengeance* (*Exemple singulier de la vengeance d'une femme*). 5 November: Diderot's library and manuscripts arrive in St Petersburg.

1792 *Jacques the Fatalist* translated into German by Christlob Mylius.

1796 Publication of *The Nun* and *Jacques the Fatalist*.

1805 Goethe publishes his translation of *Rameau's Nephew*.

THE NUN

THE Marquis de Croismare's reply, if he decides to reply, will give me the opening lines of this story. Before writing to him, I wanted to find out what sort of man he was. He is a man of the world, with a distinguished military career behind him.* He is a widower, not young, with one daughter and two sons, whom he loves and who love him too. He is well born, enlightened, intelligent, cheerful, fond of the arts, and, above all, he has a somewhat eccentric cast of mind. People have spoken to me in glowing terms of his humanity, his honour, and his integrity; and judging by the keen interest he has taken in my case, and by everything I have heard about him, I concluded that I had in no way compromised my position by writing to him. But that is not to say that he will agree to intervene on my behalf without first knowing who I am, and it is for this reason that I have resolved to put aside my pride and my diffidence and write these memoirs in which I depict some of my misfortunes, writing with neither skill nor artifice, but with the naivety of a young person of my age and with my own native honesty. Since my protector may well require it, or perhaps since I might simply decide one day to complete these memoirs at a time when the details of distant events might no longer be so fresh in my memory, I thought that the summary at the end, together with the deep impression they have made on me and will continue to make on me for the rest of my life, would be enough to allow me to remember them accurately.

My father was a lawyer.* He had married my mother quite late in life, and they had three daughters. He had more than enough money to provide for all three. But to have done that would have meant at least that he should love them equally, and that is the last thing I can give him credit for. I certainly outshone my sisters in terms of intellect, beauty, character, and ability, and this seemed to upset my parents. As both the gifts of nature and the fruits of hard work, which set me above my sisters, seemed only to create trouble, I decided at a very early age to try to be like them, in the hope of being loved, cherished, praised, and invariably excused as they were. If somebody happened to say to my mother: 'Your children are charming...', the comment was never taken to refer to me. On the rare occasion when this wrong was righted, the praise I received cost me so dear when she and I were alone that I would have been just as happy to have been met with indifference or even insults, for whenever visitors showed an interest in me, things would take a turn for the worse once they had left. Oh, how many times I wept because I was not born ugly, stupid, foolish, conceited—in a word, with all the disadvantages that earned my sisters the favour of our parents! I tried to find some explanation for this strange behaviour in a father and mother who were otherwise decent, fair, and pious. Shall I tell you what I think, Monsieur? Some words my father let slip in a fit of rage, for he was a violent man, certain incidents over the years, comments made by neighbours, and remarks by servants, all these made me suspect one reason which might go some way to excusing them. Perhaps my father had his doubts about my birth, perhaps I reminded my mother of an indiscretion she had committed and the ingratitude of a man whom she had trusted too much, how can I know? But even if these suspicions were unfounded, what would I be risking in telling you about them? You will burn this letter, and I promise to burn your replies.

Since the three of us had been born in quick succession, we grew up together. Eligible young men made themselves known to us. My eldest sister was courted by a charming young man. I soon noticed that he was more interested in me, however, and I guessed that she would quickly become just the pretext for his frequent visits. Even then I could see all the pain that his attentions might cause me, so I warned my mother. This was perhaps the only thing I ever did in my whole life that pleased her, and this is how I was rewarded. Four days later, or thereabouts, I was told that a place had been found for me in a convent, and the following day I was taken there. I was so unhappy at home that this turn of events did not trouble me at all, and I went off to Sainte-Marie,* my first convent, quite cheerfully. My sister's suitor, meanwhile, not seeing me any more, forgot all about me and duly married her. His name is Monsieur K..., and he is a notary in Corbeil, where married life is treating him rather badly. My second sister was married to a Monsieur Bauchon, a silk merchant in Paris, in the rue Quincampoix, and they are happy together.

My two sisters now being married off, I believed that thoughts would turn to me, and that I would soon be able to leave the convent. I was sixteen and a half then. My sisters had been given considerable dowries, I was convinced that I would be treated in the same way, and my head was full of enticing plans for the future, when one day I was summoned to the parlour.* It was Father Séraphin,* my mother's spiritual director. He had also been mine, so he found it easy to explain the reason for his visit: he had come to persuade me to take the veil. I bridled at this strange suggestion, and I told him plainly that I had no inclination whatsoever towards the religious life.

'Well, that is a shame,' he said, 'because your parents have spent all their money on your sisters, and I cannot see what else they could possibly do for you in their current straits. Think about it, Mademoiselle, you must either enter this convent permanently, or go to another in the provinces where you will be accepted for a modest sum,* and stay there until your parents die, which may not happen for quite some time yet...'

I complained bitterly and shed floods of tears. The Mother Superior had been informed, and she was waiting for me when I returned from the parlour. I cannot begin to explain how distraught I was. She said to me:

'What on earth is wrong, my dear child?' (She knew better than I did what was wrong with me.) 'Just look at you! I've never seen such despair! I fear the worst! Have you lost your father or mother?'

As I collapsed in her arms, I thought of saying: 'I wish to God I had!...' Instead, I simply cried out:

'Alas, I have neither father nor mother; I'm a poor, wretched girl who's hated and who's to be buried alive in this place.'

She let the torrent pass, waiting for me to calm down. I explained to her more clearly what I had just been told. She seemed to feel sorry for me, pitied me, encouraged me not to become a nun if I had no inclination, and promised to pray, remonstrate, and appeal on my behalf. Oh! Monsieur, you simply cannot begin to imagine how devious these Mothers Superior are! She did, in fact, write. She knew perfectly well what replies she would receive. She showed them to me, and it was only some time later that I began to doubt her good faith. Meanwhile the time had come for my decision, and she came to tell me so with the most studied sadness. At first she said nothing, then she uttered a few words of commiseration, from which I was able to gather the rest. There followed another scene of despair; I shall not have many others to describe. These women are highly skilled in the art of self-control. Then she said to me, in fact I think she was weeping as she did so:

'So, my child, you're going to leave us! Dear child, we'll never see each other again!...'

And so she went on, but I was not listening. I had collapsed onto a chair. One minute I was silent, the next I was sobbing. One minute I was sitting quite still, the next I was on my feet, now leaning against the wall for support, now pressing my face to her bosom as I poured out my misery. We continued like this for some time and then she added:

'But there is one thing you can do. Listen, but don't tell anyone I gave you this advice—I'm relying on your complete discretion, for I wouldn't wish to compromise my position, not for anything in the world. What are you being asked to do? To take the veil? So! why don't you? What does it commit you to? Nothing, except staying here with us for another two years.* No one knows who's going to die and who'll be alive; two years is a long time, a lot can happen in two years...'

To these insidious remarks she added so many words of affection, so many protestations of friendship, and so many sweet falsehoods. I knew where I was, but I did not know where I would be taken, she said, and I let myself be persuaded. So she wrote to my father. Her letter was very good—oh yes, nobody could write better: my misery, my suffering, and my complaints were all made very plain. I am sure that a wiser girl than I would have been taken in by it. And so my consent was finally given. How quickly all the preparations were made! The date was set, my habit made, the time for the ceremony came, and looking back today I cannot see the slightest interval between all these events.

I forgot to mention that I saw my father and my mother, that I made every effort to soften their hearts, and that I found them inflexible. It was a certain abbé Blin,* a Sorbonne doctor, who read the homily, and the Bishop of Aleppo* who gave me my habit. This ceremony is not by nature a cheerful one, and that day it was one of the saddest ever.* Although the nuns bustled around me and supported me, I felt my knees give way time and time again, and thought I would collapse on the altar steps. I heard nothing, saw nothing; I was in a daze. I was led, and I followed; I was asked questions, and others replied for me. This cruel ceremony eventually came to its end, everybody went away, and I was left with the flock which I had just joined. My companions surrounded me, embracing me and saying to each other:

'But look, Sister, look how pretty she is! Look how her black veil brings out the whiteness of her complexion! How her headband suits her! How it rounds off her face! How it makes her cheeks stand out! How her habit shows off her waist and her arms!...'

I hardly heard a word they were saying, I felt so wretched. But I must admit that, when I was alone in my cell, I remembered the fulsome things they said. I could not resist looking in my little mirror to see if what they had said was true, and it seemed to me that their flattery was not wholly without foundation. This is meant to be a day of great honour, and the point was emphasized for my benefit, but I was almost oblivious. People pretended to disbelieve me and said so, but it was clear that it was not so. In the evening, after prayers, the Superior came to my cell.

'Really,' she said, after looking at me for a short while, 'I don't know why you dislike your habit so much. It suits you perfectly, and you look charming. Sister Suzanne is a very beautiful nun, and we will love you all the more for that. Now, let's have a look at you. Turn around. You're not holding yourself quite straight; don't lean forward like that...'

She showed me how to carry myself, my head, my feet, my hands, my body, and my arms. It was almost like being given a lesson by Marcel* on convent style, for each way of life has its own. Then she sat down, and said to me:

'That's good, but now let's talk seriously. The next two years are taken care of. During that time your parents may change their minds, and you yourself will perhaps want to stay here when they want to take you away—that cannot be ruled out altogether.'

'No, Madame, don't believe that.'

'You've been with us for a long time, but you still don't know what our life is like. It certainly has its pains, but it also has its pleasures...'

You can well imagine everything she said about the world and the cloister, for it is written about everywhere, and always in the same way. Thank God I was made to read all that nonsense which the religious churn out about their way of life, which they know so well but which they hate, and all of it written to attack the world, which they love, but which they tear to shreds without actually knowing what it is like.

I will spare you the details of my noviciate. If one observed all its austerities, it would be unbearable, but it is in fact the most pleasant period of convent life. The novice mistress is the most indulgent sister imaginable. Her aim is to protect you from all the thorns of convent life; it is a lesson in seduction of the most subtle and refined kind. It is she who deepens the darkness surrounding you, who cradles you, who lulls you to sleep, who impresses you, who fascinates you; ours was particularly devoted to me. I do not think there is a single soul, young and inexperienced, who could resist this dark art. The world has its pitfalls, but I do not imagine that they are reached by such a gentle slope. If I sneezed twice, I was dispensed from the Divine Office, work, and prayer; I went to bed earlier, I got up later; the rules did not apply to me. Just imagine, Monsieur, there were days when I longed for the time to sacrifice myself. Not a single unpleasant story happens in the world outside without our being told about it; true stories are embroidered, false ones are invented, and then endless praise and thanksgiving are offered to God for saving us from such humiliations. Meanwhile the moment that I had at times wished for was approaching. Then I became pensive, I felt my resistance returning and growing stronger. I went to the Mother Superior or to the novice mistress and confided in them. These women certainly know how to avenge the trouble novices cause them; for it is wrong to think that they enjoy the hypocritical role they play or the nonsense they are forced to repeat to us. In the end it all becomes so familiar and dull to them. But they remain determined, because doing it earns the convent some thousand *écus*.* This is the main reason why they lie all their lives and prepare young, innocent girls for forty, fifty years of despair and perhaps eternal suffering. For it is certain, Monsieur, that out of every hundred nuns who die before the age of fifty, there are exactly one hundred who are damned, and of these many in the meantime become mad, weak-minded, or delirious.*

One day one of these mad nuns escaped from the cell where she had been locked up. I saw her. That was the beginning of my good or bad fortune, depending, Monsieur, on how you decide to treat me. I have never seen a sight more hideous. She was unkempt and almost naked; she was weighed down by iron chains; her eyes were wild; she tore at her hair, beat her chest with her fists, ran about, screamed, called down the most awful curses on herself and on everyone else; she looked for a window to throw herself out of. I was terrified, my whole body shook, I saw that this poor, unfortunate girl's fate would be mine too, and instantly I made up my mind that I would rather die a thousand deaths than expose myself to that. Others foresaw the effect that this event might have on my mind and they knew they must prevent it. I was told endless ridiculous and contradictory lies about this nun: that she was already mentally deranged when she was admitted to the convent; that she had had a great fright at a critical time of her life;* that she had started having visions; that she believed herself to be in touch with the angels; that she had read pernicious works which had ruined her mind; that she had listened to new thinkers peddling an unorthodox moral code, who had made her so frightened about God's judgement that her mind had been quite disturbed;* that all she saw now was demons, hell, and fiery depths; that they were unfortunate indeed; that such a thing had never been heard of before in the convent; and goodness knows what else! This had no effect on me; my mad nun was constantly on my mind, and I swore again not to take my vows.

Yet the time came when I was going to have to show if I could keep my word. One morning, after the office, I saw the Mother Superior coming into my cell. She had a letter in her hand. Sadness and despondency were written on her face, her arms trailed by her sides; it was almost as if she didn't have the strength in her hand to lift up the letter. She looked at me, her eyes appearing to fill with tears. Neither of us said anything. She was waiting for me to speak first; I was tempted, but I stopped myself. She asked me how I was, adding that the office had certainly been long today, that I had coughed a little, and that I seemed to her a little unwell. I replied: 'No, my dear Mother.' She was still holding the letter in her limp hand. As she spoke to me she placed the letter on her lap, and partly concealed it from view with her hand. Finally, having asked a few questions about my father and my mother, and realizing that I was not going to ask her what the piece of paper was, she said to me: 'I have here a letter...'. As she uttered the word I felt my heart becoming uneasy, and I added in a broken voice and with my lips trembling:

'Is it from my mother?'

'It is. Here, read it...'

I gathered myself a little, took the letter, and at first read it quite confidently. But as I read, I felt a succession of different emotions— fear, indignation, anger, bitter disappointment—and my voice kept changing, my facial expression, and my gestures. Sometimes I held the piece of paper in my fingertips; at other times I held it as if I wanted to rip it up or I gripped it violently as if I felt like screwing it up and throwing it away.

'So, my child, what have you got to say?'

'You know very well, Madame.'

'No I don't. Times are hard, your family has suffered great losses; your sisters' finances are in turmoil; between them they have lots of children and your parents have exhausted their resources in marrying them off; they continue to ruin themselves in order to support them. It is impossible for them to guarantee you a certain future. You've taken the habit; the expenses have been met; by doing this you've given them hope; word has spread in the outside world that you will shortly be taking your vows. And you can always count on my total support too. I've never drawn anyone into the religious life: it's a state that God calls us to, and it's very dangerous to mix one's own voice with his. I shan't even try to speak to your heart if God's grace isn't already speaking to it. To this day I haven't been responsible for any girl's misfortune: why would I want to start with you, my child, you who are so dear to me? I realize that it was I who persuaded you to take your first steps towards becoming a nun, and I won't permit anyone to force you into anything you don't want to do. So let's take stock, let's think about this together. Do you want to make your profession?'

'No, Madame.'

'You have no inclination for the religious life?'

'No, Madame.'

'You won't obey your parents?'

'No, Madame.'

'So what do you want to do?'

'Anything except become a nun. I don't want to be a nun, I won't be a nun.'

'Very well! You won't be a nun. So we need to compose a reply to your mother...'

We agreed on a few ideas. She wrote the letter, which she showed me. It seemed very good. Yet the convent confessor was sent to see me; the Sorbonne doctor who had given the homily when I took my habit was also sent to see me; I was recommended to the novice mistress; I saw the Bishop of Aleppo; I had to cross swords with pious ladies whom I didn't know but who meddled in my business; I had endless discussions with monks and priests; my father came to see me and my sisters wrote to me; in the end my mother came to see me: I resisted it all. Nevertheless the date for my profession was fixed. Every effort was made to obtain my consent, but when it became evident that these efforts were in vain, the decision was taken to proceed without my consent.

From that moment on I was locked in my cell. I was forced to keep silent. I was cut off from everyone else, left to my own devices, and I realized that they were resolved to deal with me as they saw fit. I did not want to become a nun, I was clear about that. All the true or false horrors with which I was endlessly confronted did nothing to weaken my resolve. Nevertheless I was in an awful state. I did not know how long it would last, and should it finally end, I knew even less about what might happen to me afterwards. In the midst of this uncertainty, I took a decision which you are free to judge as you wish, Monsieur. I no longer saw anyone, neither the Mother Superior, nor the novice mistress, nor my companions. I sent word to the Mother Superior, pretending that I was coming round to my parents' point of view. But my plan was to end this persecution in a spectacular way and to protest publicly against the violence that was being planned. So I announced that my fate was in their hands, that they could do with me what they wished, that I was expected to take my vows, and that I would do so. This brought joy to the whole house, and once again I found myself being complimented and flattered and seduced in all kinds of ways. 'God had spoken to my heart; nobody was better suited to the state of perfection than I was. Any other outcome was impossible; they had always known that this would happen. One didn't fulfil one's duties in such an edifying and devoted way if one wasn't truly destined to such a state. The novice mistress had never seen a clearer sense of vocation in any of her charges. She had been altogether surprised by my lapse, but she had always assured our Mother Superior that, with perseverance, I would come through in the end; that all the best nuns have such moments, which are provoked by the devil who intensifies his efforts when he is about to lose his prey; that I was going to be free of him; that the way ahead for me was strewn with roses; that the duties of the religious life would seem all the more bearable to me since I had formed such a very exaggerated view of them beforehand; and that this unexpected sense of the weight of the burden was a grace sent from heaven, which used this means to make it more bearable...' It seemed quite odd to me that the same thing could come from either God or the devil, depending on how they chose to look at it. There are many other similar cases in religious matters, and those who consoled me often said that my thoughts were either prompted by Satan or inspired by God. The same ill comes either from God who tests us or from the devil who tempts us.

I behaved discreetly; I thought I could take care of myself. I saw my father, who spoke to me coldly. I saw my mother, who kissed me. I received letters of congratulation from my sisters and from many others besides. I knew that a Monsieur Sornin, priest of Saint-Roch, would be giving the homily, and that Monsieur Thierry, chancellor of the University, would preside when I took my vows.* All went well until the day before the big day, except that, having discovered that the ceremony would take place behind closed doors, that there would be very few people in attendance, and that only family members would be allowed into the church, I had the doorkeeper* summon all the people in our neighbourhood, my friends, and I was allowed to write to some of my acquaintances. All these unexpected guests arrived at the church, and they had to be let in. So the congregation was of just about the necessary size for my plan to work.

Oh, Monsieur! What a night I spent before the ceremony! I did not go to bed. Instead I sat and cried out to God to help me. I raised my hands heavenwards, and I called on him to witness the violence that was being done to me. I played out in my mind the role I would perform, kneeling before the altars, a young girl crying out in protest against an event to which she seems to have given her consent; I imagined the scandal that this would cause in those present, the despair that the nuns would feel, the anger of my parents. 'Oh God, what is to become of me?...' As I uttered these words, I became utterly weak and fainted, collapsing onto my bolster. This weakness was followed by trembling, my knees shook, and my teeth chattered loudly. After the trembling I felt feverish. My mind was unsettled. I cannot remember getting undressed or leaving my cell, but I was found, naked but for a chemise, lying on the ground outside the Mother Superior's room, motionless and almost dead. I have found out these things since. In the morning I was in my cell, with the Mother Superior, the novice mistress, and those known as assistants all gathered around my bed. I was utterly exhausted. They asked me some questions, but they saw by my answers that I had no idea what had happened, so they did not tell me about it. They asked me how I was, if I still maintained my holy resolve, and if I felt up to the tiring events of the day. I said yes, and, contrary to their expectations, everything went ahead as planned.

Everything had been arranged the day before. The bells were rung to announce to everyone that a young girl was to be made to suffer. My heart was still pounding. Nuns came to get me ready: this day is a day for getting dressed up. As I recall these rituals now, it seems to me that they had about them something solemn and rather touching for an innocent young girl whose inclination led her nowhere else. I was taken to the church; mass was celebrated. The good priest, who discerned in me a resignation that I did not have, gave me a long sermon in which every single word was misconceived. Everything he said to me about my happiness, about grace, about my courage, my zeal, my fervour, and all the fine feelings he imagined me to have, was simply ridiculous. This contrast between his praise of me and what I was about to do troubled me; I had moments of uncertainty, but they soon passed. I felt now more than ever that I lacked everything that was required in order to be a good nun. Meanwhile the fateful moment arrived. When I had to enter the place where I was to make my vows, I found I could no longer walk. Two of my companions took me by the arms. I rested my head on the shoulder of one of them, and I dragged myself along. I do not know what was happening in the souls of those present, but they saw before them a young victim, close to death, being taken to the altar, and all around me I could hear sighs and tears, though not, I am sure, from my father and mother. Everyone was on their feet; some young women had climbed up on chairs and pressed themselves against the grille.* Everyone fell completely silent when the person presiding at the ceremony said to me:

'Marie-Suzanne Simonin, do you promise to tell the truth?'

'I do.'

'Are you here by your own free will?'

I replied 'No', but the nuns accompanying me replied 'Yes' on my behalf.

'Marie-Suzanne Simonin, do you swear to God that you will be chaste, poor, and obedient?'

I hesitated a moment. The priest waited. And then I replied:

'No, Monsieur.'

He repeated the question:

'Marie-Suzanne Simonin, do you swear to God that you will be chaste, poor, and obedient?'

I replied more firmly:

'No, Monsieur, no.'

He stopped and said:

'My child, calm down and listen to me.'

'Monsieur.' I said to him, 'you have asked me if I swear to God that I will be chaste, poor, and obedient. I have understood the question, and my answer is no...' And turning at that moment towards the congregation, most of whom were now muttering things, I indicated that I wanted to speak. The muttering stopped and I said:

'Gentlemen, and especially you, my father and my mother, I call on you all to witness...'

As I spoke one of the nuns drew the curtain across the grille, and I realized that it was pointless continuing. The nuns surrounded me and reproached me vigorously; I listened to them in silence. I was taken to my cell and locked in.

There, all alone with my thoughts, I started reassuring my soul. I went back over what I had done and I was not sorry for it. I realized that, after the scandal I had caused, it would be impossible for me to stay there for much longer and that perhaps nobody would dare to put me in a convent again. I did not know what would become of me, but I could see nothing worse than being a nun against one's will. I remained for quite some time without hearing any news at all. Those nuns who brought me my food would come in, put my dinner down on the ground and leave in silence. After a month I was given ordinary clothes to wear; I stopped wearing my religious habit. The Mother Superior came and told me to follow her. I followed her to the door of the convent. There I got into a carriage where my mother was waiting for me alone; I sat on the front seat and we set off. We sat facing each other in complete silence. I lowered my eyes, not daring to look at her. I do not know what was happening in my soul, but suddenly I threw myself at her feet and put my head on her knees. I said nothing, but sobbed and was hardly able to breathe. She pushed me away firmly. I did not get up. My nose started bleeding; I grabbed one of her hands, despite her efforts to avoid me, and, bathing it in my tears and my blood, I pressed my mouth to it, kissing it and saying: 'You're still my mother; I'm still your daughter...' She replied (pushing me away yet more violently and tearing her hand from mine): 'Get up, you wretched girl, get up.' I did as she said, sat down again, and pulled my headscarf down over my face. She had spoken with such authority and firmness that I felt I had to hide myself from view. My tears and the blood streaming from my nose mixed together and dripped down my arms, and I ended up covered in it without noticing. From a few things she said I realized that her gown and undergarments had been stained and that she was not pleased. We arrived at the house, where I was immediately taken to a little room that had been prepared for me. Again I knelt before my mother on the stairs and tried to stop her from leaving by clinging to her clothes, but the result was only to make her turn back and look at me with indignation written all over her face, mouth, and eyes, a look which you can imagine better than I can describe.

I entered my new prison, where I spent six months, each day pleading in vain to be allowed to speak to her, to see my father, or to write to them. I was brought my meals, I was waited on; a servant girl accompanied me to mass on feast days and then shut me in my room again. I read, worked, cried, and sometimes sang, and so the time passed. One secret feeling kept me going: that I was free and that my fate, however hard it may be, could change. But it had been decided that I was to become a nun, and so I did.

Such cruelty and obduracy on my parents' part have finally convinced me of what I initially suspected about my birth. I have never been able to find any other way of forgiving them. My mother apparently feared that one day I might challenge the distribution of the estate, that I might lay claim again to my rightful inheritance, and that I might put a natural child on a par with legitimate children. But what was only a conjecture is going to become a certainty.

While I was shut away at home, I engaged in few acts of religious devotion, but I was nevertheless sent to confession on the eve of high feasts. I told you that I had the same spiritual director as my mother. I spoke to him and told him all about how harshly I had been treated for some three years. He knew about it already. I complained most bitterly and resentfully about my mother. He had entered the priesthood late in life; he was humane; he listened to me quietly and said:

'My child, pity your mother; pity her even more than you blame her. She has a good soul; rest assured that she has acted this way despite herself.'

'Despite herself, Monsieur! And what can possibly force her to do that? Did she not bring me into this world? What's the difference between me and my sisters?'

'Considerable.'

'Considerable! I don't know what you mean.'

I was about to compare myself to my sisters, but he stopped me and said:

'Come, come now, cruelty is not your parents' vice. Try to bear your fate patiently and try at least to make something good out of it in the eyes of God. I shall speak to your mother: rest assured that I shall use whatever influence I have over her in order to help you.'

This *considerable* that he had said in reply to me was illuminating: I was no longer in any doubt that what I had thought about my birth was right.

The following Saturday, at about half past five in the evening, at dusk, the servant girl who was responsible for me came up to my room and said: 'Your mother says you must get dressed.' An hour later: 'Your mother wants you to come downstairs.' At the entrance to the house I found a carriage which the servant girl and I got into, and I learned that we were going to the Feuillants monastery,* where Father Séraphin was. He was waiting for us, alone. The servant girl left and I went into the parlour. I sat down, anxious and curious to find out what he had to say to me. This is what he said:

'Mademoiselle, I'm going to explain to you the mystery surrounding your parents' harsh treatment of you; your mother has given me permission to do so. You're sensible, intelligent, and resilient. You're at an age where you can keep a secret, even one which doesn't concern you. A long time ago I first urged your mother to tell you what you're about to learn, but she was never able to bring herself to do so. It's hard for a mother to confess a grave fault to her child. You know what she's like: she's not the sort to be able to face the humiliation of making such a confession. She thought that she could make you do what she wanted without having to resort to this measure. She was wrong, and this has angered her. Today she has accepted my advice, and she has asked me to tell you that you're not the daughter of Monsieur Simonin.'

I replied immediately: 'I thought as much.'

'Now look, Mademoiselle, think about it, weigh it up, consider whether your mother can, with or without the consent of your father, treat you in the same way as her daughters who are not your sisters, whether she can confess to your father a fact which he already suspects all too well.'

'But, Monsieur, who is my father?'

'Mademoiselle, that's something I haven't been told. What is all too clear, Mademoiselle,' he added, 'is that your sisters have been given enormously preferential treatment, that every possible step has been taken, including marriage contracts, the conversion of property, stipulations, trusts, and other means, to ensure that there is nothing left of your rightful inheritance, in case one day you take legal action in order to claim it back. If your parents die, you'll find there's not much for you. You're refusing now to enter a convent, but in the future you may well regret it.'

'That's impossible, Monsieur. I ask for nothing.'

'You have no idea what hardship, work, and destitution really are.'

'At least I know the price of freedom, and the burden of a way of life to which one isn't called.'

'I've said everything I had to say to you. It's up to you now, Mademoiselle, to think it over...'

And then he got up.

'But, Monsieur, I have one more question.'

'Go ahead.'

'Do my sisters know what you've told me?'

'No, Mademoiselle.'

'So how could they possibly decide to rob their sister of her inheritance? Because they do think I'm their sister.'

'Ah! Mademoiselle, it's for their own good! Their own good! Otherwise they would never have enjoyed the considerable advantages they have. Everyone is selfish in this world. I wouldn't advise you to count on them when your parents die. You can be sure that they'll fight you even for the small amount that is due to you, right down to the last penny. They have lots of children: this alone will be a respectable enough reason for them to reduce you to begging. And then they're helpless in the matter, for it's the husbands who deal with everything: if they felt any pity, any assistance they gave you without telling their husbands would become a source of domestic strife. I see such things all the time: abandoned children, or even legitimate children, supported at the expense of domestic peace. And then, Mademoiselle, the bread one receives is terribly dry. If you take my advice, you'll make peace with your parents; you'll do what your mother is expecting of you; you'll become a nun; you'll be given a small pension which will enable you to live the rest of your life, if not happily, at least tolerably. Besides, I shall not hide from you the fact that your mother's apparent desertion of you, her insistence on locking you away, and a number of other factors, which I forget now but which I once knew, have had exactly the same effect on your father as they have on you: he was suspicious about your birth, but he's not any more, and although he doesn't know the full truth, he is sure that you are his child only in so far as the law attributes a woman's children to the man who is her husband. So, Mademoiselle, you're good and sensible; think about what you've just learned.'

I stood up and started crying. I saw that he was moved too; he gently lifted his eyes heavenwards and led me out. The servant girl who had come with me was waiting for me; we got back in the carriage and went home.

It was late. I spent part of the night pondering what had just been revealed to me; I was still thinking about it the next day. I was fatherless; scruples had robbed me of my mother; steps had been taken to ensure that I could lay no claim to the rights that were legally mine by birth; an extremely harsh domestic captivity; no hope, no means of support. Perhaps if I had been told the truth earlier, after my sisters had been married off, if I had been allowed to stay at home, where they were still living, then there might have been someone who would have found my character, my mind, my appearance, and my abilities a sufficient dowry. This could still happen, but the scandal that I had caused in the convent made it more difficult: it is seldom understood how a girl of seventeen or eighteen years of age can have driven herself to such lengths without a rare degree of determination. Men praise this quality highly in each other, but it seems to me that they willingly forgo it in a potential wife. Yet it was a possibility worth pursuing before trying to think of something else. I decided to confide in my mother. I requested a meeting with her, which she granted.

It was winter. She was sitting in an armchair in front of the fire.

Her face looked severe, staring, and motionless. I went over to her, threw myself at her feet, and asked her to forgive me for all the wrong I had done.

'You'll earn my pardon', she said, 'by what you have to say. Get up. Your father is away, so you have all the time you need to explain yourself. You've seen Father Séraphin, so you now know who you are and what you can expect of me, if you intend not to punish me for the rest of my life for a mistake for which I have already paid so dearly. So, Mademoiselle! What do you expect of me? What have you decided to do?'

'Mother,' I replied, 'I know that I have nothing and that I can expect nothing. I've no intention of adding to your woes, of whatever kind they may be. Perhaps you'd have found me more willing to do your will if you'd told me earlier about those things which it was difficult for me to suspect. But now I know, I know who I am, and all I have to do now is behave in a way that's in keeping with my status. I'm no longer surprised by the different treatment meted out to my sisters and me. I recognize the justice of that difference, and I support it. But I'm still your child; you carried me in your womb; and I hope you won't forget that.'

'Woe betide me', she added sharply, 'if I didn't tell you as much as I am able to.'

'Very well, Mother,' I said to her, 'let me experience your goodness again; let me be with you again; let me enjoy again the tenderness of the man who thinks he's my father.'

'He's almost as sure', she added, 'as you and I are about your birth. I can't see you standing next to him without hearing his reproaches; he reproaches me by treating you harshly; you shouldn't expect him to be like a tender father with you. What's more, and I freely admit this, you remind me of a betrayal, someone else's ingratitude that I find so utterly odious that I can't bear to think about it any more. I can't help seeing this man standing between us; he repels me, and I end up feeling for you the hatred that I feel for him.'

'What!' I said. 'Can I not even hope that you, you and Monsieur Simonin, might treat me like a stranger, a waif whom you've humanely taken in?'

'Neither of us can do that. My daughter, I don't want you to poison my life any longer. If you didn't have any sisters, I know what

I'd have to do. But you have two sisters, and they both have a large family. The passion which once sustained me has long since died; now my conscience has resumed its rightful role.'

'But what about the man who fathered me?...'

'He's dead; he died without giving you a second thought; and that's the least of his failings...'

As she spoke, her expression changed, her eyes lit up, indignation was etched all over her face. She tried speaking, but she could not make the words come out properly, for her lips were trembling so much. She was sitting down; she put her head in her hands to prevent me from seeing the violent emotions she was experiencing. She stayed like that for some time, then stood up and walked around the room without saying a word. She fought back the tears which were welling up in her eyes, and she said:

'The monster! It was no thanks to him that all the hurt he caused me didn't kill you in my womb. But God saved us both so that the mother might atone for her sin through her child... My daughter, you have nothing, you'll always have nothing. The little that I can do for you is stolen from your sisters: such are the effects of my weakness. Yet I hope to have nothing to reproach myself for when I die: I'll have built up your dowry by my savings. I'm not taking advantage of my husband's indulgence; but every day I put aside what he is occasionally generous enough to give me. I've sold all my jewellery, and he's allowed me to do what I will with the money I received. I used to enjoy cards, but I've stopped playing. I used to like going to the theatre, but I do without now. I used to like socializing, but now I live a life of seclusion. I used to like the fine things in life, but I've given them up. If you become a nun, as Monsieur Simonin and I wish, your dowry will consist of all the money I put aside every day.'

'But, Mother,' I said, 'some respectable men still come here. Perhaps one of them might like me and not even expect to receive the money that you're saving for my marriage.'

'You mustn't think about that any more: the scandal you caused has been your undoing.'

'Is there nothing to be done?'

'Nothing.'

'But if I don't find a husband, does that mean I have to lock myself away in a convent?'

'Yes, unless you wish to draw out my pain and remorse until the day I die. For that day must come. On that fateful day your sisters will be at my bedside. Imagine if I saw you there too; imagine what effect your being there would have in my dying moments! My daughter, for that's what you are, whatever I may do, your sisters have the legal right to a name that you only have because of a crime: don't make your dying mother suffer; let her go to her grave in peace so that she may tell herself, as she's about to appear before the judge of all things, that she has atoned for her sin as far as she could, so that she can reassure herself that, after she is dead, you won't make trouble for her family and you won't lay claim to rights that aren't yours.'

'Mother,' I said, 'you have no need to worry. Send for a lawyer; have him draw up a deed relinquishing my claim; I shall agree to whatever you wish.'

'That's impossible: a child cannot disinherit itself; it's a punishment meted out by fathers and mothers who have just complaint. If God chose to call me to him tomorrow, tomorrow I'd have to resort to that extremity and confide in my husband so that together we might follow the same course of action. Don't force me to make a revelation to him that would make me abhorrent in his eyes and that would bring shame on you. If you outlive me, you'll have no name, no wealth, and no status. You poor girl! What do you think would become of you? What do you want me to think as I die? I shall have to tell your father... But what shall I tell him? That you're not his child!... My daughter, if only I had to throw myself at your feet to obtain from you... But you're unfeeling; you have your father's inflexible soul...'

At that point Monsieur Simonin walked in. He saw his wife's distress. He loved her. He was furious. He stopped suddenly and, turning his terrifying gaze towards me, said:

'Get out!'

If he had been my father, I would not have obeyed him, but he was not.

Speaking to the servant who was showing me out, he added:

'Tell her never to come back.'

I locked myself away again in my little prison. I reflected on what my mother had said to me. I knelt and prayed for God to inspire me. I prayed for a long time, my face pressed against the ground. The voice of God is usually only ever invoked when one does not know oneself what to do, and in those instances the voice almost always advises obedience. That was my decision. 'They want me to be a nun; perhaps that's what God wants too. Very well, I shall be a nun. Since I have to be unhappy, what does it matter where I am!' I told the servant girl to let me know when my father went out. The next day I requested a meeting with my mother. She sent a reply informing me that she had promised Monsieur Simonin that she would not see me, but that I could write to her using the pencil that the girl gave me. So I wrote on a piece of paper (this fateful piece of paper was later discovered and used against me all too effectively):

'Mother, I bitterly regret all the suffering I have caused you; please forgive me. All I want to do now is end that suffering. Tell me to do whatever you wish. If it is your will that I should become a nun, then may that be God's will too...'

The servant girl took this note to my mother. She came back to my room a little later and told me excitedly:

'Mademoiselle, since you only needed to say one word to ensure your own happiness and that of your father and mother, why have you put it off for so long? Monsieur and Madame look such as I've never seen them since I've been here: they used to argue constantly about you; thank God that I shall never experience that again...'

As she was speaking, I began to suspect that I had just signed my own death warrant. And that suspicion will come true, Monsieur, if you forsake me.

A few days went by without my hearing anything. But one morning, at about nine o'clock, my door opened suddenly. It was Monsieur Simonin, in his dressing gown and nightcap. Since I had found out that he was not my father, I felt nothing but fear in his presence. I got up and curtseyed. I felt as if I had two hearts: I could not think of my mother without being moved, without wanting to cry; I felt quite differently about Monsieur Simonin. It is true that a father inspires feelings of a kind reserved solely for him. You can only appreciate this if, as I have, you have come face to face with the man who for so long had this august character and who has just lost it. Nobody else can ever know what this is like. If I went from being with him to being with my mother, I felt as if I was a different person. He said:

'Suzanne, do you recognize this letter?'

'Yes, Monsieur.'

'Did you write it of your own accord?'

'I have to say yes.'

'Are you at least resolved to carry out what it promises?'

'I am.'

'Do you have a preference for a particular convent?'

'No, they are all the same to me.'

'Very well.'

Such were my replies, but unfortunately they were not written down. For a fortnight I was not told what was happening, though I surmised that a number of convents had been approached and that they had refused to accept me as a postulant because of the scandal caused by my behaviour in my first convent. The convent at Longchamp* was less concerned about that, no doubt because it was suggested to them that I was musical and that I could sing. I was given an exaggerated account of the difficulties that had been faced and of the kindness that was being shown to me by my acceptance into this convent. I was even urged to write to the Mother Superior. I had no sense then of what the consequences would be of this written testimony that was expected of me. Apparently it was feared that one day I would rescind my vows, so it was felt necessary to have a statement in my own hand to the effect that I had taken those vows of my own accord. Otherwise, how could this letter, which was supposed to remain in the hands of the Superior, have subsequently passed into the hands of my brothers-in-law? But let us quickly close our eyes to that matter, for it makes me see Monsieur Simonin in a way I do not want to see him: he is no longer with us.

I was taken to Longchamp, accompanied by my mother. I did not ask to say farewell to Monsieur Simonin, and I admit that the thought only occurred to me after we had left. They were expecting me: accounts both of my past and of my talents had gone before me. Nothing was said about the former, but there was a great deal of interest in finding out if this new acquisition was worth the effort. Once we had spoken about a lot of trivial things, since, after what had happened to me, you can rest assured that no reference was made to God, a vocation, the dangers of the world, or the comforts of the religious life, and not a word was uttered of the pious platitudes with which these first moments are usually filled, the Mother Superior said: 'Mademoiselle, you can read music, you can sing. We have a harpsichord. If you'd like, we could go into our parlour...' I felt a pang of anguish, but this was not the time to show my repugnance. My mother led the way, I followed her, and the Mother Superior brought up the rear with a few nuns who had come out of curiosity. It was evening, and candles were brought in for me. I sat down at the harpsichord and improvised for a long time, trying to remember one of the many pieces I knew by heart, though in vain. But the Mother Superior insisted, and so, without a second thought and out of habit, because I knew it well, I sang *Sorrowful decorations, faint candles, a light more terrible than the darkness**... I do not know what effect it had, but they did not listen to it for long. I was interrupted by words of praise which I was very surprised to have earned so quickly and with so little effort. My mother handed me over to the Mother Superior, gave me her hand to kiss, and then left.

So I found myself in another convent as a postulant, to all intents and purposes of my own free will. But you, Monsieur, knowing everything that has happened up to this point, what do you think? Most of these things were not put forward when I wanted to renounce my vows, some because they were true but unproved, others because they would have made me look odious and would not have helped my case: I would have been seen as an unnatural child who was blackening the memory of her parents in order to obtain her freedom. The evidence *against* me was well established, but that *for* me could not be put forward or proved. I did not even want the judges to be given the slightest hint about my birth. Some people, unfamiliar with the law, advised me to implicate my mother's and father's spiritual director. That was impossible. And even if it had been possible, I would not have allowed it to happen. By the way, in case I forget and your desire to help me stops you from thinking about it, I think, though I am willing to bow to your better judgement, that we should keep quiet about my musical ability and harpsichord-playing, for it would take no more than that to reveal my identity: the display of these talents is not conducive to the obscurity and security that I seek. People in my walk of life do not have such talents, and neither should I. If I am forced to go abroad, then I will make use of them. Go abroad! Why does this idea fill me with such horror? Because I do not know where to go; because I am young and inexperienced; because I am afraid of poverty, men, and vice; because I have always led a sheltered life, and if I were away from

Paris, I would feel utterly lost in the world. None of that may be true, but that is how I feel. Monsieur, whether or not I know where to go and what to do depends on you.

The Mothers Superior at Longchamp, as in most convents, change every three years. A certain Madame de Moni had just arrived when I was taken there. I cannot speak too highly of her, and yet her kindness was my undoing. She was a sensible woman who understood the human heart. She was indulgent, though nobody needed that quality less: we were all her children. She only ever saw the faults which she could not help seeing, or which were so serious that she could not overlook them. I do not speak of this out of self-interest. I was careful to do my duty, and, in fairness to me, she would say that I never did anything for which she had to punish me or forgive me. If she had her favourites, she chose them according to merit. Now that I have said that, I do not know if I should tell you that she loved me dearly and that I was not the least of her favourites. I realize that I am praising myself highly, more highly than you can imagine, since you never met her. The word favourite is used by the others to refer enviously to those whom the Mother Superior particularly loves. If I had one criticism to make of Madame de Moni, it would be that she let herself be very obviously swayed by her taste for virtue, piety, openness, gentleness, talent, and decency, and that she knew very well that those who could not lay claim to these qualities felt only more humiliated. She also had the ability, which is perhaps more common in the convent than in the world, promptly to weigh up people's characters. It was rare for her ever to like a nun whom she did not like from the outset. She was not slow to take a liking to me and from the start I put my complete trust in her. Woe betide those whose trust she did not win without her first having to make an effort: they must be bad, beyond the pale, and admit as much. She talked to me about my adventure at Sainte-Marie. As with you, I told her openly what had happened. I told her everything I have written to you, everything to do with my birth and my troubles: nothing was left out. She pitied me, consoled me, and encouraged me to hope for a happier future.

Meanwhile my time as a postulant came to an end, the time came for me to take the habit, and I took it. I undertook my noviciate without any feeling of distaste. I pass quickly over these two years because the only sadness they held for me was the feeling deep inside me that I was

moving step by step towards assuming a way of life to which I was not
suited. Sometimes this feeling would strike me with renewed force,
but whenever that happened I would run straight to my good
Mother Superior who would embrace me, put things straight for me,
explain her reasons very clearly, and always finish by saying: 'And
don't other ways of life have their thorns too? One only ever feels
one's own. Come along, my child, let us kneel down and pray.'

She would then prostrate herself and pray out loud, but with such
unction, eloquence, gentleness, elevation, and strength that she
seemed to be inspired by the spirit of God. Her thoughts, her
expressions, and her images went straight to the heart. At first you
would listen to her, but little by little you were swept along,
you found yourself becoming one with her, your soul thrilling as you
shared her ecstasy. Her aim was not to seduce, but that was certainly
the result. You would leave her room with your heart on fire, joy and
ecstasy radiating from your face, and weeping such sweet tears. She
too was affected in the same way, and for a long time, as we were. I
am not simply relying here on my own experience, but on that of all
the nuns. Some of them have told me that they felt growing within
them the need to be consoled like the need for a very great pleasure,
and I think that I too might have reached such a state if I had become
more used to the experience.

However, as the time for my profession drew near, I was overcome
by such a deep melancholy that it put my dear Mother Superior to
the severest test. Her talent failed her, as she herself admitted to me.

'I don't know', she said, 'what's happening to me. It's as if, when
you come near, God withdraws and his spirit falls silent. I stir
myself, I search for ideas, I try to lift up my soul, but it's all in vain,
for I'm just an ordinary, flawed woman. I'm afraid to carry on
speaking...'

'Oh, dear Mother!' I replied, 'what a feeling to have! Perhaps it's
God who's preventing you from speaking!...'

One day, when I was feeling more uncertain and despondent than
ever, I went to her cell. At first she was disconcerted by my presence.
She seemed to be able to tell from my eyes, indeed from everything
about me, that the deep emotion within me was more than she could
cope with, and she did not want to struggle against it without being
sure of victory. Nevertheless she took me to task, she became more
and more heated, and, as my pain dwindled, her enthusiasm grew.

She suddenly fell to her knees, and I did likewise. I thought I was going to share in her ecstasy: that is what I wanted to happen. She said a few words and then suddenly went silent. I waited in vain. She said nothing else, stood up, burst into tears, took hold of my hand, and, holding me in her arms, said: 'Oh! Dear child, what a cruel effect you've had on me! That's it, the Spirit has left me, I can feel it. Go, and may God speak to you himself, for it does not please him to do so through my mouth.'

In fact, I do not know what had happened to her, whether I had stirred in her a mistrust of her own strength which has not been dispelled since, whether I had made her afraid, or whether I had really come between her and God. Whatever had happened, she never regained her ability to console others. The day before my profession I went to see her. Her melancholy was the same as mine. I started crying, as did she. I threw myself at her feet, she blessed me, made me stand up, embraced me, and sent me on my way, saying: 'I'm tired of living; I want to die. I prayed to God that I might not see this day, but that is not his will. Run along, I'll speak to your mother. I'll spend the night praying. And you should pray too, but be sure to go to bed, I insist.'

'Let me stay with you,' I replied.

'You may stay from nine o'clock until eleven, but no longer. At half past nine I shall start praying, and so will you, but at eleven you must leave me to pray alone and you must get some rest. There, my dear child, I shall spend the rest of the night keeping watch before God.'

She tried to pray, but she could not. While I slept, this holy woman roamed the corridors, knocking on every door, waking up the nuns and making them go down to the church in silence. They all went, and once they were there she invited them to pray for me. To begin with they prayed in silence. Then she put out the lights and they all recited the *Miserere*,* apart from the Mother Superior who had prostrated herself before the altar and was cruelly mortifying her flesh,* saying: 'Oh God! If some sin I have committed has caused you to forsake me, grant me your forgiveness. I don't ask that you should give me back the gift you have taken from me, but that you yourself speak to this innocent young girl who now sleeps while I am pleading for her here. My God, speak to her, speak to her parents, and forgive me.'

Early the next morning she came to my cell. I did not hear her as I was still asleep. She sat down next to my bed. She had laid her hand lightly on my forehead. She was looking at me, her expression changing from concern to distress and then to pain. That was how she looked when I opened my eyes. She said nothing about what had happened during the night. She simply asked me if I had gone to bed early. I replied:

'At the time you told me to.'

How had I slept?

'Soundly.'

'I thought you would...' How was I feeling?

'Very well. And you, dear Mother?'

'Alas,' she said, 'I have never seen anyone become a nun without worrying about them, but I've never before felt as much disquiet for anyone as I do for you now. All I want is for you to be happy.'

'As long as you love me, I shall be.'

'Oh! If only it was as simple as that! Haven't you thought of anything during the night?'

'No.'

'You didn't even dream?'

'Not at all.'

'What's happening now in your soul?'

'I'm dazed. I'm accepting my fate with neither disgust nor inclination. I feel as if necessity is carrying me along and I'm letting myself go. Oh! My dear Mother, I feel nothing of that sweet joy, that quivering, that melancholy, that sweet anxiety that I've sometimes noticed in those in my position. I'm stunned, I can't even cry. This is what is wanted, this is what is required of me: that's all I can think about... But you're not saying anything.'

'I didn't come in order to talk to you, but to see you and to listen to you. I'm expecting your mother. Try not to distress me. Let my feelings well up in my soul, and when it's full I shall leave you. I mustn't say anything, I know what I'm like. I have only one outpouring to make, but it's a violent one, and I don't want to give vent to it here. Rest a little longer so that I can look at you. Just say a few words to me and let me take away from here what I came in search of. I shall go and God will do the rest...'

I said nothing. I laid my head on my pillow and held out my hand, which she took. She seemed to be meditating, meditating very deeply. She kept her eyes tightly shut, but sometimes she opened them, looking up at first and then back down at me. She was agitated, her soul was now full of turmoil, now composed, now troubled again. Truly this woman had been born to be a prophetess, for she had the face and character of one. She had been beautiful, but time, while making her features fall and etching deep lines, had given further dignity to her face. She had small eyes, but they seemed to be looking either into herself or into the distance, through and beyond the things around her, always into the past or the future. From time to time she squeezed my hand tightly. She suddenly asked me what time it was.

'It's nearly six o'clock.'

'Farewell, I must be going. Someone is going to come and dress you. I don't want to be here for that: it would distract me. My only concern now is to keep calm in the first few moments.'

She had only just gone when the novice mistress and my companions came in. They took off my religious habit and dressed me in secular clothes instead: you know the custom.* I did not hear a word they said: I was all but reduced to the state of an automaton,* oblivious to what was happening. But occasionally I had what seemed to be little convulsions. They told me what to do, but they had to keep repeating it because I did not hear them the first time, and I obeyed. It was not because I was thinking of something else; it was because I was absorbed: my head was weary as if I had been thinking too hard. Meanwhile the Mother Superior was talking to my mother. I still do not know what went on during this long conversation. All I was told was that, when they parted, my mother was so distressed that she could not even find her way back to the door she had come in through, and that the Mother Superior had left with her hands clenched against her forehead.

Meanwhile the bells started ringing, and I went down. There were only a few people in the church. There was a homily, but I could not say if it was good or bad: I did not hear a word of it. They did whatever they wanted with me throughout the morning, which has never been real to me, as I never knew how long it lasted. I have no idea what I did or what I said. I must have been asked questions, and I must have replied and made my vows, but I have no memory of doing so. I found I had become a nun just as innocently as I had been made a Christian. I understood no more about all the ceremony of my profession than I did about my own baptism, but with one difference: the one confers grace, the other presupposes it. And so, Monsieur, although I did not protest at Longchamp as I did at Sainte-Marie, do you think I am any more committed? I appeal to your judgement, I appeal to God's judgement. I was in a state of such complete collapse that when, a few days later, I was told that I was to sing in the choir, I did not know what that meant. I asked if it was really true that I had made my profession; I wanted to see my signature on the document. I also wanted as evidence the testimonies of the whole community and of the few outsiders who had been invited to the ceremony. I went to see the Mother Superior several times and said: 'So is it really true?...', and each time I expected her to reply: 'No, my child, you are being deceived...' Her repeated assurances did not convince me, for I could not understand how, out of a whole day, and one so tumultuous and varied, so full of strange and striking events, I could not remember a single thing, not even the faces of those who had assisted me, nor that of the priest who had given the homily, or of the one who had received my vows. The only thing I can remember is getting changed out of my religious habit and into my secular clothes. From that moment on I was what is known as physically alienated. It took several months to bring me out of this state, and I think the sheer length of this sort of convalescence made me forget entirely what happened. It is like those who have suffered a long illness, who have spoken sensibly and have received the last sacraments, but who, once restored to health, cannot remember anything of what has happened to them. I have seen several cases like this in the convent and have told myself that that must be what happened to me on the day I made my profession. But it remains to be seen whether the person involved is responsible for the actions performed and whether he is present in any real sense, even though he appears to be.

In the same year I suffered three sad losses: my father, or rather the man who had passed for my father, who was old, had worked hard, and faded away; then my Mother Superior and my own mother.

This worthy nun felt from an early stage that the hour of her death was approaching. She condemned herself to silence. She had her coffin brought into her room. She could not sleep, so spent her days and nights meditating and writing, leaving behind fifteen

Meditations which, to my mind, are very beautiful. I have a copy of them and if one day you would like to read the thoughts prompted by this time of life, I shall send them to you. They are entitled *The Last Moments of Sister de Moni*.

As her death was drawing near, she had herself dressed. She was lying on her bed, where she received the last sacraments, holding a crucifix in her arms. It was night time, and the glow of torches lit up the mournful scene. We were gathered around her, all in tears. Her cell was filled with the sound of crying, when suddenly her eyes lit up. She sat up sharply and spoke in a voice that was almost as strong as when she was healthy. The gift that she had lost had now come back to her as she reproached us for our tears, which seemed to envy her her eternal happiness. 'My children, your pain misleads you. It is there, up there,' she said, pointing heavenwards, 'that I shall serve you. I shall look down constantly on this place. I shall pray for you, and my prayers will be answered. Come closer so that I may kiss you all. Come and receive my blessing and farewell...' As she uttered these last words, this unique woman passed away, leaving behind her unending sorrow.

My mother died following a short trip she had made in late autumn to the home of one of her daughters. She was deeply distressed, and her health had been badly affected. I never found out my father's name or the circumstances of my birth. The priest who had been her spiritual director and mine gave me a little package on her behalf. It was fifty *louis* and a letter,* wrapped and sewn up in a piece of linen. The letter read: 'My child, this is not very much, but my conscience prevents me from giving you a larger sum. This is all that is left of what I have managed to save from the little gifts Monsieur Simonin gave me. Live a holy life: this is the best way for you to find happiness in this world. Pray for me. Giving birth to you is the only serious sin I have ever committed. Help me to atone for it, and pray that God, taking into account all the good works you will do, will forgive me for having brought you into the world. Above all do not upset the family, and although you did not embrace your chosen way of life as willingly as I would have liked, be wary of changing it. If only I had spent my whole life confined to a convent! I would not be so distressed by the prospect of the divine judgement that awaits me. Remember, my child, that your mother's fate in the life hereafter depends a lot on how you behave in this life. God, who sees everything, will in his justice do unto me all the good and evil that you do. Farewell, Suzanne. Ask nothing of your sisters, for they are in no position to help you. Hope for nothing from your father, for he has gone before me. He has seen the great light and is waiting for me: my presence will be less awful for him than his will be for me. Farewell once again. Oh! wretched mother! Oh! wretched child! Your sisters have come and I am not pleased with them. They are taking things, carrying things away with them. It hurts me to see that, before the very eyes of their dying mother, they are quarrelling greedily. When they come near my bed, I turn away. For what would I see in them? Two creatures in whom poverty has wiped out all trace of natural feeling. They yearn for the little that I leave behind, they ask the doctor and the nurse inappropriate questions which show how eager they are for me to be gone and to take possession of all the things around me. They suspect, I don't know how, that I have some money hidden in my mattress. They have tried every means to make me get up and they have been successful too, but thankfully my trusted friend had come the day before and I had given him this little package together with this letter that I dictated to him. Burn this letter, and when you learn that I am no more, which will be soon, have a mass said for me, and during it renew your vows, for I want you to remain a nun. The thought of your being in the world, without help or support and so young, would only cause me distress in my final moments.'

My father died on 5 January, my Mother Superior at the end of the same month, and my mother the following Christmas.

Mother de Moni was succeeded by Sister Sainte Christine. Oh, Monsieur! How different the two women were! I have already told you what the first woman was like. The latter had a petty character; she was narrow-minded and terribly superstitious. She went in for new-fangled opinions and had dealings with Sulpicians and Jesuits.* She took a dislike to all her predecessor's favourites. In an instant the convent was filled with unrest, hatred, malicious gossip, accusations, calumny, and persecution. We were made to discuss theological issues that we did not understand in the least, to subscribe to formulae and adopt strange practices. Mother de Moni disapproved of penitential mortification; she had mortified herself only twice in her whole life, once on the eve of my profession and again on a similar occasion. She said that such penances did not correct any of our failings but were merely a source of pride. She wanted her nuns to be well, to have healthy bodies and serene minds. The first thing she did on taking up office was to confiscate all hair-shirts and scourges and to forbid the spoiling of food with ashes, sleeping on the floor, and acquiring any of the confiscated instruments. The new Mother Superior, by contrast, returned to each nun her hair-shirt and scourge and confiscated her Old and New Testaments. The favourites of the old reign are never the favourites of the new. I was indifferent, to put it mildly, to the new Mother Superior because her predecessor had shown me such affection, but I soon made my lot worse by behaving in a way which you will consider either imprudent or resolute according to your point of view.

The first thing I did was to abandon myself to all the pain that I felt at the loss of our Mother Superior and to sing her praises at every opportunity, to suggest comparisons between her and the new Mother Superior which were unfavourable to the latter, to describe what the convent was like in years gone by, to recall the peace we used to enjoy, the kind treatment we enjoyed, the food that was given to us, both spiritual and temporal, and to praise the morals, feelings, and character of Sister de Moni. The second thing I did was to throw my hair-shirt on the fire and to get rid of my scourge, to tell my friends all about what I had done, and to encourage some of them to follow my example. The third thing I did was to obtain a copy of the Old and New Testaments. The fourth thing I did was to reject all sects, to content myself with being called a Christian and to refuse to be called a Jansenist or a Molinist.* The fifth thing I did was to conform strictly to the rules of the convent, refusing to do any more or less, and therefore not performing any supererogatory acts, since the obligatory ones already struck me as too harsh anyway. I chose only to go up into the organ loft on feast days and to sing only when I had to be in the choir. No longer would I allow my good will and talents to be taken advantage of, nor would I allow myself to be coerced into doing every kind of duty, every day. I read and reread the rules of the order until I knew them by heart. If I was told to do something which was either not set out clearly in the rules or not in them at all, or which seemed to me to run counter to them, I would refuse categorically. I would pick up the book and say: 'Here are the promises I've made; I haven't made any others.'

My words won over some of the other nuns. The authority of the novice mistresses was thus severely limited, and they could no longer treat us like slaves. Rarely did a day pass without there being a scene of some kind. Whenever they were unsure, my companions consulted me, and I was always for the rules and against despotism. I soon looked like, and perhaps even played the part of, a trouble-maker. The Archbishop's Vicars General* were constantly being called in. I would appear before them, defend myself and my companions, and not once was I found guilty, because I made absolutely sure that I had reason on my side. It was impossible for them to attack me concerning my duties, because I scrupulously performed them all. As to the little graces and favours that a Mother Superior is always free to refuse or grant, I never asked for any. I never went to the parlour, and I never had any visitors because I did not know anyone. But I had burnt my hair-shirt and thrown away my scourge, and I had advised others to do the same. I did not want to hear a word spoken, be it good or bad, about Jansenism or Molinism. When they asked me if I submitted to the Constitution, I replied that I submitted to the Church. When they asked me if I accepted the Papal Bull,* I replied that I accepted the Gospels. They went to my cell and found there the Old and New Testaments. I had let slip some indiscreet remarks about the suspicious intimacy between some of the favourites. The Mother Superior had long and frequent private meetings with a young cleric, and I had worked out the reason and the pretext for these. I included everything that was necessary to make myself feared and hated and to bring about my downfall, and I succeeded. They stopped complaining about me to the authorities, but instead they set about making my life a misery. The other nuns were forbidden to come near me, and I soon found myself all alone. I had a small number of friends, and it was thought that they would try secretly to frustrate the constraints that were imposed upon them by visiting me at night or at other forbidden times, since they could not speak to me during the day. We were spied upon, and I was discovered first with one friend, then with another, and they took full advantage of this foolhardiness. I was punished in the most inhumane way imaginable. I was condemned for weeks on end to stay on my knees throughout the services, cut off from the other nuns in the middle of the choir, to live off bread and water, to be locked up in my cell, and to perform the most unpleasant domestic tasks in the convent. Those who were thought of as my accomplices were treated almost as harshly. When I could not be found to be at fault, faults were invented. I was given orders that contradicted each other, and I was punished for not carrying them all out. The times of the services and meals were brought forward, disrupting the routine of convent life without my being told, so that even with the best will in the world, I got into trouble every day, and every day I was punished. I have strength of heart, but no such strength can ever withstand neglect, solitude, and persecution. Things reached such a point that to torment me became a game, a source of fun for fifty people in league against me. It is impossible for me to go into all the tiny details of this spitefulness. I was prevented from sleeping, from keeping watch, and from praying. One day some of my clothing was stolen, another time it was my keys or my breviary; my keyhole was blocked. Either I was prevented from doing things properly, or the things that I had done properly were spoilt. I was alleged to have said and done things that I had not. I was held responsible for everything, and my life was one long series of real or fabricated wrongdoings and punishments.

My health could not withstand such prolonged and hard ordeals, and I sank into exhaustion, sorrow, and melancholy. To begin with I sought strength at the altar, and sometimes I found it. I wavered between resignation and despair, sometimes accepting all the severity of my fate, sometimes thinking of finding freedom by violent means. At the bottom of the garden was a deep well. How many times did I go there! How many times did I look into it! There was a stone seat next to it. How many times did I sit there, resting my head on the edge of the well! How many times, my head spinning with thoughts, did I get up suddenly, determined to put an end to all my sufferings! What stopped me? Why did I prefer to cry, to scream out loud, to throw my veil to the ground and trample on it, to tear at my hair, and to scratch my face with my fingernails? If it was God stopping me from ending my life, why did he not stop all these other emotions too?

I am going to tell you something which may well seem very strange to you, but which is nevertheless true. It is that I am absolutely sure that my frequent visits to the well were noticed, and that my cruel enemies cherished the hope that one day I might carry out the plan that was burning away deep in my heart. Whenever I went towards the well, the others made a show of going the other way and looking elsewhere. On a number of occasions I found the garden gate left open at times when it was supposed to be locked, and especially on days when they had been particularly cruel to me, when they had stretched my violent character to breaking point and thought me out of my mind. But as soon as I thought I had guessed that this way out of life was, so to speak, being offered to me in my despair, that I was being led by the hand to the well which I would always find ready to receive me, I worried about it no more. My mind turned to other things. I stood in the corridors and measured the height of the windows. In the evenings, as I was getting undressed, quite without thinking about it, I tested the strength of my garters. Another day I refused food. I went down to the refectory and stood with my back to the wall, with my hands by my sides and my eyes closed, and I did not touch any of the food that had been put in front of me. I lost myself so completely in this state that I was left there all alone after the other nuns had gone. They made a point of withdrawing in silence and leaving me there, and then I was punished for having missed the service. What can I say? They turned me against almost every available means of killing myself, because it struck me that, far from opposing them, they were openly presenting these means to me. Apparently we do not like being forced out of this world, and perhaps I would not still be here now if they had pretended to want to stop me. When people take their own lives, perhaps they are trying to drive others to despair, and they hold back from doing it when they think it is precisely what others want them to do. There are subtle processes going on in our minds. In fact, if I can recall the state I was in when I was next to the well, it is as if I was, deep within me, screaming at those wretched women who went the other way so as to facilitate a crime: 'Just take one step in my direction, show at least the slightest desire to save me, run to stop me, and rest assured that you'll be too late.' In fact I only carried on living because they wanted me to die. The urge to torment and destroy others gradually weakens in the real world, but never in convents.

That is how I was when, thinking back over my past, I thought about having my vows rescinded. To begin with I did not think about it very seriously. Alone, abandoned, and unaided, how could I possibly succeed with such a difficult plan, even if I had all the help that I lacked? Nevertheless the idea helped to soothe me; it calmed my mind, and I felt more like myself again. I kept out of trouble and I bore with greater patience the trouble that came my way. This change in my character was remarked upon, and with some surprise. The nastiness stopped abruptly, like a cowardly enemy pursuing you whom you turn and confront when he is not expecting it. One question that I would like to ask you, Monsieur, is why, amidst all the dreadful ideas which a desperate nun has going through her mind, she never thinks of setting fire to her convent? I never thought of doing it or any other such thing, despite the fact that it would be very easy to do. All you would have to do is take a torch on a windy day to an attic, a pile of wood, or a corridor. No convent has ever burnt down, and yet if it did, the doors would be flung open and anyone who wanted to could escape. Could it be that we are afraid of the danger that this would represent both for ourselves and for those whom we love, and that we refuse a source of help which could equally benefit us and those whom we hate? This last idea may be too subtle to be true.

The more you think about a thing, the more you believe it to be just and even possible: to find oneself in such a position is to be in a position of strength. It took me just a fortnight: my mind works quickly. What did I do? I wrote a statement of my case and handed it over to be considered. Neither of these things was free from danger. Since a revolution had come about in my way of thinking, I was watched more closely than ever before. I could feel their eyes following me. I could not take a single step without it being explained, and every word I uttered was weighed up. They tried to get closer to me and sound me out. They asked me questions, feigning sympathy and friendship. They went back over my life, blamed me only slightly, and then forgave me. They hoped I would behave better now, and they sought to delude me that I would have a happier future. They would come into my cell whenever they wanted, day or night, under any pretext, suddenly and stealthily. They would open my curtains and then leave again. I had got into the habit of sleeping fully dressed; I had also got into the habit of writing out my confession. On the days appointed for confession, I would go and ask the Mother Superior for paper and ink, which she never refused me. So I waited for the day of confession, and as I waited I drafted in my mind what I wanted to say. It was a summary of everything I have just written to you, the only difference being that I used false names. But I made three silly mistakes: first, I told the Mother Superior that

I had a lot to write and so asked her for more paper than was usually allowed; secondly, I concentrated on my statement and neglected my confession; and thirdly, since I had not written out my confession and had not prepared myself for that particular religious observance, I only remained in the confessional for a moment. All of this was noticed, and the conclusion was drawn that the paper I had requested had been used for some purpose other than that I had claimed. But if it had not been used for my confession, which it clearly had not, what had I used it for?

Though I did not know how concerned they would be, I realized that I could not let such an important document be found in my cell. My first thought was to sew it in my bolster or my mattress. Then I thought of hiding it in my clothes, burying it in the garden, or throwing it on the fire. You will never believe what a hurry I was in to write it and how worried I was once I had finished it. First I sealed it and then hid it in my bosom before going off to the office, for which the bell was ringing. My every movement betrayed how nervous I was. I was sitting next to a nun who was fond of me. I had sometimes seen her looking at me pitifully, tears in her eyes. She said nothing to me, but I am sure that she was suffering. Risking all the possible consequences, I decided to entrust my statement to her. At the point in the prayers when all the nuns kneel and bow their heads and are, so to speak, buried in their stalls, I quickly pulled the paper from my bosom and handed it to her behind my back. She took it and hid it in her bosom. This was the most important thing she had ever done for me, though she had done many other things before. Without getting herself into trouble, she had spent several months removing the obstacles that were put in my way so as to prevent me doing my duties and to give the others an excuse to punish me. She would come and knock on my door when it was time to come out; she would tidy up what had deliberately been messed up; she would go and ring the bell or answer it when necessary; she was wherever I was meant to be. I knew nothing of all that then.

I had made a wise decision. As we left the choir, the Mother Superior said to me: 'Sister Suzanne, follow me.' I followed her. She stopped outside another door in the corridor and said: 'This is your cell now. Sister Saint Jerome will have your old one.' I went in and so did she. We were both sitting in silence when a nun appeared with some clothes which she put down on a chair. The Mother Superior

said to me: 'Sister Suzanne, get undressed and put on these clothes.'
I obeyed instantly. As I did so, she watched my every movement.
The sister who had brought the clothes was standing in the doorway:
she came back in; she picked up the clothes I had taken off and went
out, followed by the Mother Superior. I was not told why this was
happening, nor did I ask. Meanwhile my cell had been thoroughly
searched: they had torn open my pillow and mattress; they had
moved everything that could be moved or could have been moved;
they had retraced my steps, visiting the confessional, the church, the
garden, the well, and the stone seat. I saw some of their searching
and I guessed the rest. Nothing was found, but nevertheless they
remained convinced that there was something to be found. They
continued to spy on me for several days, going wherever I had been
and looking everywhere, but in vain. Finally the Mother Superior
thought that the only way to find out the truth was directly from me.
One day she came into my cell and said:

'Sister Suzanne, you have your faults, but lying is not one of them.
So tell me the truth. What have you done with all the paper I gave
you?'

'Madame, I've already told you.'

'But that's impossible, because you asked me for a lot of paper but
you only spent a moment in the confessional.'

'That's true.'

'So what have you done with it?'

'Exactly what I told you.'

'Very well, if you swear to me by the vow of holy obedience that
you have made before God that that is indeed the case, then, in spite
of appearances, I shall believe you.'

'Madame, you have no right to demand I swear an oath on such a
trivial matter, and I cannot do it. I cannot swear.'

'You're deceiving me, Sister Suzanne, and you don't know the risk
you're taking. What have you done with the paper I gave you?'

'I've already told you.'

'Where is it?'

'I don't have it any more.'

'What have you done with it?'

'What one normally does with these kinds of writing which are
useless once they've served their purpose.'

'Swear to me by your vow of holy obedience that you used all the paper to write out your confession and that you don't have it any more.'

'Madame, I repeat, since the second thing is just as trivial as the first, I cannot swear.'

'Swear,' she said, 'or else...'

'I will not swear.'

'You won't swear?'

'No, Madame.'

'So you're guilty?'

'And what can I possibly be guilty of?'

'Everything. There's nothing you're not capable of. You have made a great show of praising my predecessor in order to belittle me, of pouring scorn on the customs she had outlawed and the laws she had abolished and which I have thought it necessary to reinstate, of stirring up the whole community, of breaking the rules, of setting people against each other, of failing to perform your duties, and of forcing me to punish you and those whom you've seduced, and that hurts me most of all. I could have dealt ruthlessly and harshly with you, but instead I treated you considerately, believing that you would acknowledge your wrongdoing, that you would return to the spirit of your calling, and that you would come back to me, but you haven't done so. There's something going on in your mind that isn't right. You're plotting something. The interest of the convent demands that I know what it is, and I shall find out, let me assure you of that... Sister Suzanne, tell me the truth.'

'I've told you the truth.'

'I'm going now, but you should fear my return... No, I'll sit down and give you another moment to make up your mind... Your papers, if they exist...'

'I don't have them any more.'

'Or swear that only your confession was written upon them.'

'I cannot do that.'

She remained silent for a moment, then she left, before returning with four of her favourites, who looked wild and furious. I threw myself at their feet and begged their mercy. They all cried together: 'Show no mercy, Madame, don't let yourself be moved. Make her hand over her papers or have her locked away...'* I clasped the knees of each in turn. Addressing each by name, I said: 'Sister Sainte Agnes, Sister Sainte Julie, what wrong have I done you? Why are you turning my Mother Superior against me? Have I ever behaved in that way? How many times have I interceded for you? You don't remember. You had done wrong then, but I have not.' The Mother Superior stood there motionless, looking at me, and said:

'Hand over your papers, wretched girl, or tell us what was in them.'

'Madame,' they said, 'don't ask for them again. You're too kind, you don't know what she's like. She's a recalcitrant soul who can only be controlled by extreme measures. She's forcing you to take them, so much the worse for her.'

'My dear Reverend Mother,' I said, 'I have done nothing to offend God or man, I swear to you.'

'That's not what I want you to swear.'

'I imagine she's written to the Vicar General or to the Archbishop, attacking you and us. God knows how she will have portrayed life inside the convent. People are quick to believe the worst. Madame, we must take care of this creature before she takes care of us.'

The Mother Superior added: 'Sister Suzanne, you see...'

I jumped up and said: 'Yes, Madame, I've seen everything. I know I'm condemning myself, but what does it matter whether it happens sooner or later? Do whatever you want with me. Listen to their fury and satisfy your injustice.'

And at that moment I held out my arms to them. Her companions grabbed me, tore off my veil and shamelessly stripped me. They found hanging around my neck a little portrait of my old Mother Superior, which they took from me. I begged them to allow me to kiss it one last time, but they refused. They threw over a shirt, took off my stockings, covered me with a sack and led me along the corridors, with nothing on my head or feet. I screamed and cried for help, but they had rung the bell to warn people to keep away. I cried out to heaven, I fell to the ground, and they dragged me along. By the time I reached the foot of the stairs, my feet were bleeding and my legs were bruised. Even someone with a heart of stone could not fail to be moved by the state I was in. Nevertheless they took out some huge keys and unlocked the door to an underground cell, tiny and dark, and threw me on to some matting half rotten with damp. I found there a piece of black bread and a pitcher of water, together with a few crude but essential vessels. Rolling the matting up at one end provided a pillow. Standing on a block of stone were a skull and a wooden crucifix. My first instinct was to kill myself. I put my hands round my throat, I tore my clothes with my teeth, and I screamed horribly, howling like a wild animal. I banged my head against the walls and was soon covered in blood. I kept trying to kill myself until my strength gave way, which did not take long. I remained there for three days, though I thought I would have to spend the rest of my life there. Every morning one of my executioners came and said: 'Obey our Mother Superior and you will be released.'

'I have done nothing wrong, and I don't know what is being asked of me. Oh! Sister Saint Clement, if there's a God...'

At about nine o'clock in the evening on the third day, the door opened. It was the same nuns who had taken me there. After singing the praises of our kind Mother Superior, they told me that she was pardoning me and that I was to be released. 'It's too late,' I told them, 'leave me here, I want to die.' But even as I spoke they picked me up and started dragging me along. They took me back to my cell, where the Mother Superior was waiting:

'I have prayed to God about your fate and he has touched my heart. He wants me to have pity on you, and I am doing his will. Kneel down and pray for his forgiveness.'

I knelt down and said:

'My God, I ask your forgiveness for the wrong I have done, just as you prayed for forgiveness on the cross for me.'

'How arrogant!' they cried. 'She's comparing herself to Jesus Christ and us to the Jews who crucified him.'

'Look not at me,' I said, 'but at yourselves and judge.'

'That's not all,' said the Mother Superior. 'Swear to me by your vow of holy obedience that you will never tell anyone anything about what has happened.'

'What you have done must be evil, then, for you're asking me to swear that I shall say nothing about it. Nobody but your own conscience will ever know about it, I swear.'

'Do you swear?'

'Yes, I swear.'

This done, they stripped me of the clothes they had given me and left me to put on my old ones again.

I had caught a chill because of the damp. I was in a critical condition. My body was covered in bruises, for several days all I had had was a few drops of water and a little bread, and I thought that this persecution would be the last trial I would ever face. But the effect of these violent upsets was short lived, which shows how strong nature is in young women. I recovered very quickly, and I found, when I reappeared, that the rest of the community had been given to believe that I had been ill. I took up my duties again in the convent and my place in the church. I had not forgotten about my statement, nor about the young sister to whom I had entrusted it. I was convinced that she would not have abused this trust, but also that looking after it would have caused her some disquiet. A few days after my release from prison, in the choir, at precisely the point in the service when I had first handed it to her, that is to say, when we kneel down and bow our heads, disappearing in our stalls, I felt a gentle pull on my dress, I held out my hand and was given a note which read simply: 'I have been so worried about you! And what I am supposed to do with your cruel papers?' Once I had read her note, I screwed it up and swallowed it. All this happened at the start of Lent. The time was approaching when the desire to listen to the music at Longchamp brings in all the people of Paris, good and bad alike. I had a very fine voice which had hardly deteriorated. Convents are keen to foster all interests, however small. I was treated rather considerately, enjoying a little more freedom than the others, and the sisters to whom I gave singing lessons could approach me without any repercussions. I had entrusted my statement to one of these sisters. During the free time we had in the garden, I took her to one side and made her sing, and while she was singing, I said:

'You know lots of people, whereas I don't know anybody. I have no desire to make you compromise yourself. Indeed I'd far sooner die than risk your being suspected of having helped me. My dear friend, it would be your undoing, I realize that. It wouldn't save me, and even if your undoing could save me, I wouldn't want to be saved at such a price.'

'Never mind that,' she said, 'what needs to be done?'

'My document needs to be passed safely to some able lawyer, without his knowing which convent it has come from, and a reply obtained from him, which you will then give to me in church or elsewhere.'

'By the way,' she said, 'what have you done with the note I gave you?'

'Don't worry, I swallowed it.'

'And don't you worry either, I shall see what I can do to help you...'

You have to realize, Monsieur, that I sang while she spoke to me and that she sang while I was replying, so that our conversation was punctuated by singing. This young woman is still in the convent, and her happiness is in your hands. If anyone were to discover what she has done for me, she would be met with all kinds of torment. I would not wish to be responsible for having opened the door to a prison cell for her; I would sooner go back there myself. So burn these letters, Monsieur, for, apart from the interest you are kind enough to take in my fate, they contain nothing worth keeping.

That is what I told you at the time, but alas she is no more, and I am left all alone.

She lost no time in keeping her word and in keeping me informed in our usual way. Holy Week arrived, and many people attended the Tenebrae.* I sang well enough to provoke an outburst of that scandalous applause that your actors receive in their theatres and that should never be heard in the Lord's house, especially not on the solemn and mournful days when we honour the memory of his son, crucified on the cross to atone for the sins of mankind. My young pupils were well prepared, some of them had good voices, almost all of them sang expressively and with taste, and it seemed to me that the public had enjoyed listening to them and that the community was satisfied with the success of my efforts.

As you know, Monsieur, on Maundy Thursday the Blessed Sacrament is taken from its tabernacle to a special altar of repose, where it remains until Good Friday morning. Throughout that time the nuns take it in turns to kneel in adoration before the altar, either individually or in pairs. A notice indicates the time at which each nun is to make her adoration, and I was very happy to read that Sister Sainte Suzanne and Sister Sainte Ursule were to be together between two and three in the morning. I went to the altar at the allotted time, and my companion was already there. We took our places side by side on the altar steps, prostrated ourselves together, and adored God for half an hour. Then my young friend took my hand and squeezed it, saying:

'We may never again have the chance to speak at such length and so freely. God knows the constraints under which we live, and he will forgive us if we use for ourselves some of the time that we should be devoting entirely to him. I haven't read your papers, but it is not difficult to guess what they contain. I shall receive the reply very shortly, but if that reply gives you the grounds to proceed with the annulment of your vows, don't you see that you will necessarily have to confer with lawyers?'

'That's true.'

'That you'll need to be free?'

'That's true.'

'And that if you are sensible, you'll take advantage of the current arrangements in order to obtain some freedom?'

'I've thought of that.'

'So that's what you'll do?'

'I'll see.'

'And another thing: if your case is taken up, you'll find yourself subjected to the full fury of the community here. Have you thought about the torments that await you?'

'They won't be any worse than those I've already suffered.'

'I don't know about that.'

'Forgive me, but they won't. First of all, they won't dare to restrict my freedom.'

'Why not?'

'Because by then I shall be protected by the law. I shall have to appear in person, so I shall be, so to speak, halfway between the world and the cloister. I shall speak freely, I shall be free to make my complaint, I shall call you all to witness, they won't dare do anything wrong for fear of my complaining about it, and they'll make sure they don't damage their own case. I'd be only too pleased if they treated me badly, but they won't. You can rest assured that they will do quite the opposite. They'll appeal to me, they'll point out to me the wrong that I'm going to do both to myself and to the convent, and you can be sure that they will only resort to threats once they've realized that kindness and seduction are useless, and that they'll refrain from using force.'

'But it's quite incredible that you should be so averse to this way of life when you perform its duties so easily and so scrupulously.'

'I feel that aversion, I was born with it, and I shall never lose it. I shall end up becoming a bad nun, unless I do something now to prevent it.'

'But what if you are unfortunate enough to fail?'

'If I fail, I shall ask to move to another convent or I shall die here.'

'But before death there can be much suffering. Oh, my dear friend, what you are doing frightens me. I'm frightened both that your vows will be annulled and that they won't be. If they are, what will become of you? What will you do in the world? You're attractive, intelligent, and talented, but it's said that these things get you nowhere if you're also virtuous, and I know that you'll never lose that particular quality.'

'You do justice to me, but not to virtue, and it is on virtue alone that I rely. The rarer it is amongst men, the more they must respect it.'

'It is praised, but nothing is done for it.'

'Virtue encourages me and supports me in my plans. Whatever anyone says, my morals will earn respect. At least it will not be said of me, as it is of most of the other nuns, that I was driven out of my way of life by some unruly passion. I see nobody and know nobody. I want to be free because my freedom was sacrificed against my will. Have you read my statement?'

'No. I opened the package you gave me because it was not addressed, so I thought it was for me, but I realized after reading the first few lines that it wasn't, so I went no further. How inspired you were to give it to me when you did! If you'd left it a moment later, they would have found it on you. But our vigil is nearly over. Let's prostrate ourselves so that the nuns who are coming to relieve us will find us as we're supposed to be. Pray to God that he will enlighten you and guide you, and I shall join my prayers and tears with yours...'

My soul was somewhat relieved. My companion prayed kneeling in an upright position, while I prostrated myself, my forehead pressed on the bottom step of the altar, my arms stretched out on the steps above. I do not think I have ever experienced such consolation and fervour when praying to God. My heart was pounding violently, and in an instant I was oblivious to everything around me. I do not know how long I remained in that position or how much longer I would have remained there, but I must have been a very touching spectacle for my companion and the two nuns who came to relieve us. When I finally got up, I thought I was alone, but I was wrong, for the three of them were standing behind me in tears. They had not dared interrupt me, preferring instead to wait for me to emerge of my own accord from this state of ecstasy and elation in which they found me. When I turned towards them, I must have looked very striking, to judge from the effect I had on them and from what they said. They said that I reminded them of our former Mother Superior when she used to console us, and that the sight of me had filled them with the same emotion. If I had had any inclination towards hypocrisy or fanaticism and had wanted to play a role in the convent, I am sure that I would have been successful. My soul catches fire easily, becomes exalted, and is moved, and that good Mother Superior told me a hundred times as she was embracing me that nobody would have loved God like me, that I had a heart of flesh whereas the others had hearts of stone. I certainly found it extremely easy to share her ecstasy, and when she prayed aloud, I some-times started speaking too, following the train of her thoughts and encountering, as if inspired, something of what she might have said herself. The others listened to her in silence or followed her, whereas I interrupted her or anticipated what she was going to say or spoke at the same time as she did. The impression she had made on me remained with me for a very long time, and it seems that I must have given something of it back to her, for, just as one could see in others when they had spoken to her, so one could see in her when she had spoken to me. But what does any of that mean, if it has nothing to do with vocation? Our vigil ended, we made way for the nuns who had come to relieve us, and my young companion and I embraced very tenderly before going our separate ways.

The scene at the altar of repose caused a stir in the convent. Add to that the success of the Tenebrae on Good Friday, when I sang, played the organ, and was applauded. Oh how foolish nuns can be! I hardly had to do anything in order to be reconciled with the rest of the community again. They came up to me, beginning with the Mother Superior. Some people from outside the convent wanted to make my acquaintance, which fitted in too well with my plans for me to turn them down. I met the First President,* Madame de Soubise,* and a whole host of respectable people, including monks, priests, military men, magistrates, women both pious and worldly, as well as the kind of fools known as red heels,* whom I quickly got rid of. I cultivated only those acquaintances that could not be found in any way objectionable, and I left the rest to those nuns who were less particular than I am.

I forgot to tell you that the first sign of kindness shown to me was to allow me to return to my old cell. I dared to ask again if I could have back the little portrait of our former Mother Superior, and they did not dare to refuse me. It has taken its place again on my heart, and there it will stay as long as I live. Every morning the first thing I do is lift up my soul to God; the second thing I do is kiss the portrait. Whenever I want to pray but my soul feels cold, I take the portrait from around my neck, place it in front of me and look at it, and it inspires me. It really is a great shame that we never knew the holy people whose images are set before us for veneration: they would make quite a different impression on us and would not leave us as cold as we find ourselves when we kneel or stand before them.

I received the reply to my statement; it came from a Monsieur Manouri,* and it was neither favourable nor unfavourable. Before he could pronounce on the case, he wanted a large number of issues to be clarified, which would be difficult to achieve without a meeting. So I told Manouri my name and invited him to come to Longchamp. It can be difficult to find such men who are willing to travel, but he did come. We spoke at length and agreed to begin a correspondence which would allow him to send his questions to me safely and I would send him my replies. For my part I used all the time that he was spending on my case to win over people's minds, to raise interest in my fate, and to find people who would defend my cause. I said who I was and I told people about what I had done in the first convent I had lived in, what I had endured in my parents' home, how I had been made to suffer in the convent, about my protest at Sainte-Marie, my stay at Longchamp, my taking the veil, my profession, and about how cruelly I had been treated since I had finally taken my vows. I received pity and offers of help. I stored up the good will that was shown towards me for later, when I might need it, but without explaining any further. Nothing transpired in the convent. I had received from Rome permission to appeal against my vows. The case was to be heard shortly and there was great confidence about its outcome. So you can imagine how surprised my Mother Superior was when she was served with a notice of appeal against her vows in the name of Sister Marie-Suzanne Simonin, together with a request for permission to abandon her religious habit, leave the convent, and make of her life whatever she wished.

I had already foreseen that I would encounter opposition of many kinds: from the law, from the convent, and from my alarmed brothers-in-law and sisters. They had inherited all the family wealth, and, once free, I would have had a strong claim to make against them. I wrote to my sisters, pleading with them not to oppose in any way my leaving the convent and appealing to their consciences on the question of my having had little freedom of choice when taking my vows. I offered to have a legal deed drawn up confirming that I was renouncing all claim on my father's and mother's inheritance. I went to great lengths to persuade them that I was not acting out of self-interest or passion. I failed to sway their feelings. The legal deed I was offering them, if I were to make it while I was still a nun, would become invalid afterwards and my sisters were concerned that I might not abide by it once I was free. And besides, was it in their interest to agree to my proposals? Will they leave a sister with no home and no money? Will they enjoy her wealth? What will people say in the world outside? If she comes to us asking for bread, shall we refuse her? If she takes it into her head to get married, who knows what kind of man she will marry? And what if she has children? We must use all our strength to thwart this dangerous endeavour. That is what they said to themselves and what they did.

No sooner had the Mother Superior received the legal notification of my appeal than she made straight for my cell.

'What's this, Sister Sainte Suzanne?' she said. 'Do you want to leave us?'

'Yes, Madame.'

'And you're going to appeal against your vows?'

'Yes, Madame.'

'Didn't you take them of your own free will?'

'No, Madame.'

'So who forced you to take them?'

'Everything.'

'Your father?'

'My father.'

'Your mother?'

'She too.'

'And why didn't you protest when you were standing before the altar?'

'I was hardly myself. I don't even remember having been there.'

'How can you say such things?'

'I'm telling the truth.'

'What? Didn't you hear the priest asking you: "Sister Sainte Suzanne Simonin, do you swear to God obedience, chastity, and poverty?" '

'I have no recollection of it.'

'Didn't you reply "Yes"?'

'I have no recollection of it.'

'And do you imagine that people will believe you?'

'Whether they believe me or not, it is the truth.'

'My dear child, if people listened to such excuses, can you imagine the abuses that might follow? You've acted thoughtlessly, you've let yourself be swept along by feelings of revenge, all you can think about are the punishments you forced me to inflict upon you and you thought that these were enough to allow you to break your vows. But you're wrong: that simply can't happen, neither in the eyes of men nor in the eyes of God. You should reflect that perjury is the greatest of all crimes, that you've already committed it in your heart and that now you're going to commit it in reality.'

'I shan't be committing perjury, for I've sworn nothing.'

'We may have done you wrong in the past, but haven't we made up for it now?'

'That's not what has made me decide to do this.'

'Then what has?'

'My lack of vocation and my lack of freedom of choice when taking my vows.'

'If you weren't called to be a nun, if you were being forced into it, why didn't you say so at the time?'

'And what good would that have done?'

'Why didn't you show the same strength of purpose that you showed at Sainte-Marie?'

'Can we control our resolve? I was resolute the first time, but the second time I was weak.'

'Why didn't you summon a lawyer? Why didn't you protest? You had the usual twenty-four hours to declare that you had done the wrong thing.'

'What did I know about the formalities? Even if I had known about them, was I in any fit state to have recourse to them? And even if I had been in a fit state, would I have been able to do so? Why,

Madame, didn't you yourself notice the deranged state I was in? If I call you as a witness, will you swear that I was in sound mind?'

'Yes, I will.'

'Well in that case, Madame, it will be you who'll be committing perjury, not me.'

'My child, you're going to cause an unnecessary scandal. Come to your senses, I beseech you, both for your own good and for the good of the convent. Pursuing these kinds of cases only ever causes scandalous publicity.'

'That won't be my fault.'

'People out in the world are nasty. The most unfavourable conclusions will be drawn about your mind, your heart, and your morals. They will believe...'

'Whatever they like.'

'But speak openly now. If you have some secret reason for being dissatisfied, whatever it is, there is a remedy for it.'

'I was, I am, and I always will be dissatisfied with my way of life.'

'Perhaps the devil, who is always and everywhere around us and who tries to bring about our ruin, has taken advantage of the excessive freedom that you have been granted recently to inspire in you some wicked yearning?'

'No, Madame, you know that I don't swear an oath lightly, and I declare before God that my heart is innocent and that it never harboured any shameful feeling.'

'That's difficult to believe.'

'On the contrary, Madame, nothing is easier to believe. Everyone has their own character and I have mine. You love the monastic life and I hate it. You have received from God all the grace required for your way of life and I have received none. You would have been lost in the world, so here you ensure your salvation, but I would be lost here and I hope to save myself in the world. I am, and I will be, a bad nun.'

'But why? Nobody fulfils their duties better than you do.'

'But I do so with difficulty and reluctantly.'

'You deserve better.'

'Nobody knows better than I do what I deserve, and I'm forced to admit to myself that by being totally submissive, I deserve nothing. I'm tired of being a hypocrite. By doing what saves others I only hate and condemn myself. In short, Madame, the only true nuns I know are those who are kept here by their taste for a life of seclusion and who would remain here even if there were no bars or walls around them to keep them here. I am far from being one of those nuns. I am here, but my heart isn't: it is outside, and if I had to choose between dying and being shut away for the rest of my life, I'd have no hesitation in dying. That's how I feel.'

'What! Without the slightest compunction you'll abandon that veil and that habit which have marked you out for Jesus Christ?'

'Yes, Madame, because I took them without thinking and without any freedom of choice...'

I answered her with a great deal of self-control, for that was not what my heart was telling me to say, which was: 'Oh! if only I could tear them up now and throw them away!...'

But my reply brought about a change in her. She blanched, she tried to speak, but her lips were trembling and she had no idea what she wanted to say. I strode up and down my cell, and she cried:

'Oh my God! What will our sisters say? Oh Jesus! Look down on her with pity! Sister Sainte Suzanne?'

'Yes, Madame?'

'So you've made up your mind? You want to bring shame on us, make a public laughing stock of us and yourself, and bring about your own ruin!'

'I want to leave here.'

'But if it's simply the convent you don't like...'

'It's the convent, it's my life here, it's religious life in general. I don't want to be shut away here or anywhere else.'

'My child, you're possessed by the devil. He's the one who's stirring you up, making you speak like this, and driving you mad. That's what it is: just look at the state you're in!'

And so I looked at myself and realized that my dress was in disarray, that my wimple was almost back to front, and that my veil had fallen around my shoulders. I was annoyed by what this wicked Mother Superior had said in the soft and false tone of voice that she always adopted when speaking to me. I replied angrily:

'No, Madame, no, I don't want this habit any more, I just don't want it...'

As I spoke, I tried to rearrange my veil, but my hands were trembling, and the more I tried to adjust it, the more untidy it became. I lost my patience, grabbed hold of it, ripped it off and threw it to the ground. I stood there in front of the Mother Superior, the band still around my forehead and my hair dishevelled. Meanwhile, not knowing whether to stay or leave, she walked up and down saying:

'Oh Jesus! She is possessed, that's what it is, she's possessed...'

And the hypocrite signed herself with the cross on her rosary.

I quickly came to my senses. I realized what an indecent state I was in and how imprudent my words had been. I composed myself as best I could, picked up my veil and put it back on, and then turned to her and said:

'Madame, I am neither mad nor possessed. I am ashamed of my acts of violence and I ask for your forgiveness. But that should make you realize how ill suited I am to life in a convent and how right it is that I should try to get out if I can.'

But she was not listening to me, and she went on saying: 'What will people outside say? What will our sisters say?'

'Madame,' I said, 'do you want to avoid a scandal? There might be a way of doing just that. I'm not asking for my dowry. All I want is to be free. I'm not telling you to open the gates for me, but all you need to do today, tomorrow, or some time thereafter, is see that they're poorly guarded, and then leave it as late as you can before noticing that I've escaped.'

'You audacious wretch! What on earth are you suggesting?'

'It's a suggestion that a good and wise Mother Superior ought to follow with all those for whom the convent is a prison, and that's exactly what this convent is for me, albeit a thousand times worse than those which hold criminals. I must escape or perish here... Madame,' I said, adopting a serious tone and looking at her confidently, 'listen. If the laws to which I have appealed fall short of my expectations, and if, driven by that despair which I know only too well... you have a well... there are windows in the convent... there are walls in front of you wherever you go... our habits can be cut up... we can use our hands...'

'Stop there, you wretched girl! You're terrifying me. What, you could...'

'I could, for want of anything which would put a speedy end to life's woes, refuse my food. It is entirely up to us whether we eat, drink, or do neither... Given what I've just told you, if it so happened that I had the courage, which, as you know, I don't lack and which one sometimes needs more of in order to live than to die;

imagine yourself facing God on the day of judgement and tell me whether the nun or the Mother Superior would be the more guilty in his eyes... Madame, I am not asking for anything back from the convent, and I never shall. Save me from a crime, and save yourself from endless remorse. Let's help each other...'

'Do you really think, Sister Sainte Suzanne, that I will fail in my most important duty, that I will lend my hand to a crime, that I will be party to a sacrilege?'

'The real sacrilege, Madame, is what I commit every day by profaning through contempt the sacred habit that I wear. Take it away from me, for I am unworthy of it. Send someone to the village to fetch the rags of the poorest peasant woman, and leave the gates of the convent ajar for me.'

'And where will you go to lead a better life?'

'I don't know where I'll go, but we are badly off only where God doesn't want us to be, and God doesn't want me to be here.'

'You have nothing.'

'That's true, but poverty isn't what I'm most afraid of.'

'But you should be afraid of the troubles it can lead to.'

'My past is the best guarantee of my future. If I'd behaved in a criminal manner, I'd be free now. But if I decide that I must leave this convent, I shall do so either with your blessing or on the authority of the law. It's your decision.'

This conversation had lasted for some time. When I recalled it later I was embarrassed by the indiscreet and absurd things I had done and said, but it was too late. The Mother Superior was still exclaiming—'What will people outside say? What will our sisters say?'—when the bell rang calling us to church and bringing the meeting to an end. As she left, she said:

'Sister Sainte Suzanne, go into church and ask God to touch you and to fill you again with the spirit of religion. Examine your conscience and believe what it tells you, because it will undoubtedly reproach you. I don't want you to sing in the choir.'

We went down almost together. The office ended, and as it did so, when all the nuns were about to go their separate ways, she tapped on her breviary and stopped them.

'My sisters,' she said, 'I invite you to kneel before the altar and beg God to have mercy on a nun whom he has abandoned, a nun who has lost her inclination to, and the spirit of, the religious life and who is on the point of doing something which is sacrilegious in the eyes of God and shameful in the eyes of man.'

I cannot portray for you the general state of surprise. In an instant each nun, without moving, had looked around at the faces of all her companions to try to work out from her disquiet who was the guilty party. They all prostrated themselves and prayed in silence. After quite a considerable period of time, the prioress intoned softly the *Veni Creator*.* Then, after another silence, the prioress tapped on her stall and everyone left.

You can imagine the stir that was created in the community: 'Who is it? Who isn't it? What has she done? What does she want to do?' These suspicions did not last long. My request was beginning to be talked about in the outside world. I received an endless stream of visitors. Some of them came to reproach me; others came to offer advice. Some of them approved; others rebuked me. I had only one way of justifying myself to everyone and that was to tell them how my parents had treated me, and you can imagine how delicately I had to handle that. I could only be completely open with those few people who remained sincerely devoted to me, and with Monsieur Manouri who had taken on my case. When I was frightened by the suffering I was threatened with, I remembered in all its hideousness that cell that I had once been dragged into, and I knew how frenzied the nuns could be. I told Monsieur Manouri of my fears and he said:

'It will be impossible for you to avoid all sorts of trouble: you will inevitably confront it, you must have been expecting to do so. Your defence must be your patience and your support must be the hope that it will all end. As far as that cell is concerned, I promise you that you will never go back there: I shall see to that.'

And indeed he did, for a few days later he brought a directive to the Mother Superior ordering her to let me appear whenever she was called upon to do so.

The next day, after the office, I was again commended to the public prayers of the community. They prayed in silence and the same hymn as the previous day was recited softly. The same ceremony took place on the third day, but with one difference: I was told to stand in the middle of the choir and they recited the prayers for the dying and the litanies of the saints with the refrain *Ora pro ea*.* On the fourth day there was a ploy which revealed the Mother Superior's peculiar character. At the end of the office I was made to lie down in a coffin in the middle of the choir, with candlesticks and a stoup of holy water placed beside me. I was covered with a shroud and they recited the office for the dead, after which each nun, as she left, sprinkled me with holy water and said *Requiescat in pace*.* You have to understand the language of convents in order to understand the particular kind of threat that was implicit in those words. Two nuns removed the shroud, blew out the candles and left me there soaked to the skin with the water that they had maliciously thrown on me. My clothes dried on me as I had nothing to change into.

This mortification was followed by another. The community gathered. They considered me a reprobate, my behaviour was presented as apostasy, and it was forbidden as an act of disobedience for any nun to speak to me, to help me, to come near me, or even to touch anything I had used. These orders were carried out to the letter. Our corridors are narrow and in some places it is difficult for two people to walk side by side. If I was walking along and a nun was coming towards me, either she would turn round and go back or she would press herself against the wall, clutching her veil and habit for fear of their brushing against mine. If anything had to be taken from me, I had first to put it on the ground and then it would be picked up with a cloth. If anything had to be given to me, it was thrown. If anyone had the misfortune to touch me, they thought themselves sullied and they would go and make their confession and receive absolution from the Mother Superior. It has been said that flattery is vile and base, but more than that, it is cruel and ingenious when it sets out to please someone by inventing mortifications. How many times have I recalled the words of my saintly Mother de Moni: 'Out of all these creatures you see around me, so docile, so innocent, and so gentle, well, my child, there is scarcely one, scarcely a single one that I could not turn into a wild animal; a strange metamorphosis to which one is all the more susceptible the younger one enters religion and the less one knows of life in society. These words surprise you: may God preserve you from ever finding out how true they are. Sister Suzanne, the good nun is the one who brings with her into the cloister some great sin to expiate.'

I was deprived of all my duties. In church the stalls either side of mine were left empty. I sat alone in the refectory but nobody served me, so I had to go into the kitchen and ask for my portion. The first time I went in, the cook shouted at me: 'Don't come in here, get back...' I did as she said.

'What do you want?'

'Something to eat.'

'Something to eat! You don't deserve to live...'

Sometimes I left and ate nothing the whole day. On other occasions I insisted, and food was left for me on the doorstep that one would have been ashamed to give to animals. I picked it up in tears and left. Whenever I arrived last at the door to the choir, I would find it shut, so I would kneel down and wait there for the office to end. But if it was the door to the garden, I would go back to my cell. However, with my strength being sapped by my eating so little and by the poor quality of the food I did eat, and also by how difficult I found it to endure so many repeated acts of inhumanity, I felt that if I persisted in suffering without complaining, then I would never see my lawsuit through to its conclusion. And so I resolved to speak to the Mother Superior. I was half dead with terror. I nevertheless went and knocked gently on her door, which she opened. As soon as she saw me she took several steps back and cried:

'Apostate, get back...' I stepped back.

'Further.' I stepped further back.

'What do you want?'

'Since neither God nor men have condemned me to death, I want you, Madame, to order that I be kept alive.'

'Alive?', she said, repeating what the cook had said. 'Do you deserve that?'

'Only God knows that, but I warn you that if I am refused food, I shall be forced to lodge my complaint with those who have taken me into their care. I am only here provisionally until my fate and my condition have been decided.'

'Go away,' she said, 'don't defile me by looking at me. I'll see to it...'

I left and she slammed the door shut. Apparently she gave her orders, but I was hardly better looked after as a result. They took pride in disobeying her. I was thrown the most disgusting food, which they spoilt still further by mixing in ashes and all kinds of filth.

That is the kind of life I led while my lawsuit was going on. I was not completely forbidden to go into the parlour. I could not be denied the freedom to speak with my judges or my lawyer, but even Monsieur Manouri was forced several times to resort to threats in order to gain access to me. Another nun used to accompany me on these occasions. She would complain if I spoke too softly and grow impatient if I stayed too long. She would interrupt me, refute what I had said, contradict me, and she repeated my words to the Mother Superior, though she altered them, and poisoned them, even claimed I had said things that I had not, and so on. It even got to the stage of my being robbed and deprived of my belongings, and my chairs, bedding, and mattress were taken away. I was no longer given fresh undergarments, my clothes were torn, and I had almost worn out my stockings and sandals. It was difficult for me to obtain water, and on several occasions I was forced to go and fetch it for myself from the well, the one that I have told you about. My utensils had been smashed, so I had to drink the water that I had drawn there and then because I could not take it away with me. Whenever I walked beneath windows I had to hurry or have waste thrown at me from the cells. Some nuns spat in my face. I had become horribly dirty. Since it was feared that I might complain to our spiritual directors, I was forbidden to go to confession. One particular feast day, it was Ascension Day, I think, the lock on my door had been tampered with and I could not go to mass, and I might have missed all the other services if I had not been visited by Monsieur Manouri, who was told at first that nobody knew what had happened to me, that nobody saw me any more, and that I had abandoned my Christian observances. But I struggled with it and eventually managed to break open the lock, and I went down to the door to the choir which I found closed, as it always was whenever I was not one of the first to arrive. I lay on the ground, with my head and back against one of the walls and my arms crossed across my chest, and with the rest of my body I stretched out and blocked the passageway when the office finished and the nuns came to leave. The first one stopped short and the others followed behind her. The Mother Superior guessed what had happened and said:

'Walk over her, she's just a corpse.'

Some of them obeyed and trampled on me, others were less inhuman, but not one of them dared to stretch out her hand to help me up. While I was away from my cell, my prayer stool, my portrait of our founder, my other pious images, and my crucifix were all taken away, and I was left only with the crucifix on my rosary, which was also soon taken from me. So I found myself living within four bare walls, in a room with no door or chair, my only option being to stand or to lie on a straw mattress, with no essential utensils, forced to go out at night in order to meet the call of nature, and accused in the morning of disrupting the convent, of wandering about, and of going mad. Since the door to my cell could no longer be closed, nuns would burst in during the night, shouting, pulling my bed, smashing my windows, and doing all sorts of terrifying things to me. The noise could be heard both upstairs and downstairs, and those nuns who were not part of the conspiracy said that strange things were going on in my room, that they had heard doleful voices, screams, and the jangling of chains, that I was conversing with ghosts and evil spirits, that I must have made some pact, and that all the other nuns there should leave my corridor forthwith. There are weak-minded people in all religious communities; in fact they are in the majority. They believed what they were told and did not dare walk past my door; I was a hideous vision in their troubled imaginations. They crossed themselves whenever they saw me and ran away screaming: 'Get away from me, Satan! Help me, dear God.' At the far end of the corridor was one of the youngest nuns. I went to see her and there was no way she could avoid me. She was gripped by the most dreadful panic. At first she pressed her face against the wall, muttering in a trembling voice: 'My God! My God! Jesus! Mary! Jesus! Mary!...' As she spoke, I went towards her, and when she felt me close by her, she was so afraid of the very sight of me that she buried her face in her hands, then threw herself towards me, rushing violently into my arms and screaming: 'Help me! Help me! Have mercy upon me! I am lost! Sister Sainte Suzanne, don't harm me, Sister Sainte Suzanne, have pity on me...' And as she spoke, she fell backwards, half dead, onto the floor. Her cries drew the attention of the other nuns and they carried her away. I cannot tell you how this episode was misrepresented. It was turned into the most criminal story. They said that I had been possessed by the devil of impurity and they credited me with intentions and actions which I dare not name and bizarre desires which were meant to account for the young nun's obvious distress. To be frank, I am not a man and I do not know what can be imagined about one woman and another, and still less about a woman on her own. But since my bed had no curtains and since nuns came into my room at all hours of the day and night, what can I say, Monsieur? Despite their outward reserve, their modest looks, and their chaste expression, these women must have truly corrupt hearts. Or at least they know that unseemly acts can be committed on one's own, whereas I do not. So I have never really understood what they were accusing me of, and they spoke in such an obscure way that I had no idea how to respond. I could go on for ever describing in detail how I was persecuted. Oh Monsieur, if you have any children, let my fate be a warning to you about the fate you would be preparing for them if you allowed them to enter the religious life without showing signs of the strongest and most committed vocation. How unjust people are to allow a child to take responsibility for her own freedom at an age when she is not even allowed to spend an *écu*.* Kill your daughter rather than imprison her against her will in a convent, yes, kill her. How often have I wished that my mother had smothered me at birth! It would have been less cruel of her. Would you believe that they took away my breviary and forbade me to pray to God? As you may well expect, I disobeyed them. Alas, that was my only consolation. I lifted up my hands to God, I cried out loud, and I was bold enough to hope that my cries were heard by the only Being who saw all my suffering. They listened at my door, and one day, as I was praying to him, my heart utterly downcast, and calling upon him to help me, one of them said to me:

'There's no point calling on God. There's no God for you any more. Die in despair and be damned...'

Others added: 'Amen on the apostate, amen on her.'

But here is something which you will find stranger than anything else. I do not know if it was out of malice or self-delusion, but, although I did nothing to suggest that my mind was deranged, and even less that my mind was possessed by the devil, they discussed amongst themselves whether or not I should be exorcized, and it was decided by a majority that I had renounced my chrism and my baptism, that the devil was in me, and that he was leading me away from divine service. Another nun added that when certain prayers were said in church I gnashed my teeth and trembled and that at the elevation of the Blessed Sacrament I contorted my arms. Another said that I trampled on the crucifix and that I no longer carried my rosary with me (which had been stolen from me), that I uttered blasphemies which I dare not repeat to you. And all said that there was something unnatural happening to me and that the Vicar General should be told about it, and so he was.

The Vicar General went by the name of Monsieur Hébert,* a mature and experienced man, brusque but fair and enlightened. He was told in great detail about the unrest in the convent. It was clear that it was considerable and that, if I had caused it, I had done so quite innocently. You will no doubt imagine that the statement that was sent to him included mention of my nocturnal wanderings, my absences from the choir, the commotion in my room, what this nun had seen and what that nun had heard, my aversion to divine things, my blasphemies and the obscene conduct that I was accused of, and as for what happened with the young nun, they took full advantage of that. The accusations were so weighty and so numerous that, for all his good sense, Monsieur Hébert could not help giving them some credence and thinking that there was a good deal of truth in them. He found the case serious enough for him to want to find out more about it for himself. He had the convent notified of his visit and he duly arrived with two young clergymen who had been assigned to him and who helped him to perform his onerous duties.

A few days earlier, I heard someone creep into my room in the middle of the night. I said nothing and waited for them to speak. They called out to me in a soft and trembling voice:

'Sister Sainte Suzanne, are you asleep?'

'No, I'm not. Who's there?'

'It's me.'

'Who?'

'It's your friend who is frightened to death and who risks condemning herself in order to give you some advice which may well be useless. Listen: tomorrow or some time later the Vicar General is coming. You'll be accused, so be ready to defend yourself. Farewell, be brave, and may the Lord be with you.'

Having spoken, she parted as discreetly as a shadow. You see, everywhere, even in convents, there are a few compassionate souls whom nothing can harden.

Meanwhile my case attracted feverish attention. A host of people from all walks of life, of both sexes and of all callings, none of whom I knew, took an interest in my fate and intervened on my behalf. One of them was you, and perhaps you know the story of my case better than I do, since towards the end I was no longer allowed to speak with Monsieur Manouri, who was told that I was ill. He suspected that he was being deceived, and he feared that I had been thrown into the dungeon. He contacted the Archbishop's palace but was not given so much as a hearing, for they had already been told that I was mad or perhaps worse. He went back to the judges and insisted that the directive given to the Mother Superior be enforced, which required her to have me appear dead or alive whenever she was called upon to do so. The civil judges broached the question with the ecclesiastical judges, who were well aware of the consequences that this incident could have if they did not proceed as necessary, and this seems to have ensured the prompt visit of the Vicar General, since men like him, weary of the endless squabbles in convents, are usually in no hurry to get involved in them, for experience tells them that their authority is always evaded and undermined.

I took advantage of my friend's advice and prayed for God's help, calmed my soul, and prepared my defence. All I asked from God was that I might be fortunate enough to be questioned and heard in an impartial way. My prayer was answered, but at a cost, as you will see.

Since it was in my interest to appear innocent and sensible before my judge, it was no less important to my Mother Superior that I should be seen as wicked, possessed by the devil, guilty, and mad. So, whilst I was doubly fervent and prayerful, they were doubly nasty: I was given only enough food to stop me from starving to death, they overwhelmed me with mortifications, and terrified me more and more on every side; I was totally deprived of sleep at night; they did all they could to weaken my health and to derange my mind: you cannot begin to imagine how well they had perfected the art of cruelty. But you can form some impression from this incident. One day as I was coming out of my cell to go to church or somewhere else, I saw a pair of fire tongs on the floor in the corridor. I bent down to pick them up so that I could put them where whoever had lost them could easily find them. Because of the light, I could not see that they were almost red hot. I picked them up, but as I dropped them they ripped all the skin off the palm of my bare hand. At night obstacles were left for me wherever I went, either on the floor or at head-height. I was hurt a hundred times, and I do not know how I managed not to kill myself. I had no means of lighting my way, so I had to walk along, tentatively stretching my arms out in front of me. Glasses were smashed and the shards scattered beneath my feet. I was determined to say all this and did so, more or less. I used to find the door to the conveniences locked and had to go down several floors and run down to the bottom of the garden, when the gate was open. But when it was locked... Oh, Monsieur! What wicked creatures they are, those cloistered women who always assist their Mother Superior in her hatred and who believe that they are serving God by driving you to despair! It was time for the Archdeacon to come; it was time for my case to be decided.

This was the most terrible moment in my life, for you must remember, Monsieur, that I had absolutely no idea how I had been portrayed to this cleric and that he was coming in order to see a girl who was possessed or who was pretending to be so. The nuns thought that only some great torment could reduce me to such a state, and this is how they meted it out to me.

Early in the morning on the day of his visit, the Mother Superior came into my cell, accompanied by three nuns, one of whom was carrying a stoup of holy water, the other a crucifix, and the third some rope. The Mother Superior said in a loud and threatening voice:

'Get up. Kneel down and commend your soul to God.'

'Madame,' I replied, 'before I do as you say, could I ask you what is to become of me, what you have decided for me, and what I have to ask God for?'

A cold sweat enveloped the whole of my body: I was trembling and felt my knees giving way. I looked in terror at her three dreadful companions. They were standing in a line, their faces grave, their lips set, and their eyes closed. Fear made me pronounce each word in my question separately, and I judged from their silence that they had not understood me. I started to repeat just the last part of the question, as I did not have the strength to repeat it all, so I said in a weak, faltering voice:

'What favour do I have to ask God for?'

The reply came: 'Ask him to forgive you all the sins you have ever committed; speak as if the time had come for you to appear before him.'

Hearing this, I thought that they had deliberated and had decided to get rid of me. I had certainly heard that this sort of thing sometimes happened in certain monasteries, where a monk would be judged, condemned, and tortured to death. I did not think that this inhuman form of trial had ever been practised in a convent. But then there were so many other things that went on that I had not imagined possible! Believing my death to be imminent, I wanted to scream, but I opened my mouth and no sound came out. I went towards the Mother Superior, holding my arms out in supplication, and my feeble body fell backwards. I collapsed on the ground, but did not land heavily. In such moments of stupor when all one's strength imperceptibly drains away, one's limbs give way and collapse, so to speak, on top of each other, and since nature cannot sustain herself, she seems to try to weaken gently. I lost all consciousness and feeling. All I could hear was confused and distant voices buzzing around me. Whether it was the nuns talking or my ears ringing, all I could make out was that constant buzzing. I do not know how long I remained in this condition, but I was brought round by a sudden chill which made me jump slightly and take a deep breath. I was soaked in water, which dripped from my clothes onto the floor, water that had been thrown over me from a large stoup. I was lying on my side in this puddle of water, with my head against the wall, my mouth half open, and my eyes lifeless and half closed. I tried to open them and look around, but it was as if I was surrounded by a thick haze through which all I could see was flapping habits, which I tried to focus on in vain. I attempted to move my arm that was not supporting me and tried to raise it, but it was too heavy for me. My extreme weakness gradually retreated, and I lifted myself up and sat with my back against the wall, my hands in the puddle of water and my head resting on my chest, and I gave an inarticulate, broken, painful groan. The way the women looked at me betrayed their determination and their intransigence, and it robbed me of the courage to appeal to them for mercy. The Mother Superior said:

'Lift her up.'

They took hold of me under my arms and lifted me up. Then she said:

'Since she refuses to commend herself to God, so much the worse for her. You know what you have to do, so do it...'

I thought that they had brought rope with them in order to strangle me, and as I looked at them, my eyes filled with tears. I asked if I could kiss the crucifix, but they would not let me. I asked if I could kiss the rope, and they held it out in front of me. I leant forward, took the Mother Superior's scapular in my hand and kissed it. I said:

'My God, have mercy upon me, my God, have mercy upon me. Dear sisters, try not to make me suffer...'

And I offered my neck to them. I cannot tell you what happened to me or what they did to me. Those who are led out to execution, and I thought that I was one of them, are surely already dead before they are executed. I ended up sitting on the straw mattress which I used as a bed, with my hands tied behind my back and a big iron crucifix on my lap... Monsieur le Marquis, I can tell from here all the trouble I am causing you, but you did want to know if I was in any way worthy of the compassion that I am expecting of you.

It was then that I came to feel that Christianity was superior to all the other religions in the world. What profound wisdom there was in what benighted philosophy calls the folly of the cross.* In the state I was in, how would the image of a happy and glorious lawgiver have helped me? I saw that innocent man, his side pierced, his head crowned with thorns, his hands and feet pierced with nails, and dying in agony, and I said to myself: 'This is my God, and yet I dare to feel sorry for myself!...' I clung to this idea and felt a renewed sense of consolation in my heart. I knew the vanity of life and found myself only too happy to lose it rather than have the time to commit yet more sins. But I counted up my years and, realizing that I was barely twenty years old, I sighed. I was too weak and exhausted for my mind to rise above the horror of death. I think that had I been in full health, I would have been able to be bolder in my resolve.

Meanwhile the Mother Superior and her minions had returned. They found that I had more presence of mind than they had expected or would have liked. They pulled me up and fixed my veil over my face. Two of them held me under my arms, a third pushed me from behind, and the Mother Superior ordered me to walk. I set off not knowing where I was going, but thinking that I was going to be executed, and I said: 'My God, have mercy upon me. My God, give me strength. My God, do not forsake me. My God, forgive me if I have sinned against you.'

I entered the church. The Vicar General had just finished celebrating Mass. The whole community was gathered there. I forgot to tell you that when I was at the door to the church, the three nuns who were leading me held me tightly, pushed me about violently, appeared to be struggling all around me, and some of them dragged me by the arms while others held me from behind, to make it look as if I was resisting and refusing to enter the church, which was not the case at all. I was led towards the altar steps. I could hardly stand up and they dragged me on my knees to make it look as if I was refusing to stand there, and they kept hold of me as if I was about to run away. The *Veni Creator* was sung, the Blessed Sacrament was exposed, and benediction was said. At that point in benediction when everyone bows in veneration, the nuns who had grabbed me by the arms made it look as if they were forcing me to bow, and the others pressed down on my shoulders. I could feel all these different movements, but I found it impossible to tell why they were making them. It all became clear in due course.

After benediction, the Vicar General removed his chasuble, put on simply his alb and stole, and walked towards the altar steps where I was kneeling. He was flanked by the two priests, with his back to the altar where the Blessed Sacrament was exposed, and facing me. He came up to me and said:

'Sister Suzanne, stand up.'

The nuns holding me pulled me up sharply, and others stood around me with their hands around my waist as if they were frightened that I would escape. He went on:

'Untie her.'

They did not obey him, but pretended instead to see only the problem or even the danger in letting me go. But I told you that this man was brusque, and he repeated in a firm, hard voice:

'Untie her.'

They obeyed him. No sooner had my hands been freed than I gave a sharp, pained cry which made him go pale, and the hypocritical nuns standing near me scattered as if in terror. He regained his composure, the sisters returned, apparently trembling, and I remained still. He said to me:

'What is wrong?'

I replied by simply showing him my two arms. The rope that had been used to tie them together had almost cut right through my flesh, and they were purple where the blood supply had been cut off and where the veins had burst. He realized that I had let out a cry because of the sudden pain caused by the blood being allowed to flow again. He said:

'Remove her veil.'

I had not realized that they had sewn it up in various places, and this ensured that an otherwise simple task required yet more fuss and physical force. They wanted the priest to see me obsessed, possessed, or mad. However they pulled so much that the thread snapped in some places, my veil or habit was torn in others, and my face was visible. I have a touching appearance; the intense pain I had experienced had altered it but had not robbed it of any of its character. The sound of my voice also touches people, and they feel that when I speak, I am telling the truth. The combination of these qualities struck pity in the hearts of the Archdeacon's two young acolytes, but the Archdeacon himself was a stranger to such feelings: he was fair, but he was not very sensitive. He was one of those people unfortunate enough to be born to be virtuous but without ever experiencing the pleasure it can bring: such people do good routinely, in the same way as they think. He took the end of his stole and, placing it on my head, said to me:

'Sister Suzanne, do you believe in God the Father, the Son, and the Holy Spirit?'

'I do,' I replied.

'Do you believe in the Holy Mother Church?'

'I do.'

'Do you renounce Satan and all his works?'

Instead of replying, I suddenly moved forwards and screamed loudly, and the end of his stole came away from my head. He was unnerved and his companions went pale. Some of the nuns ran away and the others, who were in their stalls, left in a great commotion. He gestured to them to calm down. As all this was going on, he looked at me, expecting me to do something extraordinary. I reassured him by saying:

'Monsieur, there's nothing wrong. One of the nuns jabbed me with something sharp.'

And raising my eyes and hands heavenwards, and with tears streaming down my face, I added:

'One of them hurt me just as you were asking me if I renounced Satan and his works, and I know why.'

They all protested via the Mother Superior that they had not touched me. The Archdeacon placed the end of his stole on my head again. The nuns were about to gather round again but he gestured to them to keep back, and then he asked me again if I renounced Satan and all his works, and I replied resolutely:

'I renounce him, I renounce him.'

He had a crucifix brought to him and he held it out to me to kiss it, and I kissed it on the feet, the hands, and the wound in Christ's side. He ordered me to worship it aloud. I laid it on the ground and, kneeling before it, I said:

'My God, my Saviour, you who died on the cross for my sins and for those of all mankind, I worship you. Grant me the rewards that come from the suffering you endured, and let a drop of the blood you shed fall on me so that I may be made clean. Forgive me, my God, as I forgive all my enemies...'

Then he said:

'Make an act of faith...', and I did so.

'Make an act of love...', and I did so.

'Make an act of hope...', and I did so.

'Make an act of charity...', and I did so.

I cannot remember how they were expressed, but I think they must have been very moving, because I made some of the nuns sob, the two young priests wept, and the Archdeacon, in his amazement, asked me where the prayers that I had just recited had come from. I replied:

'From the bottom of my heart: they are my thoughts and my feelings. I swear to God who hears us everywhere and who is present on this altar. I am a Christian, and I am innocent. If I have sinned, then God alone knows what those sins are, and he alone can call me to account and punish me.'

At these words, he looked witheringly at the Mother Superior.

The ceremony, during which God's majesty had been insulted, the most sacred things profaned, and a minister of the Church treated with scorn, came to an end and the nuns went away, apart from the Mother Superior, me, and the young priests. The Archdeacon sat down and took out the statement against me which had been given to him and he read it aloud, questioning me on the claims it contained.

'Why', he said, 'don't you go to confession?'

'Because I'm prevented from doing so.'

'Why don't you go near the sacraments?'

'Because I'm prevented from doing so.'

'Why don't you come to mass or the Divine Office?'

'Because I'm prevented from doing so.'

The Mother Superior tried to speak, but he said in his usual tone: 'Madame, be quiet... Why do you leave your cell at night?'

'Because I have been deprived of water, jug, and all utensils necessary for the calls of nature.'

'Why can noise be heard at night in your dormitory and in your cell?'

'Because they try to keep me awake.'

The Mother Superior tried again to interrupt, and for the second time he said: 'Madame, I have already told you to be quiet. You will answer when I question you.'

'What is all this about a young nun who was torn away from you and found lying on the floor in the corridor?'

'That occurred because she was made to be terrified of me.'

'Is she a friend of yours?'

'No, Monsieur.'

'So you've never been in her cell?'

'Never.'

'And you've never done anything indecent either to her or to any of the other nuns?'

'Never.'

'Why were you tied up?'

'I don't know.'

'Why can't you shut the door to your cell?'

'Because I broke the lock.'

'Why did you break it?'

'So that I could open the door and attend the office on Ascension Day.'

'So you did go to church that day?'

'Yes, Monsieur...'

The Mother Superior said:

'Monsieur, that is not true, the whole community...'

I interrupted her:

'Will tell you that the door to the choir was shut, that they found me lying in the doorway, and that you ordered them to walk on me, which some of them did, but I forgive them and you, Madame, for having ordered them to do so. I have not come here to accuse anybody, but to defend myself.'

'Why don't you have a rosary or a crucifix?'

'Because they've been taken away from me.'

'Where's your breviary?'

'It's been taken away from me.'

'So how do you pray?'

'I pray with my heart and my spirit, despite the fact that I have been told not to pray.'

'Who told you not to pray?'

'Madame...'

The Mother Superior made to speak again.

'Madame,' he said, 'is it true or false that you told her she could not pray? Answer yes or no.'

'I believed, and I was right to believe...'

'I'm not interested in that. Did you tell her she could not pray, yes or no?'

'I told her not to, but...'

She was about to go on.

'But,' the Archdeacon interrupted, 'but... Sister Suzanne, why do you have nothing on your feet?'

'Because I haven't been given any stockings or sandals.'

'Why are your undergarments and clothes so shabby and dirty?'

'Because for more than three months now I've been refused fresh undergarments and have been forced to sleep with my clothes on.'

'Why do you sleep with your clothes on?'

'Because I don't have any curtains, mattresses, blankets, sheets, or nightwear.'

'Why don't you have any?'

'Because they've been taken away from me.'

'Are you given food?'

'I ask for it.'

'So you're not fed?'

I said nothing, and he added:

'I simply cannot believe that you've been treated so harshly without your having done something wrong to deserve it.'

'All I have done wrong is not to be called to the religious life and to seek to rescind the vows which I made against my will.'

'It is up to the law to rule on this matter, but whatever is decided, you must in the meantime perform the duties of the religious life.'

'Nobody, Monsieur, is more assiduous than I am.'

'You must enjoy the same fate as all your fellow nuns.'

'That is all I ask.'

'Do you not have a complaint to bring against anyone?'

'No, Monsieur, as I told you, I did not come here to accuse anyone, but to defend myself.'

'You may go now.'

'Where, Monsieur?'

'To your cell.'

I took a few steps, but then I turned back and threw myself at the feet of the Mother Superior and the Archdeacon.

'My,' he said, 'whatever's wrong?'

Showing him the bruises all over my head, my bloody feet, my pale, skinny arms and my dirty, torn clothes, I said: 'Just look at me!'

I can hear you now, Monsieur le Marquis, you and most of those who will read these memoirs,* saying: 'So many horrors, so varied and so continuous! A succession of such calculated atrocities in religious souls! It's so implausible,' they will say, you will say. And I agree, but it is true. And may God be my witness and judge me with all his severity and cast me down into the eternal flames if I have allowed even the slightest shadow of calumny to tarnish just one line of what I have written. Although I have lengthy experience of how a Mother Superior's dislike can act as a violent spur to natural perversity, especially when such perversity could become a merit and be applauded and boast of its crimes, resentment will not stop me from being fair. The more I think about it, the more I convince myself that what was happening to me had not happened to anyone before and would perhaps never happen again. Once (and please God may it be the first and last time!) Providence, whose ways are a mystery to us, saw fit to pour down on one unfortunate girl the whole weight of its cruel acts which its impenetrable decrees had otherwise destined to be shared by the infinite multitude of wretched girls who had gone before her in a convent and who would come after her. I have suffered. I have suffered a great deal, but the fate of my persecutors seems to me, and has always seemed to me, more pitiful than mine. I would prefer, or I would have preferred, to die rather than to abandon my role in order to play theirs. My suffering will end; your kindness gives me that hope. The memory and shame of their crime and their remorse will remain with them until they die. They are already accusing themselves, believe me. They will accuse themselves for the rest of their lives, and terror will go to their graves with them. In the meantime, Monsieur le Marquis, my current situation is deplorable and life is a burden to me. I am a woman, and I have the weak mind of those of my sex. God may abandon me, and I do not feel that I have either the strength or the courage to endure for very much longer what I have already endured. Monsieur le Marquis, beware of another fateful moment. Even if you wore out your eyes in weeping over my fate, even if you were wrecked by remorse, I would still not emerge from the abyss into which I had fallen, and it would close for ever over me in my despair.

'You may leave,' said the Archdeacon. One of the priests held out his hand to help me up, and the Archdeacon added:

'I have questioned you, I shall now question your Mother Superior, and I shan't leave this place until order has been re-established.'

I left. I found the rest of the house in a state of great alarm. All the nuns were standing in the doorways to their cells, talking to one another across the corridors. As soon as I appeared, they quickly went inside their cells, creating a resounding noise as, one after another, they slammed their doors shut. I went back into my cell, knelt down facing the wall and prayed that God would see how restrained I had been when speaking to the Archdeacon and would show him my innocence and the truth.

I was praying when the Archdeacon, his two companions, and the Mother Superior came into my cell. As I have told you, I had no wall hangings, no chair, no prayer stool, no curtains, no mattress, no blankets, no sheets, no utensils whatsoever, no door that could be closed, and hardly a pane of glass in my windows. I got up, and the Archdeacon stopped short and looked indignantly at the Mother Superior, saying:

'Well, Madame?'

She replied: 'I didn't realize.'

'You didn't realize! You're lying. Has there been a single day when you haven't been in here, and hadn't you just been here when you came to see me? Sister Suzanne, tell me, has Madame not been here today?'

I said nothing. He did not press, but the young priests dropped their arms and looked down, their eyes apparently fixed to the floor, showing quite clearly how distressed and surprised they were. They all went out, and I heard the Archdeacon in the corridor saying to the Mother Superior:

'You are unworthy of your office, you deserve to be dismissed, and I shall lodge my complaint about you with the Bishop. All this disorder must be sorted out before I leave.'

And walking along, shaking his head, he added:

'It's chilling. Christians! Nuns! Human beings! It's chilling.'

From that moment on I never heard another word about anything, but I was given some undergarments, other clothes, curtains, sheets, blankets, utensils, my breviary, my devotional books, my rosary, my crucifix, and new panes of glass, in short everything I needed to restore my condition to that of the other nuns. I was also allowed to go into the parlour again, but only to discuss my case.

My case was going badly. Monsieur Manouri published his first account which made little impact. It was too intellectual, not moving enough, and there were almost no justifications. The blame cannot be laid entirely at this able lawyer's door. I absolutely insisted that he must not attack my parents' reputation, and I wanted him to handle carefully the religious life and above all the convent that I was in. I did not want him to cast my brothers-in-law and my sisters in too odious a light. All I had in my favour was my first protest, which was certainly solemn, but which had been made in another convent and had not been repeated since. When one imposes such tight limits on one's defence and when one is dealing with people for whom the best form of defence is attack, who trample underfoot both the just and the unjust, who make allegations and denials with equal impudence, and who are not ashamed to deal in accusations, suspicions, scandalmongering, or calumny, then it is difficult to win, particularly in courts that have become so used to, and so bored with, cases that they rarely examine at all scrupulously, even the most important ones, and where claims like mine are always looked upon unfavourably by the judge who, thinking politically, worries that the success of one nun appealing against her vows would lead to a whole host of others trying to do the same thing. It is secretly felt that if the gates to these prisons were allowed to be flung open for one unfortunate nun, then a whole army of nuns would surge forward and try to force them open. Determined efforts are made to discourage us and to make us all resign ourselves to our fate, in despair of ever being able to change it. 'Yet it seems to me that in a well-governed state, the opposite should be the case: it should be difficult to enter the religious life and easy to leave it. And why not add this case to all those others where the slightest error in procedure negates the whole process, however justified that process may be? Are convents so essential to the constitution of a state? Did Jesus Christ institute monks and nuns? Can the Church really not do without them? What need has the bridegroom of so many foolish virgins,* and what need has the human race of so many victims? Will the need never be felt to narrow the opening to these chasms in which future generations will be lost? Are all the routine prayers which are said there worth as much as the penny that charity gives to the poor? Does God, who created man as a social being, approve of him locking himself away? Can God, who created man as such a fickle and fragile being, allow such rash vows? Can these vows, which fly in the face of our natural inclinations, ever be properly observed by anyone other than a few abnormal creatures in whom the seeds of passion have withered and whom we should rightly consider as monsters, if the current state of our knowledge allowed us to understand the internal structure of man as easily and as well as we understand his external form? Do all those doleful ceremonies that are performed at the taking of the habit and at the profession, when a man or woman is dedicated to the monastic life and to misfortune, actually suspend our animal instincts? On the contrary, are not those very instincts stirred up in the silence, constraint, and idleness, and with a violence unknown to people in the world outside who are swept along by a host of distractions? Where does one see minds obsessed by impure visions which haunt them and torment them? Where does one see that profound boredom, that pallor, and those skeletal forms which are all symptoms of nature languishing and wasting away? Where are nights troubled by groans and days filled with tears shed needlessly and preceded by some mysterious melancholy? Where does nature, revolted by a constraint for which it is not intended, smash the obstacles put in its way, become enraged, and throw the whole animal system into incurable disarray? Where have spite and whim destroyed all social qualities? Where are there no fathers, no mothers, no brothers, no sisters, no relatives, and no friends? Where does man, considering himself but an ephemeral, transitory being, treat the sweetest relationships of this world with disinterest, as a traveller treats the things he comes across? Where is the dwelling place of coercion, disgust, and hysteria? Where is the home of servitude and despotism? Where is undying hatred? Where are the passions nurtured in silence? Where is the home of cruelty and curiosity? We do not know the true story of these retreats,' Monsieur Manouri went on in his address, 'we simply do not know.' Elsewhere he added: 'To make a vow of poverty is to swear to be an idler and a thief. To make a vow of chastity is to swear to God constantly to break the wisest and most important of his laws. To make a vow of obedience is to renounce man's inalienable prerogative: freedom. If you keep these vows, you are a criminal; if you do not keep them, you are guilty of perjury before God. To live the cloistered life, you have to be either a fanatic or a hypocrite.'*

A girl asked her parents' permission to enter our convent. Her father told her that he agreed, but he gave her three years to think about it. The young girl, full of fervour, found her father's ruling difficult to accept, but accept it she must. Not having wavered in her vocation, she went back to her father and told him that the three years had passed. 'Very good, my child,' he replied. 'I gave you three years to test you, and I hope now that you will be good enough to give me the same amount of time to make up my mind.' She found that more difficult still and she wept, but her father was a firm man who stood his ground. After six years she entered the convent and made her profession. She was a good nun, simple, pious, and scrupulous in performing all her tasks, but the confessors took advantage of her openness to find out from her in the confessional what was going on in the convent. Our superiors guessed as much, so she was locked away, cut off from religious observances, and she went mad. For how can the mind withstand being persecuted by fifty people, all of whom devote every minute of the day to tormenting you? Previously they had set her mother a trap which is a good illustration of how greedy convents are. They instilled into the nun's mother the idea of coming to the convent and visiting her daughter in her cell. She asked the Vicars General, who granted her the permission she sought. She came in and ran to her daughter's cell, but just imagine her surprise when she found there nothing but four bare walls! Everything had been taken away, and they felt sure that this loving and sensitive mother would not leave her daughter in such a state. And indeed she did not, for she refurnished the cell, gave her daughter new clothes and undergarments, and protested to the nuns that her desire to visit had cost her too much to come a second time, and that three or four such visits a year would spell the ruin of the girl's brothers and sisters. This is the place where ambition and the love of luxury sacrifice one part of a family in order to ensure that the other has a more comfortable life. It is the sink into which the dregs of society are thrown. How many mothers like mine atone for a secret crime by committing another!

Monsieur Manouri published a second account, and this made a somewhat greater impact. Strenuous efforts were made. Once again I offered to let my sisters have full and unhindered rights to my parents' inheritance. At one point the progress of my case took a most favourable turn and I hoped to obtain my freedom, but I was only all the more cruelly deceived as a result. My case was heard in court and lost. The whole community was informed of this even before I was. There was much bustling and commotion, joy, secret little conversations, with the nuns coming and going in and out of the Superior's room and each other's cells. I was trembling all over, and I felt unable to stay in my cell or to leave it, for there was not a single friend into whose arms I could throw myself. How cruel the morning of the verdict in a big case is! I wanted to pray, but I could not. I knelt down, collected my thoughts, and started reciting a prayer, but my mind soon wandered off, in spite of my best efforts, into the midst of the judges. I could see them, I could hear the lawyers, I spoke to them, and I interrupted what mine was saying, as I found that my case was being poorly defended. I did not know any of the magistrates, but I nevertheless painted all kinds of pictures of them in my mind, some of them favourable, but others sinister, and yet others indifferent. I was agitated and in a state of unimaginable mental distress. The noise gave way to a deep silence. The nuns had stopped talking to each other. It sounded to me as if their voices in the choir were brighter than normal, at least those who were singing, for some of them were not. At the end of the office they all left in silence. I convinced myself that the waiting was troubling them just as much as it was me. But suddenly in the afternoon the noise and the commotion started up again all over the convent. I could hear doors opening and closing, nuns coming and going, the murmur of people talking softly to each other. I put my ear to the keyhole, but it seemed to me as if they were deliberately falling silent and tiptoeing past. I had a feeling then that I had lost my case; there was no doubt about it. I started walking silently round and round in my cell, feeling as if I was suffocating, unable to raise a murmur. I folded my arms over my head. I leant my head first against one wall, then against another. I wanted to lie down and rest on my bed, but I could not because my heart was beating so heavily, so heavily in fact that I am sure that I could hear it and that it was making my clothes go up and down. That is the state I was in when I was summoned to appear. I went downstairs, but I hardly dared walk forward. The nun who had fetched me was so cheerful that I decided that the news I was about to hear could only be very bad, but I went ahead neverthe-less. I stopped short as I came to the parlour door and I threw myself into the corner, unable to stand up any longer. Nevertheless I went in. Nobody was there, so I waited. The man who had had me sum-moned had been prevented from getting there before me. They felt sure that he had been sent by my lawyer, and they wanted to know what business he had with me, so they had gathered together to listen to him. When he came into the room, I was sitting down, my head on my arms, resting against the grille.

'I've come on behalf of Monsieur Manouri,' he said.

'You've come to tell me that I've lost my case,' I replied.

'I don't know anything about that, Madame. But he has given me this letter for you. He looked troubled when he handed it to me, and I came as quickly as I could, as he told me to.'

'Give it to me...'

He handed me the letter, I took it without moving or looking at him, I placed it on my lap and remained as I was. But the man asked me:

'Is there no reply?'

'No,' I said, 'you may go.'

He went away, and I stayed where I was, unable to move or to resolve to leave.

In a convent you are not allowed to write or receive letters without the permission of the Mother Superior, to whom one has to give both the letters one receives and those one writes. So I had to take mine to her, and I set off to do so. I thought I would never get there. A condemned man who leaves his cell to go and hear his sentence walks no more slowly, with no heavier a heart than I did. But there I was at her door. The nuns watched me from a distance, not wanting to miss any of the spectacle of my pain and humiliation. I knocked and the door opened. Never daring to lift up my eyes in her presence, I could see from the bottom of their gowns that the Mother Superior was with some other nuns. Trembling, I handed her my letter, which she took, read, and then gave back to me. I went back to my cell and threw myself on my bed, my letter by my side, and I lay there without reading it, without getting up to eat, without making even the slightest movement until it was time for the afternoon office, for which the bell rang at half past three, alerting me to go down to the church. A few nuns had already arrived before me, and the Mother Superior, standing at the entrance to the choir, stopped me and ordered me to kneel outside; meanwhile the rest of the community arrived and the door was closed. At the end of the service, they all left, I let them go past, and I got up in order to follow behind. From that moment on I started to condemn myself to whatever they wanted. No sooner had they forbidden me to go into the church than I forbade myself to go to the refectory or to recreation. I considered the position I was in from every angle, and I decided that my only hope lay in their need of my talents and in my submission. I would have been content with the kind of oblivion to which I had been condemned for several days. A few visitors came, but I was only allowed to see Monsieur Manouri. When I went into the parlour, I found him in exactly the position I had been in when I received his messenger, his head resting on his arms and his arms against the grille. I recognized him, but I said nothing to him. He hardly dared look at me or speak to me:

'Madame,' he said, without moving, 'I wrote to you, and you've read my letter.'

'I received it, but I haven't read it.'

'So you don't know...'

'No, Monsieur, I know full well. I've guessed what my fate is, and I'm resigned to it.'

'How are they treating you?'

'They're not giving me a moment's thought just now, but the past shows me what the future has in store. My one consolation is that, deprived of the hope that sustained me, I couldn't possibly suffer as much as I've suffered already, for I shall die. My wrongdoing is not of the kind that can be forgiven in a nun. I don't ask God to soften the hearts of those to whose discretion he has chosen to abandon me, but I do ask him to grant me the strength to suffer, to save me from despair, and to call me unto himself without delay.'

'Madame,' he said, crying, 'I couldn't have done more for you even if you'd been my own sister...'

He is a kind-hearted man.

'Madame,' he added, 'if I can help you in any way, I am at your service. I shall go and see the First President, who thinks highly of me. I shall go and see the Vicars General and the Archbishop.'

'Monsieur, go and see nobody. It's over.'

'But what if we could get you moved to another convent?'

'There are too many obstacles in the way.'

'What obstacles?'

'Obtaining permission, which would be difficult, and arranging a new dowry or taking back the old one from this convent. And after all that, what will I find in another convent? My stubborn heart, ruthless Mothers Superior, nuns who will be no better than they are here, the same duties, the same suffering. It is better that I should end my days here, where they will be shorter.'

'But, Madame, you have aroused the interest of many decent people, and most of them are wealthy. Nobody will want to keep you here if you're able to leave and take nothing away with you.'

'So I believe.'

'A nun who leaves or dies increases the well-being of the other nuns who are left behind.'

'But these decent people, these wealthy people, have forgotten all about me now, and you'll find them very cool if they're asked to give their own money to support me. Why do you expect it to be easier for people in the world outside to help a nun with no vocation to leave a convent than for pious people to help a nun with a genuine vocation to enter a convent? Is it easy to find dowries for the latter? Why, Monsieur, everybody has disappeared, and since I lost my case nobody comes to see me any more!'

'Madame, just leave all this with me; I shall be more successful this time.'

'I ask for nothing, I hope for nothing, I stand in the way of nothing. My last hope has been shattered. If only I could convince myself that God would change me and that, with all my hope of leaving gone, my heart might be filled with all the qualities necessary for the religious life... But that's impossible; this nun's habit has attached itself to my skin and bones and irks me all the more. Oh! What fate is mine! To be a nun for ever more, and to feel that I will only ever be a bad nun. To spend my whole life banging my head against the bars of my prison cell!'

At that point I started screaming. I tried to stifle it, but I could not. Shocked by my emotions, Monsieur Manouri said to me:

'Madame, dare I ask you a question?'

'Please do, Monsieur.'

'Is there a hidden explanation for your violent pain?'

'No, Monsieur, I hate the solitary life, I feel deep down that I hate it and that I shall always hate it. I shall never be able to subject myself to all the drudgery that fills a nun's waking hours: it is nothing but an endless round of childish things which I despise. I would have got used to it by now if I had been capable of getting used to it. I've tried a hundred times to deceive myself, to break my resistance, but I simply cannot. I have envied, and asked God for, the blissful stupidity of my companions, but I have not obtained it and he will not grant it me. I do everything badly and say everything wrong. My every deed lays bare the fact that I have no vocation, and it's plain for all to see. Everything I do is an insult to the religious life. They call my inability to do things properly pride, and they spend their time humiliating me. My wrongdoings and punishments become ever more frequent, and I spend my days gauging with my eyes how high the walls are.'

'Madame, I can't knock those walls down for you, but there is something else I can do.'

'Monsieur, don't do anything.'

'You must go to another convent. I'll see to it and come back and see you again. I hope they won't keep you away from me. You'll hear from me very soon. Rest assured that if you agree to this, I shall succeed in getting you out of here. If they treat you too harshly, you must let me know.'

It was late when Monsieur Manouri left. I went back to my cell. Before long the bell rang for the evening office. I was one of the first to arrive. I let the other nuns go ahead of me and took it for granted that I had to remain at the door. And indeed, the Mother Superior closed the door in my face. That evening, at supper, as she came in she signalled to me to sit on the floor in the middle of the refectory, which I did, and I was served only bread and water. I ate a little of the bread, soaked in my tears. The following day they held a conclave. The whole community was summoned to pass judgement on me, and I was sentenced to go without recreation, to listen to services from the other side of the choir door for a month, to eat on the floor in the middle of the refectory, to make a public confession of guilt for three days in succession, to renew the taking of my habit and my vows, to wear a hair-shirt, to fast every other day, and to mortify my flesh after the evening office every Friday. I was kneeling, with my veil over my face, as this sentence was passed.

The next day the Mother Superior came to my cell with a nun who was carrying over her arm a hair-shirt and the gown made of rough cloth that I had been made to change into when I was taken down to the dungeon. I understood what this meant. I undressed, or rather my veil was torn off me, I was stripped and I put on the gown. I had nothing on my head or my feet, my long hair fell about my shoulders, and all I had to wear was the hair-shirt I had been given, a very coarse chemise, and the long gown which went from my neck right down to my feet. That is what I wore during the day and how I appeared at all the religious exercises.

That evening, after I had returned to my cell, I heard people approaching, singing litanies. It was the whole community, walking in double file. They entered, I presented myself. A rope was placed around my neck, and with one hand I was made to hold a flaming torch, with the other a scourge. One of the nuns took hold of the other end of the rope and pulled me along between the two lines, and the procession made its way towards a little inner oratory dedicated to St Mary. They had come singing softly; now they walked in silence. When I had reached the oratory, lit by two lamps, I was ordered to ask both God and the community to forgive me for the scandal I had caused. The nun who had led me there said the words I had to repeat, and I repeated them all. Then the rope was removed, I was stripped down to the waist, they took my hair, which was hanging down over my shoulders, and pulled it to one side of my neck, they placed in my right hand the scourge I had been carrying in my left, and they started reciting the *Miserere*. I knew what was expected of me, and I did it. Once the *Miserere* was over, the Mother Superior gave me a short exhortation. The lamps were put out, the nuns withdrew, and I put my clothes back on.

When I returned to my cell, I felt an excruciating pain in my feet. I looked down and saw that they were covered in blood from cuts made by the shards of glass that had been maliciously scattered in my path.

I made the same public confession of guilt on the next two days, except that on the second day a psalm was added to the *Miserere*.

On the fourth day my habit was returned to me with almost the same formality as when one first takes it at the solemn ceremony in public.

On the fifth day I renewed my vows. I spent a month doing the rest of the penance that I had been given, after which I more or less returned to my normal role in the community. I took my place again in the choir and in the refectory, and in my turn I went about the various tasks in the convent. But imagine my surprise when I happened to see the young friend who had taken such an interest in my fate! She seemed to me to have changed almost as much as I had. She was terribly thin, her face was deathly pale, her lips where white, and her eyes were almost lifeless.

'Sister Ursule,' I whispered to her, 'what's wrong with you?'

'What's wrong with me?' she replied. 'I love you, do you really need to ask? It was high time that your ordeal ended; it would have killed me if it had gone on any longer.'

The reason I had not cut my feet on the last two days of my public confession of guilt was that she had been thoughtful enough secretly to sweep the corridors, pushing to either side the pieces of glass. On the days when I was condemned to take nothing but bread and water, she deprived herself of some of her food, which she wrapped in a piece of white cloth and threw into my cell. The nun who would lead me on the rope had been chosen by drawing lots, and the task had fallen to her. She had the strength of mind to go and see the Mother Superior and to swear to her that she would sooner die than fulfil that unspeakable and cruel task. Fortunately for her, this young girl was from a highly esteemed family, she enjoyed a handsome allowance which she used as the Mother Superior saw fit, and for the price of a few pounds of sugar and coffee she was able to find a nun to take her place. I would not presume to think that the hand of God had weighed down on that unworthy girl; she went mad and is now locked up; but the Mother Superior lives on, remains in charge, continues to torment, and is in good health.

My health could not possibly withstand such prolonged and difficult ordeals, and I fell ill. It was at this point that Sister Ursule really demonstrated what a good friend she was to me. I owe her my life. Not that my life was altogether worth saving, and she said as much herself from time to time, but she did me every possible good turn on those days when she was on duty in the infirmary. On the other days I was not neglected, thanks to the interest she took in me and to the little rewards she gave to those looking after me, depending on how satisfied I was with them. She had asked if she could keep watch over me at night, and the Mother Superior had refused, claiming that she was too delicate to cope with the strain; this caused her a good deal of distress. All her attention could not prevent me from deteriorating; I was at death's door, and I received the last sacraments. A few moments earlier I asked if I could see the whole community, and my wish was granted. The nuns gathered around my bed, the Mother Superior standing in the midst of them, and my young friend sat at my bedside and held my hand, weeping over it. They assumed that I had something to say, so I was lifted up into a sitting position, with two pillows supporting me. Then I spoke to the Mother Superior and asked her to give me her blessing and to forget the sins I had committed. I asked all my companions to forgive me for the scandal I had brought upon them. I had asked them to bring to my bedside lots of trinkets which either adorned my cell or were for my own private use, and I asked the Mother Superior if I could give them away. She agreed, and I gave them to those nuns who had been her minions when I had been thrown into the dungeon. I asked the nun who had led me on the rope on the day of my public confession of guilt to come over to me, and as I embraced her and gave her my rosary and crucifix, I said to her:

'Dear Sister, remember me in your prayers and rest assured that I shall not forget you before God.'

So why did God not take me at that moment? I was approaching him fearlessly. It is such a great joy, and who can possibly expect it twice? Who knows what I shall be like when I reach my final moment? But reach it I must. May God renew my suffering once more and grant that that moment may be as peaceful as it was then. I saw the heavens wide open, and they doubtless were; for one's consciousness at such times is highly acute, and mine promised me eternal bliss.

Once the final sacraments had been administered, I fell into a kind of lethargy. They despaired of my life all that night. From time to time somebody came and checked my pulse; I could feel hands running over my face, and I could hear different voices saying, as if in the distance:

'It's rising again... Her nose is cold... She won't survive the night... The rosary and the crucifix will be yours...'

And another voice, saying angrily:

'Go away! Go away! Let her die in peace. Haven't you made her suffer enough?'

It was a wonderful moment for me when I awoke from this crisis and opened my eyes to find myself in the arms of my friend. She had not left me; she had supported me throughout the night, saying over and over again the prayers for the dying, and making me kiss the crucifix before taking it from my lips and pressing it against her own. She thought, as she saw me opening my eyes wide and sighing deeply, that I was breathing my last, and she started crying out, calling me her friend, and saying:

'My God, have pity on her and on me; my God, receive her soul. My dear friend, when you're before God, remember Sister Ursule.'

I looked at her and smiled sadly, shed a tear and squeezed her hand. At that moment Monsieur B...,* the convent doctor, arrived. This man is apparently able, but he is also tyrannical, arrogant, and inflexible. He pushed my friend out of the way; and felt my pulse and my skin. He was accompanied by the Mother Superior and her favourites. He asked a few monosyllabic questions about what had happened, and then said:

'She'll pull through...', and, looking at the Mother Superior, who was not pleased to hear the news, he said: 'Yes, Madame, she'll pull through, her skin is fine, the fever has abated, and her eyes are beginning to show signs of life again.'

As he spoke, a look of joy came across my friend's face, whereas the faces of the Mother Superior and her companions showed an indescribable displeasure, thinly disguised by the constraints of decency.

'Monsieur,' I said to him, 'I don't want to live.'

'Well that's hard luck,' he replied. Then he prescribed something and left. I have heard that on several occasions during my lethargy I had said: 'Dear Mother, you're calling me to you, and so I'm going to join you and I shall tell you everything.' Apparently I was speaking to my old Mother Superior, and I am sure I was. I did not give her portrait to anybody; I wanted to take it with me to the grave.

Monsieur B...'s diagnosis proved accurate. The fever abated, quelled finally by heavy sweating, and my recovery was no longer in doubt. I did indeed recover, but I had to convalesce for a very long time.

It was said that in that convent I would suffer in every possible way. There had been something spiteful in my illness. Sister Ursule had hardly left my side. As I regained my health and strength, she began to lose hers; her digestion was upset; in the afternoons she was laid low by bouts of fainting, which sometimes lasted a quarter of an hour. Whenever she fainted, she looked as if she had died, her eyes became lifeless, her forehead was covered in a cold sweat, forming drops which ran down her cheeks; her limp arms hung, motionless, by her sides; the only way to give her a little relief was to undo and loosen her clothing. When she came round after fainting, her first instinct was to look for me at her side, where she always found me; and sometimes, when she still had a little feeling and was not entirely unconscious, she even ran her hand around her, without opening her eyes. The significance of this gesture was so clear that those nuns who had reached out to touch her hand as it groped around, but whom she clearly did not recognize since her hand simply fell motionless, said to me: 'Sister Suzanne, it's you she wants, come closer...' I threw myself at her knees and drew her hand to my forehead, where it rested until she came round. When she regained consciousness, she said to me: 'So, Sister Suzanne, I'm the one who's going to depart this world and you're going to stay; I shall be the first to see her again, and I shall talk to her about you, and she'll be in tears as she listens (if tears can be bitter, they can also be sweet); and if there is love up there, then why shouldn't there be crying?' Then she leant her head on my shoulder, wept copiously, and went on: 'Farewell, Sister Suzanne, adieu, my friend. Who will share your suffering when I am gone? Who... Oh! My dear friend, how I pity you! I'm going, I can feel it, I'm going. If you were happy, I'd be so sorry to die!'

Her condition terrified me; I spoke to the Mother Superior. I wanted her to be moved to the infirmary and excused from the services and the other arduous duties in the convent, and I wanted a doctor to be called, but the reply always came that there was nothing wrong with her and that her fainting fits would pass of their own accord; and dear Sister Ursule wanted nothing more than to fulfil her duties and to participate in the communal life of the convent. One day, after matins, which she had attended, she failed to reappear. I thought she must be very ill. As soon as the morning office was over, I rushed to her room. I found her lying on her bed, fully dressed. She said to me:

'Is that you, dear friend? I knew you'd come, and I was waiting for you. Listen. I couldn't wait for you to come! I was so very feeble for so long that I thought I wouldn't recover and that I'd never see you again. Here, this is the key to my oratory; go and open the cupboard, lift up the little plank of wood that divides the bottom drawer in two, and behind it you'll find a bundle of papers; I could never bring myself to part with them, no matter how dangerous it was to keep them and how painful it was to read them: Alas! my tears have almost blotted out all the writing. When I'm gone, you must burn them.'

She was so weak and had such difficulty breathing that she could not string together two words of what she was saying, but had instead to pause after almost every syllable, and she also spoke so softly that I had difficulty hearing her, even though I was almost pressing my ear to her mouth. I took the key, pointed to the oratory, and she nodded. Then, realizing that I was going to lose her and convinced that her illness had been caused either by mine, or by all the trouble she had taken, or by the care she had shown me, I started crying and was overwhelmed by grief; I kissed her on her forehead, her eyes, her face, and her hands, and asked her to forgive me. But she seemed to be elsewhere; she could not hear me; one of her hands rested on my face and stroked it; I do not think she could see me any more, and perhaps she even thought I had left the room, for she called out to me:

'Sister Suzanne?'

'I'm here,' I replied.

'What time is it?'

'It's half past eleven.'

'Half past eleven? You should go and eat. Go, but come straight back afterwards.'

The bell rang for dinner, so I had to leave her. When I reached the door, she called me back; I went back to her. She strained to offer me her cheeks, and I kissed them; she took my hand and held it tight, as if she did not want to, or could not, leave me. 'But it must be so,' she said, letting go of my hand, 'it's God's will. Farewell, Sister Suzanne. Give me my crucifix.' I placed it in her hands, and I left.

We were about to leave at the end of the meal. I spoke to the Mother Superior, telling her in front of all the other nuns about the danger that Sister Ursule was in, and I urged her to go and see for herself. 'Very well,' she said, 'I should see her.' She went upstairs, accompanied by some other nuns, and I followed them; they went into her cell; the poor sister had passed away. She was lying on her bed, fully clothed, her head resting on her pillow, her mouth half open, her eyes closed, and the crucifix in her hands. The Mother Superior looked at her coldly and said: 'She's dead! Who would have thought that she was so close to her end? She was a fine girl. The bell must be rung for her and she must be buried.'

I stayed alone at her bedside. I cannot describe the pain I was in; yet I envied her fate; I drew closer to her, offering her my tears and kissing her several times, and then I pulled the sheet over her face, which was beginning to change. Then I remembered that I had to carry out what she had asked me to do; so that I would not be interrupted while I was doing this, I waited until everyone was in church. I opened the oratory, I removed the plank of wood, found quite a considerable bundle of papers, rolled up, and burned them that evening. This young girl had always been melancholy, and I cannot remember ever having seen her smile, except once, during her illness.

I found myself all alone in the convent, and in the world, for I did not know a single person who was interested in me. I had heard no more of the lawyer Manouri; I assumed that he had been either put off by the difficulties or distracted by some amusements or by his own business; the offers of help that he had made me were now far from his thoughts, and I did not really hold that against him; I am by nature inclined to be indulgent and I can forgive men anything, apart from injustice, ingratitude, and inhumanity. So I forgave the lawyer Manouri as much as I could, as well as all those people in the world outside who had shown such excitement during my case and for whom I did not now exist, and you too, Monsieur le Marquis. But at that point our ecclesiastical superiors came to visit the convent.

They come in, they look round the cells, they ask the nuns questions; they enquire about the temporal and spiritual administration of the convent and, depending on how they approach their task, they either put any disorder right or make it worse. So I saw once again the decent but severe Monsieur Hébert with his two young and sympathetic acolytes. They seemed to remember the dreadful state I had been in when I last appeared before them, for their eyes became moist, and I could tell by their faces that they were moved and delighted. Monsieur Hébert sat down and made me sit in front of him; his two companions stood behind his chair, staring at me. Monsieur Hébert said:

'So, Sister Suzanne, how are they treating you these days?'

'Monsieur, they've forgotten all about me,' I replied.

'Good.'

'Indeed, I couldn't wish for anything more. But I have an important favour to ask of you: it's to summon my Mother Superior here.'

'Why?'

'Because if any complaint is made to you about her, she'll be sure to blame me.'

'I understand. But tell me anyway what you know about her.'

'Monsieur, I beg you to have her called so that she can listen to your questions and my answers.'

'Tell me anyway.'

'Monsieur, you're going to bring about my downfall.'

'No, don't be afraid. From now on you're no longer under her authority; before the week is out you'll be transferred to Sainte-Eutrope, near Arpajon.* You have a good friend.'

'A good friend, Monsieur? I don't know that I have one.'

'I'm talking about your lawyer.'

'Monsieur Manouri?'

'The very same.'

'I thought he'd forgotten all about me.'

'He has been to see your sisters, the Archbishop, the First President, and all the people known for their piety. He has provided you with a dowry at the convent I've just told you about, and you'll be leaving here very shortly. So, if you know of any irregularity, you can tell me about it without compromising yourself, and indeed I order you to do so as an act of holy obedience.'

'I don't know of any.'

'What! Have you been treated with restraint since you lost your case?'

'It was believed, and necessarily so, that I had done wrong by appealing against my vows, and I was made to ask God to forgive me for having done so.'

'But it's precisely the circumstances of this plea for forgiveness that I want to know about.'

As he spoke, he shook his head and frowned, and I realized then that I was in a position to pay back the Mother Superior with some of the disciplinary measures that she had had taken against me; but I had no intention of doing so. The Archdeacon realized that he would get nothing out of me, so he left, advising me to say nothing about what he had told me about my move to Sainte-Eutrope d'Arpajon. As this decent man walked off alone down the corridor, his two companions turned round and bowed to me in a very affectionate, sweet way. I do not know who they are, but may God grant that they keep their gentle and compassionate character, which is so rare in men in their position and which is so fitting in those in whom men confide their weakness and who intercede on their behalf for the mercy of God. I thought that Monsieur Hébert was busy consoling, questioning, or reprimanding some other nun when he walked back into my cell. He said to me:

'How do you know Monsieur Manouri?'

'Through my case.'

'Who put you in touch with him?'

'It was Madame la Présidente ***.'

'So you must have talked to him often during your case.'

'No, Monsieur, I hardly saw him.'

'How did you give him his instructions?'

'By means of a few handwritten statements.'

'Did you keep copies of these statements?'

'No, Monsieur.'

'Who passed the statements on to him?'

'Madame la Présidente ***.'

'And how do you know her?'

'I met her through Sister Ursule, my friend, who was related to her.'

'Have you seen Monsieur Manouri since you lost your case?'

'Once.'

'That's not very much. Hasn't he written to you?'

'No, Monsieur.'

'Haven't you written to him?'

'No, Monsieur.'

'I'm sure he'll tell you what he's done for you. I order you not to see him in the parlour, and, if he writes to you, whether directly or indirectly, you must send me his letter without opening it, you understand, without opening it.'

'Yes, Monsieur, I shall do as you say.'

Whether Monsieur Hébert's mistrust was directed at me or at my benefactor, it hurt me.

Monsieur Manouri came to Longchamp that evening. I kept my word to the Archdeacon and refused to speak to him. The next day he wrote to me through his representative. As soon as I received the letter, I sent it on, unopened, to Monsieur Hébert. That was on the Tuesday, if I remember rightly. I eagerly awaited the outcome of the Archdeacon's promise and Monsieur Manouri's efforts. Wednesday, Thursday, and Friday came and went without my hearing any news. How long those days seemed to me! I was terrified that some obstacle had emerged which had spoilt everything. I was not regaining my freedom, I was simply moving from one prison to another, but that is something in itself. One happy event makes us hope for another, and that's perhaps where the proverb comes from: that *one good thing leads to another*.

I knew what the companions I was leaving behind were like, and it was easy for me to imagine that living with a different set of prisoners would be an improvement; whoever they were, they could not be any more cruel or malicious. On the Saturday morning, at about nine o'clock, there was a great commotion in the convent; it does not take much to throw nuns' minds into confusion. They were coming and going, whispering to each other, and the dormitory doors were opening and closing: all the signs, as you have already seen, of upheavals in a convent. I was alone in my cell; I was waiting; my heart was pounding; I listened at my door and looked out of my window; I was darting about, not knowing what I was doing; trembling with joy, I told myself: 'They've come to get me; I shall be gone from here any minute now...' And I was right.

Two people whom I had not seen before introduced themselves to me: they were a nun and the doorkeeper from Arpajon. They told me in a word why they had come. I feverishly gathered up my few belongings and flung them all together into the gatekeeper's apron, which she bundled up. I did not ask to see the Mother Superior;

Sister Ursule was dead; I was not leaving anybody behind; I went downstairs; after my belongings had been inspected, the gates were opened for me, I got into a carriage and left.

The Archdeacon and his two young priests, Madame la Présidente, and Monsieur Manouri had met in the Mother Superior's room, where they were informed of my departure. As we travelled, the nun talked to me about the convent, and to each sentence of this hymn of praise the gatekeeper added as a refrain: 'It's absolutely true.' She was pleased to have been chosen to come and collect me and she wanted to be my friend. So she told me some secrets and gave me some advice about how I should behave. She apparently followed her own advice, but it could be of no use to me. I do not know if you have ever seen the convent at Arpajon. It is a square building, one side of which looks out onto the main road, the other onto the countryside and gardens. One, two, or three nuns were peering out of every window at the front of the convent, and this alone told me far more about the way it was run than everything the nun and her companion had told me about it. They apparently recognized our carriage, for in a split second all the veiled heads disappeared, and I arrived at the door to my new prison. The Mother Superior came out to meet me, with outstretched arms, and embraced me, and then she took me by the hand and led me into the common room where some of the nuns had arrived before me, and others flocked in after me.

This Mother Superior is called Madame ***.* I simply cannot deny myself the pleasure of painting her portrait for you before I go any further. She is a short, plump woman, yet quick and lively in her movements; she never keeps her head still; there is always something wrong with her clothes; her appearance is not unattractive; her fiery eyes are always darting about, and one of them, the right one, is higher and bigger than the other; she swings her arms to and fro as she walks; when she wants to speak, she opens her mouth before she has thought out what she wants to say, so she stutters a little; when she is sitting down, she fidgets in her chair as if something is bothering her. Forgetting all sense of decorum, she lifts up her wimple so that she can scratch herself, and she crosses her legs; she asks you questions and you answer her, but she does not listen; as she speaks to you, she loses her train of thought and stops suddenly, unable to remember what she has said, and she gets cross and calls you a silly ass, stupid, or foolish if you do not remind her what she was saying. Sometimes she addresses you informally; sometimes she is imperious and scornfully self-righteous. Her moments of dignity are short lived; one minute she is compassionate, the next stony-hearted. Her drawn face illustrates all the disjointedness of her mind and all the unevenness of her character; so order and disorder succeed each other in the convent. There were some days when everything was confused, the boarders mixed in with the novices,* and the novices with the nuns; days when people ran in and out of each other's rooms; days when people gathered to have tea, coffee, chocolate, and alcohol; days when the services were conducted with the most unseemly haste; and then in the midst of all this hubbub, the Mother Superior's face changes suddenly, the bell rings, everyone withdraws and retires to their cells, and the noise, screams, and commotion give way to the deepest silence, such that you would think that everything had suddenly died. At such times, if a nun does the slightest thing wrong, the Mother Superior summons her to her cell, deals with her harshly, and orders her to get undressed and to give herself twenty strokes with her scourge; the nun obeys, gets undressed, picks up her scourge, and mortifies her flesh, but no sooner has she given herself a few strokes than the Mother Superior, overwhelmed with pity, snatches the instrument of penitence from her and starts crying; how dreadful it is for her to have to punish people! She kisses her on the forehead, eyes, mouth, and shoulders, caresses her, and sings her praises: 'Oh but how white and soft her skin is! What a beautifully full figure! What a beautiful neck! What a beautiful nape! Sister Sainte Augustine, don't be silly, there's no need to be ashamed, undo your undergarments, I am a woman and your Mother Superior... Oh what a beautiful breast! How firm it is!... And to think of letting it be cut by the spikes of a scourge? No, no, certainly not...' She kisses her again, lifts her up, puts her clothes back on for her, says the sweetest things to her, gives her permission not to attend the services, and sends her back to her cell. It is very difficult being with women like that, as you never know what they are going to like or dislike, what you need to avoid doing or what you need to do. Nothing is fixed: either you are served copious amounts of food or you are left to starve to death; the administration of the convent gets into a muddle, and your objections are either badly received or ignored. You always find yourself either too close to or too remote from

Mothers Superior like that; there is no sense of proper distance or balance; you pass from disgrace to favour and from favour to disgrace without knowing why. Let me tell you about one small thing which is typical of how she runs the convent in general. Twice a year she would run from cell to cell and would have all the bottles of alcohol she found thrown out of the windows, but four days later she would send bottles back to most of the nuns. This was the woman to whom I had made my solemn vow of obedience, for we take our vows with us from one convent to the next.

I went inside with her; she accompanied me with her arm round my waist. Light refreshments were served: fruits, marzipan, and preserves. The solemn Archdeacon began to speak in praise of me, but she interrupted him, saying: 'It was wrong, it was wrong, I know...' The solemn Archdeacon tried to continue, but the Mother Superior interrupted him again, saying: 'How could they part with her? She is the very image of modesty and gentleness. I hear she's extremely talented...' The solemn Archdeacon tried to finish what he was saying, but the Mother Superior interrupted him once more and whispered in my ear: 'I utterly adore you, and once these bores have all left, I shall gather together the sisters and you'll sing a little tune for us, won't you?' I wanted to laugh, and the solemn Monsieur Hébert was a little disconcerted; his two companions smiled at his embarrassment and at mine. However Monsieur Hébert regained his usual disposition and abruptly ordered her to sit down and be quiet. She sat down but was restless; she fidgeted in her chair; she scratched her head; she fixed her clothes when they were not even out of place; she yawned; and meanwhile the Archdeacon spoke sensibly about the convent I had left and the troubles I had endured there, about the convent I was joining, and about how much I owed to those who had helped me... At that point I looked at Monsieur Manouri; he looked down. Then people started talking to each other and the painful silence that had been imposed on the Mother Superior came to an end. I went over to Monsieur Manouri and thanked him for what he had done for me; I was trembling and stammering and did not know how I should promise to acknowledge my gratitude for his help; my confusion, my awkwardness, and my emotional state, for I was truly touched, a mixture of tears and joy, in fact my whole demeanour spoke to him more eloquently than I could ever have done. His response was no more coherent than my words had been, and he was as flustered as I was. I do not know what he was saying to me, but I heard him say that he would be more than rewarded if he had done something to lessen the severity of my lot, that he would look back on what he had done with more pleasure than I would, that he was only sorry that his duties at the Palais de Justice in Paris* prevented him from visiting the convent at Arpajon very often, but that he hoped that the Archdeacon and the Mother Superior would allow him to enquire after my health and situation. The Archdeacon did not hear him say that, but the Mother Superior replied: 'Monsieur, as often as you wish; she will do whatever she wants. We shall try to make up here for the distress that she has been caused...', and then she whispered to me: 'My child, you really have suffered a great deal! But how could those creatures at Longchamp dare to mistreat you? I used to know your Mother Superior, she and I were boarders together at Port-Royal,* and she was the bane of everyone else's life. We'll have time to be with each other and you can tell me all about it...' And as she spoke she held one of my hands and gently patted it. The young priests also paid me their compliments. It was late; Monsieur Manouri took his leave of us, the Archdeacon and his companions went to the home of Monsieur ***, lord of Arpajon, who had invited them to stay, and I was left alone with the Mother Superior, but not for long. All the nuns, novices, and boarders ran in together, and in an instant I was surrounded by about a hundred people. I did not know whom to listen to or whom to answer. There were people of all kinds, and they were saying all sorts of things. But I could tell that they were not disappointed by my replies or by me.

When this awkward conversation had gone on for some time and their initial curiosity had been satisfied, some of the crowd began to disperse, the Mother Superior sent the rest away, and she herself came and settled me in my new cell. She did the honours, in her own way: she showed me the oratory and said: 'That's where my little friend will pray to God. We need to put a cushion on this step so that she doesn't hurt her little knees... There's no holy water in this stoup: that Sister Dorothée is always forgetting things... Try this chair; see if you find it comfortable...' And as she said this, she made me sit down, leant my head against the back of the chair, and kissed my forehead. Then she went over to the window to check that the sashes opened and closed smoothly, and to my bed, opening and closing the curtains to see that they worked properly. She examined the blankets... 'They are fine.' She picked up the bolster and, plumping it up, said: 'This sweet head of yours will be quite comfortable on this... These sheets aren't soft, but they're all we have in our convent... This mattress is good...' Having done that, she comes over to me, kisses me, and then leaves. During this episode I said to myself: 'Oh, what a mad creature!' And I expected good and bad days.

I settled myself into my cell. I went to the evening office, and then to supper and recreation afterwards. Some nuns came up to me, while others kept away. Those who came up were counting on my influence with the Mother Superior to protect them; those who kept away were already alarmed by the favour she had shown me. The first few minutes were devoted to our praising each other and to the nuns asking me about the convent I had left and trying to find out more about my character, my preferences, my tastes, and my mind; they paw you all over; they set you a whole series of little traps and draw from them the most accurate conclusions. For example, someone says something disparaging about someone else and then they look at you; someone starts telling a story and they wait for you either to ask what happened next or not to pick up on it. If you say something quite ordinary, they find it charming, although they all know it is nothing of the sort; they praise you or criticize you quite deliberately. They try to work out your innermost thoughts; they ask you about what you read, they offer you some sacred books and some secular ones, and they make a note of which one you choose. They encourage you to bend the rules; they tell you secrets; they say a few words here and there about the Mother Superior's odd behaviour; everything is stored up and repeated. They drop you and then they become interested in you again; they sound you out about your feelings on morals, piety, the world, religion, monastic life, everything in fact. These repeated tests enable them to come up with an epithet which sums you up and which they tag on to your first name like a surname. So I was called Sainte Suzanne the shy.

On the first evening, the Mother Superior came to visit me; she came in as I was getting undressed. It was she who took off my veil and wimple and brushed my hair for bed; it was she who undressed me. She said a hundred sweet things to me and stroked me a thousand times, which made me feel rather awkward, but I do not know why, because I did not know what was happening, and neither did she, and even now as I think back over it, what could we have possibly known? Nevertheless I told my confessor and he reacted to this intimacy, which to me seemed, and does indeed still seem, innocent, in a very serious way and solemnly ordered me not to let it happen again. She kissed my neck, shoulders, and arms, she praised the fullness of my figure and my waist, and she put me to bed; she tucked in the blankets on both sides, kissed my eyes, drew the curtains, and left. I forgot to tell you that she assumed that I was tired and so gave me permission to stay in bed as long as I wanted.

I took her at her word. That was, I think, the only good night's sleep I ever had in a convent, although I spent most of my life in them. The next morning, at about nine o'clock, I heard someone tapping softly on my door. I was still in bed; I answered and someone came in; it was a nun who told me, rather testily, that it was late and that the Mother Superior wanted to see me. I got up, quickly got dressed, and went.

'Good morning, my child,' she said. 'Did you sleep well? This coffee was made an hour ago, but I think it will still be fine. Drink it quickly and then we can have a talk.'

And as she spoke she laid out a handkerchief on the table, laid another across my lap, and poured out a cup of coffee and put in some sugar. The other nuns did the same in each other's cells. While I was having my breakfast she talked to me about my fellow nuns, describing them according to her likes and dislikes. She was extremely friendly towards me and asked me hundreds of questions about the convent I had left, my parents, and the unpleasant experiences I had had; she accorded praise or blame as she saw fit, and she never listened to any of my replies in full. I did not contradict her; she was very pleased with my intelligence, my judgement, and my discretion. Meanwhile a nun came in, and then another, and then a third and a fourth and a fifth. One of them talked about the Mother Superior's birds, another about Sister ***'s habits; they talked about all the funny little ways of those nuns who were not there, and they became rather merry. There was a virginal in one corner of the cell and I distractedly ran my fingers over it, since, as a newcomer to the convent, I did not know any of the nuns they were joking about, so what they were saying was not very amusing, and even if I had been better informed, what they were saying would still not have been very amusing. To make a really good joke requires too much wit, and after all, is there anybody who does not have a ridiculous side to them? While they were laughing, I played some chords, and gradually attracted their attention. The Mother Superior came over to me and, tapping me on the shoulder, said: 'Come along, Sainte Suzanne, entertain us. Play first, and then you can sing afterwards.' I did what she told me. I played a few pieces which I knew off by heart, I improvised, and then I sang a few verses from Mondonville's setting of the Psalms.*

'That's splendid,' said the Mother Superior, 'but we have as much holiness as we want in church. We're by ourselves here. These are my friends, and they'll be yours too. Sing us something more cheerful.'

Some of the nuns said: 'But perhaps that's all she knows; she's tired after her journey, we must spare her. That's quite enough for one occasion.'

'No, no,' said the Mother Superior, 'she plays marvellously, and she has the most beautiful voice in the world' (it is true that my voice is not ugly; it is accurate, sweet, and flexible rather than strong and wide in range) 'and I shan't let her off until she's sung something else for us.'

I was a little put out by what the nuns had said, and I told the Mother Superior that the sisters were no longer enjoying my music.

'But I still am.'

I thought she would say that. So I sang a rather dainty little song, and they all applauded, praised me, kissed me, caressed me, and asked me to sing another: these were all false little affectations dictated by the Mother Superior's answer. Given the opportunity, almost every one of them would have robbed me of my voice and broken my fingers. Women who had perhaps not listened to a note of music in their entire lives now took it upon themselves to pronounce judgements on my singing that were as ridiculous as they were unpleasant, but they had no effect on the Mother Superior.

'Be quiet,' she said to them. 'She plays and sings like an angel, and I want her to come here every day. I used to be able to play the harpsichord a little, and I want her to help me take it up again.'

'Oh! Madame,' I said, 'once you've learnt to play, you never forget completely...'

'Quite right. Move aside...'

She improvised and played things that were mad, bizarre, and as

disjointed as her ideas were, but despite all the faults in her performance I could see that her touch was infinitely lighter than mine. I told
her as much, because I like to praise people, and I have rarely missed
the opportunity to do so when it is entirely justified, because it is
such a nice thing to do! One after another the nuns disappeared, and
I was left almost entirely alone with the Mother Superior, talking
about music. She was seated, I was standing. She took my hands and,
squeezing them, said:

'But not only does she play well; she also has the prettiest fingers
in the world. Just look, Sister Thérèse...'

Sister Thérèse looked down, blushed, and stammered. But
whether or not I had pretty fingers, and whether the Mother
Superior was right or wrong to comment on them, what did it have
to do with this nun? The Mother Superior put her arms around me
and decided that I had the prettiest waist. She had pulled me
towards her and made me sit on her knee. She lifted up my head with
her hands and invited me to look at her. She praised my eyes, my
mouth, my cheeks, and my complexion. I said nothing in reply. I
looked down and let myself be caressed like an idiot. Sister Thérèse
was agitated and restless; she walked up and down; she kept touching things quite unnecessarily, and she did not know what to do with
herself; she looked out of the window; she thought she had heard
someone knocking at the door; and the Mother Superior said to her:

'Sainte Thérèse, you can leave if you're bored.'

'Madame, I'm not bored.'

'It's just that I have a thousand things I want to ask this child.'

'I can believe it.'

'I want to know everything about her. For how can I possibly make
up for the suffering that has been inflicted on her if I know nothing
of it? I want her to tell me absolutely everything. No doubt it will
break my heart to hear and I shall cry, but never mind. Sainte
Suzanne, when will you tell me all about it?'

'Madame, whenever you ask me to.'

'I would ask you to tell me now, if we had time. What time is it?'

'Madame, it is five o'clock and the bell will soon be ringing for
vespers,' replied Sister Thérèse.

'Let her start anyway.'

'But, Madame, you had promised me a moment of consolation
before vespers. I'm having distressing thoughts and I really want to

open my heart to my dear Mama. If I go to the service before I've had a chance to do so, I shan't be able to pray and I shall be agitated.'

'No, no,' said the Mother Superior, 'you're so silly with all these ideas of yours. I bet I know what it is. We'll talk about it tomorrow.'

'Ah! Dear Mother,' said Sister Thérèse, throwing herself at the Mother Superior's feet and bursting into tears, 'let me speak to you now.'

'Madame,' I said, getting up from the Mother Superior's knee, where I had remained throughout, 'grant my sister's request and put an end to her suffering; I shall withdraw now. There's still plenty of time for me to satisfy the interest that you're kindly taking in me. And when you've heard my sister Thérèse, she'll no longer be suffering.'

I moved towards the door to leave, but the Mother Superior held me back with one hand, while Sister Thérèse, on her knees, had seized the other and was kissing it and weeping. And the Mother Superior said to her: 'Really, Sainte Thérèse, you are a nuisance with all your worrying. I've told you before, I don't like it, it upsets me. I don't want to be upset.'

'I know, but I can't control the way I feel. I'd like to, but I can't...'

By now I had withdrawn, leaving the young nun with the Mother Superior. I could not help looking at her in church. She was still dejected and sad. Our eyes met several times, and she seemed to find it difficult being looked at by me. As for the Mother Superior, she had dozed off in her stall.

The service was over in the twinkling of an eye. Of all the places in the convent, the choir was not, it seemed to me, the one that the nuns enjoyed being in the most. They left with as much speed and jabbering as a flock of birds escaping from an aviary, and the sisters ran off to each other's cells, laughing and talking. The Mother Superior locked herself away in her cell, and Sister Thérèse paused in her doorway, watching me as if she was wondering what I was going to do. I went back to my cell, and it took a little time for the door to Sister Thérèse's cell to be shut softly. It occurred to me that this young woman was jealous of me and that she feared I would usurp the position of favour and intimacy that she enjoyed with the Mother Superior. I watched her for several days on end, and when I felt that my suspicions had been adequately confirmed by her little fits of anger and her childish panic, by her insistence on following me around, watching me, coming between the Mother Superior and me, interrupting our conversations, belittling my good points and highlighting my bad, and even more so by her pallor, her grief, her tears, and the deterioration in her health and even in her state of mind, I went to see her and said:

'Dear friend, what's wrong with you?'

She said nothing. My visit took her by surprise and embarrassed her. She did not know what to say or do.

'You're not being altogether fair to me. You're afraid, aren't you, that I'm going to take advantage of the affection that our Mother Superior has for me and make her love you less. You've nothing to fear, that's not in my nature. If I were ever fortunate enough to gain some hold over her mind...'

'You'll have as much hold over her as you wish. She loves you. She's doing for you today precisely what she did for me to begin with.'

'Well, you can be sure that I shall only ever use the trust she places in me to ensure that she cherishes you all the more.'

'But will that be up to you?'

'Why wouldn't it be?'

Instead of replying, she flung her arms around my neck and, sighing, said: 'It's not your fault, I know that perfectly well, and I tell myself so constantly. But promise me...'

'What do you want me to promise you?'

'That...'

'Go on. I'll do whatever I can.'

She hesitated, put her hands over her eyes and, in a voice so hushed that I could hardly hear it, said:

'That you'll see her as little as possible.'

This seemed to me such a strange request that I could not help replying:

'And what difference does it make to you if I see our Mother Superior often or rarely? I don't get angry because you see her all the time, so you shouldn't be angry either if I do likewise. Isn't it enough for me to assure you that I'll never do anything to malign you or anybody else in her eyes?'

Her only reply was to utter these anguished words as she tore herself away from me and collapsed onto her bed: 'This is the end for me.'

'The end! Why? You really must think I'm the most wicked creature in the world.'

At that very moment, the Mother Superior walked in. She had gone to my cell and, discovering that I was not there, she had searched almost the whole convent, but in vain. She had not even thought that I might be in Sainte Thérèse's cell. When those she had sent to look for me told her where I was, she came running. She looked somewhat perturbed, but then her whole bearing was rarely untroubled! Sainte Thérèse was sitting silently on her bed, and I was standing. I said to her:

'My dear Mother, please forgive me for coming here without asking permission.'

'It's true,' she replied, 'that it would have been better if you'd asked.'

'But I felt sorry for this dear sister, I saw that she was suffering.'

'Suffering from what?'

'Shall I tell you? Why wouldn't I tell you? She's suffering from a weakness which reflects well on her soul and which is a clear sign of how attached she is to you. The kindnesses which you have shown me have given her love cause for alarm, and she was afraid that I would become dearer to you than she is. This feeling of jealousy, which is, it must be said, so honest, so natural, and so flattering for you, dear Mother, had, or so it seemed to me, become painful for my sister, and I was reassuring her.'

Having listened to me, the Mother Superior suddenly became severe and imposing, and said:

'Sister Thérèse, I have loved you and I still love you. I have no grievance with you, and you should have none with me, but I cannot bear these exclusive claims you make. Be done with them, otherwise you risk extinguishing what remains of my affection for you. And remember what happened to Sister Agathe...'

Then, turning to me, she said:

'That's the tall, dark woman you'll have seen sitting opposite me in the choir.' (I had been so unsociable, I had been in the convent for such a short time, and I was so new that I still did not know the names of all my fellow nuns.) She added:

'I used to love Agathe when Sister Thérèse arrived and I began to be fond of her too. She had the same worries; she did the same foolish things. I warned her about her conduct, but she did nothing about it, so I was forced to resort to harsh measures which have lasted for too long and which are quite out of keeping with my character, for all the nuns will tell you that I am good and that I only ever mete out punishments reluctantly...'

Then, speaking to Sainte Thérèse, she added: 'My child, I don't want to be upset, as I've already told you. You know me; don't make me act out of character.'

Then, leaning on my shoulder with one hand, she said to me: 'Come on, Sainte Suzanne, come back with me.'

We left. Sainte Thérèse tried to follow us, but the Mother Superior, looking back casually over my shoulder, said to her in authoritarian tones: 'Go back to your cell, and don't leave it until I tell you that you may do so.' She did as she was told, slammed her door shut, and spluttered some words which made the Mother Superior shudder, though I do not know why, as they were meaningless. I saw how angry she was and I said to her:

'Dear Mother, if you have any kindly feeling for me, then forgive my sister Thérèse. She's lost her mind and doesn't know what she's saying or what she's doing.'

'You want me to forgive her? Gladly, but what will you give me in return?'

'Ah! Dear Mother, could I possibly be fortunate enough to have anything you might like and that would placate you?'

She looked down, blushed, and sighed. To tell the truth, she was behaving like a lover. Then, leaning on me nonchalantly as if she felt faint, she said: 'Bring your forehead nearer so that I may kiss it...' I lent over and she kissed my forehead. From that moment on, whenever a nun did something wrong, I would intercede for her, and I was sure to obtain her forgiveness by doing her some innocent favour: it was always a kiss, either on the forehead, or on the neck, or on the eyes, or on the cheeks, or on the mouth, or on the hands, or on the breast, or on the arms, but most often on the mouth; she thought I had fragrant breath, white teeth, and fresh red lips. I would really be very beautiful if I deserved even an ounce of the praise she lavished on me. If it was my forehead she was kissing, then it was white, smooth, and beautifully shaped; if it was my eyes, they were bright; if it was my cheeks, they were pink and soft; if it was my hands, they were small and plump; if it was my breast, it was as firm as stone and admirably formed; if it was my arms, nobody had better shaped and rounder ones than I did; if it was my neck, then none of the sisters had a neck that was better made or more exquisitely, more peculiarly beautiful. I cannot remember everything she used to say. There was certainly some truth in her praise; I took much of it with a pinch of salt, but not all. Sometimes, looking me up and down with a look of satisfaction such as I had never seen in any other woman, she would say to me: 'No, it is the greatest joy that God has called her to the cloistered life; with a figure like that in the outside world she would have driven every man she set her eyes on to damnation, and she would have been damned with them. All God's ways are just.'

Meanwhile we approached her cell, and I was expecting to leave her, but she took hold of my hand and said: 'It's too late for you to start telling the story of what happened to you at Sainte-Marie and at Longchamp, but do come in and give me a little harpsichord lesson...' I followed her in. In an instant she had opened the harpsichord, produced a book, and pulled up a chair, for she moved briskly. I sat down. She thought I might be cold, so she took a cushion from one of the chairs and placed it in front of me, then bent down, took my feet and placed them on the cushion; then she went and stood behind my chair and leant against it. At first I played some chords, then I played some pieces by Couperin, Rameau, and Scarlatti.* While I was playing, she had lifted up a corner of my gimp,* her hand was now resting on my bare shoulder and the ends of her fingers were touching my breast. She sighed, it was as if she felt oppressed, she had difficulty breathing. The hand she had placed on my shoulder at first held me tightly, then not at all, as if all strength and life had drained from her, and her head fell against mine. In truth, though mad, she was extremely sensitive and had the keenest interest in music. I have never known anybody on whom music has had such an extraordinary effect.

We were enjoying ourselves in this simple, sweet way when suddenly the door burst open. I was terrified, and so was the Mother Superior. It was the wild Sainte Thérèse. Her clothes were in disarray, she had a disturbed look in her eyes, she stared at both of us in the oddest way; her lips were trembling, she could not speak. Eventually she came to her senses and she threw herself at the Mother Superior's feet. I added my plea to hers, and again ensured that she was forgiven. But the Mother Superior declared in no uncertain terms that this was the last time, at least as far as offences of this kind were concerned, and the two of us left together.

On the way back to our cells, I said to her: 'Dear Sister, do be careful, you're going to turn our Mother against you. I'll never abandon you, but you're going to exhaust the influence I have over her, and I shall despair at not being able to help you or anyone else again. But what are you thinking?'

No answer.

'What do you have to fear from me?'

No answer.

'Can't our Mother love both of us equally?'

'No, no,' she replied angrily, 'that's impossible. She will soon loathe me, and I shall die of grief. Oh! Why did you come here? You won't be happy here for long, I'm sure of that, and I shall be unhappy for ever.'

'But,' I said, 'I know how awful it is to have lost the good will of one's Mother Superior, but I know that it's even worse to have deserved such a loss. Do you have nothing to blame yourself for?'

'Oh, please God that were true!...'

'If you're secretly accusing yourself of some offence, then you must make amends for it, and the surest way of doing that is to bear the penalty with fortitude.'

'I can't, I can't. And is it up to her to punish me for it?'

'Up to her! Sister Thérèse, up to her! Is that how one talks about a Mother Superior? That's not right, you're forgetting yourself. I'm sure that offence is more serious than anything else you're accusing yourself of.'

'Oh, please God that were true,' she repeated, 'please God that were true!'

And we went our separate ways, she to go and grieve in her cell, I to go and ponder in mine on how strange women's minds are. Such is the effect of cutting oneself off from society.* Man is born to live in society. Separate him, isolate him, and his way of thinking will become incoherent, his character will change, a thousand foolish fancies will spring up in his heart, bizarre ideas will take root in his mind like brambles in the wilderness. Put a man in a forest and he will become wild; put him in a cloister, where the idea of coercion joins forces with that of servitude, and it is even worse. You can leave a forest, but you can never leave a cloister; you are free in the forest, but you are a slave in the cloister. It perhaps takes even more strength of character to withstand solitude than it does poverty. A life of poverty is degrading; a life cut off from society is depraving. Is it better to live in humility than in madness? I would not dare decide between them, both must be avoided.

I saw the affection that the Mother Superior had conceived for me grow day by day. I was constantly in her cell or she in mine. If I had the slightest ailment, she would order me to go to the infirmary, she would excuse me from attending the services and send me to bed early or forbid me to say morning prayers. In the choir, in the refectory, and during recreation she would find ways of showing me signs of her friendship. In the choir, if there happened to be a verse which expressed some affectionate and tender emotion, she would sing it to me or she would look at me if somebody else was singing it. In the refectory she always sent me some of the delicious food she was served. During recreation she would put her arms around my waist and say the sweetest and kindest things. I shared every present she was given: chocolate, sugar, coffee, alcohol, snuff, undergarments, handkerchiefs, whatever it happened to be. She had removed prints, utensils, furniture, and a whole host of pleasant and useful things from her cell in order to put them in mine. I could scarcely leave my cell for a moment without returning to find it enriched with some gifts. I would go and see her to thank her for them, and words cannot describe how pleased she would be. She would embrace me, caress me, make me sit on her knee, confide in me about the most private matters in the convent, and say her life would be a thousand times happier than that she would have had in the outside world, as long as I loved her. Then she would pause, look at me, her eyes full of emotion, and say: 'Sister Suzanne, do you love me?'

'How could I possibly not love you? I'd have to be terribly ungrateful.'

'That's true.'

'You show me such kindness...'

'Or rather, such fondness for you...'

And as she spoke she would look down, with the hand she had round my waist she would squeeze me more tightly still, pressing down more firmly with the hand she had placed on my knee, she would pull me towards her, my face would be against hers, she would sigh, fall back in her seat, trembling, as if she wanted to tell me something but did not dare, she would be crying, and then she would say: 'Oh! Sister Suzanne, you don't love me!'

'I don't love you, dear Mother?'

'No.'

'Tell me what I have to do to prove it you.'

'You have to guess.'

'I'm trying to, but I can't think...'

By that point she had lifted up her gimp and had placed one of my hands on her breast. She said nothing, and neither did I. She seemed to be experiencing the most intense pleasure. She would ask me to kiss her forehead, her cheeks, her eyes, and her mouth, and I would obey. I do not think there was anything wrong in doing that. As I did so, her pleasure would increase, and since I wanted nothing more than to add to her happiness in such an innocent way, I would kiss her again on the forehead, the cheeks, the eyes, and the mouth. Her hand, which she had placed on my knee, would now wander up and down all over my clothes, from the tips of my toes to my waist, pressing me here, then there. Stammering and in a faltering, soft voice, she would urge me to caress her even more, and I would do so. Eventually there came a point, and I do not know if this was out of pleasure or pain, when she went deathly pale, her eyes shut, her whole body tensed violently, her lips tightened at first, slightly mois-tened as if by some kind of foam, then her mouth opened and she gave a deep sigh, as if she was dying. I jumped up, I thought she was unwell, I was going to leave and call for help. She half opened her eyes and said in a faint voice: 'Innocent one, there's nothing wrong. What are you doing? Stop...' I looked at her, with big, dazed eyes, unsure if I would stay or go. She opened her eyes again but could not speak a word. She gestured to me to come over to her and to sit on her knee again. I do not know what was going on inside me. I was afraid, I was trembling, my heart was pounding, I could hardly breathe, I felt anxious, constrained, agitated, I was frightened, I felt as if my strength had drained away and I was about to faint. But I could not say that what I was feeling was pain. I went over to her and again she gestured to me with her hand to sit on her lap; I sat down. It was as if she was dead, as if I was going to die. Both of us remained in this peculiar state for quite some time. If one of the nuns had found us, she would certainly have had quite a fright. She would have thought either that we had been taken ill or that we had fallen asleep. Eventually the good Mother Superior, for it is impossible to be so sensitive and not to be good, seemed to come round. She was still lying back in her chair and her eyes were still shut, but her face had lit up with the loveliest colour. She took hold of one of my hands, kissed it, and I said to her:

'Oh! Dear Mother, you really scared me...'

She smiled sweetly without opening her eyes.

'But haven't you been in pain?'

'No.'

'I thought you had.'

'The innocent girl! Oh! The dear innocent girl! I like her so much!'

As she said these words she sat up straight in her chair, threw her arms around my waist, kissed me hard on both cheeks, and then said to me:

'How old are you?'

'Nearly nineteen.'

'I can't believe it.'

'Dear Mother, it's absolutely true.'

'I want to know all about your life. Will you tell me?'

'Yes, dear Mother.'

'Everything?'

'Everything.'

'But somebody might come. Let's sit at the harpsichord and you can give me a lesson...'

We did so, but, and I do not know how this happened, my hands were trembling and all I could see on the paper was a confused jumble of notes. I simply could not play anything. I told her so, and she started laughing. She took my place, but it was even worse: she could hardly raise her arms.

'My child,' she said, 'I can see that you're in no fit state to teach me, and neither am I to learn. I'm a little tired, I must rest. Goodbye. Tomorrow, without further delay, I want to know everything that has happened in that dear little soul of yours. Goodbye...'

In the past when I left her, she would come with me as far as her door and then watch me as I walked down the corridor to my door; she would blow me a kiss and go back inside her cell only when I had gone into mine. On this occasion she hardly even stood up, and it was all she could manage to get to the armchair next to her bed. She sat down, laid her head on her pillow, blew me a kiss, her eyes closed, and I left.

My cell was almost directly opposite Sainte Thérèse's. Her door was open and she was waiting for me. She stopped me and said:

'Oh! Sainte Suzanne, you've been with our Mother Superior.'

'Yes,' I replied.

'You were with her for a long time.'

'As long as she wanted me to be.'

'That's not what you'd promised me.'

'I didn't promise you anything.'

'Dare you tell me what you did while you were with her?'

Although my conscience was clear, I nevertheless have to admit, Monsieur le Marquis, that her question perturbed me. She realized as much, pressed the point, and I replied:

'Dear Sister, you might not believe me, but perhaps you'll believe our dear Mother, so I shall ask her to tell you.'

'My dear Sainte Suzanne,' she replied sharply, 'you mustn't do that. You don't want to make me suffer, for she would never forgive me. You don't know what she's like, she's capable of being compassionate one minute, ferocious the next. I don't know what would become of me. Promise me you won't say anything to her.'

'Is that what you want?'

'I'm on my knees begging you. I'm desperate. I know that I have to be firm, and I shall be firm. Promise me you won't say anything to her.'

I helped her to her feet and gave her my word; she trusted me, rightly so. And so we locked ourselves away, she in her cell and I in mine.

Back in my cell I was lost in thought. I wanted to pray but could not. I tried to busy myself, beginning one task only to abandon it in favour of another and then to abandon that too in favour of yet another; my hands stopped all by themselves and it was as if I was in a daze. I had never felt like that before. My eyes closed of their own accord; I had a little nap, even though I never normally sleep during the day. When I woke up, I went over in my mind what had happened between the Mother Superior and me. I examined my conscience; as I did so again I thought I glimpsed... but they were such vague, stupid, ridiculous ideas that I dismissed them. Thinking it over brought me to the conclusion that it was perhaps an illness she was suffering from. Then I had another idea: that this illness was possibly contagious, that Sainte Thérèse had caught it, and that I too would catch it.

On the following day, after matins, our Mother Superior said to me:

'Sainte Suzanne, today's the day when I hope to learn everything that has happened to you. Come with me...'

I went with her. She made me sit down in her armchair next to her bed, and she sat on a slightly lower chair. I dominated her a little because I am taller and because I was higher up. She was sitting so close to me that her knees embraced mine, and she was leaning on her bed. After a brief silence, I said:

'Although I'm very young, I've suffered a great deal. I shall soon have been alive and suffering for twenty years. I don't know if I'll be able to tell you everything, or if you'll have the heart to hear me out. Suffering at the hands of my parents, suffering in the convent of Sainte-Marie, suffering in the convent at Longchamp, suffering everywhere. Dear Mother, where do you want me to start?'

'With your earliest suffering.'

'But, dear Mother,' I said, 'it's a long, sad story, and I wouldn't want to make you upset for such a long time.'

'Never fear, I like crying: shedding tears is a delicious state for a sensitive soul to be in. You must like crying too. You will wipe away my tears, and I yours, and perhaps we'll find happiness in the midst of your account of your suffering. Who knows where our emotions might lead us?...'

And as she spoke these last words she looked me up and down, her eyes already moist with tears, she took hold of my hands and came even closer to me so that we were touching each other.

'Tell me everything, my child,' she said, 'I'm waiting, I'm very much in the mood for emotion. I don't think I've ever known a more affecting and moving day in my whole life...'

So I began my account rather as I have just written it for you. I cannot describe the effect it had on her, the sighs she gave, the tears she shed, her expressions of indignation against my cruel parents, the awful nuns at Sainte-Marie, and those at Longchamp. I should be sorry if the smallest part of the ills she wished on them ever actually came about: I would not wish to have plucked a single hair from the head of my worst enemy. From time to time she interrupted me, got up, walked around, then sat back down again. At other points she raised her eyes and hands heavenwards and then buried her head in my lap. When I told her about what happened to me in the dungeon, and the exorcism and my public confession, she almost screamed. When I had finished, I said nothing and for a while she remained there, bent forward on her bed, her face hidden in her blanket and her arms stretched out above her head. So I said to her:

'Dear Mother, forgive me for all the suffering I've caused you. I did warn you, but it's what you wanted...'

And all she said in reply was:

'The wicked creatures! The wicked creatures! Only in convents could humanity sink so low. When hatred joins forces with a characteristically bad temper, there's no telling how far things will go. Fortunately I'm a gentle woman, I like all my nuns. They have all, to different degrees, taken on something of my character, and they all like each other. But how did your failing health withstand such torments? How did all your little limbs not end up broken? How has this delicate machine not been destroyed? How has the sparkle in your eyes not been washed away by tears? The cruel women! Tying up these arms with rope!...' And she took hold of my arms and kissed them. 'Bathing these eyes in tears!...' And she kissed them. 'Wringing moans and groans from this mouth!...' And she kissed it. 'Condemning this charming and serene face to be constantly clouded by sadness!...' And she kissed it. 'Making these rosy cheeks fade!...' And she stroked them and kissed them. 'Spoiling this head! Tearing out this hair! Darkening this forehead with anguish!...' And she kissed my head, my forehead, my hair. 'Daring to tie a rope round this neck and cutting these shoulders with sharp points!...' And she pushed aside my gimp and wimple and opened up the top of my gown. My hair fell loose over my bare shoulders, my breast was half naked, and her kisses spread over my neck, bare shoulders, and half-naked breast. I could tell then from the trembling that gripped her, from the confusion in her speech, from the wild movements of her eyes and hands, from her knee pressing against mine, from the way she was clutching me fervently and embracing me violently that her illness would soon be upon her. I do not know what was going on inside me, but I was gripped by a terror, a trembling, and a dizziness which confirmed in my mind my suspicion that her illness was contagious. I said to her:

'Dear Mother, just look at the state you've reduced me to! What if somebody came along now?'

'Stay here, stay here,' she said in a feeble voice, 'nobody will come...'

Nevertheless I tried hard to get up and tear myself away from her, and I said to her:

'Dear Mother, be careful, your illness is coming on. Let me go...'

I wanted to go, I really wanted to, that is certain, but I could not. I had no strength left, and my knees were giving way beneath me. She was seated and I was standing. She pulled me towards her, and I was afraid I might fall on top of her and hurt her. I sat on the edge of her bed and said to her:

'Dear Mother, I don't know what's wrong with me, I don't feel well.'

'Neither do I', she said. 'But rest a while, it will pass. It won't be anything serious...'

And indeed my Mother Superior regained her composure and so did I. Both of us were exhausted. I laid my head on her pillow, she rested hers on one of my knees, her forehead on one of my hands. We stayed like that for a few moments. I do not know what she was thinking. I was not thinking anything, I simply could not, I was overwhelmingly weak. We remained silent, but it was the Mother Superior who spoke first:

'Suzanne, from what you told me about your first Mother Superior, it seemed to me that she was very dear to you.'

'Very.'

'She didn't love you any more than I do, but you loved her more... Have you got nothing to say?'

'I was unhappy and she eased my suffering.'

'But where does your aversion to the religious life come from? Suzanne, you haven't told me the whole story.'

'Forgive me, Madame, but I have.'

'What! It's not possible, as lovely as you are, for you are very lovely, my child, you don't realize just how much, that nobody has ever told you so.'

'I have been told so.'

'And you didn't dislike the person who told you?'

'No.'

'And did you grow to like him?'

'Not in the least.'

'What! Have you never been in love?'

'Never.'

'What! Isn't there some passion you've kept secret or that your parents disapproved of that has provoked your aversion to convent life? Tell me all about it, I won't judge you.'

'Dear Mother, there's nothing like that for me to tell you.'

'But I ask you again, where does your aversion to the religious life come from?'

'From the life itself. I hate its duties, its tasks, the seclusion, and the constraint. It seems to me that I'm called to something else.'

'But what makes you feel like that?

'The overwhelming boredom. I'm deeply bored.'

'Even here?'

'Yes, dear Mother, even here, despite all the kindness you show me.'

'But do you feel any emotions or desires within you?'

'No.'

'I believe you. It seems to me as if you have a very even temperament.'

'Fairly.'

'Cold even.'

'I wouldn't know.'

'Don't you know what the world outside is like?'

'I hardly know it at all.'

'So what possible attraction can it hold for you?'

'I don't really know, but it must have some.'

'Is it the freedom that you miss?'

'Yes, it's that, and perhaps lots of other things besides.'

'And those other things, what are they? My friend, be honest with me: would you like to get married?'

'I'd prefer that to being as I am now, that's for sure.'

'Why would you prefer it?'

'I don't know.'

'You don't know? But tell me, what effect does the company of a man have on you?'

'None whatsoever. If he's intelligent and speaks well, I enjoy listening to him. If he's attractive, I notice.'

'And your heart remains calm?'

'So far it has remained unmoved.'

'What! When they fixed you with their lively eyes, you didn't feel...'

'Sometimes they made me feel awkward and I would look down.'

'But you felt no agitation?'

'None.'

'And your senses weren't telling you anything?'

'I don't know what the language of the senses is.'

'And yet they do have one.'

'Maybe.'

'And you don't know it?'

'Not at all.'

'What! You... It's a very tender language. Would you like to learn it?'

'No, dear Mother. What use would it be to me?'

'It would put an end to your boredom.'

'Or it might add to it. And then, what does this language of the senses mean, without an object?'

'Whenever one speaks, it's always to someone else, which is undoubtedly better than talking to oneself, though that isn't totally devoid of pleasure either.'

'I don't understand what you're saying.'

'If you wanted me to, dear child, I would explain myself more clearly.'

'No, dear Mother, no. I don't know anything, and I prefer that to gaining knowledge which might make me even more wretched than I already am. I have no desires, and I don't want to seek any which I couldn't satisfy.'

'But why couldn't you satisfy them?'

'But how could I?'

'As I do.'

'As you do! But there's nobody in this convent...'

'I'm here, dear friend, and so are you.'

'Very well, what do I mean to you? And what do you mean to me?'

'How innocent she is!'

'Oh yes, it's true, dear Mother, I am very innocent, and I'd sooner die rather than stop being so.'

I do not know what she found distressing about my words, but they made her face change in an instant. She became serious and embarrassed; her hand, which she had placed on one of my knees, first stopped pressing, then moved away; she kept her eyes lowered. I said to her:

'My dear Mother, what have I done? Have I happened to say something which has upset you? Forgive me. I'm taking advantage of the freedom you've given me. Nothing I say to you is studied, and even if I were more studied, I wouldn't say anything differently; perhaps I'd even speak less well. I find the things we're talking about so strange! Forgive me...'

As I finished speaking, I threw my arms round her neck and laid my head on her shoulder. She put her arms round me and held me very tenderly. We stayed like that for a little while. Then, tender and serene once more, she said:

'Suzanne, are you sleeping well?'

'Very well,' I replied, 'especially recently.'

'Do you fall asleep as soon as you go to bed?'

'Usually.'

'But when you don't fall asleep straight away, what do you think about?'

'About my life so far and my future, or I pray to God, or I cry, what else?'

'And in the mornings, when you wake up early?'

'I get up.'

'Without delay?'

'Without delay.'

'You don't like daydreaming?'

'No.'

'Lying back on your pillow?'

'No.'

'Enjoying the gentle warmth of your bed?'

'No.'

'Have you never...'

She stopped at that point, which was the right thing to do, for what she was going to ask me was not proper, and perhaps I shall do much more harm by repeating it, but I have resolved to hide nothing...

'Have you never been tempted to consider with some satisfaction how beautiful you are?'

'No, dear Mother. I don't know if I'm as beautiful as you say I am, but even if I were, one is beautiful for others, not for oneself.'

'Have you never thought of running your hands over your breast, your thighs, your stomach, your flesh, so firm, so soft, so white?'

'Oh certainly not, for that's sinful, and if I had done, I don't know how I would ever have admitted it in confession...'

I cannot remember what else we said to each other before someone came to tell her that there was a visitor for her in the parlour. I thought that the arrival of this visitor annoyed her and that she would have preferred to continue talking to me, though what we were saying was hardly worth a regret. At all events we went our separate ways.

The community had never been happier than since I had joined it. The Mother Superior no longer seemed to be as unpredictable as she used to be, and it was said that I had had a settling effect on her. She even established on my account several days of recreation and what were called feast days, when we were given rather better food than usual, the services were shorter, and all the time in between was devoted to recreation. But that happy time was to come to an end both for the others and for me.

The scene that I have just depicted was followed by a large number of similar scenes, about which I shall say nothing. Here is what happened after the first one.

Anxiety began to take hold of the Mother Superior. She lost her cheerfulness, her fullness of figure, and her peace of mind. The next night, when everyone was asleep and the convent was silent, she got up. After wandering along the corridors for a while, she came to my cell. I sleep lightly, and I thought I recognized her. She stopped. She seemed to be pressing her forehead against my door in order to make enough noise to wake me up, if I had been asleep. I remained silent. I thought I could hear a plaintive voice, somebody sighing. At first I trembled slightly, then I decided to say *Ave;** but instead of replying, whoever was there tiptoed away. She came back a little while later. The moans and the sighs started again. I said *Ave* again, and again she went away. I composed myself and fell asleep. While I was asleep, someone came in and sat down by my bed. My curtains were half open, and the light from the little candle she was holding lit up my face, and the woman who was holding it watched me sleeping, or at least this is what I surmised when I opened my eyes and saw her there. It was the Mother Superior. I sat up with a start. Seeing how frightened I was, she said to me:

'Don't worry, Suzanne, it's me...'

I lay back down on my pillow and said:

'Dear Mother, what are you doing here at this hour? What can have brought you here? Why aren't you asleep?'

'I can't sleep,' she replied, 'and I shan't sleep for a long time. I'm tormented by bad dreams. No sooner have I closed my eyes than the sufferings you've been through come to mind again. I can see you in the hands of those inhumane women; I can see your hair falling over your face; I can see your feet bleeding, the flame in your hand, the rope round your neck, and I think they're going to take your life. I shudder and tremble, my whole body breaks out in a cold sweat. I want to go and help you; I cry out; then I wake up, and I wait in vain to fall asleep again. That's what has happened to me tonight. I was afraid that the heavens were giving me a sign that some misfortune had befallen my friend. I got up and came to your door, I listened, I thought you weren't asleep. You spoke and I went away. I came back, you spoke again, and I went away again. I came back a third time, and when I thought you were asleep, I came in. I've been sitting next to you for quite some time now, frightened of waking you up. I hesitated at first about opening your curtains. I wanted to leave for fear of disturbing your sleep, but I couldn't resist the desire to see if my dear Suzanne was fine. I've been watching you. You're so beautiful to look at, even when you're asleep!'

'My dear Mother, how good you are!'

'I've caught a chill, but at least I know that I've nothing nasty to fear for my child, and I think I'll be able to sleep now. Give me your hand.'

I gave her my hand.

'How calm her pulse is! How steady! Nothing troubles it!'

'I'm sleeping quite peacefully.'

'How fortunate you are!'

'Dear Mother, you'll get even more of a chill like that.'

'You're right. Farewell, sweet friend, farewell, I'm going now.'

But she did not move; instead she continued to look at me. Tears fell from her eyes.

'Dear Mother,' I said, 'what's wrong? You're crying. I'm angry with myself for having told you about my suffering.'

At that point she shut my door, blew out her candle, and threw herself onto me. She held me in her arms, lying next to me on top of the bed, her face pressed against mine, and her tears moistened my cheeks. She sighed and said in a plaintive, broken voice:

'Dear friend, have pity on me.'

'Dear Mother,' I replied, 'what's wrong? Are you ill? What should I do?'

'I'm trembling,' she said, 'I'm shaking; my whole body has become deathly cold.'

'Do you want me to get out of bed so that you can take my place?'

'No,' she said, 'there's no need for you to get up. Just pull back your blanket a little so that I can get close to you, warm myself, and feel better.'

'Dear Mother,' I replied, 'that's not allowed. What would people say if they found out? I've seen nuns given penance for far lesser offences. One night in the convent of Sainte-Marie a nun went into the cell of another nun, her good friend, and I can't tell you just how badly this was viewed. My confessor has sometimes asked me if anyone has ever suggested coming to sleep with me, and he earnestly advised me to say no to anyone who did. I've even told him about your caresses, which I find very innocent, but which he doesn't. I don't know how I forgot his advice, because I'd intended to speak to you about it.'

'Dear friend,' she said, 'everyone's asleep, nobody will know a thing. I'm the one who gives out rewards and punishments, and whatever your confessor may think, I don't see what harm there is in one friend welcoming beside her another friend in the grip of fear, who has woken up and come to her cell in the middle of the night, in spite of the bitterly cold weather, to see if her beloved friend was in any danger. Suzanne, did you never share a bed with one of your sisters when you were living with your parents?'

'No, never.'

'But if the opportunity had arisen, would you not have done so without any hesitation? If your sister had come, anxious and freezing cold, and asked to lie next to you, would you have turned her away?'

'I don't think so.'

'And am I not your dear Mother?'

'Yes, you are, but it's still not allowed.'

'Dear friend, I'm the one who forbids others to do it, but I allow you to do it and I'm asking you to do it. Just let me warm myself for a moment and then I'll leave. Give me your hand...'

I gave her my hand.

'Here,' she said, 'feel me, see for yourself, I'm trembling, I'm shaking, I'm stone cold...'

And indeed she was.

'Oh! My dear Mother', I said, 'will get ill like that. Just a moment, I'll move over to the far side of the bed and you can lie where it's warm.'

I moved over to the side, I lifted up the blanket and she lay down where I had been. Oh, how poorly she was! Her body was trembling all over. She wanted to talk to me and get closer to me, but she could neither speak nor move. She whispered:

'Suzanne, my friend, come a little closer...'

She stretched out her arms. I rolled over, turning my back to her. She took hold of me gently, pulled me towards her, wrapping her arms round my body, and said:

'I'm frozen. I'm so cold that I'm afraid to touch you in case I hurt you.'

'Dear Mother, don't be afraid.'

As soon as I had said this, she put one of her hands on my chest and the other round my waist. Her feet were underneath mine and I pressed down on them to warm them, and the dear Mother said to me:

'Oh, dear friend, my feet have warmed up quickly because there's nothing between them and yours.'

'But,' I said, 'what's stopping you from warming your whole body in that way?'

'Nothing, if that's what you want.'

I had turned back towards her. She had opened up her nightdress, and I was about to do the same when suddenly there were two violent knocks at the door. Terrified, I instantly jumped out of the bed on one side and the Mother Superior jumped out on the other side. We listened and heard someone tiptoeing back to the next-door cell.

'Ah,' I said, 'it's my sister Sainte Thérèse. She must have seen you walk down the corridor and come in here. She must have been listening; she must have overheard us. What will she say?...'

I was half-dead with fright.

'Yes, it's her,' said the Mother Superior, annoyed, 'it's her, I'm sure of it, but I hope she'll never forget just how foolhardy she's been.'

'Oh, dear Mother,' I said, 'don't do anything to hurt her.'

'Suzanne,' she replied, 'farewell and goodnight. Go back to bed and sleep well. I don't expect you to be at morning prayer. I'm going to go and see that foolish girl. Give me your hand...'

I held out my hand to her across the bed. She lifted up my sleeve and, sighing, kissed me all along my arm, right from the tips of my fingers to my shoulder. And as she left she vowed that the foolhardy girl would regret daring to disturb her. I moved straight over to the other side of the bed, nearer the door, and listened. She went into Sister Thérèse's cell. I was tempted to get up and intervene between Sister Sainte Thérèse and the Mother Superior, should things turn violent. But I was so distressed and felt so uneasy that I decided to stay in bed, though I did not sleep. I thought that I was going to become the talk of the convent; that what had happened, which in itself could not have been more straightforward, would be recounted in the most unfavourable way possible; that the situation here would become even worse than it had been at Longchamp, where I had been accused of all manner of things; and that the authorities would get to hear about what we had done wrong, that our Mother Superior would be dismissed and that both of us would be severely punished. Meanwhile I kept my ears open and was impatient for our Mother Superior to leave Sister Thérèse's cell. The problem must have been difficult to deal with, because she ended up spending almost the whole night there. I felt so sorry for her! She was naked but for a chemise, and bristling with anger and cold.

In the morning I was very keen to take advantage of the special dispensation she had given me to stay in bed, but the thought came to me that I should do nothing of the sort. I dressed at great speed and was the first to arrive in the choir, but neither the Superior nor Sainte Thérèse appeared, which I was very happy about, first because I would have found it difficult to see my sister without feeling embarrassed, and secondly because, as she had been given permission not to attend the service, she must have been forgiven, and on conditions which could only reassure me. I had guessed correctly, for no sooner was the service over than the Mother Superior sent for me. I went to see her. She was still in bed, looking exhausted. She said:

'I've been ill and haven't slept. Sainte Thérèse is mad, and if she behaves like that again, I'll lock her up.'

'Oh, dear Mother,' I said, 'don't ever lock her up.'

'It depends on how she behaves. She's promised me that she'll behave better and I'm counting on that. And you, dear Suzanne, how are you?'

'I'm well, dear Mother.'

'Have you rested a little?'

'Only a little.'

'I'm told that you were in the choir. Why didn't you stay in bed?'

'I wouldn't have felt right, and besides I thought it was better to...'

'No, there was no problem. But I feel as if I want to take a nap now, and I'd advise you to go and do the same in your cell, unless you'd prefer to accept a place next to me.'

'Dear Mother, I'm terribly grateful to you. I'm used to going to bed alone, and I couldn't sleep with anybody else.'

'Run along then. I shan't come down to the refectory for dinner; food will be brought to me here instead. Perhaps I shall stay in bed for the rest of the day. You must come and see me, together with a few other nuns I've asked.'

'And is Sister Sainte Thérèse one of those nuns?' I asked.

'No' she replied.

'Good.'

'Why?'

'I don't know; it's as if I'm frightened of seeing her.'

'Don't worry, my child. I can assure you that she's more frightened of you than you need be of her.'

I left her and went to rest. In the afternoon I went to the Mother Superior's room, where I found quite a large gathering of the convent's youngest and most beautiful nuns; the others had already made their visit and left. You know about painting, and I can assure you, Monsieur le Marquis, that it was quite a pleasant picture to behold. Imagine a studio with ten to twelve people in it, the youngest of whom was probably fifteen years old, the oldest not yet twenty-three; a Mother Superior, nearly forty, white, fresh, of full figure, sitting up in bed, with a double chin, which she bore quite elegantly, arms as round as if they had been turned on a lathe, slender and dimpled fingers, and big dark eyes, bright and tender, hardly ever wide open, but instead half closed, as if their owner was too weary to open them; rosy-red lips and milk-white teeth, the prettiest cheeks, and a very pleasant head, sunk into a deep soft pillow, her arms lying feebly by her sides, with little cushions supporting her elbows. I was sitting on the edge of her bed, doing nothing. Another nun was in an armchair with a little embroidery frame on her knees. Other nuns were near the windows, making lace; some were sitting on the floor on cushions from the chairs, sewing, embroidering, unpicking threads* or spinning on the little wheel. Some of them had blond hair, others brown. None looked alike, although they were all beautiful. Their characters were as varied as their looks: some were calm, others were cheerful, yet others were serious, melancholy, or sad. They were all doing something, apart from me, as I told you. It was not difficult to distinguish between those nuns who were friends and those who were indifferent to each other or who were enemies. The friends were sitting side by side or facing each other and they were chatting as they did their needlework, giving each other advice, exchanging furtive glances, squeezing each other's hands as they pretended to hand over a pin, a needle, or a pair of scissors. The Mother Superior glanced at them. She reproached one nun for not applying herself to her work, another for being lazy, another for being indifferent, and another for being sad. She had them bring over their needlework and she would praise it or criticize it. She fixed one nun's headwear: 'This veil is too far forward... You've covered too much of your face... We can't see enough of your cheeks... These creases will hurt you...' She offered everyone a few words of praise or blame.

While all this was going on, I heard a tapping at the door and I went to see who it was. The Mother Superior said to me:

'Sainte Suzanne, you will come back, won't you?'

'Yes, dear Mother.'

'Make sure you do, because I've got something important to tell you.'

'I'll be straight back...'

It was poor Sainte Thérèse at the door. She stood there for a little while saying nothing, and so did I, then I said:

'Dear Sister, are you looking for me?'

'Yes.'

'How can I help you?'

'I'll tell you. I've incurred our dear Mother's displeasure. I had reason to believe that she had forgiven me. But now you're all gathered in her room, apart from me, and I've been told to stay in my cell.'

'Would you like to come in?'

'Yes.'

'Would you like me to go and ask the Mother Superior's permission?'

'Yes.'

'Wait here, dear friend, I'll go and ask.'

'Really? Will you speak to her for me?'

'Yes, of course, why ever shouldn't I promise to do such a thing? And why ever wouldn't I do it having promised to do it?'

'Ah!' she said, looking at me affectionately, 'I forgive her. I forgive her for liking you, for you have all the charms, the most beautiful soul and the most beautiful body.'

I was delighted to be able to do her this little favour. I went back in. While I had been out of the room, another nun had taken my place on the edge of the Superior's bed and was leaning towards her, her elbow resting between her thighs, showing her her needlework. The Superior, her eyes almost shut, was saying 'Yes' and 'No' while hardly looking at her, and though I was standing next to her, she did not notice me. But her mind soon stopped wandering. The nun who had taken my place gave it back to me and I sat down again. Then, leaning gently towards the Superior, who had sat up a little on her pillows, I said nothing, but I looked at her as if I wanted to ask a favour.

'So,' she said, 'what is it? Tell me, what do you want? How can I refuse you anything you ask?'

'Sister Sainte Thérèse...'

'I see... I'm very annoyed with her, but since Sainte Suzanne is interceding for her, I forgive her. Go and tell her that she can come in.'

I ran to tell her. The poor little sister was waiting at the door. I told her to come in; she did so, trembling. Her eyes were downcast; she was carrying a long piece of muslin pinned to a pattern, which slipped out of her hands as soon as she stepped forward. I picked it up for her, took her by the arm, and led her over to the Mother Superior. She fell to her knees, seized one of the Mother Superior's hands, kissed it, sighing and shedding a tear, and then took hold of one of my hands, which she joined with the Mother Superior's, and kissed them both. The Mother Superior gestured to her to get up and to sit wherever she wanted, which she did. Refreshments were served. The Mother Superior got up. She did not sit with us, but instead walked around the table, placing her hand on one nun's head, gently tilting it backwards and kissing her on the forehead; lifting up another nun's gimp, placing her hand underneath it and leaning against the back of her chair; walking past another nun and as she did so letting one of her hands stray over her or touch her mouth; and nibbling some of the food that had been served and then offering it to this nun or that. Having circulated like that for a little while, she stopped in front of me and looked at me very affectionately and tenderly, and as she did so the other nuns, and particularly Sister Sainte Thérèse, lowered their eyes as if they were afraid of holding her back or distracting her. After the refreshments, I sat at the harpsichord and accompanied two sisters who sang in their untrained way, but with taste, accurately, and with good voices. I also sang and played myself. The Mother Superior sat by the harpsichord and seemed to take enormous pleasure in listening to me and watching me. The others listened to me as they stood around doing nothing, or they got on with their needlework again. That evening was delightful.

When it was over, all the nuns left. I was leaving too, but the Mother Superior stopped me.

'What time is it?' she asked.

'Nearly six o'clock.'

'Some of the senior nuns who sit on our convent council* are about to arrive. I've been thinking about what you told me about your departure from Longchamp. I've told them what I think, they agree, and we have a proposal to put to you. We are bound to succeed, and if we do, it will benefit the convent a little and will be rather nice for you.'

At six o'clock the said nuns arrived. The senior nuns are always very decrepit and very elderly. I got up and they sat down, and the Mother Superior said to me:

'Sister Sainte Suzanne, didn't you tell me that you are indebted to the kindness of Monsieur Manouri for the dowry paid for you here?'

'Yes, dear Mother.'

'So I was right. And the sisters at Longchamp have kept the dowry that you paid them when you entered their convent?'

'Yes, dear Mother.'

'They haven't returned any of it?'

'No, dear Mother.'

'They're not paying you an allowance out of it?'

'No, dear Mother.'

'That's not fair. That's what I've told the senior nuns, and they agree with me that you are entitled to ask them either to return the dowry to you so that our convent might benefit from it or to pay you an allowance out of it. What you have on account of the interest that Monsieur Manouri has taken in your fate has nothing to do with what the sisters at Longchamp owe you. He didn't provide your dowry so as to dispense them from doing so.'

'No, I don't think so, but in order to be sure the easiest thing to do is to write to him.'

'Indeed, but if his reply is what we want to hear, then these are the proposals we have to put to you. We shall undertake the case on your behalf against the convent of Longchamp. Our convent will meet the costs, which will not be very heavy because it's highly likely that Monsieur Manouri will agree to take on the case. And if we win, the convent will share the money or the allowance equally with you. What do you think, dear Sister?... You're not answering; you're daydreaming.'

'I'm thinking that the sisters at Longchamp did me a great deal of harm and I would despair if they thought I was acting out of revenge.'

'It's not a question of revenge. It's about asking to be given back what is owed to you.'

'Making a public spectacle of myself again...'

'That's a minor problem, for you'll hardly be mentioned. Besides, our community is poor and that at Longchamp is rich. You'll be our benefactress, at least as long as you're alive. Not that we need such a reason to concern ourselves with your well-being, we all love you...'

And all the senior nuns chimed in together: 'And who wouldn't love her? She's perfect.'

'I could die at any moment. Another Mother Superior might not have the same feelings for you as I do; indeed I'm sure she wouldn't. You could have some minor ailment or small needs; it's very nice to have a little money one can use to offer oneself some relief or to give to others.'

'Dear Mothers,' I said, 'these considerations should not be ignored, because you've been kind enough to mention them. There are others which concern me more, but I'm willing to sacrifice for you anything that I find objectionable. The only favour I would ask of you, dear Mother, is that you wouldn't start anything without having discussed it first in my presence with Monsieur Manouri.'

'That's perfectly proper. Would you like to write to him yourself?'

'Dear Mother, that's up to you.'

'You write to him then, and so that we don't have to discuss this all over again, since I don't like cases of this kind, for they bore me to death, you should write to him immediately.'

I was given a pen, ink, and paper, and there and then I asked Monsieur Manouri if he would kindly make his way to Arpajon as soon as his commitments allowed him, for I needed his help and advice once again in a matter of some importance, and so on. The assembled council read my letter, approved it, and it was sent off.

Monsieur Manouri came a few days later. The Mother Superior explained the situation to him, he instantly concurred with her, and my scruples were dismissed as ridiculous. It was decided that a writ would be issued against the nuns at Longchamp the following day. And so it was. In spite of myself, my name appeared again in legal documents, statements, and court hearings, complete with details, conjectures, lies, and all the aspersions that can make a creature lose favour in the eyes of judges and appear hateful in the eyes of the public. But, Monsieur le Marquis, are lawyers allowed to malign people as much as they want? Can no action be taken against them? If I could have foreseen all the bitterness that this case would rake up, I swear that I would never have agreed to it in the first place. The documents published against me were deliberately sent to several nuns in our convent. They came in a steady stream to ask me for details about horrible events which had not even a shadow of truth in them. The more ignorance I showed of them, the more they thought me guilty. Since I did not explain anything or admit anything, and since I denied everything, they thought it was all true. They smiled. They spoke to me in a convoluted but nevertheless very offensive way. They shrugged their shoulders at the idea of my innocence. I wept and was disconsolate.

But troubles never come singly. The time came for me to go to confession. I had already confessed the Mother Superior's earliest caresses; the confessor had very expressly forbidden me to allow any repetition. But how can one say no to things which give great pleasure to someone on whom one depends utterly and with which one can personally see nothing wrong?

Since this confessor will play an important role in the rest of my memoirs, I think it is right that you should know something about him.

He is a Franciscan called Father Lemoine and is forty-five years old at most. He has one of the most handsome faces imaginable: gentle, calm, open, cheerful, pleasant, when he is not self-conscious; but when he becomes self-conscious, his forehead becomes lined, he frowns and lowers his gaze, and his expression becomes severe. I do not know two men more dissimilar than Father Lemoine at the altar and Father Lemoine in the parlour, alone or in company. Moreover all religious people are like that, and even I have caught myself on a number of occasions, as I am about to reach the grille, stopping just short, fixing my veil and headband, composing my face, my eyes, my mouth, my hands, my arms, my bearing, and my gait, and affecting a deportment and a modesty that were intended for certain individuals and that I maintained for as long as I spoke to them. Father Lemoine is tall, well built, cheerful, and very pleasant when he forgets himself. He speaks wonderfully well. He has a reputation in his monastery as a great theologian and in the world as a great preacher. His conversation is delightful. He is very well informed about all sorts of subjects quite outside those to do with his vocation. He has the most beautiful voice. He knows music, history, and languages. He is a doctor of the Sorbonne. Although he is young, he has risen up the main ranks of his order. I believe him to be free from intrigue and ambition. He is liked by his colleagues. He had applied to become the abbot of the monastery at Étampes* because he saw it as a quiet post where he could devote himself freely to some studies he had begun, so he had been given the position. The choice of a confessor is an important matter for a convent. Nuns must have as their confessor an important and noteworthy man: every effort was made to secure the services of Father Lemoine, and these were duly secured, on rare occasions at least.

On the eve of high feasts the convent's carriage was sent to collect him and he came. The excitement that his imminent arrival caused throughout the whole community simply had to be seen: how thrilled they were, how they shut themselves away, how they worked hard at examining their consciences, how they prepared to take up as much of his time as possible.*

It was the day before Pentecost and he was expected. I was troubled; the Mother Superior noticed this and talked to me about it. I did not hide from her the reason for my anxiety. She seemed more alarmed by this than I was, although she did her utmost to hide this from me. She called Father Lemoine a ridiculous man and made fun of my scruples. She asked me if Father Lemoine knew more than our own consciences about the innocence of her feelings and mine and if my conscience was reproaching me for something. I said no. 'Very well,' she said, 'I am your Mother Superior, you must obey me, and I order you to say none of these silly things to him. There's no point in your going to confession if you're only going to talk nonsense.'

Meanwhile Father Lemoine arrived and I got ready for confession while some of the more eager ones had already got hold of him. It was nearly my turn when the Mother Superior came to me, pulled me aside, and said:

'Sainte Suzanne, I've been thinking about what you said to me. Go back to your cell; I don't want you to go to confession today.'

'But why not, dear Mother?' I replied. 'Tomorrow is a high feast; it's a day when we all take communion. What do you expect people will think if I'm the only one not to go up to the altar?'

'Never mind, they can say what they like, but you're not going to confession.'

'Dear Mother,' I said, 'if you really love me, don't humiliate me in this way, I beg you.'

'No, no, it's quite impossible. You'd get me into trouble with that man and I'm not having any of it.'

'No, dear Mother, I won't.'

'So promise me... It's useless. Come to my room tomorrow morning and make your confession to me. There's no sin you've committed that I cannot pardon and absolve you of, and then you can take communion with the rest of the nuns. Run along.'

So I went away and I was in my cell, sad, troubled, lost in thought, not knowing what to do, whether to go to Father Lemoine in spite of what my Mother Superior had said or to wait for her absolution the next day, and whether to make my devotions with the rest of the convent or to abstain from the sacraments, regardless of what people might say, when she came in. She had made her confession, and Father Lemoine had asked her why he had not seen me and if I was ill. I do not know what she said in reply, but the result was that he was waiting for me in the confessional. 'Go on then,' she said, 'since you must, but promise me you won't say anything.' I hesitated and she insisted: 'Come along, foolish girl!' she said. 'What harm do you think there can be in keeping quiet about something that there was no harm in doing?'

'And what harm is there in talking about it?' I replied.

'None at all, but there is a risk in doing so. Who knows what importance that man may attach to it? So promise me...'

I hesitated again, but in the end I promised to say nothing as long as he did not question me, and off I went.

I made my confession and then fell silent, but the confessor pressed me and I held nothing back from him. He asked me a thousand strange things which even now, as I recall them, I still do not understand. He was kind to me, but he talked about the Superior in terms which made me shudder. He called her unworthy, dissolute, a bad nun, a pernicious woman, and a corrupt soul, and he ordered me on pain of mortal sin never to be alone with her or to accept any of her caresses.

'But, Father,' I said, 'she's my Mother Superior. She can come into my room and summon me to hers whenever she wants.'

'I know, I know, and I'm sorry. My dear child,' he said, 'praise be to God, who has saved you until now! Without daring to explain myself to you more clearly for fear of my becoming an accomplice of your unworthy Mother Superior and, with the poisonous breath that would come from my lips in spite of myself, of causing a delicate flower to fade, a flower that is only kept fresh and spotless until your age by the special protection of Providence, I order you to keep away from your Mother Superior, to reject utterly her caresses, never to go into her room alone, to close your door to her, especially at night, and, if she comes into your room in spite of you, to get out of bed, go out into the corridor, cry out if need be, go down naked to the foot of the altar, fill the convent with your screams, and do whatever the love of God, the fear of crime, the sanctity of your calling, and your concern for your salvation would inspire you to do if Satan himself had appeared and was pursuing you. Yes, my child, Satan, that's how I'm forced to depict your Mother Superior. She is sunk in the abyss of crime and she's trying to drag you down into it too, and you could already have been with her if your very innocence had not filled her with terror and stopped her.'

Then, looking heavenwards, he cried out:

'Dear God, continue to protect this child!... Say with me: *Satana, vade retro; apage, Satana.** If this wretched woman questions you, tell her everything, repeat to her what I've said to you. Tell her that it would be better if she had never been born or if she threw herself into hell by a violent death.'

'But, Father,' I replied, 'you've just heard her confession.'

He said nothing but, sighing deeply, he put his arms against one side of the confessional and rested his head on them like a man filled with pain, and he stayed like that for some time. I did not know what to think, my knees were shaking, and I was agitated and confused in a way that I cannot comprehend. I felt like a traveller walking in the dark between chasms he cannot see, beset from all sides by voices crying out from the deep to him: 'You are doomed.' Then he looked at me, calm but compassionate, and said:

'Are you in good health?'

'Yes, Father.'

'So you wouldn't be too distressed by going without sleep for a night?'

'No, Father.'

'Very well,' he said, 'tonight you won't go to bed. Straight after your supper, go to the church and prostrate yourself before the altar, and spend the night there praying. You don't realize the danger you've been in, so thank God for having kept you safe, and tomorrow you'll go to the holy table with the rest of the nuns. The only penance I give you is to keep away from your Mother Superior and to reject her poisonous caresses. Run along now. I shall join my prayers with yours. You're going to cause me such anxiety! I appreciate all the consequences of the advice I'm giving you, but I owe it you and to myself. God is our master, and we have only one law.'

I have only a very imperfect recollection, Monsieur, of everything he said. Now that I come to compare what he said as I have just reported it to you with the terrible impact it had on me at the time, there is no comparison, but that is because it is now broken up and disconnected and there are lots of things I have forgotten, because I had no clear idea about them and did not see, and still do not see, the significance of those things to which he took the strongest exception. For example, what did he find so strange about what happened when I was playing the harpsichord? Are there not people who are strongly affected by music? I myself have been told that certain tunes and modulations caused my facial expression to change completely. At such times I was utterly beside myself and hardly knew what was happening to me. I do not believe that I was any the less innocent for that. Why could it not have been the same with my Mother Superior who, despite all her manias and unpredictability, was certainly one of the most sensitive women in the world? She could not hear even a remotely sad story without bursting into tears. When I told her about my past, I reduced her to a pitiful state. Why did he not turn her compassion into a crime too? And the things that happened that night, the consequences of which he awaited in mortal fear... That man really is too harsh.

Be that as it may, I followed to the letter what he had told me to do, the immediate consequence of which he had no doubt foreseen. As soon as I left the confessional I went and prostrated myself before the altar. My head was racked with fear and I stayed there until supper. Worried about what had become of me, the Mother Superior sent for me and was told that I was at prayer. She came to the door of the choir several times, but I had pretended not to see her. The bell rang for supper and I went to the refectory. I ate quickly, and as soon as supper was over I went straight back to the church. I did not go to recreation that evening, and when it was time to retire and go to bed, I did not go up to my room. The Mother Superior knew very well what had become of me. It was the middle of the night and all was quiet in the convent when she came down to see me. I remembered the way the confessor had depicted her and I started trembling all over. I did not dare look at her, for I thought that she would have a hideous face and be surrounded by flames, and I kept saying to myself: *Satana, vade retro, apage, Satana*. Dear God, preserve me, take this demon away from me...

She knelt down and, having prayed for a while, said:

'Sainte Suzanne, what are you doing here?'

'Madame, you can see very well what I'm doing.'

'Do you know what time it is?'

'Yes, Madame.'

'Why didn't you go back to your room at the usual time?'

'Because I was getting ready to celebrate the great feast tomorrow.'

'So you were intending to spend the whole night here?'

'Yes, Madame.'

'And who gave you permission to do that?'

'The confessor told me to do it.'

'The confessor can't tell you to do anything that's against the rules of the convent. So I'm telling you to go to bed.'

'Madame, this is the penance that he gave me.'

'You will do other things instead.'

'That's not something I can choose to do.'

'Come along, my child,' she said, 'come with me. The cold in the church at night is not good for you. You can say your prayers in your cell.'

Then she tried to take hold of my hand, but I moved away sharply.

'You're avoiding me,' she said.

'Yes, Madame, I'm avoiding you.'

Emboldened by the holiness of the place, by the divine presence, and by the innocence of my heart, I dared to look up at her, but as soon as I saw her I shrieked and started running round the choir like a madwoman, shouting: 'Get thee behind me, Satan!...' She did not follow me; instead she stayed where she was and said, tenderly stretching her arms out towards me and speaking so very touchingly and softly:

'What's wrong? Why are you so frightened? Stop it. I'm not Satan; I'm your Mother Superior and your friend.'

I stopped, turned and looked at her again, and I realised that I had been terrified by a bizarre apparition that my own imagination had conjured up. For she was so positioned with respect to the lamp in the church that only her face and the tips of her fingers were lit up and the rest of her was in darkness, which made her look strange. I had gathered myself a little and threw myself into a stall. She came over to me and was about to sit in the stall next to me when I stood up and moved to the next stall down. So I travelled from one stall to the next, and so did she, right up to the end. There I stopped and begged her to leave a least one seat empty between us. 'Of course,' she said. We both sat down, separated by a stall. The Mother Superior spoke first:

'Could you tell me, Sainte Suzanne, why my being here causes you such terror?'

'Dear Mother,' I said, 'forgive me. It's not me, it's Father Lemoine. He painted your affection for me and your caresses in the most awful colours, though I have to say I can see nothing wrong with these things. He ordered me to keep away from you, not to be alone with you in your room any more, and to leave my cell if you come in. He has put in my mind an image of you as the devil, and he's said all sorts of things on the subject.'

'So you've told him?'

'No, dear Mother, but I couldn't avoid answering his questions.'

'So now you find me utterly hideous?'

'No, dear Mother, I can't help loving you, feeling how important your kindness is to me, and asking you to continue to be kind to me, but I must obey my confessor.'

'So you're not going to come and see me any more?'

'No, dear Mother.'

'And you won't let me come and see you in your cell any more?'

'No, dear Mother.'

'Will you refuse my caresses?'

'It will be very difficult for me to do so, for I was born affectionate and I like being caressed, but I must. I've promised my confessor and I made a vow before the altar. If only I could give you a sense of how he explains things... He's a pious man, an enlightened man. What purpose would it serve him to point out to me danger where there is none, to alienate a nun's heart from that of her Mother Superior? But perhaps he sees in our very innocent actions a seed of secret corruption which he believes to be fully developed in you and which he fears you're developing in me. I shan't deny that when I think back on what I have sometimes felt... Why, dear Mother, was I agitated and lost in thought whenever I left you and returned to my cell? Why could I never bring myself to pray or to do anything with myself? Why did I feel a kind of languor that I'd never felt before? Why did I, who have never before slept during the day, feel very sleepy? I thought that it was a contagious disease in you which was beginning to have its effect on me. Father Lemoine sees it very differently.'

'So how does he see it?'

'He sees in it all the guilt of crime: your certain downfall, and mine on its way; and goodness knows what else.'

'Well,' she said, 'your Father Lemoine is a visionary. This is not the first reproach of this kind that that I have suffered at his hands. All I have to do is develop a tender friendship with someone and he does his best to turn her mind against me. He very nearly drove poor Sainte Thérèse mad. It's starting to annoy me, and I shall have to get rid of this man. Besides, he lives ten leagues from here, it's difficult getting him to come, and he's not here when we want him. But we can talk about that when we're more relaxed. So, don't you want to come back up?'

'No, dear Mother. Please let me spend the rest of the night here. If I failed in this duty, tomorrow I wouldn't dare go near the sacraments with the rest of the community. But what about you, dear Mother, will you take communion?'

'Of course.'

'But hasn't Father Lemoine said anything to you?'

'No.'

'But how so?'

'Because he wasn't in a position to speak to me. One only goes to confession to confess one's sins, and I see no sin in the tender love of a child as lovable as Sainte Suzanne. If there were a fault, it would be that I focus on her alone a feeling that should be spread equally over all those who make up the community, but that's not my fault. I can't help singling out merit wherever it lies and being instinctively drawn towards it. I ask God to forgive me, and I can't understand how your Father Lemoine sees my eternal damnation stamped in a kind of predilection that is so natural and so difficult to resist. I try to ensure that all the nuns are happy, but there are some whom I respect and love more than others because they are more lovable and more deserving. That's the only crime I've committed with you. Do you find it that bad, Sainte Suzanne?'

'No, dear Mother.'

'Very well, dear child, let's each say another little prayer before leaving.'

I begged her a second time to allow me to spend the night in the church. She agreed, on condition that it would not happen again, and she left.

I went back over what she had said. I asked God to grant me understanding. I thought it over and came to the conclusion that, all things considered, although two people might be of the same sex, there could nevertheless be some indecency in the way in which they expressed their friendship for each other, and that the austere Father Lemoine had perhaps exaggerated things, but that he had nevertheless given me good advice when he told me to avoid being excessively familiar with my Mother Superior by exercising considerable reserve, and I resolved to follow his advice.

In the morning, when the nuns came down to the choir, they found me in my place. They all went up to the holy table, led by the Mother Superior, which finally convinced me that she was innocent, but it did not make me waver from the decision I had taken. And moreover I was far from feeling for her all the attraction that she felt for me. I could not help comparing her with my first Mother Superior. What a difference! She had none of the piety, seriousness, dignity, fervour, intelligence, or taste for order.

In the space of just a few days two important events occurred: first, I won my case against the nuns at Longchamp and they were ordered to pay the convent of Sainte-Eutrope, where I was, an allowance corresponding to my dowry; and second, a new confessor was appointed. It was the Mother Superior herself who told me about this latter event.

However I now only went to see her in the presence of somebody else, and she never came to my cell on her own. She always looked for me, but I avoided her. She realized this and reproached me for it. I do not know what was going on inside her, but it must have been something extraordinary. She used to get up in the night and walk along the corridors, especially mine. I could hear her going up and down, stopping outside my door, moaning and sighing. I would tremble and bury myself under the bedclothes. During the day, if I was out walking or in the workroom or the recreation room and could not see her, she would spend hours gazing at me. She watched my every move: if I went downstairs, she would be there at the bottom, and she would be waiting for me at the top when I went back up. One day she stopped me. She just looked at me and said nothing, tears streaming down her face, and then suddenly she threw herself to the floor, seized one of my knees with both hands and said:

'Cruel Sister, ask me for my life and I shall give it to you, but don't avoid me. I can't live without you.'

Seeing her like that made me feel sorry for her. Her eyes were lifeless, she had lost weight and colour. This was my Mother Superior, lying at my feet, her head pressed against my knee, which she grasped. I held out my hands to her and she seized them passionately and kissed them, and then she looked at me and then kissed them again and then looked at me again. I helped her up. She was unsteady on her feet and had difficulty walking and I led her back to her cell. When the door was open, she took me by the hand and pulled me gently to make me go in with her, but she said nothing and did not look at me.

'No,' I said, 'dear Mother, no. I've promised myself; it's best for both of us. I've taken up too great a place in your soul, and that leaves less room for God, to whom you should give yourself entirely.'

'Is it your place to reproach me for that?'

As I spoke, I tried to pull my hand free from hers.

'So you don't want to come in with me?' she said.

'No, dear Mother, no.'

'You don't want to? Sainte Suzanne, you don't realize what could happen, no, you don't realize. You're going to kill me...'

These last words inspired in me a feeling quite contrary to that which she had in mind. I pulled my hand away sharply and fled. She turned round, watched me go a few steps, went back into her cell, leaving the door open, and started wailing in the most piercing way. I could hear her and her cries penetrated me. For a moment I did not know whether I should carry on walking away or go back; however some kind of aversion made me walk away, but not without feeling pain at the state in which I was leaving her: I am by nature compassionate. I shut myself away in my cell but I was ill at ease. I did not know what to do with myself. I walked up and down a few times, feeling distracted and uneasy. I went out and came back in again. In the end I went and knocked on my neighbour Sainte Thérèse's door. She was having a private conversation with another young nun, one of her friends. I said to her:

'Dear Sister, I'm sorry to interrupt you, but could I talk to you for just a moment, as I've got something to tell you...'

She followed me into my cell and I said to her:

'I don't know what's wrong with our Mother Superior. She's disconsolate. If you went to see her, perhaps you could console her...'

She said nothing in reply. Leaving her friend in her cell and closing her door, she ran to see our Mother Superior.

Meanwhile this woman's suffering grew worse day by day. She became melancholy and serious. The jollity that had always characterized the convent since my arrival disappeared in an instant. In all things the most austere order was re-established: the Divine Office was said with due dignity; outsiders were almost entirely excluded from the parlour; nuns were no longer allowed to visit each other in their cells; religious exercises were resumed with the most painstaking rigour; there were no more gatherings in the Mother Superior's room and no more refreshments; the most trivial offences were punished severely; nuns sometimes turned to me to win the Mother Superior's favour, but I refused absolutely to seek it. Everybody knew what had caused this revolution. The older nuns were untroubled, but the young ones were in despair and looked at me disapprovingly. But my mind was at ease about my behaviour and I paid no attention to their ill temper and their reproaches.

The Mother Superior, whom I could neither help nor stop myself from pitying, passed successively from melancholy to piety and from piety to delirium. I shall not go through each of the different stages of her development, because that would require me to give you endless details. Suffice to say that in the first stage one minute she sought me out, the next she avoided me; sometimes she treated us all with her customary gentleness, but at other times she would switch suddenly to the most extreme severity; she would summon us and then send us away; she would allow recreation and the next moment she would go back on what she had ordered; she would summon us to the choir and when everybody obediently started moving, the bell would toll again sending us all back to our cells. It is difficult to imagine how confused our life was. We would spend the day leaving our cells and going back to them, picking up our breviaries and then putting them down again, going upstairs and downstairs, lowering our veils and then raising them again. The night was almost as disrupted as the day.

Some of the nuns came to me and tried to make me see that with a little more kindness and consideration on my part for the Mother Superior, everything would return to normal, though what they should have said is that it would return to the normal confusion. I answered them sadly: 'I feel sorry for you, but tell me plainly what I have to do.' Some of them went away, their heads lowered and saying nothing, but others advised me to do things that I found it impossible to reconcile with the advice that our confessor had given me, that is, the confessor that had been dismissed, since we had not yet seen his successor.

The Mother Superior no longer left her room at night. Weeks went by without her appearing at services, in the choir, in the refectory, or at recreation. She remained shut up in her room. She would wander along the corridors or go down to the church; she would go and knock on her nuns' doors and say dejectedly: 'Sister so and so, pray for me; Sister so and so, pray for me.' The rumour spread that a general confession was imminent.

One day, as I was the first to go down to the church, I saw a piece of paper attached to the curtain over the grille; I went over and read it: 'Dear Sisters, you are invited to pray for a nun who has strayed from her duties and who wants to find her way back to God.' I was tempted to tear it down, but instead I left it there. A few days later, there was another piece of paper on which was written: 'Dear Sisters, you are invited to pray for God's mercy on a nun who has acknowledged her transgressions. They are grievous.' Another day brought another invitation which read: 'Dear Sisters, you are implored to ask God to free from her despair a nun who has lost all trust in divine mercy.'

I was deeply saddened by all these invitations depicting the cruel vicissitudes of this tormented soul. One day I stood in front of one of these notices as if I was rooted to the spot. I had wondered what the transgressions for which she was reproaching herself might be, what the cause of this woman's great dread could be, what crimes she could be reproaching herself for. I went back over the confessor's exclamations, remembered the expressions he had used, tried to find a meaning in them, but in vain, and I remained somehow wrapped up in my thoughts. Some nuns who were looking at me talked amongst themselves, and if I am not mistaken, they were looking at me as if I was about to be threatened by the same terrors.

The poor Mother Superior only appeared with her veil lowered over her face. She no longer got involved in the affairs of the convent. She spoke to nobody, though she had frequent meetings with the newly appointed confessor. He was a young Benedictine. I do not know if it was he who told her to mortify her body in all the ways that she did: she fasted for three days a week, she scourged herself, and she sat in the lower stalls for services. We had to walk past her door on the way to the church, and there we would find her prostrate, her face pressed to the ground, and she would only get up when everybody had gone. At night she would go down in her nightdress and bare feet. If Sainte Thérèse or I happened to come across her, she would turn away and press her face against the wall. One day, as I was leaving my cell, I found her prostrate, her arms outstretched and her face to the ground. I stopped and she said to me: 'Carry on, keep walking, walk right over me; it's the only way I deserve to be treated.'

As the months passed and this illness continued, the rest of the community had plenty of time to suffer and to turn against me. I shall not dwell again on the difficulties endured by a nun who is hated in her convent, for you should know all about that by now. Gradually I felt my revulsion for my condition coming back. I confided in the new confessor about this revulsion and my suffering. His name is Dom Morel.* He is a passionate man in his late thirties. He seemed to listen to me attentively and with interest. He wanted to know what had happened to me in my life. He made me go into great detail about my family, my tastes, my character, the convents I had been in, the one I was in now, and what had happened between the Mother Superior and me. I told him everything. He did not seem to attach the same importance to the Mother Superior's conduct towards me as Father Lemoine had. He said very little about it to me, and he regarded the matter as closed. What he was most interested in was what I secretly felt about the religious life. The more I opened up to him, the more he trusted me. If I confessed things to him, he confessed things to me. What he told me about his suffering corresponded precisely to mine. He had entered the religious life against his will, he endured his condition with the same revulsion as I did, and he was almost as much to be pitied as I was.

'But, dear Sister,' he added, 'what can we do? There's only one thing we can do, and that's to minimize the disagreeable aspects of our condition as much as we can.' And then he gave me the advice that he himself followed, and it was wise. 'That way,' he added, 'we don't avoid sorrows, but we simply resolve to tolerate them. People in the religious life only find happiness by making a virtue before God of the crosses they bear. Then they find joy in them and they invite mortifications: the more bitter and frequent they are, the happier they make them feel. They have chosen to exchange their happiness in the here and now for happiness in the life to come: they promise themselves the latter by willingly sacrificing the former. When they have suffered much, they say: "*Amplius, Domine*, Lord, give me more..." And this is a prayer that God rarely fails to answer. But while their sufferings are just the same as ours, we can't be sure of the same reward, for we don't have the one thing that would make them worthwhile: compliance. That's sad. Alas! How shall I ever inspire in you the virtue that you lack and that I don't have either! But without it we risk being damned in the hereafter, having lived a miserable life in the here and now. In the midst of penances we're ensuring our damnation almost as certainly as people out in the world in the midst of pleasures. We're depriving ourselves while they're enjoying themselves, but after this life the same torment is awaiting us. How distressing is the life of a monk or a nun who doesn't have a calling!* But that's our life and we're powerless to change it. We've been burdened with heavy chains which we're con-demned to rattle for ever but with no hope whatsoever of being able to break them. Let's try, dear Sister, to drag them along. Now, be on your way. I'll come back and see you again.'

He came back a few days later. I saw him in the parlour and questioned him more closely. He finished telling me a whole host of things about his life, as I did about mine, and these became points of contact and similarity between us. He had endured the same domestic and religious persecution as I had. I did not realize that the way he depicted his revulsion was unlikely to help dispel my own, but in fact it did have precisely this effect on me, and I think the way I depicted my revulsion had the same effect on him. So it was that, with the similarity of our characters combining with the similarity of the events in our lives, the more we saw each other, the more we came to like each other. The story of his life was the story of mine; the story of his feelings was the story of mine; the story of his soul was the story of mine.

When we had talked for a long time about each other, we also talked about other people and in particular about the Mother Superior. The fact that he was a confessor made him very guarded, but I could tell from what he said that the woman's current state would not last much longer, that she was fighting a losing battle with herself, and that one of two things would happen: either she would at any moment revert to her old ways, or she would go mad. I was very curious to know more. He might well have been able to help me to understand questions that I had asked myself but had never been able to answer, but I did not dare to ask him. All I ventured to do was to ask if he knew Father Lemoine.

'Yes,' he said, 'I know him. He's a talented man, a very talented man.'

'One moment he was with us, the next moment he was not.'

'That's true.'

'Couldn't you tell me what happened?'

'I should be sorry if that became known.'

'You can rely on me to be discreet.'

'I think a letter was sent to the Archbishop complaining about him.'

'What possible complaints could there have been?'

'That he lived too far away from the convent, that he wasn't here when he was needed, that he was morally too austere, that there was some justification for suspecting him of being in sympathy with the new thinking,* that he was spreading discord in the convent, and that he was turning the nuns against their Mother Superior.'

'And how do you know all that?'

'He told me.'

'So you see him then?'

'Yes, I see him. He has sometimes talked to me about you.'

'What did he say?'

'That you were much to be pitied, that he couldn't understand how you had withstood everything you had suffered, that although he had only had the chance to talk to you once or twice he didn't believe that you would ever be able to settle into the religious life, and that he had in mind...'

At the point he stopped short, and I added:

'What did he have in mind?'

Dom Morel replied: 'It's too confidential for me to be at liberty to say any more.'

I did not press the point, but I simply added:

'It's true that it was Father Lemoine who was responsible for my distancing myself from the Mother Superior.'

'And rightly so.'

'Why?'

'My Sister,' he replied, becoming serious, 'follow his advice and try to remain ignorant of the reason for the rest of your life.'

'But the way I see it is, if I knew what the danger was, I would be all the more careful to avoid it.'

'But the opposite might also be true.'

'You must have a very low opinion of me.'

'I have the opinion that I must have of your morals and your innocence, but you have to realize that there is sinister knowledge that you could not acquire without some harm. It is precisely your innocence that impressed your Mother Superior; if you'd been more knowing, she would have respected you less.'

'I don't understand what you mean.'

'Good.'

'But where's the danger in one woman's intimacy with and caresses for another woman?'

Dom Morel said nothing.

'Am I not just the same as I was when I came here?'

Dom Morel said nothing.

'Wouldn't I have carried on being the same? So where's the harm in loving one another, in saying so and in showing it? It's so pleasant!'

'That's true,' said Dom Morel, looking up at me, having kept his eyes lowered while I was talking.

'And is that really so common in convents? My poor Mother Superior! What a state she has fallen into!'

'It's a shame, and I fear that things will only get worse. She was not cut out for her way of life, and this is what happens sooner or later. When you go against the general inclination of nature, the constraint deflects it into depraved affections which are all the more violent for lacking firm foundations. It's a kind of madness.'

'She's mad?'

'Yes, she is, and she'll get worse yet.'

'And do you think that's the fate that awaits all those who take on a way of life for which they have no calling?'

'No, not all of them. Some of them die first. Others have flexible characters and are able eventually to adapt. And yet others are kept going for a while by vague hopes.'

'And what hopes are there for a nun?'

'What hopes? First, to have her vows annulled.'

'And when that hope has gone?'

'The hope that one day she'll find the doors open, that mankind will stop absurdly locking up in tombs young creatures who are full of life, and that convents will be abolished; that the convent will catch fire, that the cloister walls will collapse and that someone will come and rescue them. All these ideas go round and round in their heads, they talk about them, and as they walk in the garden they instinctively look up at the walls to see how high they are. If they're in their cells, they grab the bars over the window and shake them gently and distractedly. If the road runs beneath their window, they look at it. If they hear someone going past, their hearts race and, unheard by anyone, they yearn for someone to liberate them. If there's some commotion outside and they hear it inside, they start to hope. They count on falling ill so that they might see a man or be sent to take the waters.'

'It's true, it's true,' I cried, 'you can read what's deep down in my heart. I have harboured these illusions, and I still do.'

'But when thinking about them destroys them, because these salutary vapours with which the heart shrouds reason are dispelled from time to time, it's at that point that they realize the true depth of their misery. They hate themselves and they hate other people. They weep, wail, and howl; they feel the onset of despair. Then some of them go and throw themselves at their Mother Superior's knees and seek solace; others prostrate themselves in their cells or before the altar and cry out to heaven for help; others rip off their clothes and tear out their hair; others look for a deep well, a very high window, or a length of rope, and sometimes they find it; others, who've been anxious for a long time, sink into a kind of daze and remain numb; others, with weak and delicate organs, waste away in languor; and there are yet others whose constitution is upset, whose minds are disturbed, and who go raving mad. The luckiest ones are those in whom the same consoling illusions keep recurring and who can nurture them almost until death: they spend their lives in a mixture of error and despair.'

'And the unluckiest ones,' I added, apparently sighing deeply, 'are they the ones who experience all of these states in turn?... Oh! Father, I'm so sorry I've listened to you!'

'Why's that?'

'I didn't know myself, but now I do, and my illusions won't last so long. There are times...'

I was going to go on, but another nun came in, and then another, and then a third, and then a fourth, a fifth, a sixth, and goodness knows how many more. Everybody joined in the conversation. Some of the nuns looked at the confessor; others listened to him with their heads bowed; several asked him questions all at the same time; and all of them exclaimed at the wisdom of his answers. Meanwhile I had withdrawn into a corner of the room where I let myself drift into a deep daydream. In the middle of the conversation, in which each nun was trying to make herself look good and to use her advantages to win the holy man's special attention, somebody could be heard walking up slowly, stopping now and again, and sighing. Listening out, somebody whispered: 'It's her, it's our Mother Superior.' And then there was silence and everyone sat down in a circle. Indeed it was her. She came in, her veil falling right down to her waist, her arms crossed on her chest and her head bent. I was the first one she saw; instantly she pulled out one hand from under her veil, covered her eyes, and, turning away a little, she gestured with her other hand for us all to leave. We left in silence, leaving her alone with Dom Morel.

I can tell now, Monsieur le Marquis, that you are going to have a low opinion of me, but since I did not feel ashamed of what I did, why should I blush to admit it? And how can I leave out of my account an event the consequences of which are still being felt? Let us say, then, that I have a very unusual turn of mind. When I am writing about things that could earn your respect or increase your sympathy for me, I may write well or badly, but always with incredible speed and ease. I am cheerful in heart, words come to me easily, and my tears flow gently. I feel as if you are present, as if I can see you and you are listening to me. But if, on the other hand, I am forced to present myself to you in an unfavourable light, then I have difficulty in thinking, the words do not come to me, my pen falters, the very nature of my writing is affected, and I only carry on because I secretly flatter myself that you will not read those parts. Here is one of them.

When all our sisters had gone... 'Well, what did you do?' Can't you guess?... No, you're too honest for that. I tiptoed downstairs and quietly stood outside the door to the parlour and listened to what was being said inside... 'That's very bad', you will say... And yes, it is very bad. I tell myself that, and my unease, the precautions I took to ensure that I would not be seen, the number of times I stopped, the voice of my conscience urging me with every step I took to turn back, all of these gave me no room to doubt that. And yet my curiosity got the better of me and I went. But if it is bad to have been listening in on the conversation of two people who thought they were alone, is it not even worse to tell you what they were saying? Here is another of those parts that I am writing because I flatter myself that you will not read it. I know that is not true, but I have to persuade myself that it is.

The first thing I heard, after quite a long silence, made me shudder. It was: 'Father, I am damned...' I composed myself. I listened, and the veil that had until that point shielded me from the danger I had been in was being ripped asunder, when somebody called me. I had to go, and so I did. But, oh! I had already heard too much. What a woman, Monsieur le Marquis! What a dreadful woman!...

At this point Suzanne's memoirs come to a stop. What follows is just the notes for what she apparently intended to use in the rest of her account. It seems that her Mother Superior went mad and that the fragments I am about to transcribe must relate to her unfortunate state.*

After this confession we had a few days of calm. Joy returns to the community, on which I am complimented, which I reject indignantly.

She no longer avoided me, she even watched me; my presence seemed no longer to upset her.

I did my best to conceal from her the horror that she had inspired in me ever since my fortunate or fatal curiosity had taught me more about her.

She soon becomes silent, saying only yes or no. She walks about on her own.

She refuses food. Her temperature rises, she is overcome by fever, and the fever gives way to delirium.

Alone, in bed, she sees me, speaks to me, asks me to come closer, says the most affectionate things to me.

If she hears someone walking round her room, she cries out: 'It's her going past, it's her footsteps, I recognize her. Go and call her... No, no, leave her be.'

The strange thing is that she was never wrong and never mistook another nun for me.

She would burst out laughing, and the next moment she would

burst into tears. Our sisters gathered around her in silence, and some of them were also in tears.

She would suddenly say: 'I haven't been to church, I haven't prayed to God. I want to get up. I want to get dressed; somebody get me dressed.' If anyone objected, she would add: 'At least give me my breviary.' She would be given it and she would open it, turning over the pages with her finger and still turning even when there were no pages left. And all the time there was a wild look in her eyes.

One night she went down to the church on her own; some of our sisters followed her. She prostrated herself on the altar steps and started moaning, sighing, and praying out loud. She left and came back in again. She said: 'Go and fetch her! She's such a pure soul! She's such an innocent creature! If she joined her prayers with mine...' And then, addressing the whole community and facing some empty stalls, she would cry: 'Get out, get out, all of you, and leave her on her own with me. You're not worthy to go near her. If your voices mixed with hers, your profane incense would corrupt the sweetness of hers before God. Go away, go away...' And then she would urge me to ask for heaven's help and forgiveness. She could see God, the heavens seemed to her to be streaked with lightning, to open up and rumble overhead, with angels flying down in wrath, and the face of the Lord made her tremble. She ran about in all directions and hid in the dark corners of the church. She asked for mercy. She pressed her face to the ground and dropped off to sleep. The dank coldness of the place had overcome her and she was carried back to her cell as if she was dead.

The next day she knew nothing about the terrible scene of the night before. She said: 'Where are our sisters? I can't see anyone. I'm all alone in this convent; they've all abandoned me, even Sainte Thérèse. And they were right... As Sainte Suzanne isn't here anymore, I can go out without meeting her. Oh! But what if I did meet her! But she's not here anymore, is she? She isn't, is she?... Happy the convent that has her in it!... She'll tell her new Mother Superior everything. What will she think of me?... Has Sainte Thérèse died? I heard the bell tolling for the dead all last night. The poor girl! She's lost for ever, and it's my fault, it's my fault... One day I shall be brought face to face with her. What will I say to her? What will I reply? Woe is she! Woe is me!'

On another occasion she would say: 'Have our sisters come back? Tell them I'm very ill... Lift up my pillow... Loosen my nightdress... I can feel something weighing down on me there... My head's burning; take off my nightcap... I want to get washed... Fetch me some water. Pour it out, keep on pouring... They are white, but the stain on the soul still lingers... I wish I were dead, I wish I hadn't been born; that way I wouldn't have seen her.'

One morning she was found barefoot, in her nightdress, dishevelled, screaming, foaming at the mouth, and running around her cell, her hands over her ears, her eyes closed, and her body pressed against the wall. 'Keep away from the abyss. Can you hear those cries? That's hell. I can see flames shooting up out of this deep chasm, and from the midst of the flames I can hear confused voices crying out to me... Oh my God, have pity on me!... Hurry up, ring the bell, and call everyone together. Tell them to pray for me, and I shall pray too... But it's hardly light yet and our sisters are asleep. I haven't had a moment's sleep all night; I want to sleep, but I can't.'

One of our sisters said: 'Madame, something's troubling you. Tell me what it is; it might make you feel better.'

'Sister Agathe, listen, come closer... closer... closer still... We mustn't be overheard. I'm going to tell you everything, everything, but keep it secret. Have you seen her?'

'Who, Madame?'

'Isn't it true that nobody is as sweet as she is? The way she walks! What decency! What nobility! What modesty!... Go to her and say... Oh! no, don't say anything, don't go, you couldn't go up to her. Heaven's angels are guarding her and keeping watch over her. I've seen them, and if you saw them, you'd be just as afraid of them as I was. Stay here... If you went, what would you say to her? Think of something that won't make her blush!...'

'But, Madame, would you like to speak to our confessor?'

'Yes... oh yes... No, no. I know what he'll tell me, I've heard it so many times... What will I talk to him about? If only I could lose my memory!... If only I could die or be born again!... Don't call the confessor. I'd prefer it if someone read me the Passion of our Lord Jesus Christ. Read it... I'm starting to breathe again... Just one drop of this blood is all that's needed to purify me... Look, it's gushing forth from his side... Hold that sacred wound over my head... His blood is flowing onto me but passing straight over... I'm lost!... Take that crucifix away... Bring it back...' It was brought back. She held it tightly in her arms, kissed it all over, and then added: 'These are her eyes; this is her mouth. When shall I see her again?... Sister Agathe, tell her I love her, describe for her the state I'm in, and tell her that I'm dying.'

She was bled and bathed, but each treatment seemed to make her illness worse. I dare not describe for you all the indecent things she did, nor repeat all the obscene things that escaped from her mouth in her delirium. She kept on putting her hand up to her forehead as if she was trying to get rid of troublesome ideas and images, goodness knows what images! She buried her head in the bed and covered her face with the sheets. 'It's the devil,' she said, 'it's him. How strange he looks! Get some holy water; sprinkle some holy water on me... Stop, stop, he's gone now.'

She was soon locked away, but her prison was not so well guarded that she did not manage to escape one day. She had torn off her clothes and was wandering along the corridors completely naked, with just two little lengths of torn rope hanging from her arms. She shouted: 'I am your Mother Superior. You've all sworn an oath to obey and you must do so. You've imprisoned me, you wretches! So this is the reward I get for my kindness! You're hurting me because I'm too good. Well I won't be any longer... Fire!... Murder!... Thief!... Help me!... Help me, Sister Thérèse!... Help me, Sister Suzanne!...'

But she was seized, taken back to her prison, and she said: 'You're right, you're right. I've gone mad, I can feel it.'

Sometimes she seemed to be haunted by visions of different kinds of suffering. She saw women with rope round their necks or with their hands tied behind their backs. She saw women holding torches and she joined with those making their public confession. She thought that she was being led to her death, and she said to the executioners: 'I deserve my fate, I deserve it. If only this torment were the last. But an eternity! An eternity of flames awaits me!'

I am telling you nothing that is not true, and all the other true things that I should tell you either I have forgotten them or I would be ashamed to sully the paper with them.

Having lived in this deplorable state for several months, she died. And what a death, Monsieur le Marquis! I saw it, I saw the terrible picture of despair and crime in her final hour. She thought she was surrounded by spirits from hell waiting to take her soul. Barely audible, she said: 'There they are! There they are!', holding out her crucifix on all sides to ward them off. She screamed and cried: 'My God!... My God!...' Sister Thérèse died shortly after her, and we had another Mother Superior, elderly and terribly ill tempered and superstitious.

I am accused of having bewitched her predecessor. She believes it, and my troubles start all over again.

The new confessor is also being persecuted by his superiors, and he persuades me to escape from the convent.

My escape is planned. I go into the garden between eleven and midnight. Ropes are thrown over the wall to me, I tie them around me, but they break and I fall. My legs are grazed and I have a painful bruise on my lower back. A second and then a third attempt finally manages to lift me up to the top of the wall and I get down the other side. But what a surprise I had! Instead of finding the post-chaise I hoped to be met by, I find an awful public coach. There I was on my way to Paris with a young Benedictine.* I quickly realized from his indecent tone and from the liberties he was taking that none of the conditions I had stipulated was being respected. So then I regretted having left my cell and felt the full horror of my situation.

This is where I shall depict the scene in the carriage. What a scene! What a man!

I scream, and the driver comes and helps me. A violent brawl between the driver and the monk.

I arrive in Paris. The cab stops in a little street outside a narrow doorway opening onto a dark, dirty alleyway. The landlady comes out to meet me and takes me to a little room on the top floor which has just about all the furniture I need. I am visited by the woman who lives on the first floor... 'You're young, you must be bored, Mademoiselle... Come down to my room. There's a good crowd of men and women, not all as nice as you, but almost all as young. We're chatting, playing cards, singing, dancing, and having all sorts of fun. If you turn the heads of all our young gentlemen, I swear that our ladies won't be jealous or annoyed. Come on, Mademoiselle.' The woman who said this to me was middle-aged. She looked affectionate, her voice was soft, and what she said was very astute.

I spend two weeks in that house, badgered by my deceitful abductor and witness to all the riotous things that go on in a house of ill repute, constantly looking out for an opportunity to escape.

One day I eventually found one. It was the middle of the night.

If I had been near my convent, I would have gone back there. I run off, not knowing where I am going. Some men stop me. I am gripped by fear and I collapse, exhausted, on the doorstep of a candle-maker's shop. Someone comes and helps me. When I come round, I find myself lying on a bed of straw, surrounded by several people. I was asked who I was, but I do not know what I replied. The servant girl of the house was told to take me. I take her arm and off we go. We had already gone a long way when the girl said to me:

'Mademoiselle, I suppose you know where we're going?'

'No, my child. To the poorhouse,* I suppose.'

'The poorhouse! Have you been thrown out of your home?'

'Alas, yes!'

'What did you do to get thrown out at this time of night?... But here we are at St Catherine's.* Let's see if they'll let us in. But don't worry: whatever happens, you won't be left on the street; you can come and stay with me.'

I go back to the candle-maker's. The servant girl's horror when she sees my legs so dreadfully grazed after my fall when I was leaving the convent. I spend the night there. The following evening I go back to St Catherine's. I spend three days there, after which I am told that I must either go to the poorhouse or take the first job I am offered.

The danger I was in at St Catherine's from both men and women, for it is there, as I have learnt since, that dissolute men and the town's brothel-keepers go to find recruits. The prospect of poverty did not make the crude seduction I was exposed to there any more attractive. I sell my clothes and choose some that are more in keeping with my situation.

I take a job with a laundress, whom I am staying with at the moment. I take in the washing and do the ironing. My days are hard. The board and lodging are bad, as is the bed, but on the other hand I am treated humanely. The husband works as a coachman. His wife is a little offhand, but otherwise kind. I would be fairly happy with my lot if I could hope to enjoy it in peace.

I found out that the police had captured my abductor and handed him over to his superiors. The poor man! He is more to be pitied than I am. His crime has caused a stir, and you do not realize how cruelly the religious orders punish misdemeanours that create a scandal: he will spend the rest of his life in a dungeon. And that is the fate that awaits me too, if I am caught, but he will live there longer than I would.

I am feeling the pain caused by my fall. My legs are swollen and I cannot walk a step. I work sitting down, because I would have difficulty standing up. But I am dreading getting better, for what excuse will I have then for not going out? And what risks will I run if I do go out? But thankfully I still have some time left yet.

My relatives, who can be in no doubt that I am in Paris, must be making all sorts of enquiries. I had decided to ask Monsieur Manouri to come and see me in my attic and to take and follow his advice, but he had died.

I live in a state of constant fear. The slightest noise in the house, on the staircase, or in the street fills me with terror, I tremble like a leaf, my legs give way beneath me, and I drop whatever I am working on.

Almost all my nights are sleepless, and if I do manage to sleep, then it is in a fitful way: I talk, I call out, I shout. I cannot understand why the people around me have still not worked out who I am.

My escape seems to be public knowledge. I knew it would be. One of my friends at work was talking to me about it yesterday, adding to her account horrible details and terribly hurtful comments. Thankfully she was hanging the wet washing out on the line, with her back turned to the light, so she could not see my distress. But my mistress noticed that I was crying and said:

'Marie, what's wrong?'

'Nothing,' I replied.

'What!', she went on. 'You're not stupid enough to feel sorry for a bad nun with no morals and no religion who falls head over heels in love with a nasty monk with whom she escapes from her convent? You must really be very sympathetic. All she had to do was drink, eat, pray to God, and sleep. She was fine where she was. Why didn't she stick with it? If only she'd be down to the river three or four times in this weather, that would have made her appreciate her way of life.' I replied that the only sufferings one really understood were one's own. I should have said nothing, because then she would not have added: 'Come off it, she's a hussy and God will punish her...'

At that I leant over on my table and stayed there until my mistress said: 'But Marie, what are you daydreaming about? While you're dozing, the work's not getting done.'

I was never suited to being in a cloister, and it shows clearly in what I am doing now, but I did become accustomed to certain religious practices which I now repeat automatically. For example, what do I do when I hear a bell ring? I either make the sign of the cross or kneel down. When someone knocks at the door? I say *Ave*. When I am asked a question? My answer always ends with yes or no, dear Mother Superior, or my Sister. If a stranger comes up to me, my arms form a cross on my chest and, instead of curtseying, I bow. My friends at work start laughing and think I am having fun by pretending to be a nun. But they cannot persist in their mistake: my blunders are bound to give me away and I shall be undone.

Monsieur, make haste to help me. No doubt you will say to me, tell me what I can do for you. This is what you can do, and my ambition is not great. What I need is to be taken on as a lady's maid or as a housekeeper, or even as a mere servant, as long as I can live in obscurity in the countryside, in the depths of the provinces, with decent people who do not have a wide circle of friends. I shall not be concerned about the wages; security, rest, bread, and water are all I want. Rest assured that my work will be satisfactory. I learnt to work in my father's house and in the convent I learnt to obey. I am young and very gentle. As soon as my legs have healed I shall be more than strong enough to carry out the work required. I can sew, spin, embroider, and launder, and when I was in the world I used to mend my own lace and could quickly get used to doing it again. I am in no way clumsy and no task is beneath me. I can sing and read music, I can play the harpsichord well enough to entertain any mother who would like me to, and I could even give lessons to her children. But I would be worried about giving myself away with these signs of an advanced education. If I had to learn how to dress someone's hair, I have good taste, I would take on a teacher and would quickly develop this little talent. Monsieur, any bearable position, or any position at all, that is all I need, I wish for nothing more. You can count on my morals, for despite appearances I do have some, I am even pious. Oh Monsieur, all my woes would be over and I would have nothing more to fear from mankind, if God had not stopped me. How many times I visited the deep well at the bottom of the convent garden! The only reason I did not throw myself down it is that I was completely free to do so. I do not know what fate has in store for me, but if one day I have to go back into a convent, then I cannot promise anything, for there are wells everywhere. Monsieur, have pity on me and do not store up regrets for the future.*

P.S. I am overwhelmed by tiredness, I am surrounded by terror, and rest escapes me. I have just reread at leisure these memoirs that I wrote in haste, and I have realized that, though it was utterly unintentional, I had in each line shown myself to be as unhappy as I really was, but also much nicer than I really am. Could it be that we believe men to be less sensitive to the depiction of our suffering than to the image of our charms, and do we hope that it is much easier to seduce them than it is to touch their hearts? I do not know them well enough and I have not studied myself enough to know the answer. But if the Marquis, who is credited with being a man of exquisite taste, were to persuade himself that I am appealing not to his charity but to his lust, what would he think of me? This thought worries me. In fact he would be quite wrong to attribute to me personally an impulse that is characteristic of all women. I am a woman, perhaps a little flirtatious for all I know. But it is natural and unaffected.

PREFACE

TO THE PRECEDING WORK

TAKEN FROM

MONSIEUR GRIMM'S *LITERARY CORRESPONDENCE*, 1760*

THIS charming Marquis* had left us at the beginning of 1759 to go to his estate in Normandy, near Caen. He had promised us that he would stay there only as long as it took him to put his affairs in order. But his stay got gradually longer and longer. He had moved his children there; he liked his local priest a lot; he had become a passionate gardener; and since a mind as lively as his needed real or imaginary things to cling on to, he had suddenly thrown himself into a life of the utmost piety. Nevertheless he was still very fond of us, but we would probably never have seen him again in Paris if he had not lost each of his two sons in turn, one after the other. This event brought him back to us about four years ago, after an absence of more than eight years. His piety vanished just as everything vanishes in Paris, and now he is nicer than ever.

Since losing him affected us immeasurably, in 1760, having been without him for more than fifteen months, we discussed how to make him come back to Paris. The author of the preceding memoirs remembered that a little while before he left there had been much interested talk in society of a young nun at Longchamp who was making a legal appeal against her vows, which she had been forced to take by her parents. This poor recluse moved our Marquis so much that, without having seen her, without knowing her name, and without even checking if the facts were true, he went and spoke in her favour to all the councillors in the Grand'chambre of the Parlement de Paris.* Unfortunately, despite his generous intervention, Sister Suzanne Simonin* somehow lost her case and her vows were pronounced valid.

Monsieur Diderot decided to resurrect this adventure for our own ends. He pretended that the nun in question had been fortunate enough to escape from her convent, and consequently wrote in her name to Monsieur de Croismare, asking him to help and protect her. We did not despair of seeing him come in great haste to help his nun, or, if he saw through the trick straight away and our plan failed, we were sure that it would at least give us plenty of fun. This infamous trick turned out quite differently, as you will see from the correspondence that I am about to reproduce between Monsieur Diderot or the supposed nun and the loyal and charming Marquis de Croismare, who at no point suspected a base deed that we have had on our consciences for a long time. We would spend our evenings reading and bursting with laughter at letters which were supposed to reduce our good Marquis to tears, and we also read and laughed just as much at the polite replies that this worthy and generous friend sent. However, as soon as we realized that the fate of our poor young girl was starting to move her affectionate supporter too much, Monsieur Diderot decided to kill her off, preferring to cause the Marquis some grief than to run the clear danger of tormenting him perhaps more cruelly by letting her live any longer. Since he returned to Paris, we have confessed this wicked plot to him; he laughed about it as you can imagine, and the poor nun's misfortune has served only to tighten the bonds of friendship between those who have outlived her. But he has never spoken to Monsieur Diderot about it. By no means the least strange aspect of the whole thing is that, while the practical joke stirred up our friend in Normandy, it had the same effect on Monsieur Diderot too. Convinced that the Marquis would not give refuge in his home to a young woman without knowing her first, he started writing in great detail our nun's life story. One day when he was absorbed in this work, Monsieur d'Alainville,* one of our mutual friends, paid him a visit and found him deep in sorrow, his face bathed in tears.

'What ever is the matter with you?' asked Monsieur d'Alainville. 'Just look at you!'

'What's the matter with me?' replied Monsieur Diderot. 'I'm deeply distressed by a story I'm writing.'*

If he had finished that story, it would certainly have become one of the truest, most touching and moving novels we have. It was impossible to read a page of it without crying. And yet it was not about love. It was a work of genius that bore throughout the strongest stamp of the author's imagination, a work that would be useful to the public and more generally, for it was the cruellest satire ever written of cloisters, a satire that was all the more dangerous as the first part of it was entirely favourable: his young nun was as pious as an angel and held in her simple and loving heart the most sincere respect for everything that she had been taught to respect. But this novel only ever existed in fragments and has remained that way. It is lost just like a whole host of other works by a rare man who would have secured for himself immortal renown by twenty masterpieces, if he had used his time more wisely and had not squandered it on a thousand chatterboxes, all of whom I shall cite at the Last Judgement, where they will answer to God and to mankind for the crime of which they are guilty.

(And I shall add, for I know Monsieur Diderot a little, that he did in fact finish that novel and that it is the memoirs that you have just read, in which you no doubt noticed how important it was to be wary of tributes to friendship.*)

So this correspondence and our contrition are all that remain of our poor nun. Please bear in mind that the letters signed Madin or Suzanne Simonin were written by that child of Belial,* and that the letters from the cloistered nun's generous protector are real and were written in good faith, something of which it took all the effort in the world to persuade Monsieur Diderot, who thought the Marquis and his friends were making fun of him.

NOTE

FROM THE NUN TO MONSIEUR LE COMTE DE CROISMARE, GOVERNOR OF THE ÉCOLE ROYALE MILITAIRE

AN unfortunate woman in whose lot Monsieur le Marquis de Croismare took an interest three years ago, when he was living near the Académie de Musique, has found out that he is now staying at the École Militaire.* She is writing to find out whether or not she might still count on his kindness, now that she is more to be pitied than ever before.

A word in reply, if he would. Her situation is serious, and it is crucial that the person who delivers this note to him should suspect nothing.

REPLY:

That there had been a mistake and that the Monsieur de Croismare in question was now in Caen.

THIS note was written in the hand of a young woman whom we used throughout the correspondence. A local messenger took it to the École Militaire and brought back the verbal response. Monsieur Diderot thought that this first step was essential for a number of good reasons. The nun seemed to be confusing the two cousins and to be unaware of how to spell their name properly, and naturally she learnt in this way that her protector was in Caen. It was possible that the governor of the École Militaire would tease his cousin on the occasion of this note and send it to him, giving an important air of truth to our virtuous adventuress. This governor, as agreeable as everyone with the same name, was just as irritated by the absence of his cousin as we were, and we hoped to bring him on board as one of the conspirators. After receiving his reply, the nun sent a letter to Caen.

LETTER

FROM THE NUN TO MONSIEUR LE MARQUIS DE CROISMARE
IN CAEN

MONSIEUR, I do not know to whom I am writing, but in my distress I am writing to you, whoever you are. If I have been correctly informed by the École Militaire and you are the generous Marquis I am looking for, then I shall bless God. If it is not you, then I do not know what I shall do. But I am reassured by your name. I hope that you will help a poor girl whom you, Monsieur, or another Monsieur de Croismare other than the one at the École Militaire, supported by your intervention in a vain attempt she made two years ago to get out of an interminable prison sentence to which her parents, in their cruelty, had condemned her. Despair has now led me to follow a different course of action, which you will no doubt have already heard about: I have escaped from my convent. I could no longer stand the suffering, and this was the only way, other than committing a still greater crime, to obtain for myself the freedom that I had hoped to obtain through the justice of the legal system.

Monsieur, if you were my protector in the past, may my current situation touch you now and stir in your heart some feelings of pity! Perhaps you will think it indiscreet to turn to somebody one does not know in a situation like mine. Alas! Monsieur, if you knew the state of neglect to which I have been reduced, and if you had some idea of how inhumanely scandals are punished in convents, you would forgive me. But you have a sensitive soul and you will not want to remember one day an innocent creature thrown for the rest of her life into a deep dungeon. Help me, Monsieur, help me. You will remember with satisfaction this good deed for the rest of your life and God will reward you for it in this world or the next. Above all, Monsieur, remember that I live in a state of constant fear and that I shall be counting the minutes. My relatives can be in no doubt that I am in Paris and they must be making all sorts of enquiries in their attempt to find me. Do not give them enough time to find me. Until now I have lived off my work and the help I have received from a worthy woman who was my friend and to whom you can send your reply. She is called Madame Madin and lives in Versailles.* This good friend will give me everything I need for my journey, and when I have a job I shall no longer need anything and shall no longer be dependent on her. Monsieur, my behaviour will justify your protection. Whatever you say in your reply to me, I shall complain only about my fate.

Here is Madame Madin's address: *Madame Madin, Pavillon de Bourgogne, rue d'Anjou, Versailles.*

Please be so kind as to send two envelopes, one with her address on it, the other with a cross on it.

Oh God, how I want to receive a reply from you! I am constantly apprehensive.

Your very humble and obedient servant.

Signed, SUZANNE SIMONIN.

This letter can be found in a longer form at the end of the novel, where Monsieur Diderot inserted it when he resolved to rework the rough draft that had fallen into his hands after he had forgotten all about it for twenty-one years.*

We needed an address to which the replies could be sent, and we chose a certain Madame Madin, the wife of a former infantry officer who really did live in Versailles. She knew nothing about our mischievous trick or about the letters we subsequently made her write herself, which we got another young person to write out for us. All that Madame Madin was told was that she had to receive and pass on to me all the letters postmarked *Caen*. As chance would have it, Monsieur de Croismare, after returning to Paris some eight years after our misdemeanour, came across Madame Madin one morning at the home of one of our female friends who had been in on the plot.* It was a real moment of revelation: Monsieur de Croismare was intending to find out all he could about a poor young girl whose lot had moved him so much and whose very existence was unknown to Madame Madin. It was also at that point that we all confessed and he forgave us.

REPLY

FROM MONSIEUR LE MARQUIS DE CROISMARE

MADEMOISELLE, your letter has reached the very person you were seeking. You were not wrong about his feelings and you can set off straight away for Caen, if you are happy to take up a position with a young lady.

Your lady friend should write to me to tell me that she is sending me a lady's maid of the kind I am looking for with whatever tribute she wishes to pay to your qualities, without giving any other details about your status. She should also indicate to me the name that you will be using, the coach in which you will arrive, and, if possible, when you are setting off. If you were to take the coach based in Caen, you would need to leave early on the Monday morning to arrive here on the Friday. The coachman stays in Paris in the rue Saint-Denis at the Grand Cerf. If nobody meets you when you arrive in Caen, you should go, while you are waiting, to Monsieur Gassion's, opposite the Place Royale, telling him that I told you to do so. Since it is extremely important that we all keep this a secret, your lady friend should return this letter to me, and although it is unsigned you can put your entire faith in it. Just keep the seal which will allow you to identify yourself in Caen to the person you will be going to see.

Follow exactly and diligently, Mademoiselle, the instructions in this letter. And to be safe, do not bring with you any papers, letters, or other things which could possibly identify you: it will be easy enough to have all that kind of thing brought over later. You can rely with complete confidence on the good intentions of your servant.

. . . , near Caen, Wednesday 6 February 1760.

This letter was addressed to Madame Madin. On the other envelope was a cross, as had been agreed. The seal depicted a Cupid holding a flame in one hand and two hearts in the other, with a motto that was illegible because the seal had been damaged when the letter was opened. It was only to be expected that a young nun, a stranger to love, should take this image for that of her guardian angel.

REPLY

FROM THE NUN TO MONSIEUR LE MARQUIS DE CROISMARE

MONSIEUR, I have received your letter. I think I have been very ill, very ill indeed. I am very weak. If God takes me unto himself, I shall pray constantly for your salvation; if I recover, I shall do whatever you tell me to. My dear Monsieur! What a worthy man! I shall never forget your kindness.

My worthy friend is due to arrive from Versailles and she will tell you everything.

This holy Sunday in February.

I shall guard the seal with care. It is the image of a holy angel; it is you, it is my guardian angel.

As Monsieur Diderot was unable to attend the meeting of the conspirators, this reply was sent without his involvement. He did not approve of it, and claimed that it would give away the trick. He was mistaken and he was, I think, wrong not to like the reply. But to satisfy him, we entered in the minutes of our rogues' council the following reply, which was never sent. Moreover, her illness was crucial in allowing us to delay her departure for Caen.

EXTRACT FROM THE MINUTES

Above is the letter that was sent, and here is the one that Sister Suzanne should have written:

MONSIEUR, thank you for your kindness. There is nothing more to be considered, for everything is about to end for me: in a moment I shall be before the God of mercy, where I shall remember you. They are deciding whether or not to bleed me a third time; they will do to me whatever they want. Farewell, my dear Monsieur. I hope that the place I am going to will be a happier one; we shall see each other there.

LETTER

FROM MADAME MADIN TO MONSIEUR LE MARQUIS DE CROISMARE

I AM sitting at her bedside and she is urging me to write to you. She has been at death's door but my position in Versailles prevented me from coming to her aid any earlier. I knew that she was very ill and abandoned by everyone, but I could not leave. You are right in thinking, Monsieur, that she had suffered a great deal. She suffered a fall, which she concealed from me. She suddenly fell victim to a burning fever which was only brought under control by bleedings. I think she is out of danger. But what worries me now is the fear that her convalescence will be lengthy and that she will not be able to get away for another month or even six weeks. She is already very weak, and will get weaker still. So try, Monsieur, to gain some time, and let us work together to save the most unfortunate and pathetic creature in the world. I cannot tell you what effect your note had on her. She cried a great deal and wrote down Monsieur Gassion's address on the back of an image of St Suzanne in her breviary, and then, despite being weak, she wanted to write you a reply. She was just emerging from a very bad phase and I do not know what she would have said to you, for she was quite out of her poor little mind. Forgive me, Monsieur, for I am writing at speed. I feel sorry for her and I would like not to leave her, but I cannot stay here for days on end. Here is the letter you sent her. I am sending another pretty much as you requested: in it I do not talk about her lively talents, for they are not appropriate to the position that she is going to occupy, and, it seems to me, she will have to give them up for good, if she wants to live in anonymity. Still, everything I have told you about her is true. No, Monsieur, no mother could fail to be delighted to have such a child. My first concern, as you might imagine, has been to put her out of harm's way, and that I have done. I shall only let her leave when she has fully regained her health, but that cannot be for another month or six weeks yet, as I have already mentioned, and that is as long as nothing unforeseen occurs. She has kept the seal from your letter and has put it in her Book of Hours under her pillow. I have not dared tell her that it was not yours. I had broken yours when I opened your reply, so I replaced it with mine. Given the sorry state she was in, I could not risk giving her your letter without having read it first. Might I be so bold as to ask you to send her a brief word to encourage her in her hopes, for they are her only hopes, and I could not answer for her life if she were to lose them. If you could be so kind as to send me separately a few details about the household where she will be working, then I could tell her and help calm her down. Do not worry about your letters, for they will all be sent back to you just as punctiliously as the first one was, and take heart that it is in my own self-interest too not to do anything rash. We will comply fully with your instructions, unless you wish to change them. Farewell, Monsieur. The poor dear girl prays for you whenever she feels up to it.

I look forward to receiving your reply, Monsieur, at the Pavillon de Bourgogne, rue d'Anjou, Versailles.

16 February 1760.

LETTER OF RECOMMENDATION

FROM MADAME MADIN, AS MONSIEUR LE MARQUIS DE CROISMARE HAD REQUESTED

MONSIEUR, the person I am proposing to you is called Suzanne Simonin. I love her as if she were my own child. But still you can take what I am going to tell you about her literally because it is not in my nature to exaggerate. She is an orphan, having lost both her father and her mother. She is from a good family and her education has not been neglected. She can do all the little tasks that one learns when one is able and likes being busy. She speaks rarely, but quite well, and she writes naturally. If the person for whom you intend her to work wanted to be read to, then she reads wonderfully well. She is neither tall nor small; she has a very becoming figure; and as far as her facial features are concerned, I have hardly seen any girl more attractive. She might be thought to be a little young, for I think she has only just turned seventeen,* but if she lacks the experience that comes with age, she makes up for it with the experience that comes from misfortune. She is very discreet and unusually wise. I can vouch for her good morals. She is pious, but in no way bigoted. She has a simple nature, is pleasantly cheerful, and never ill tempered. I have two daughters of my own, and if her particular circumstances did not prevent Mademoiselle Simonin from staying in Paris, I would not need to look any further for a governess for them; I do not expect to be able to find another so good. I have known her since she was a child and I have watched her grow up. She will leave here with a good supply of clothes. I shall meet the small cost of her journey and even of her return, should she be sent back: that is the least I can do for her. She has never been outside Paris, she does not know where she is going, she thinks she is lost, and I am having great difficulty in reassuring her. A word from you, Monsieur, about the person to whom she will be attached, about the house she will be living in, and about the tasks she will have to undertake, will have a greater effect on her mind than anything I can say. Am I expecting too much of your kindness in asking this? All she fears is that she will not succeed: the poor child hardly knows herself.

I have the honour to be, Monsieur, with all the respect you deserve, your very humble and obedient servant.

Signed, MOREAU MADIN.

Paris, 16 February 1760.

LETTER

FROM MONSIEUR LE MARQUIS DE CROISMARE TO
MADAME MADIN

MADAME, I received, two days ago, a short letter informing me of Mademoiselle Simonin's illness. Her sorry fate makes me weep and the state of her health worries me. May I ask you to console me by informing me of her condition and by telling me what she plans to do, that is to say, what her reply is to the letter I sent her? Your kindness and the interest that you take in this matter give me great hope.

Your very humble and obedient etc.

Caen, 19 February 1760.

ANOTHER LETTER

FROM MONSIEUR LE MARQUIS DE CROISMARE TO
MADAME MADIN

I WAS eager for news, Madame, and thankfully your letter has put my mind at rest about the condition of Mademoiselle Simonin, who is, you assure me, out of danger and not likely to be discovered. I shall write to her, and you can assure her again of my lasting feelings for her. I had found her letter striking and, seeing her in that difficult position, I thought that the best thing I could possibly do was to ask her to join me here and put her to work for my daughter, who unfortunately no longer has her mother. So this, Madame, is the house to which I intend her to come. I am sure of myself and confident that I shall be able to lessen her suffering without giving away the secret, which other people would perhaps have more difficulty with. I shall not be able to prevent myself from lamenting her condition and the fact that my own circumstances will not allow me to do all that I should like, but what can one do when one is bound by the laws of necessity? My home is two leagues from the town and set in quite pleasant countryside, where I live a very secluded life with my daughter and eldest son, who is a sensitive and religious boy, but I shall not tell him anything about her. As for my servants, they have been working for me for a long time, with the result that our life here is all very peaceful and uneventful. I should also add that she need only think of the position I am offering her as her last resort: if she were to find something better, I have no intention of holding her to a contract. But she should know that she will always find in me a guarantee of help. May she recover her strength, therefore, without worrying about anything. I shall await her, and in the meantime I should be delighted to hear her news at frequent intervals.

It is my honour, Madame, to be etc.

Caen, 21 Feburary 1760.

LETTER

FROM MONSIEUR LE MARQUIS DE CROISMARE TO SISTER SUZANNE. (THERE WAS A CROSS ON THE ENVELOPE.)

NOBODY, Mademoiselle, can be more moved than I am by your present plight. I cannot but be ever more concerned to find some consolation for you in the midst of the sorry fate that plagues you. Set your mind at rest, regain your strength, and you can always rely with complete confidence on my feelings for you. Your only concern now should be to recover your health and to remain in obscurity. If it were possible for me to make your lot an easier one, I would, but your situation places constraints on me and I can but bemoan the harshness of necessity. The person for whom I intend you to work is one of the people I love most dearly, and it is principally to me that you will be answerable. In that way, and as far as possible, I shall be able to lessen the little difficulties that are an inevitable aspect of the position that you will adopt. You should trust me, and I shall put my entire trust in you. This pledge should put your mind at rest and prove to you my way of thinking and the sincere feelings with which I am, Mademoiselle, your etc.

Caen, 21 February 1760.

I am writing to Madame Madin too, who will be able to explain further.

LETTER

MONSIEUR, our dear invalid is finally getting better. No more fever, no more headaches: all is set fair for a most speedy convalescence and the best of health. Her lips are still a little pale, but her eyes are regaining their sparkle. The colour is starting to come back to her cheeks, and her skin is fresh and will soon be firm again. All has been going well since her mind has been at rest. It is now, Monsieur, that she appreciates the full value of your kindness, and nothing could be more touching than the way she talks about it. I wish I could describe to you what went on between us when I took her your latest letters. She took hold of them; her hands were trembling, she was hardly breathing as she read them, and she stopped at the end of every line. When she had finished, she threw her arms round my neck and, weeping copiously, said: 'So, Madame Madin, God has not abandoned me after all, at last he wants me to be happy! Yes, it was God who prompted me to contact this dear Monsieur. Who else in the whole world would have taken pity on me? Let us thank God for these initial mercies, so that he may grant us yet more...' And she sat on her bed and started to pray. Then, looking back at several parts of your letters, she said: 'He's entrusting me with the care of his daughter! Oh! Mama, she will be like him, she will be gentle, kind, and sensitive, as he is...' After this, she became a little worried and said: 'Her mother has died! I'm sorry I don't have the necessary experience, I don't know anything about that, but I shall do my best. I shall remind myself morning and night of my debt to her father. Gratitude must make up for lots of things. How much longer shall I be ill? When shall I be allowed to eat? I can't feel the effects of my fall any more, not at all in fact.' I offer you these little details, Monsieur, because I hope you will enjoy them. Her words and her actions displayed such innocence and enthusiasm that I was overjoyed. I do not know what I would not have given to have enabled you to see and hear her. No, Monsieur, either I know nothing about these things or you will have a unique creature who will be a blessing in your home. What you were kind enough to tell me about yourself, your daughter, your son, and your circumstances fits perfectly with what she was wishing for. She is adamant about what she first suggested to you: all she asks is food and clothing, and you can take her at her word, if that suits you; though I am not rich, I shall see to everything else. I love this child, I have taken her into my heart, and the little that I do for her in my lifetime will continue after my death. I shall not keep from you the fact that your words *only her last resort, and I shall let her take something better, should the opportunity arise* hurt her, and I was not distressed to see this sign of humility in her. I shall not fail to keep you informed of the progress of her convalescence, but I have a grand plan which I might hope will succeed while she is recovering, as long as you could put me in touch with one of your friends: you must have many here. I need a man who is wise, discreet, shrewd, and not too eminent, a man who could make contact, either directly or through his friends, with some important people whom I shall tell him about, a man who has access to the court but is not a member of it. As I see things, he would not be told about our secret and he would help us without knowing how. Even if my attempt proved fruitless, we would still benefit from it by persuading people that she has gone abroad. If you can put me in touch with someone, do please tell me who he is and where he lives, and then write to him to tell him that Madame Madin, whom you have known for a long time, is going to come and ask a favour of him and that you would be very grateful if he could help her if at all possible. If you know of nobody suitable, then never mind, but do give it some thought, Monsieur. Otherwise, you can rely on my interest in our poor girl and on the discretion that I have gained with experience. The excitement that your last letter brought her has made her pulse slightly irregular, but it will be fine.

I have the honour to be, with all the respect you deserve, Monsieur, your etc.

Signed, MOREAU MADIN.

Paris, 3 March 1760.

Madame Madin's idea about her being put in touch with one of the generous protector's friends was a devilish plan, by means of which the conspirators hoped to prompt their friend in Normandy to get in touch with me and to share with me the whole secret business. And that is exactly what happened, as you will see from the rest of this correspondence.

LETTER

FROM SISTER SUZANNE TO MONSIEUR LE MARQUIS DE CROISMARE

Monsieur, Mama Madin has given me the two replies that you have been kind enough to send me, and she has also told me about the letter that you sent her. I accept, I accept: it is a hundred times more than I deserve, yes, a hundred times, a thousand times even. I am so unaccustomed to moving in polite society and so inexperienced, and I am so keenly aware of everything I need in order to be worthy of your trust in me. But I hope for everything from your indulgence, my enthusiasm, and my gratitude. My position will be the making of me, and Madame Madin says that it is even better than if I was already made for my position. My God, how eager I am to get better, to go and throw myself at the feet of my benefactor and to serve him and his dear daughter in whatever way I can! I am told that I shall have to wait at least another month yet. A month! That is a long time. My dear Monsieur, store up your kindness until then. I am beside myself with joy, but they do not want me to write; they prevent me from reading, they control me, they drown me in herbal tea and starve me, and all that is meant to be for my good. God be praised! But I am obeying them against my better judgement.

I am, with my grateful heart, Monsieur, your very humble and obedient servant.

Signed, Suzanne Simonin.

Paris, 3 March 1760.

LETTER

FROM MONSIEUR LE MARQUIS DE CROISMARE TO MADAME MADIN

A number of ailments over the past few days have prevented me, Madame, from replying to you sooner and letting you know how pleased I am to learn of Mademoiselle Simonin's convalescence. I dare to hope that you will very soon be good enough to let me know that she has recovered completely, as I earnestly wish. But I am terribly sorry not to be able to assist you in executing the plan that you have devised for her benefit. Though I know nothing about it, I can only approve of it, given the good sense of which you are capable and the interest which you take in it. I socialized only a very little in Paris, and even then only amongst a small group of people, who were just as little known as I was, and the kind of acquaintance that you have in mind is not easy to find. Do please, I pray you, continue to send me news of Mademoiselle Simonin, whose interests will always be dear to me. It is my honour to be etc.

13 March 1760.

REPLY

FROM MADAME MADIN TO MONSIEUR LE MARQUIS DE CROISMARE

MONSIEUR, I was perhaps wrong not to explain myself with respect to my plan, but I was so eager to press ahead with it. So this is what I had thought of. First, you need to know that the Cardinal de *** was the family's protector. They all lost a great deal when he died, above all my Suzanne, who had been introduced to him at a very early age. The old cardinal liked pretty children: he had been struck by her charms and had taken it upon himself to be responsible for her welfare. But once he had died, she was treated in the way you now know, and her guardians thought they were doing their duty by the young girl by marrying off her elder sisters. So I had thought that if it were possible to make some contact with Madame la Marquise de T***, who is said to be, if not compassionate, at least very active (but it does not really matter who helps) and who did her utmost to support my child during her legal case, and to describe to her the sad situation of a young woman enduring all the ill effects of poverty in a distant, foreign land, then we might in this way be able to obtain a small allowance from the two brothers-in-law, who have pocketed all the family wealth and have little intention of helping us. In truth, Monsieur, it would certainly be worthwhile you and I thinking about this again. You see, with that little allowance, with what I have just obtained for her, and with what you in your kindness will give her, she would be fine for the time being and not badly off in the future, and I would feel less regret in seeing her leave. But I know neither

Madame la Marquise de T***, nor the late cardinal's secretary, who is said to be a man of letters, nor anyone who knows him, and it was the child herself who suggested I should ask you. Otherwise, I cannot say that her convalescence is going quite as I would wish. She had injured her lower back, as I think I have already told you. The pain from her fall, which had gone, has now returned, and it comes and goes. It is accompanied by some internal shivering, but her pulse is not showing any signs of fever: the doctor shakes his head and I do not like the way he looks. Next Sunday she is going to mass, as she wishes, and I have just sent her a large bonnet which will keep her wrapped up to the tip of her nose; with that, she will, I think, be able to spend half an hour in a gloomy little church in the neighbourhood without being in danger. She longs for the time to come when she can leave, and I am sure that she will ask God for nothing more fervently than to be completely cured and still assured of her benefactor's kindness. If she were to be in a fit state to leave between Easter and Low Sunday,* I would not fail to let you know. Besides, Monsieur, her absence would not prevent me from acting, if I were to find amongst my acquaintances someone who might speak to Madame de T*** and Dr A***,* who has a great deal of influence over her thinking.

I am, in unbounded gratitude on her behalf and for myself, Monsieur, your very humble etc.

Signed, MOREAU MADIN.

Versailles, 25 March 1760.

P.S. I have refused to let her write to you for fear of inconveniencing you, for that is the only thought that can possibly restrain her.

REPLY

FROM MONSIEUR LE MARQUIS DE CROISMARE TO MADAME MADIN

MADAME, your plan for Mademoiselle Simonin seems very admirable and I like it all the more since I should earnestly like to see her, in her misfortune, guaranteed an acceptable way of life. I do not despair of finding a friend who might be able to speak to Madame de

T***, or to Dr A*** or to the late cardinal's secretary, but it requires both time and caution, in order both to avoid giving away the secret and to allow me to be sure that the people whom I think I could approach will be discreet. I shall not forget about it. Meanwhile, if Mademoiselle Simonin continues to feel the way she does now, and if her health is sufficiently restored, then nothing should stop her from setting off. She will find that my feelings for her are the same as I have already indicated and I am still eager to lessen the harshness of her lot, if at all possible. The current state of my own affairs and the difficult times we are going through mean that I have to remain quite cut off in the countryside with my children for reasons of economy; so we lead a very simple life. That is why Mademoiselle Simonin will be able to forgo having to spend money on clean or expensive clothes: ordinary things are enough where we live. It is in this countryside, in this uneventful, simple condition, that she will find me and where I hope she will experience some comfort and some pleasure, despite the vexing precautions that I shall be obliged to take on her account. Please be so kind, Madame, as to let me know when she sets off, and in case she has lost the address I had sent her, it is Monsieur Gassion, opposite the Place Royale, in Caen. But if I am told in time when she will be arriving, somebody will meet her and bring her here without her having to make a halt.

It is my honour, Madame, to be your very humble etc.

31 March 1760.

LETTER

FROM MADAME MADIN TO MONSIEUR LE MARQUIS DE CROISMARE

IF she continues to feel the way she does now, Monsieur! Can you be in any doubt about it? What could possibly be better for her than to go and spend time in happiness and peace with a good man and a good family? Is she not extremely fortunate that you have remembered her? And where would she turn to if she did not have the refuge that you have so generously offered her? These are her very own words, Monsieur, and I am simply repeating them to you. She insisted on going to mass on Easter Sunday, although I told her not to, and it went very badly for her: she came home with a fever, and since that sad day she has not been at all well. Monsieur, I shall not send her to you until she is in good health. She currently feels hot in her lower back where she injured herself when she fell. I have just had a look and cannot see anything, but her doctor told me the day before yesterday, as we were coming downstairs together, that he was afraid that the wound was beginning to throb and that we would have to wait and see what happened. But she has no shortage of appetite, she sleeps well, and her weight is keeping up. Only occasionally do I see that she has a little more colour in her cheeks and a little more sparkle in her eyes than normal. But her impatience distresses me. She gets out of bed and tries to walk, but as soon as she puts weight on her bad side, she lets out a heart-rending cry. Nevertheless I remain hopeful, and I have used the time to put together her little trousseau.

There is a dressing gown made of English calamanco,* which she will be able to wear on its own during the warm weather and under which she will have to wear something else in the winter, along with the blue cotton gown she is wearing at the moment.

Fifteen chemises with lace sleeves, some made of cambric,* others of muslin. In about the middle of June I shall send her everything she needs to make another six out of a piece of fabric that is currently being laundered for me at Senlis.

Several white skirts, two of which are mine, made of dimity* and trimmed with muslin.

Two matching bodices, which I had made for my youngest daughter and which turned out to fit her perfectly. That is all she will need by way of clothes for the summer.

Some corsets, aprons, and neckerchiefs.

Two dozen handkerchiefs.

Several nightcaps.

Six scalloped shawls for daytime wear, with eight pairs of cuffs with one tuck and three with two.

Six pairs of fine cotton stockings. This was the very best I could do. I took it all to her on Easter Monday, and I cannot tell you how moved she was when I gave it to her. She looked at one thing and tried on another, and she took my hands and kissed them. But she simply could not hold back her tears when she saw my daughter's bodices. 'Oh!' I said to her, 'what are you crying for? Haven't you always been one of my daughters?' 'It's true,' she replied, and then she went on: 'Now that I can hope to be happy, I feel as if I would find it hard to die. Mama, will this burning sensation in my side never go away? What if they put something on it?' I am delighted, Monsieur, that you do not disapprove of my plan and that you can see a way to make it succeed. I leave everything to your wisdom, but I feel I should warn you that Madame la Marquise de T∗∗∗ is leaving for the countryside, that Monsieur A∗∗∗ is distant and bad-tempered, that the secretary, terribly proud at having been made a member of the Académie Française after twenty years of trying,* is going back to Brittany, and that in three or four months' time we shall be forgotten about. People lose interest in things so quickly in this country! We are hardly spoken about now, and soon we will not be spoken about at all. Don't worry about her losing the address you sent her. She never opens her Book of Hours without looking at it. She would be more likely to forget her own name than Monsieur Gassion's. I asked her if she wanted to write to you and she told me that she had started writing you a long letter telling you everything that she would have to tell you if God had mercy on her, cured her, and allowed her to see you, but that she had the foreboding that she would never see you.

'It's going on too long, Mama,' she added, 'and I shall never reap the benefits of your kindness or his: either Monsieur le Marquis will change his mind, or I shan't get better.'

'Utter madness!' I replied. 'Do you realize that if you insist on entertaining these gloomy notions, then your fears will come true?'

She said: 'May God's will be done.'

I asked her to show me what she had written. I was horrified: it is a whole volume, a huge volume.

'That's what's killing you,' I said to her, angrily.

She replied: 'What do you expect me to do? Either I am unhappy or I am bored.'

'And when have you found the time to scribble all that down?'

'A little bit now and then. Whether I live or die, I want people to know everything I've suffered.'

I have forbidden her to continue, and her doctor has done likewise. I would ask you, Monsieur, to add your authority to my requests, for she considers you to be her dear master and she is sure to obey you. However, since I realize that the hours are very long for her and that she must have something to do, if only to prevent her from writing more, from daydreaming, and from fretting, I have had an embroidery frame delivered and I suggested that she start making a waistcoat for you. She liked the idea very much indeed and set about it immediately. May God grant that she should not be here long enough to finish it! Send a word, please, forbidding her to write or work too hard. I had decided to go back to Versailles this evening, but I am anxious: the onset of the throbbing worries me and I want to be with her tomorrow, when the doctor comes to see her again. Unfortunately I have some faith in the forebodings of sick people; they instinctively know the truth about their condition. When I lost Monsieur Madin,* all the doctors reassured me that he would get better, but he himself said that he would not, and what the poor man said was only too true. I shall stay here and shall be honoured to write to you. If I had to lose her, I do not think I would ever get over it. You, Monsieur, would be so fortunate not to have seen her. It's now that those wretches who made her decide to escape will be feeling the loss they have suffered, but it is too late.

It is my honour to be, Monsieur, with feelings of respect and gratitude on her account and mine, your very humble etc.

Signed, MOREAU MADIN.

Paris, 13 April 1760.

REPLY

FROM MONSIEUR LE MARQUIS DE CROISMARE TO MADAME MADIN

I AM truly moved and share, Madame, your concern about Mademoiselle Simonin's illness. Her unhappy state had always touched me immensely, but the details that you were kind enough to give me about her qualities and her feelings so predispose me in her favour that it would be impossible for me not to take the keenest interest in her. So, far from possibly changing my feelings about her, I would ask you to undertake to repeat to her those feelings that I have expressed in my letters to you and that will never change. I thought that it was wise not to write to her, so as not to give her any opportunity to write a reply. All activities are, without doubt, harmful to her in her frail condition, and if I had any power over her, I would use it to stop her from doing anything. There is nobody better than you, Madame, to let her know on my behalf what I think on this score. It is not that I should not be delighted to receive news directly from her, but I could not allow her to do something out of pure politeness which could possibly slow down her recovery. The interest that you take in her, Madame, saves me having to ask you again on this score. You should always be sure of my sincere affection for her and of the special respect and true esteem with which I am honoured to be, Madame, your very humble etc.

25 April 1760.

I shall write at once to one of my friends whom you may approach regarding Madame de T***. He is called Monsieur G***;* he is the personal secretary to Monsieur le Duc d'Orléans and lives in rue Neuve de Luxembourg, near the rue Saint-Honoré, in Paris. I shall inform him that you are going to take the trouble to visit him and I shall make it clear to him that I am very much in your debt and that I want nothing more than to be able to show you my gratitude. He does not usually dine at home.

LETTER

FROM MADAME MADIN TO MONSIEUR LE MARQUIS DE CROISMARE

Monsieur, I have suffered terribly since I was honoured to write to you last! I have never been able to bring myself to let you know about my own sufferings, and I hope that you will be grateful to me for not having put your sensitive soul to such a cruel test. You know how dear she was to me. Imagine, Monsieur, that I have watched her for almost two weeks nearing her end in the most intense pain. Finally God has, I believe, taken pity on her and on me. The poor, sad girl is still alive, but surely not for much longer. Her strength has gone, and although her pain has in fact subsided, the doctor says that it is so much the worse. She hardly speaks now and her eyes can barely open. All she has now is her patience that has not abandoned her. What will become of us if her patience gives out? My hope that she would get better faded rapidly. An abscess formed on her side,

which had been surreptitiously growing since her fall. She could not
bear its being lanced when the time came, and when she finally
agreed, it was too late. She can feel her last moment approaching.
She sends me away, and I have to admit that I am in no state to watch
this spectacle. She received the last rites last night between ten and
eleven; this was at her own request. After the sad ceremony, I stayed
alone at her bedside. She could hear me sighing, she felt for my
hand, which I gave her, she took it and lifted it up to her lips, and,
pulling me towards her, said so softly that I could hardly hear her:
'Mama, one last favour.'

'What is it, my child?'

'Bless me and then leave.' She added: 'Monsieur le Marquis...
Be sure to thank him.'

These will have been her last words. I gave my instructions and
went to a friend's house, where I am waiting constantly. It is one
o'clock in the morning. Perhaps we now have a friend in heaven.

I am, Monsieur, respectfully your very humble etc.

Signed, Moreau Madin.

The previous letter was written on 7 May, but it was not dated.

LETTER

FROM MADAME MADIN TO MONSIEUR LE MARQUIS DE CROISMARE

The dear child is no more, her sufferings are ended, and ours may
have a long time still to run. She parted from this world and into the
world where we are all awaited, last Wednesday, between three and
four o'clock in the morning. Just as her life was innocent, so her final
moments were peaceful, despite everything that was done to trouble
them. May I thank you for the affectionate interest that you took in
her fate; that is the only duty which remains for me to do for her.
Herewith all the letters that you graciously wrote to us; I had kept
some of them and I found the others amongst the papers that she
had handed over to me a few days before she died. The papers
contained, as she explained to me, the story of her life with her
parents and at the three convents where she stayed and an account of

what happened after she had left. I shall not be able to read them for some time yet. I cannot look at any of her belongings, not even at what I had given her, as her friend, without feeling great pain.

If I were ever fortunate enough, Monsieur, to be able to help you in any way, I should be flattered if you remembered me. I am, Monsieur, with the feelings of respect and gratitude that are owed to men of mercy and kindness, your etc.

Signed, MOREAU MADIN.

10 May 1760.

LETTER

FROM MONSIEUR LE MARQUIS DE CROISMARE TO MADAME MADIN

I KNOW, Madame, what it means to a sensitive and caring heart to lose the object of one's affection and the privileged opportunity to bestow favours so worthily earned both by misfortune and by the charming qualities which were those of the dear young woman who today causes your grief. I share that grief, Madame, with the greatest emotion. You knew her, and that is what makes your separation from her so hard to bear. Even without having enjoyed that advantage, I was keenly touched by her misfortune and was able to anticipate the pleasure of being able to add to the peacefulness of her existence. If God has ordained it differently and seen fit to deprive me of that longed-for pleasure, then I must praise him for it, but I cannot be unmoved. You have at least the consolation of having behaved towards her with the noblest feelings and in the kindest possible way, which I have admired and which it would have been my ambition to emulate. All I feel now is the keen desire to have the honour to meet you and to tell you in person how enchanted I have been by your grandeur of soul and with what respectful esteem it is my honour to be, Madame, your very humble etc.

18 May 1760.

Everything relating to the memory of our ill-fated friend has become extremely dear to me. Would it be asking too great a sacrifice of you to ask you to send me the memoirs and the notes that she wrote about her various misfortunes? I ask you this favour, Madame, all the more confidently since you indicated to me that I was entitled to do so. I shall be sure to send them back to you, together with all your letters, at the first opportunity, if you so wish. Please be kind enough to send them to me via the driver of the Caen coach, who stays at the Grand Cerf, rue Saint-Denis, in Paris, and departs on Mondays.

Here ends the story of the likeable and ill-fated Sister Suzanne Saulier (known as Simonin in the story and in this correspondence). It is very sad that no fair copy has been written of the memoirs of her life, as they would have made interesting reading. In the end, Monsieur le Marquis de Croismare must be grateful to his deceitful friends for having given him the opportunity to help another's misfortune with such nobility and affection and a simplicity truly worthy of him. The role that he plays in this correspondence is not the least touching aspect of the novel.

We will perhaps be criticized for having inhumanely hastened Sister Suzanne's end, but this measure had become necessary because of the information we received from the Château de Lasson* to the effect that a room was being furnished in preparation for the arrival of Mademoiselle de Croismare, whom her father was about to remove from the convent where she had been since her mother's death. This information added that they were expecting a lady's maid to come from Paris who was also going to be the young girl's governess, and that Monsieur de Croismare was also trying to provide some other work for the servant who had until that point been attending to his daughter. This information left us with no choice about the next step to take, and so neither the youthfulness nor the beauty nor the innocence of Sister Suzanne, nor her gentle, sensitive, and caring soul, which could touch even those hearts most lacking in compassion, could save her from an inevitable death. But since we had all developed the same feelings as Madame Madin for this pitiful creature, the grief that her death caused us was hardly less intense than that of her respectable protector.

If there are some slight contradictions between this account and the memoirs, it is because most of the letters were written after the novel, and it will be acknowledged that if ever there were a useful preface, it is the one that you have just read, and that it is perhaps the only preface that had best be read at the end of the work.

QUESTION TO PEOPLE OF LETTERS*

HAVING spent his mornings composing letters that were well written, well conceived, very moving, and very novelistic, Monsieur Diderot spent days spoiling them by deleting, on the advice of his wife and his fellow conspirators, everything in them that was striking, overdone, and contrary to utter simplicity and complete verisimilitude; so that if somebody had picked up the first version of the letters in the street, they would have said: 'They're beautiful, really beautiful', and if they had picked up the final version, they would have said: 'They're really true.' Which are the good ones? Those that would perhaps have earned admiration? Or those that were certain to create the illusion of reality?

EXPLANATORY NOTES

3 *a distinguished military career behind him*: an allusion to the Marquis de Croismare's service as a captain in the King's regiment (for further details on the Marquis de Croismare, see the Introduction, pp. xii–xiii).

My father was a lawyer: there are both similarities and differences between Suzanne's family and the family of Marguerite Delamarre, on whose real-life case Suzanne's fictional story is partly based. Marguerite's father Claude was a goldsmith in Paris; he had one son and three daughters; he and his wife treated Marguerite less well than her sisters, which led her to conclude, quite wrongly, that she was illegitimate.

4 *Sainte-Marie*: an allusion to the Convent of the Visitation on the rue du Bac in Paris. It was established in 1673 and had particularly large grounds. Marguerite Delamarre was sent there in 1724 at the age of 7, leaving only in 1731. Queen Marie-Antoinette laid the foundation stone for the new chapel in 1775. The convent was destroyed in the Revolution.

5 *I was summoned to the parlour*: convents had parlours in which outside visitors could be entertained, with the permission of the Mother Superior; nuns and visitors were separated, as in church, by a grille.

Father Séraphin: a cleric of this name did exist—he was a Capuchin serving in Rome on behalf of the Bishop of Marseille and the Archbishops of Arles and Aix—though it is unclear whether or not Diderot is alluding to him.

for a modest sum: some convents did rent out accommodation, not just to girls of well-to-do families in need of an education, but also to widows and wealthy women involved in scandalous affairs or unhappy marriages. In addition, some well-connected ladies rented rooms in convents where they could live permanently or have a second home, entertain, and run a salon: for example, Madame du Deffand had an apartment at St Joseph's, and Madame Geoffrin had one at Saint-Antoine-des-Champs. So Father Séraphin is making it clear to Suzanne that, even if she chooses not to become a nun at Sainte-Marie, she will still be expected to live in a convent.

6 *for another two years*: this is the period known as the noviciate, the time between a young woman's entering a convent and taking her vows. But at the Convent of the Visitation, to which Diderot is alluding, the noviciate would actually have lasted only one year.

a certain abbé Blin: there was a Canon Blin at the cathedral in Orléans, but it is unclear whether or not Diderot is alluding to him.

the Bishop of Aleppo: Aleppo (in French, Alep) is Syria's second city.

'Alep' may be a mistake for the French medieval town of Alet, on the banks of the Aude in the Languedoc-Roussillon, which did have a bishop.

6 *that day it was one of the saddest ever*: Suzanne's account of her physical and mental distress at being forced to become a nun might be an ironic echo of Julie's ecstatic account of her religious conversion during her wedding ceremony in part III of Rousseau's *Julie or The New Eloise* (*Julie ou La Nouvelle Héloïse*), first published in 1761, though Diderot was able to read parts of it as early as 1757. Like Suzanne, Julie finds herself 'trembling and about to faint', but for her, this is because of the transcendental quality of the liturgy; Suzanne suffers the same physical symptoms for (ironically) different reasons.

7 *like being given a lesson by Marcel*: an allusion to the famous eighteenth-century dancing master who gave lessons to the young Louis XV in 1726; he died in 1759. Marcel is reputed to have said: 'In other countries people jump; it's only in Paris that people dance.'

8 *doing it earns the convent some thousand écus*: an allusion to the fact that new nuns brought dowries with them. This practice was forbidden by the Lateran Council of 1215 and the Council of Trent, but it was authorized in France by royal decree in 1693. Dowries provided the basic wealth upon which religious communities were built, and the amounts paid varied, not least according to the social status of the postulants. The reference here is to a sum of 6,000 *livres*, since the value of an *écu* (a silver coin) was fixed in 1726 at 6 *livres* (or *francs*). In 1764 the statesman and economist Jacques Turgot drew up a table of upper levels of wealth, in which he indicated that an annual income of 6,000 *livres* (in the outside world) was decent, but by no means rich; in the provinces, 12,000 *livres* was the minimum income with which one could be considered rich, in Paris, 15,000. At the other end of the spectrum, a manual labourer could expect to earn 1 *livre* a day. While payment was a burden to some families, paying a dowry to a convent was far cheaper than providing a dowry for a suitable marriage: sending a daughter to a convent was an excellent money-saving device for parents (cf. the reference to the 'considerable dowries' given to Suzanne's half-sisters on their marriage, p. 4).

mad, weak-minded, or delirious: the spectacle of nuns' madness in the novel may be informed by Diderot's own experience of the deleterious effects of convent life. One of his sisters, Angélique, became a nun in Langres and went mad and died in 1748.

9 *at a critical time of her life*: a possible allusion to the menopause. The original French, 'dans un temps critique', is echoed in the modern French euphemism for the menopause, 'l'âge critique'.

her mind had been quite disturbed: possibly an allusion to Jansenists, followers in the Roman Catholic Church of the doctrine of Cornelis Jansen (1585–1638), a Dutch theologian who defended the teachings of St Augustine, especially on free will, grace, and predestination. The idea that the mad nun may have lost her mind through fear of divine judgement could point to the effect of Jansenism's emphasis on eternal damnation for those whom God has not predestined for eternal life. Though Jansenism was declared a heresy in the Papal Bull *Unigenitus* in 1713, it nevertheless took hold in some convents, only to be repressed by the authorities. Interestingly, there is an account in 1758 in the Jansenist periodical *Nouvelles ecclésiastiques* of a Jansenist nun at a convent of the Visitation of the Blessed Virgin Mary in Paris being driven mad, not by Jansenist teachings, but by the persecutions of her Mother Superior.

12 *would preside when I took my vows*: Diderot inserted these names when he was revising the text for publication in 1780–2. Sornin has hitherto not been identified, but Thierry was a contemporary chancellor of the University of Paris.

the doorkeeper: doorkeepers were salaried employees who, since they took no solemn vows, were free to come and go between the community and the world outside.

13 *pressed themselves against the grille*: a grille separated the nuns from outside visitors.

16 *the Feuillants monastery*: a Cistercian monastery in Paris in the rue Saint-Honoré, near the Tuileries, established in 1587. The Cistercians took the name 'Feuillants' from the name they gave in the twelfth century to their abbey in a leafy valley near Toulouse. From the late sixteenth century onwards the Feuillants grew significantly, and by 1791, at the time of the suppression of the religious orders, they possessed twenty-four abbeys in France.

23 *The convent at Longchamp*: situated in the Bois de Boulogne (near the present-day racetrack), the royal abbey at Longchamp, founded in 1256 by Isabelle of France, daughter of Blanche of Castile and sister of King Louis IX, was a prestigious convent belonging to the Order of St Clare. It had become known by the eighteenth century for the musical ability of its nuns, who were instructed by the famous opera singer Mlle Le Maure, such that attending services there soon became a fashionable activity for the elite and affluent. Having been closed down in the Revolution, the abbey was destroyed in 1794. Marguerite Delamarre took her vows at Longchamp in 1736 at the age of 19. In 1752 she made an official request to the religious authorities in Paris that she be relieved of them, but they rejected her request in 1756, and her appeal to the Parlement de Paris in 1758 also failed.

24 '*Sorrowful decorations, faint candles, a light more terrible than the dark-ness...*': the opening of the aria ('Tristes apprêts, pâles flambeaux, jour plus affreux que les ténèbres') sung by Telaira, daughter of the sun, in act II, scene ii of Jean-Philippe Rameau's third opera *Castor et Pollux*, first performed in October 1737 and revised in 1754. Castor and Telaira are in love, but Telaira is betrothed to Castor's brother Pollux. On discovering that Castor loves Telaira, Pollux gives her up to him. But Castor is killed by a family rival moments after the betrothal. A distraught Telaira sings

mournfully at Castor's tomb in the subterranean mausoleum as final preparations are made for his funeral; she goes on to address the sun, expressing her wish to die. Her lament is perhaps the most famous aria in the opera and one of the most famous in all French baroque opera.

27 *they all recited the Miserere*: the name given to Psalm 51, which begins with the words 'Miserere mei Deus' ('Have mercy upon me, O God'). As the great psalm of penitence and mourning, it is commonly recited at funerals.

cruelly mortifying her flesh: the religious practice of mortifying the flesh is condemned as a 'sad superstition' in the *Encyclopaedia* article 'Mortification' ('Macération'). The article is tentatively attributed to Diderot.

29 *you know the custom*: it was the custom in many religious orders for the novice or postulant, at the moment of her profession, to be presented by her family, dressed in her finest secular clothes, which she would subsequently change for her religious habit, which had earlier been blessed by the bishop presiding at the ceremony.

I was all but reduced to the state of an automaton: a possible allusion to the work of the inventor Jacques Vaucanson (1709–82), who built a number of automata in the 1750s. In 1757 Vaucanson and Diderot were both candidates for a vacancy in the Académie des Sciences: the King chose Vaucanson. Vaucanson was also familiar with the convent at Longchamp: he may have acted as an intermediary between the authorities there and Marguerite Delamarre's mother after Marguerite had begun the process of annulling her vows.

31 *It was fifty louis and a letter*: 1 *louis* (a gold coin) was the equivalent of 4 *écus* or 24 *livres*. On the significance of these values, see the note to p. 8.

32 *Sulpicians and Jesuits*: Sulpicians were members of the Society of Saint-Sulpice, a movement founded in 1642 by Jean-Jacques Olier (1608–57) and dedicated to training ordinands (the Society was named after the parish where Olier was priest, Saint-Sulpice in Paris). Jesuits were members of the Society of Jesus, founded in 1540 by Ignatius Loyola (1491–1556); they too were associated with education and training. The Sulpicians and the Jesuits also had in common their opposition to Jansenism: it is implicitly Mother Sainte Christine's anti-Jansenist opinions that are here labelled as 'new', in contrast to Jansenism, which self-consciously defined itself in terms of an older, purer form of Christian teaching.

33 *a Jansenist or a Molinist*: a Molinist was a follower of the teachings of the sixteenth-century Spanish theologian Luis Molina (1535–1600). Molina sought to reconcile the Augustinian teaching on predestination (an idea developed, of course, by the Jansenists) with the idea of the freedom of human will by arguing that the Christian may accept grace through an exercise of free will. Molinism therefore found favour with the Jesuits, but was opposed by the Jansenists. Suzanne, by contrast, insists on being known simply as a Christian, and she refuses to engage in theological controversy.

34 *The Archbishop's Vicars General*: the vicar general is second in command to a diocesan bishop (or archbishop); he has executive power over the whole diocese, acting in the name of the bishop.

the Papal Bull: an allusion to the Papal Bull *Unigenitus* of 1713, in which Clement XI condemned Jansenist doctrines as heretical.

40 *have her locked away...*: the original French here is 'qu'elle aille en paix', a euphemism meaning 'have her locked in an *in pace*'. An *in pace*, a pun on the biblical injunction *Vade in pace* ('Go in peace'), was a dungeon in a convent where a nun guilty of a serious misdemeanour would be locked away.

44 *the Tenebrae*: the name given to the office of matins and lauds on the last three days of Holy Week, commemorating the death of Jesus Christ and his lying three days and three nights in the tomb; the candles lit at the beginning of the service are extinguished one by one after each psalm, in remembrance of the darkness at the time of the crucifixion. In mid-eighteenth-century Paris, attendance at the Tenebrae at the convent of Longchamp was a fashionable Easter pursuit.

47 *the First President*: the chief judge, by royal appointment, of the Grand'chambre of the Parlement de Paris, the most prestigious law court in France; the First President between 1757 and 1763 was Mathieu-François de Molé. The Grand'chambre was the senior and most illustrious of the eight chambers into which the Parlement de Paris was organized. It was composed of the First President, the *présidents à mortier* (so called because of the black mortars they wore), and thirty-three councillors, twelve of whom were clerics. It was in the Grand'chambre that the most important cases were judged and appeals from the other chambers of the court were heard.

Madame de Soubise: an allusion to Anna Viktoria of Hesse-Rheinfels-Rotenburg (1728–92), the third (and final) wife of Charles de Rohan, Prince de Soubise (1715–87), a favourite of Louis XV and one of the protégés of his official mistress, Madame de Pompadour.

red heels: a reference to fashionable young members of the nobility whose red-heeled shoes were a mark of their elegance.

48 *Monsieur Manouri*: the name might have been inspired by that of Louis Mannory, who between 1718 and 1751 had been a well-known lawyer in the Paris Parlement. Between 1759 and 1766 he published his monumental, eighteen-volume *Speeches and Statements* (*Plaidoyers et mémoires*).

55 *Veni Creator*: 'Come Creator', a hymn of invocation to the Holy Ghost, sung at vespers and at such solemn ceremonies as the election of popes, the consecration of bishops, the ordination of priests, and the dedication of churches.

Ora pro ea: Latin phrase, meaning 'Pray for her'.

56 *Requiescat in pace*: Latin phrase, meaning 'May she rest in peace'. For another meaning of 'in pace', see the note to p. 40.

60 *at an age when she is not even allowed to spend an écu*: though the legal age
    of majority in France was 25, the minimum age at which a girl could
    become a nun was 16, as decided by the Council of Trent in 1563. This
    lower limit was raised by royal edict to 18 in 1768. On the *écu*, see the
    note to p. 8.

61 *Monsieur Hébert*: a possible allusion to Charles-Roland Hébert, a doctor
    of the Sorbonne, though not Vicar General.

65 *the folly of the cross*: cf. St Paul's bold claim that 'this doctrine of the cross
    is sheer folly to those on their way to ruin, but to us who are on the way to
    salvation it is the power of God' (1 Corinthians 1: 18).

71 *and most of those who will read these memoirs*: Diderot added this phrase
    when revising his text for publication in 1780–2. On the implications
    of Suzanne's awareness of a wider reading public, see the Introduction,
    pp. xxiv–xxv.

74 *What need has the bridegroom of so many foolish virgins*: an allusion to the
    parable of the wise and foolish virgins (Matthew 25: 1–13), which teaches
    that Christians need to be always ready for Christ's second coming.
    Diderot exploits the ambiguity in the original French of the phrase
    'vierges folles', meaning both 'foolish virgins' and 'mad virgins'.

75 *you have to be either a fanatic or a hypocrite*: Diderot added the quotation
    marks around Manouri's words (beginning on p. 73) when revising the
    novel for publication in 1780–2, seemingly wanting to make clear the
    distinction between Manouri's voice and Suzanne's. The final section
    (from 'Elsewhere he added') was also added at this stage.

84 *Monsieur B...*: in the autograph manuscript of 1760, the doctor is
    named as Bouvart, a reference to Michel-Philippe Bouvart (1711–87), a
    well-known and irascible doctor of the time who gradually gave up teach-
    ing at the Collège Royal in favour of a lucrative medical practice amongst
    the Parisian elite. He was a sworn enemy of the successful doctor
    Théophile de Bordeu (1722–76), whom Diderot depicts in *D'Alembert's
    Dream*.

88 *Sainte-Eutrope, near Arpajon*: a religious community, of the Order of the
    Annunciation of the Ten Virtues of Our Lady, had existed at Saint-
    Eutrope-lès-Arpajon, south of Paris, since the beginning of the sixteenth
    century; Marguerite Delamarre might have been sent there from
    Longchamp after the failure of her appeal. Despite Diderot's feminine
    spelling (*Sainte*-Eutrope), the patron saint was a man: the third-century
    missionary and martyr Eutropius, a Persian of royal descent who was
    ordained and sent by Pope St Clement to Gaul, where he became the first
    Bishop of Saintes, in western France; there he converted Eustelle, the
    daughter of the local Roman governor, who promptly had his head split
    open with an axe. Diderot's feminization of the saint may have been
    deliberate, since he probably would have known that Eutropius was a
    man, having read the 1765 *Encyclopaedia* article 'Immunity' ('Immunité'),
    which describes the beleaguered missionary taking refuge in a church.

91 *Madame ✱✱✱*: a character possibly based on Louise-Adélaïde d'Orléans (1698–1743), daughter of Philippe d'Orléans, the sexually adventurous (and ambiguous) Regent of France; she was abbess of Chelles, east of Paris, between 1719 and 1734.

92 *the boarders mixed in with the novices*: some girls were sent to convents as boarders (*pensionnaires*) simply to be educated.

94 *his duties at the Palais de Justice in Paris*: the Palais de Justice, on the Île de la Cité in the very heart of Paris, was home to the Parlement de Paris (see note to p. 47) and a number of other distinguished courts; the cramped surroundings were home not only to judges, lawyers, and litigants, but also to prostitutes, booksellers, and artisans who plied their respective wares there.

Port-Royal: the two Mothers Superior were educated at one of the convents most intimately linked with Jansenism. The allusion here is specifically to the community of Port-Royal in Paris, which survived well into the eighteenth century, whereas its older sister establishment, Port-Royal des Champs, in the countryside near Versailles, with which Jean Racine and Blaise Pascal had been connected in the seventeenth century, had been closed and razed to the ground in 1709 as part of Louis XIV's campaign against Jansenism.

97 *Mondonville's setting of the Psalms*: Jean-Joseph Cassanéa de Mondonville (1711–72) was a composer who first came to the attention of the Paris public in 1734 as a violinist in the Concert Spirituel, a series of concerts established in Paris in 1725 with the aim of performing sacred music during periods, such as Lent, when other performances were forbidden; Mondonville went on to direct the Concert between 1755 and 1762. He composed sacred cantatas drawn from the Psalms, most famously his setting of the penitential psalm 'De Profundis' (Psalm 130), which forms part of the Roman Catholic funeral liturgy. If it was his sacred music that won him greatest acclaim, he was nevertheless known as a dramatic composer: his 1753 opera *Titon et l'Aurore* made a significant pro-French contribution to the 'War of the Bouffons', the controversy that from 1752 to 1754 divided musical Paris into those who upheld French serious opera in the tradition of Lully and Rameau, and those who upheld Italian comic opera (*opera buffa*), who included Jean-Jacques Rousseau, d'Alembert, and Diderot himself.

103 *Couperin, Rameau, and Scarlatti*: François Couperin (1668–1733), Jean-Philippe Rameau (1683–1764), and Domenico Scarlatti (1685–1757) were all well known for their compositions for harpsichord.

gimp: a piece of linen covering the neck, shoulders, and breast, and worn by a nun.

104 *Such is the effect of cutting oneself off from society*: this paragraph can be read as an implicit riposte to the perceived misanthropy of Jean-Jacques Rousseau (see the Introduction, p. xviii).

115 *Ave*: an exclamation, in Latin, of greeting or farewell.

121 *unpicking threads*: parfilage—the unravelling of gold or silver thread from laces, epaulettes, and tassels—was a fashionable pastime for women in late eighteenth-century France; this is another example of the relaxed, even luxurious life that the nuns lead at Sainte-Eutrope.

123 *our convent council*: each convent had a council, consisting of the Mother Superior and a small number of senior nuns, which was responsible both for the day-to-day management of the community and for its spiritual welfare. The term in the original French for these senior nuns is 'discrètes', denoting the qualities of discretion and good judgement that they were supposed to bring to their role.

126 *Étampes*: a small town between Paris and Orléans.

127 *how they prepared to take up as much of his time as possible*: the nuns' excitement at the imminent arrival of a (male) confessor is a topos of libertine convent fiction. In Godard d'Aucour's *Thémidore* (1744), for example, the eponymous hero disguises himself as a priest in order to gain access to his beloved Rozette in her convent, much to the excitement of the nuns, who, as soon as he arrives, are eager to join him in the eroticized space of the confessional. And Diderot's *The Indiscreet Jewels* includes Sélim's account of entering a convent in Baruthi, disguised as a young widow, only to find there a hothouse of pent-up sexuality waiting to be satisfied: 'Zirziphile [a young and sexually inexperienced novice] got me talking at every opportunity about marriage and the pleasures of having a husband; . . . I deftly pricked her curiosity, and as she asked more and more questions, I eventually got her to put into practice what I was teaching her'; he ends up making her pregnant and is forced to escape from the convent by climbing over the wall, an anticipation of Suzanne's escape.

129 *Satana, vade retro; apage, Satana*: 'Get thee behind me, Satan' (Mark 8: 33), Christ's stern response to Peter when the latter rebukes him for speaking of his forthcoming death; 'vade retro' is the Latin translation of the Greek 'apage'. The phrase recalls Christ's rebuke to Satan during the Temptation (Matthew 4: 10).

138 *Dom Morel*: a possible allusion to the well-known Benedictine monk Robert Morel (1653–1731), who spent much of his life at Saint-Denis, near Paris. His reputation was such that his portrait was painted shortly before his death by Jean Restout, an artist much admired by Diderot. The portrait is now lost, but a contemporary engraving by Nicolas de Larmessin survives, showing Morel, a committed Jansenist, sitting next to his copy of the works of St Augustine. Morel was the author of numerous ascetic works, including the popular manual *On the Happiness of a Simple Monk who Likes his Condition and his Duties* (*Du bonheur d'un simple religieux qui aime son état et ses devoirs*), first published in 1727; a third edition appeared in 1752.

139 *How distressing is the life of a monk or a nun who doesn't have a calling!*: a possible (ironic) echo of the opening of Robert Morel's *On the Happiness*

of a Simple Monk, where he acknowledges that 'there is hardly any situation less happy than that of a monk who does not like his way of life'; he goes on to describe the cloister as a prison for anyone who does not want to be there, before extolling its delights for the happy monk.

140 *the new thinking*: another veiled allusion to Jansenism (cf. note to p. 9).

144 *the fragments I am about to transcribe must relate to her unfortunate state*: this surprising intrusion of an unidentified (and unidentifiable) editorial voice is one of the loose ends in Diderot's novel.

148 *a young Benedictine*: in the original version of the novel, Diderot had Suzanne escape with a Franciscan monk, but he subsequently changed him to a young Benedictine. The original reference might have been intended to remind the reader of Father Lemoine; the reference in the final version might imply that Suzanne has escaped with Dom Morel.

149 *To the poorhouse*: the French word here is 'l'hôpital', an allusion to L'Hôpital-Général, created in the seventeenth century to serve as a poorhouse for homeless, aged, and mentally sick people and, originally at least, for former prostitutes. It was also known as the Salpêtrière (saltpetre works), because it was built on the former site of a gunpowder factory. At the beginning of Prévost's *Manon Lescaut*, the eponymous 'heroine' is on her way from the Salpêtrière to be deported to America.

St Catherine's: the hospital of St Catherine, on the corner of the rue Saint-Denis and the rue des Lombards in the centre of Paris, was an establishment run since the sixteenth century by Augustinian nuns. They provided free board and lodging for impoverished women coming to Paris from the countryside to look for work; they also had the task of burying people who drowned in the Seine, who were killed on the streets of Paris, or who died in the city's prisons. The hospital was closed during the Revolution.

152 *do not store up regrets for the future*: this whole paragraph, in a slightly different form, was originally part of the first letter to be sent from the (at that stage anonymous) nun to the Marquis de Croismare in Caen (see the note to p. 157).

153 *MONSIEUR GRIMM'S LITERARY CORRESPONDENCE, 1760*: the year is an error: 1760 was the year in which the exchange of letters took place, but Grimm published them, together with his explanatory comments, in the *Literary Correspondence* of 15 March 1770. For further discussion of this preface, see the Introduction, pp. xxxi–xxxiii.

This charming Marquis: the Marquis de Croismare.

the Grand'chambre of the Parlement de Paris: see the note to p. 47.

Sister Suzanne Simonin: when this correspondence was first published by Grimm in 1770, the nun referred to was Marguerite Delamarre, the historical nun on whose case the hoax was based. Only when revising the prefatory material for publication with the rest of the novel, in 1782, did Diderot substitute the name of his fictional heroine.

154 *Monsieur d'Alainville*: Henri-Louis d'Alainville (1732–1801), an actor, known particularly for his tragic roles; he made his début at the Comédie-Française in 1758.

'*I'm deeply distressed by a story I'm writing*': Diderot inserted this anecdote for publication in 1782, referring to himself in the third person.

155 *be wary of tributes to friendship*: Diderot inserted this paragraph for publication in 1782.

Belial: a Hebrew term meaning worthless; it is found in 2 Corinthians 6: 15, where St Paul uses it to refer to the devil.

the École Militaire: the École Royale Militaire (Royal Military Academy) was founded by Louis XV in 1751, with the help of Madame de Pompadour and the financier Pâris-Duverney, in order to offer a military training to men from humble backgrounds. The building was designed by Jacques-Ange Gabriel.

157 *She is called Madame Madin and lives in Versailles*: Michelle Madin, née Moreau (1714–79), was a real person who, in 1758, having separated from her husband, was living in Versailles, probably employed in the royal household. Though seemingly unaware of her role in the conspiracy, she appears to have allowed her address to be used.

he had forgotten all about it for twenty-one years: Diderot added this paragraph for publication in 1782. A substantial section after the words 'Help me, Monsieur, help me' was at the same time moved, with some changes, to near the end of Suzanne's memoir (see note to p. 152).

158 *one of our female friends who had been in on the plot*: presumably Madame d'Épinay (1725–83), Grimm's mistress and a close friend of Diderot; the original plot had been hatched in her house.

162 *she has only just turned seventeen*: the internal chronology of the novel would suggest that Suzanne must be about 25 years old at this point, but Diderot is at pains to stress her youthfulness and, implicitly, her innocence: he substituted 17 for earlier versions of 22 and 19. On Diderot's playful disruption of conventional chronology, see the Introduction, pp. xxiii, xxviii–xxix.

169 *Low Sunday*: the Sunday after Easter.

*Madame de T*** and Dr A****: the four important individuals referred to in this letter are usually presumed to be the Marquise de Tencin, the Cardinal de Tencin, the abbé Trublet, and Dr Jean Astruc. The Marquise de Tencin (1681–1749) was, as a young girl, forced to become a nun, though she managed to obtain a papal rescript releasing her, and quickly made up for lost time by writing novels, becoming a famous literary hostess, and earning a reputation for sexual indiscretions; most famously, Jean le Rond d'Alembert, Diderot's fellow editor of the *Encyclopaedia* until 1758, was her illegitimate son (she abandoned him at birth outside the church of Saint-Jean-le-Rond in Paris, hence his second name). The Cardinal de Tencin (1680–1758) was the Marquise's brother and an

infamous political intriguer. The abbé Trublet (1697–1770), sometime
secretary to the Cardinal, was an essayist and well-known opponent of
the *philosophes*. Jean Astruc (1684–1766) was a famous doctor: he was
consulting doctor to the King in 1730, and from 1731 until his death he
was professor at the Collège Royal; he was also doctor to, and friend of,
the Marquise de Tencin. He was particularly interested in specific dis-
eases of women and children, and he wrote the first great treatise on
syphilis, in addition to an influential enquiry into the textual authenticity
of the Book of Genesis, *Conjectures on the Book of Genesis* (*Conjectures sur
la Genèse*, 1753), which remains in print today. Significantly, these names
replace different names in the original version of the correspondence: the
Cardinal de Fleury, the Marquise de Castries, the Marquis de Castries,
and the Duc de Fleury. The Cardinal de Fleury (1653–1743) was a prelate
and politician, sometime tutor to the young Louis XV and later his First
Minister. His great nephew, André-Hercule de Rosset (1715–88),
acceded to the title of Duc de Fleury in 1748. In 1743 the latter's sister,
Gabrielle-Isabeau-Thérèse (1728–1800), married the fourth Marquis de
Castries (1727–1801), a friend of Grimm's who enjoyed a successful
military career. Diderot substitutes for these aristocrats from the south of
France four high-profile figures in Parisian society. This is one example
of how Diderot fictionalizes the authentic correspondence and success-
fully incorporates it into the composite whole that is *The Nun*.

171 *English calamanco*: a woollen fabric popular in the eighteenth century,
silky on one side and woven on the other.

cambric: a fine white linen.

dimity: a strong cotton fabric.

172 *terribly proud at having been made a member of the Académie Française after
twenty years of trying*: in 1761, and much to the dismay of the *philosophes*,
the abbé Trublet (see note to p. 169) was made a member of the Académie
Française, the institution established under Richelieu in 1634 to monitor
and police linguistic usage and literary standards.

173 *When I lost Monsieur Madin*: in 1758 the real Madame Madin had separated from her husband, but he was still alive in 1760; she seems to have
preferred to pass herself off as a widow.

174 *Monsieur G****: Frédéric-Melchior Grimm.

177 *the Château de Lasson*: the seat of the Marquis de Croismare in
Normandy.

178 *QUESTION TO PEOPLE OF LETTERS*: Diderot added this final
paragraph for publication in 1782.

American Literature

British and Irish Literature

Children's Literature

Classics and Ancient Literature

Colonial Literature

Eastern Literature

European Literature

Gothic Literature

History

Medieval Literature

Oxford English Drama

Poetry

Philosophy

Politics

Religion

The Oxford Shakespeare

A complete list of Oxford World's Classics, including Authors in Context, Oxford English Drama, and the Oxford Shakespeare, is available in the UK from the Marketing Services Department, Oxford University Press, Great Clarendon Street, Oxford OX2 6DP, or visit the website at www.oup.com/uk/worldsclassics.

In the USA, visit www.oup.com/us/owc for a complete title list.

Oxford World's Classics are available from all good bookshops. In case of difficulty, customers in the UK should contact Oxford University Press Bookshop, 116 High Street, Oxford OX1 4BR.

GUY DE MAUPASSANT	A Day in the Country and Other Stories
	A Life
	Bel-Ami
	Mademoiselle Fifi and Other Stories
	Pierre et Jean
PROSPER MÉRIMÉE	Carmen and Other Stories
MOLIÈRE	Don Juan and Other Plays
	The Misanthrope, Tartuffe, and Other Plays
BLAISE PASCAL	Pensées and Other Writings
ABBÉ PRÉVOST	Manon Lescaut
JEAN RACINE	Britannicus, Phaedra, and Athaliah
ARTHUR RIMBAUD	Collected Poems
EDMOND ROSTAND	Cyrano de Bergerac
MARQUIS DE SADE	The Crimes of Love
	The Misfortunes of Virtue and Other Early Tales
GEORGE SAND	Indiana
MME DE STAËL	Corinne
STENDHAL	The Red and the Black
	The Charterhouse of Parma
PAUL VERLAINE	Selected Poems
JULES VERNE	Around the World in Eighty Days
	Captain Hatteras
	Journey to the Centre of the Earth
	Twenty Thousand Leagues under the Seas
VOLTAIRE	Candide and Other Stories
	Letters concerning the English Nation

ÉMILE ZOLA

L'Assommoir
The Attack on the Mill
La Bête humaine
La Débâcle
Germinal
The Kill
The Ladies' Paradise
The Masterpiece
Nana
Pot Luck
Thérèse Raquin